# Wives and
# Daughters

Elizabeth Gaskell

# Wives and Daughters

COMPACT EDITIONS

PHOENIX

A PHOENIX PAPERBACK
COMPACT EDITIONS

This paperback edition, a condensed version of the original,
first published in Great Britain in 2007
by Phoenix,
an imprint of Orion Books Ltd,
Orion House, 5 Upper St Martin's Lane,
London WC2H 9EA

1 3 5 7 9 10 8 6 4 2

A CIP catalogue record for this book
is available from the British Library.

ISBN 978-0-7538-2272-2

Typeset by Deltatype Ltd,
Birkenhead, Merseyside

Printed and bound in Great Britain by
Clays Ltd, St Ives plc

The Orion Publishing Group's policy is to use papers
that are natural, renewable and recyclable products and
made from wood grown in sustainable forests. The logging
and manufacturing processes are expected to conform to
the environmental regulations of the country of origin.

www.orionbooks.co.uk

# Contents

## Wives and Daughters
### *An Every-day Story*

# About the Author

Elizabeth Gaskell was born in Chelsea, London, in 1810. Her father was first a Unitarian minister and then a writer, and her mother died thirteen months after her birth. Unable to raise her himself, her father sent the young Elizabeth to live with her aunt, Hannah Lumb, in Knutsford, Cheshire, a town she later immortalized as Cranford in the book of that name (1853).

In 1832, when staying in Manchester, Elizabeth met and married William Gaskell, the minister of the Cross Street Unitarian Chapel. Most of William Gaskell's parishioners were textile workers and Elizabeth was deeply shocked by the poverty she witnessed in industrial Manchester. The circles in which they moved included social reformers and both the Gaskells were very involved in charity work in Manchester. Elizabeth started writing after the death of her baby son when her husband suggested it might help her recover from her grief. Her first novel, *Mary Barton*, dealt with social issues such as poverty and trade unionism. When it was published in 1848 it was greatly admired by other writers such as Thackeray and Charles Dickens, who serialized some of Gaskell's other work in his journal, *Household Words*. Elizabeth published many other books, including *North and South* in 1855 and a biography of Charlotte Brontë in 1857. She died in 1865 in Hampshire, before she had completed *Wives and Daughters*, in a house she had bought as a surprise for her husband. She had intended that they would spend their retirement there. Other important novels are *Ruth* (1853) which deals with a fallen but really virtuous woman and *Sylvia's Lovers* (1863), set at the time of the Napoleonic Wars.

# Chronology of Elizabeth Gaskell's Life

| Year | Age | Life |
|------|-----|------|
| 1810 | | Born 29 September, second surviving child of William and Elizabeth Stevenson, in Chelsea, London. (An older brother, John) |
| 1811 | 1 | October. Her mother dies. In November Elizabeth is taken to Knutsford, Cheshire, where she will be brought up by her aunt, Hannah Lumb |
| 1812 | | |
| 1815 | | |
| 1820 | | |
| 1821 | 10 | Goes to the Misses Byerleys' school at Barford, Warwickshire |
| 1826 | 16 | June. Leaves school |
| 1828 | 18 | Her brother John disappears on a voyage to India. Elizabeth goes to Chelsea to live with her father and stepmother |
| 1829 | 19 | March. William Stevenson dies. Elizabeth goes to stay with Rev. William Turner, Newcastle upon Tyne |
| 1830 | 20 | Spent in Knutsford and Newcastle |
| 1831 | 21 | In Manchester meets Rev. William Gaskell, junior minister at Cross Street Unitarian Chapel |
| 1832 | 22 | 30 August. Marries William Gaskell, moves to Manchester |
| 1834 | 24 | 12 September. Her daughter Marianne is born. |
| 1837 | 27 | January. 'Sketches among the Poor' (with William) in Blackwood's Edinburgh Magazine. 5 February. Margaret Emily (Meta) born. May. Aunt Lumb dies |
| 1839 | 29 | Infant son dies |
| 1842 | 32 | 7 October. Florence Elizabeth (Flossy) born |

# Chronology of her Times

| Year | Literary Context | Historical Events |
|------|------------------|-------------------|
| 1810 | | |
| 1811 | | |
| 1812 | Birth of Charles Dickens | |
| 1815 | | Battle of Waterloo |
| 1820 | | George III dies; succeeded by George IV |
| 1821 | | |
| 1826 | Fenimore Cooper, *Last of the Mohicans* | |
| 1828 | | |
| 1829 | | |
| 1830 | Tennyson, Poems, *Chiefly Lyrical* Charles Lyell, *Principles of Geology* | George IV dies; succeeded by William IV |
| 1831 | Ebenezer Elliot, *Corn Law Rhymes* | Russell introduces first Reform Bill |
| 1832 | Deaths of Sir Walter Scott and Goethe | First Reform Act passed |
| 1834 | | Slavery ended in British possessions |
| 1837 | Dickens, *Oliver Twist* | William IV dies; succeeded by Queen Victoria |
| 1839 | Carlyle, *Chartism* | Chartist petition presented to Parliament |
| 1842 | | Hong Kong ceded to Britain. Widespread Chartist riots |

| Year | Age | Life |
|------|-----|------|
| 1844 | 34 | 23 October. Birth of her son, William |
| 1845 | 34 | William dies, aged 10 months. |
| 1846 | 36 | 3 September. Fourth daughter, Julia Margaret Bradford born |
| 1848 | 38 | November, *Mary Barton* |
| 1849 | 39 | Visits London: meets Dickens, Carlyle, Forster |
| 1850 | 40–41 | Begins to write for Dickens's *Household Words* First meeting with Charlotte Brontë |
| 1851 | 41 | Cranford in *Household Words* |
| 1853 | 42 | May. Visit to Paris. September – Visit to Haworth |
| 1854 | 43–4 | *North and South* in *Household Words* |
| 1855 | 44 | Patrick Brontë asks her to write Charlotte's *Life* |
| 1857 | 46 | The *Life* completed; holiday in Italy |
| 1859 | 49 | 'Lois the Witch' |
| 1862 | 52 | Autumn. Intense relief work in the Manchester 'cotton famine' the American Civil War |
| 1863 | 53 | *Sylvia's Lovers* September. Florence Gaskell marries |
| 1865 | 54–5 | *Wives and Daughters* begins in the *Cornhill Magazine* 12 November. Elizabeth dies of a heart attack at her newly bought house, 'The Lawn', in Hampshire |

| Year | Literary Context | Historical Events |
|------|------------------|-------------------|
| 1844 | Disraeli, *Coningsby* | |
| 1845 | Disraeli, *Sybil* | Beginning of potato famine in Ireland |
| 1846 | Edward Lear, *Book of Nonsense* | Repeal of Corn Laws in Britain |
| 1848 | Thackeray, *Vanity Fair* | France: the Republic is proclaimed. |
| 1849 | Charlotte Brontë, *Shirley* | Garibaldi enters Rome |
| 1850 | Dickens, *David Copperfield* Tennyson becomes Poet Laureate | Australian Constitution Act |
| 1851 | Melville, *Moby-Dick* | First women's suffrage petition presented to House of Commons |
| 1853 | Charlotte Brontë, *Villette* Dickens, *Bleak House* | France: Napoleon III proclaimed Emperor |
| 1854 | Thoreau, Walden | France and Britain declare war on Russia |
| 1855 | Death of Charlotte Brontë | Paris World Exhibition |
| 1857 | Dickens, *Little Dorrit* Trollope, *Barchester Towers* | 'Indian Mutiny': Massacre of Cawnpore, loss of Delhi |
| 1859 | Darwin, *The Origin of Species* | Revolutions against Austrian rule in Parma, Modena and Tuscany |
| 1862 | | Bismarck appointed Prussian Premier |
| 1863 | Tolstoy begins *War and Peace* | |
| 1865 | Lewis Carroll, *Alice's Adventures in Wonderland* Dickens, *Our Mutual Friend* | Lincoln assassinated: Confederate Army surrender. Palmerston dies: Russell Prime Minister |

# CHAPTER I

# The Dawn of a Gala Day

To begin with the old rigmarole of childhood. In a country there was a shire, and in that shire there was a town, and in that town there was a house, and in that house there was a room, and in that room there was a bed, and in that bed there lay a little girl; wide awake and longing to get up, but not daring to do so for fear of the unseen power in the next room – a certain Betty, whose slumbers must not be disturbed until six o'clock struck. It was June, and the room was full of sunny warmth and light.

On the drawers opposite to the little white dimity bed in which Molly Gibson lay, was a bonnet-stand, on which was hung a bonnet made of solid straw, its only trimming a plain white ribbon. Still, there was a neat little quilling inside, every plait of which Molly knew; for had she not made it herself the evening before, with infinite pains? and was there not a little blue bow in this quilling, the very first bit of such finery Molly had ever had the prospect of wearing?

Six o'clock now! the brisk ringing of the church bells told that; calling everyone to their daily work. Up jumped Molly, and ran across to the window; and let in the sweet morning air. The dew was already off the flowers in the garden below, but still rising from the long hay-grass in the meadows directly beyond. At one side lay the little town of Hollingford, into a street of which Mr Gibson's front door opened; and puffs of smoke were already beginning to rise from many a cottage chimney, where some housewife was already up, and preparing breakfast for the bread-winner of the family.

Molly Gibson saw all this; but all she thought about it was, 'Oh!

it will be a fine day! I was afraid it never would come; or that, if it ever came, it would be a rainy day!' Pleasures in a country town were very simple, and Molly had lived for twelve long years without the occurrence of any event so great as that which was now impending. Poor child! It is true that she had lost her mother, which was a jar to the whole tenour of her life; but that was hardly an event in the sense referred to; and, besides, she had been too young to be conscious of it at the time. The pleasure she was looking forward to today was her first share in a kind of annual festival in Hollingford.

The little straggling town faded away into country on one side, close to the entrance-lodge of a great park, where lived my Lord and Lady Cumnor: 'the earl' and 'the countess', as they were always called by the inhabitants of the town; where a very pretty amount of feudal feeling still lingered. 'The earl' was lord of the manor, and owner of much of the land on which Hollingford was built; he and his household were fed, and doctored, and, to a certain measure, clothed by the good people of the town; their fathers' grandfathers had always voted for the eldest son of Cumnor Towers, and, following in the ancestral track, every man-jack in the place gave his vote to the liege-lord, totally irrespective of such chimeras as political opinions.

This was no unusual instance of the influence of the great landowners over humbler neighbours in those days before railways, and it was well for a place where the powerful family were of so respectable a character as the Cumnors. The simple worship of the townspeople was accepted by the earl and countess as a right. But they did a good deal for the town, and were often thoughtful and kind in their treatment of their vassals. Lord Cumnor was a forbearing landlord; putting his steward a little on one side sometimes; which meant that occasionally the earl asked his own questions of his own tenants, and used his own eyes and ears in the management of the smaller details of his property. But his tenants liked my lord all the better for this habit of his. Lord Cumnor had certainly a little time for gossip. But, then, the countess made up by her unapproachable dignity for this weakness of the earl's. Once a year she was condescending. She and the ladies, her daughters, had set up a school of the kind we should call 'industrial', where girls are taught to sew beautifully, to be capital housemaids, and pretty fair cooks, and, above all, to dress neatly – ready curtseys, and 'please, ma'ams', being *de rigueur*.

Now, as the countess was absent from the Towers for a considerable part of the year, she was glad to enlist the sympathy of the Hollingford ladies in this school. And the various unoccupied gentlewomen of the town responded to the call of their liege lady, and gave her their service as required. In return, there was a day of honour set apart every summer, when, with much stately hospitality, Lady Cumnor and her daughters received all the school visitors at the Towers, the great family mansion. The order of this annual festivity was this. About ten o'clock, one of the Towers carriages rolled through the lodge, and drove to different houses, wherein dwelt a woman to be honoured; picking them up by ones or twos, till the loaded carriage drove back again through the ready portals, bowled along the smooth, tree-shaded road, and deposited its covey of smartly dressed ladies on the great flight of steps leading to the ponderous doors of Cumnor Towers. Back again to the town; another picking-up, and another return, and so on, till the whole party were assembled either in the house or in the really beautiful gardens. After the proper amount of exhibition on the one part, and admiration on the other, had been done, there was a collation for the visitors, and some more display and admiration of the treasures inside the house. Towards four o'clock, coffee was brought; this was a signal of the carriage that was to take them back to their own homes; whither they returned with the happy consciousness of a well-spent day, but with some fatigue at the long-continued exertion of behaving their best. Nor were Lady Cumnor and her daughters free from something of the same self-approbation, and something, too, of the fatigue that always follows on conscious efforts to behave as will best please the society you are in.

For the first time, Molly Gibson was to be included among the guests at the Towers. She was much too young to be a visitor at the school, but it had so happened that, one day when Lord Cumnor was on a 'pottering' expedition, he had met Mr Gibson, *the* doctor of the neighbourhood, coming out of the farm-house my lord was entering; and, having some small question to ask the surgeon (Lord Cumnor seldom passed anyone of his acquaintance without asking a question of some sort – not always attending to the answer), he accompanied Mr Gibson to a ring in the wall to which the surgeon's horse was fastened. Molly was there too, sitting square and quiet on her rough little pony. Her grave eyes opened large and wide at the close neighbourhood and advance of 'the earl'; for to her imagination the grey-haired, red-faced, somewhat clumsy man, was a cross between an archangel and a king.

'Your daughter, eh, Gibson? – nice little girl; how old? Pony wants grooming, though,' patting it as he talked. 'What's your name, my dear? He's sadly behindhand with his rent, as I was saying; but, if he's really ill, I must see after Sheepshanks, who is a hardish man of business. You'll come to our school-scrimmage on Thursday, little girl – what's-your-name? Mind you send her, or bring her, Gibson.' And off the earl trotted.

Mr Gibson mounted, and he and Molly rode off. Then she said, 'May I go, papa?' in rather an anxious little tone of voice.

'Where, my dear?' said he.

'To the Towers – on Thursday, you know. That gentleman' (she was shy of calling him by his title) 'asked me.'

'Would you like it, my dear? It has always seemed to me rather a tiresome piece of gaiety – rather a tiring day, I mean – beginning so early.'

'Oh, papa!' said Molly reproachfully.

'You'd like to go then, would you?'

'Yes; if I may! Don't you think I may?'

'Well! We'll see – yes! I think we can manage it, if you wish it so much, Molly.'

Then they were silent again. By-and-by, Molly said – 'Please, papa – I do wish to go – but I don't care about it.'

'I suppose you mean you don't care to go, if it will be any

trouble to get you there. I can easily manage it, however; so you may consider it settled. You'll want a white frock; you'd better tell Betty you're going, and she'll see after making you tidy.'

Now, there were two or three things to be done by Mr Gibson, before he could feel quite comfortable about Molly's going to the festival at the Towers; so, the next day, he rode over to the Towers, ostensibly to visit some sick housemaid, but, in reality, to throw himself in my lady's way, and get her to ratify Lord Cumnor's invitation to Molly. He chose his time, with a little natural diplomacy; which, indeed, he had often to exercise in his intercourse with the great family. He rode into the stable-yard about twelve o'clock, a little before luncheon-time, and yet after the worry of opening the post-bag and discussing its contents was over. After he had put up his horse, he went in by the back-way to the house; the 'House' on this side, the 'Towers' at the front. He saw his patient, gave his directions to the housekeeper, and then went out, with a rare wild-flower in his hand, to find one of the ladies Tranmere in the garden, where, according to his hope and calculation, he came upon Lady Cumnor too – now talking to her daughter about the contents of an open letter which she held in her hand, now directing a gardener about certain bedding-out plants.

'I was calling to see Nanny, and I took the opportunity of bringing Lady Agnes the plant I was telling her about as growing on Cumnor Moss.'

'Thank you so much, Mr Gibson! Mamma, look! this is the *Drosera rotundifolia* I have been wanting so long.'

'Ah! yes; very pretty, I daresay. Nanny is better, I hope? We can't have anyone laid up next week, for the house will be quite full of people – and here are the Danbys writing to offer themselves as well. One comes down for a fortnight of quiet, at Whitsuntide, and leaves half one's establishment in town; and, as soon as people know of our being here, we get letters without end, longing for a breath of country-air.'

'We shall go back to town on Friday the 18th,' said Lady Agnes, in a consolatory tone.

'Yes! as soon as we have got over the school visitors' affair.'

'By the way!' said Mr Gibson, availing himself of the good opening thus presented, 'I met my lord at the Crosstrees Farm yesterday, and he was kind enough to ask my little daughter, who was with me, to be one of the party here on Thursday; it would give the lassie great pleasure, I believe.'

'Oh, well! if my lord asked her, I suppose she must come; but I wish he was not so amazingly hospitable! Not but what the little girl will be quite welcome; only, you see, he met a younger Miss Browning the other day, of whose existence I had never heard. I knew there was one visitor of the name of Browning; I never knew there were two, but, of course, as soon as Lord Cumnor heard there was another, he must needs ask her; so the carriage will have to go backwards and forwards four times now to fetch them all. So your daughter can come quite easily, Mr Gibson, and I shall be very glad to see her for your sake. She can sit bodkin with the Brownings, I suppose? You'll arrange it all with them; and mind you get Nanny well up to her work next week!'

Just as Mr Gibson was going away, Lady Cumnor called after him, 'Oh! by-the-bye, Clare is here; you remember Clare, don't you? She was a patient of yours, long ago.'

'Clare!' he repeated, in a bewildered tone.

'Miss Clare, our old governess,' said Lady Agnes. 'About twelve years ago, before Lady Cuxhaven was married.'

'Oh, yes!' said he. 'Miss Clare, who had the scarlet fever here; a pretty, delicate girl. But I thought she was married!'

'Yes!' said Lady Cumnor. 'She was a silly little thing, and went and married a poor curate, and became a stupid Mrs Kirkpatrick; but we always kept on calling her "Clare". And now he's dead, and left her a widow, and she is staying here; and we are racking our brains to find out some way of helping her to a livelihood, without parting her from her child. She's somewhere about the grounds, if you like to renew your acquaintance with her.'

'Thank you, my lady. I'm afraid I cannot stop today; I have a long round to go.'

Long as his ride had been that day, he called on the Miss Brownings in the evening, to arrange about Molly's accompanying them to the Towers. They were tall, handsome women, past their first youth, and inclined to be extremely complaisant to the widowed doctor.

'Eh, dear! Mr Gibson, but we shall be delighted to have her with us. You should never have thought of *asking* us such a thing,' said Miss Browning the elder.

'I'm sure I'm hardly sleeping at nights, for thinking of it,' said Miss Phoebe. 'You know I've never been there before. Somehow, though my name has been down on the visitors' list these three years, the countess has never named me in her note; and you know I could not go to such a grand place without being asked; now, could I?'

'I told Phoebe last year,' said her sister, 'that I was sure it was only inadvertence on the part of the countess, and that her ladyship would be as hurt as anyone when she didn't see Phoebe among the school visitors; but Phoebe has got a delicate mind, Mr Gibson, and, for all I could say, she stopped here at home; and it spoilt all my pleasure, I do assure you.'

'I had a good cry after you was gone, Sally,' said Miss Phoebe; 'but for all that, I think I was right in stopping away from where I was not asked. Don't you, Mr Gibson?'

'Certainly,' said he.

'Molly will know she's to put on her best clothes,' said Miss Browning. 'We could perhaps lend her a few beads, or artificials, if she wants them.'

'Molly must go in a clean white frock,' said Mr Gibson, rather hastily; for he did not admire the Miss Brownings' taste in dress, and was unwilling to have his child decked up according to their fancy. Miss Browning had just a shade of annoyance in her tone as she drew herself up, and said, 'Oh! very well.' But Miss Phoebe said, 'Molly will look very nice in whatever she puts on, that's certain.'

## CHAPTER 2

# A Novice Amongst
# the Great Folk

At ten o'clock on the eventful Thursday, the Towers carriage began its work. Molly was ready long before it made its first appearance, although it had been settled that she and the Miss Brownings were not to go until the last, or fourth, time of its coming. Her face had been soaped, scrubbed, and shone brilliantly clean; her frills, her frock, her ribbons were all snow-white. She had on a black mode cloak that had been her mother's; it was trimmed round with rich lace, and looked quaint and old-fashioned on the child. For the first time in her life she wore kid gloves; hitherto she had only had cotton ones. She trembled many a time, and almost turned faint once with the long expectation of the morning, and after two hours the carriage came for her at last. She had to sit very forward to avoid crushing the Miss Brownings' new dresses; and yet not too forward, for fear of incommoding fat Mrs Goodenough and her niece, who occupied the front seat: so that Molly felt herself to be very conspicuously placed in the centre of the carriage, a mark for all the observation of Hollingford. It was far too much of a gala day for the work of the little town to go forward with its usual regularity. Maidservants gazed out of upper windows; shop-keepers' wives stood on the door-steps; cottagers ran out, with babies in their arms; and little children, too young to know how to behave respectfully at the sight of an earl's carriage, huzza-ed merrily as it bowled along. The woman at the lodge held the gate open, and dropped a low curtsey to the liveries. And now they were in the Park; and now they were in sight of the Towers, and silence fell upon the ladies, only broken by one faint remark from Mrs Goodenough's niece, a stranger to the town, as they drew up before the double semicircular flight of steps which led to the door of the mansion.

'They call that a *perron*, I believe, don't they?' she asked. But the only answer she obtained was a simultaneous 'hush'. It was very awful, and Molly half wished herself at home again. But she lost all consciousness of herself when the party strolled out into the beautiful grounds. Green velvet lawns, bathed in sunshine, stretched away on every side into the finely wooded park. Near the house there were walls and fences; but they were covered with climbing roses, and rare honeysuckles and other creepers just bursting into bloom. Molly held Miss Browning's hand very tight, as they loitered about in company with several other ladies, marshalled by a daughter of the Towers, who seemed half amused at the voluble admiration showered down upon every possible thing and place. Molly said nothing, as became her age and position; but every now and then she relieved her full heart by drawing a deep breath. Presently, they came to the long glittering range of greenhouses and hothouses, and Lady Agnes expatiated on the rarity of this plant, and the mode of cultivation required by that, till Molly began to feel very faint. At length, afraid of making a greater sensation, she caught at Miss Browning's hand, and gasped out –

'May I go back, out into the garden? I can't breathe here!'

'Oh, yes, to be sure, love! I daresay it's hard understanding for you, love; but it's very fine and instructive, and a deal of Latin in it too.'

She turned hastily round, not to lose another word of Lady Agnes's lecture on orchids; and Molly turned back and passed out of the heated atmosphere. She felt better in the fresh air; and went from one lovely spot to another, till at length she grew very weary, and wished to return to the house, but did not know how. The hot sun told upon her head, and it began to ache. She saw a great wide-spreading cedar-tree, and the black repose beneath its branches lured her thither. There was a rustic seat in the shadow; and weary Molly sate down and fell asleep.

She was startled from her slumbers after a time, and jumped to her feet. Two ladies were standing by her, talking about her. And, with a vague conviction that she had done something wrong, and also because she was worn out with hunger, fatigue, and the morning's excitement, she began to cry.

'Poor little woman! She has lost herself; she belongs to some of the people from Hollingford, I have no doubt,' said the oldest-looking who appeared to be about forty, though she did not really number more than thirty years. She was plain-featured, and had rather a severe expression on her face; her dress was as rich as any morning dress could be; her voice deep and unmodulated – what in a lower rank of life would have been called gruff; but that was not a word to apply to Lady Cuxhaven, the eldest daughter of the earl and countess. The other lady was in fact some years the elder; at first sight Molly thought she was the most beautiful person she had ever seen. Her voice was soft and plaintive as she replied –

'Poor little darling! she is overcome by the heat.'

Molly now found voice to say –

'I am Molly Gibson, please. I came here with Miss Brownings;' for her great fear was that she should be taken for an unauthorised intruder.

'Miss Brownings?' said Lady Cuxhaven to her companion.

'I think they were the two tall, large young women that Lady Agnes was talking about.'

'Oh, I daresay. Have you had anything to eat, child, since you came? You look a very white little thing; or is it the heat?'

'I have had nothing to eat,' said Molly, rather piteously; for, indeed, before she fell asleep she had been very hungry.

The two ladies spoke to each other in a low voice; then the elder said, 'Sit still here, my dear; we are going to the house, and Clare shall bring you something to eat before you try to walk back.' So they went away, and Molly sat upright, waiting for the promised messenger. She did not know who Clare might be, and she did not care much for food now; but she felt as if she could not walk without some help. At length she saw the pretty lady coming back, followed by a footman with a tray.

'Look how kind Lady Cuxhaven is,' said she who was called Clare. 'She chose you out this little lunch herself; and now you must try and eat it, and you'll be quite right when you've had some food, darling. You need not stop, Edwards; I will bring the tray back with me.'

There was some bread, and cold chicken, and some jelly, and a glass of wine, and a bottle of sparkling water, and a bunch of grapes. Molly put out her trembling little hand for the water; but she was too faint to hold it. Clare put it to her mouth, and she took a long draught and was refreshed. But she could not eat; her headache was too bad. Clare looked bewildered. 'Take some grapes, they will be the best for you; you must try and eat something, or I don't know how I shall get you to the house.'

'My head aches so,' said Molly, lifting her eyes wistfully.

'Oh, dear, how tiresome!' said Clare, still in her sweet gentle voice. 'You see, I don't know what to do with you here, if you don't eat enough to enable you to walk home. And I've been out for these three hours, trapesing about the grounds till I'm as tired as can be, and I've missed my lunch and all.' Then, as if a new idea had struck her, she said – 'You lie back for a few minutes, and try to eat the bunch of grapes; and I'll wait for you, and just be eating a mouthful meanwhile.'

Molly leant back, picking at the grapes, and watching the good appetite with which the lady ate up the chicken and jelly, and drank the glass of wine. She was so pretty and so graceful in her deep mourning, that even her hurry in eating, as if she was afraid of some one coming to surprise her in the act, did not keep her little observer from admiring her in all she did.

'And now, darling, are you ready to go?' said she, when she had eaten up everything on the tray. 'Now, if you will come with me to the side-entrance, I will take you up to my own room, and you shall lie down for an hour or two; and, if you have a good nap, your headache will be gone.'

So they set off, Clare carrying the empty tray, rather to Molly's shame; but the child had enough work to drag herself along.

The 'side-entrance' was a flight of steps leading up into a private ante-room in which were deposited the light garden-tools and the bows and arrows of the young ladies of the house. Lady Cuxhaven met them in this hall as soon as they came in.

'How is she now?' she asked; then glancing at the plates and glasses, she added, 'Come, I think there can't be much amiss! You're a good old Clare, but you should have let one of the men fetch that tray in.'

Molly could not help wishing that her pretty companion would have told Lady Cuxhaven that she herself had helped to finish up the ample luncheon; but she only said – 'Poor dear! she is not quite the thing yet. I am going to put her down on my bed, to see if she can get a little sleep.'

Molly saw Lady Cuxhaven say something in a half-laughing manner to 'Clare', as she passed her; and the child could not keep from tormenting herself by fancying that the words spoken sounded wonderfully like 'Overeaten herself, I suspect.' However, she felt too poorly to worry herself long; the little white bed in the cool and pretty room had too many attractions for her aching head. The muslin curtains flapped softly in the scented air that came through the open windows. Clare covered her up with a light shawl, and as she was going away, Molly roused herself to say, 'Please, ma'am, don't let them go away without me! I am to go back with Miss Brownings.'

'Don't trouble yourself about it, dear; I'll take care,' said Clare, kissing her hand to little anxious Molly. And then she went away, and thought no more about it. The carriages came round at half-past four, hurried a little by Lady Cumnor, who had suddenly become tired of the business of entertaining.

'Why not have both carriages out, Mamma, and get rid of them all at once?' said Lady Cuxhaven. So, at last, there had been a great hurry and an unmethodical way of packing off everyone at once. Miss Browning had gone in the chariot, and Miss Phoebe, along with several other guests, in a great roomy family conveyance, of the kind which we should now call an 'omnibus'. Each thought that Molly Gibson was with the other.

Mrs Kirkpatrick, *née* Clare, coming to her bed-room to dress for dinner, stood aghast at the sight of Molly.

'Why, I quite forgot you!' she said. 'Nay, don't cry; you'll make yourself not fit to be seen. Of course, I must take the consequences of your over-sleeping yourself; and, if I can't manage to get you back to Hollingford tonight, you shall sleep with me, and we'll send you home tomorrow morning.'

'But papa!' sobbed out Molly. 'He always wants me to make tea for him; and I have no night-things.'

'Well, don't go and make a piece of work about what can't be helped now! I'll lend you night-things, and your papa must do without your making tea for him tonight. And, another time, don't over-sleep yourself in a strange house; you may not always find yourself among such hospitable people as they are here. I'll ask if you may come in to dessert with Master Smythe and the little ladies. You shall go into the nursery, and have some tea with them. I think it is a very fine thing for you to be stopping in such a grand house as this; many a little girl would like nothing better.'

During this speech she was arranging her toilette for dinner – taking off her black morning-gown; putting on her dressing-gown; shaking her long soft auburn hair over her shoulders, and glancing about in search of various articles of her dress.

'I have a little girl of my own, dear! I don't know what she would not give to be staying here at Lord Cumnor's with me; but, instead of that, she has to spend her holidays at school; and yet you are looking as miserable as can be at the thought of stopping for just one night. I have been as busy as can be with those tiresome – those good ladies, I mean, from Hollingford – and one can't think of everything at a time.'

Molly – only child as she was – had stopped her tears at the mention of that little girl of Mrs Kirkpatrick's; 'Are you married, ma'am; I thought she called you Clare?'

In high good-humour, Mrs Kirkpatrick made reply – 'I don't look as if I was married, do I? Everyone is surprised. And yet I have been a widow for seven months now; and not a grey hair on my head, though Lady Cuxhaven, who is younger than I, has ever so many.'

'Why do they call you "Clare"?' continued Molly.

'Because I lived with them when I was Miss Clare. It is a pretty name, isn't it? I married a Mr Kirkpatrick; he was only a curate, poor fellow; but he was of a very good family; and, if three of his relations had died without children, I should have been a baronet's wife. But Providence did not see fit to permit it; and we must always resign ourselves to what is decreed.'

'You have a little girl?' asked Molly.

'Yes: darling Cynthia! she is my only comfort. But I must go now. It does not do to keep Lady Cumnor waiting. Now I shall ring this bell; and, when the housemaid comes, ask her to take you into the nursery, and to tell Lady Cuxhaven's nurse who you are. And then you'll have tea with the little ladies, and come in with them to dessert. There! I'm sorry you've over-slept yourself, but give me a kiss, and don't cry – you are rather a pretty child, though you've not got Cynthia's colouring! Oh, Nanny, would you be so very kind as to take this young lady – (what's your name, my dear? Gibson?) – Miss Gibson, to Mrs Dyson, in the nursery, and ask her to allow her to drink tea with the young ladies there; and to send her in with them to dessert? I'll explain it all to my lady.'

Nanny's face brightened when she heard the name Gibson; and, having ascertained from Molly that she was 'the doctor's' child, she showed more willingness to comply with Mrs Kirkpatrick's request than was usual with her.

Molly was fond of children; so, as long as she was in the nursery, she got on pretty well, being obedient to the wishes of the supreme power, and even very useful to Mrs Dyson, by playing at tricks, and thus keeping a little one quiet, while its brothers and sisters were being arrayed in lace and muslin.

At length Mrs Dyson, in a rustling silk gown, marshalled her convoy, and set sail for the dining-room door. There was a large party of gentlemen and ladies sitting round the decked table, in the brilliantly lighted room. Each child ran up to its mother, or aunt, or particular friend; but Molly had no one to go to.

'Who is that tall girl in the thick white frock? Not one of the children in the house, I think?'

The lady addressed put up her glass, gazed at Molly, and dropped it in an instant. 'A French girl, I should imagine. I know Lady Cuxhaven was inquiring for one to bring up with her little girls, that they might get a good accent early. Poor little woman, she looks wild and strange!' And the speaker, who sat next to Lord Cumnor, made a sign to Molly to come to her; Molly crept up to her as to the first shelter; but, when the lady began talking to her in French, she blushed violently, and said in a very low voice –

'I don't understand French. I'm only Molly Gibson, ma'am.'

'Molly Gibson!' said the lady, as if that was not much of an explanation.

Lord Cumnor caught the words and the tone.

'Oh, ho!' said he. 'Are you the little girl who has been sleeping in my bed?'

He imitated the deep voice of the fabulous bear, who asks this question of the little child in the story; but Molly had never read the 'Three Bears', and fancied that his anger was real; she drew nearer to the kind lady who had beckoned her as to a refuge. Lord Cumnor was very fond of getting hold of what he fancied was a joke, and working his idea threadbare; so, all the time the ladies were in the room, he kept on his running fire at Molly, alluding to the Sleeping Beauty, the Seven Sleepers, and any other famous sleeper that came into his head. He had no idea of the misery his jokes were to the sensitive girl. All the girl thought of was, how little they wanted her in this grand house; how she must seem like a careless intruder. Once or twice she wondered where her father was, and whether he was missing her; but the thought brought such a choking in her throat, that she felt she must not give way to it, for fear of bursting out crying.

She followed the ladies out of the dining-room, almost hoping that no one would see her. But that was impossible, and she immediately became the subject of conversation between the awful Lady Cumnor and her kind neighbour at dinner.

'Do you know, I thought this young lady was French? she has

got the black hair and eyelashes, and grey eyes, and colourless complexion one meets with in some parts of France, and I knew Lady Cuxhaven was trying to find a well-educated girl who would be a pleasant companion to her children.'

'No!' said Lady Cumnor, looking very stern, as Molly thought: 'She is the daughter of our medical man at Hollingford; she came with the school visitors this morning, and she was overcome by the heat and fell asleep in Clare's room, and did not waken up till all the carriages were gone. We will send her home tomorrow morning; but for tonight she must stay here, and Clare is kind enough to say she may sleep with her.'

There was an implied blame running through this speech, that Molly felt like needle-points all over her. Lady Cuxhaven came up at this moment. Her manner of speaking was as abrupt as her mother's, but Molly felt the kinder nature underneath.

'How are you now, my dear? You look better than you did under the cedar-tree. Clare, don't you think we could find some of those books of engravings that would interest Miss Gibson?'

Mrs Kirkpatrick came gliding up to the place where Molly stood; and began petting her with pretty words and actions, while Lady Cuxhaven turned over heavy volumes in search of one that might interest the girl.

'Poor darling! I saw you come into the dining-room, looking so shy; and I wanted you to come near me, but I could not make a sign to you, because Lord Cuxhaven was speaking to me at the time, telling me about his travels. Ah, here is a nice book – *Lodge's Portraits*; now I'll sit by you and tell you who they all are, and all about them. Don't trouble yourself any more, dear Lady Cuxhaven; I'll take charge of her; pray leave her to me!'

Molly grew hotter and hotter. If they would only leave her alone, and not labour at being kind to her; would 'not trouble themselves' about her! These words of Mrs Kirkpatrick's seemed to quench the gratitude she was feeling to Lady Cuxhaven for looking for something to amuse her.

By-and-by, Mrs Kirkpatrick was called away to accompany Lady Agnes's song, and then Molly really had a few minutes' enjoyment. She could look round the room, unobserved, and, sure, never was any place out of a king's house so grand and magnificent! Large mirrors, velvet curtains, pictures in their gilded frames, a multitude of dazzling lights decorated the vast saloon; and the floor was studded with groups of ladies and gentlemen, all dressed in gorgeous attire. Suddenly, Molly bethought her of the children whom she had accompanied into the dining-room – where were they? Gone to bed an hour before, at some quiet signal. Molly wondered if she might go, too – if she could ever find her way back to the haven of Mrs Kirkpatrick's bed-room. But she was at some distance from the door; a long way from Mrs Kirkpatrick. So Molly sate on, her heart growing heavier. Presently a footman entered and went up to Mrs Kirkpatrick, where she sate at the pianos. She came now towards Molly, and said to her –

'Do you know, darling, your papa has come for you, and brought your pony for you to ride home; so I shall lose my little bedfellow, for I suppose you must go?'

Go! was there a question of it in Molly's mind, as she stood up quivering, sparkling, almost crying out loud?

'You must go and wish Lady Cumnor good-night, you know, my dear, and thank her ladyship for her kindness to you. She is there, near that statue, talking to Mr Courtenay.'

Yes! she was there – forty feet away! All that blank space had to be crossed; and then a speech to be made!

'Must I go?' asked Molly, in the most pitiful voice.

'Yes; make haste about it; there is nothing so formidable in it, is there?' replied Mrs Kirkpatrick, in a sharper voice than before, aware that they were wanting her at the piano.

Molly, looking up, said softly –

'Would you mind coming with me, please?'

'No! not I!' said Mrs Kirkpatrick, seeing that her compliance was likely to be the most speedy way of getting through the affair; so she took Molly's hand, and, in passing the group at the piano, she said, smiling, in her pretty genteel manner –

'Our little friend here is shy and modest, and wants me to

accompany her to Lady Cumnor to wish good-night; her father has come for her, and she is going away.'

Molly did not know how it was, afterwards; but she pulled her hand out of Mrs Kirkpatrick's on hearing these words, and, going a step or two in advance, came up to Lady Cumnor, grand in purple velvet, and dropping a curtsey, she said –

'My lady, papa is come, and I am going away; and, my lady, I wish you good-night, and thank you for your kindness.'

Mr Gibson was in the housekeeper's room, when Molly ran in. She threw her arms round her father's neck. 'Oh, papa, papa, papa! I am so glad you have come!' and then she burst out crying, stroking his face almost hysterically.

'Why, what a noodle you are, Molly! Did you think I was going to give up my little girl to live at the Towers all the rest of her life? You make as much work about my coming for you, as if you thought I had. Make haste, now, and get on your bonnet!'

Once out into the park, Molly struck her pony, and urged him on as hard as he would go. Mr Gibson called out at last –

'Molly! Stop! We're getting into the shadow of the trees, and it's not safe riding fast here.'

'Oh! papa, I never was so glad in all my life. I felt like a lighted candle when they're putting the extinguisher on it.'

'Did you? How d'ye know what the candle feels?'

'Oh, I don't know, but I did.'

He laid his hand upon hers.

'Oh! I am so glad to feel you. Papa, I should like to get a chain, just as long as your longest round, and then I could fasten us two to each end of it, and when I wanted you I could pull; and, if you didn't want to come, you could pull back again; but I should know you knew I wanted you, and we could never lose each other.'

'In that plan of yours, if I make out rightly, I am to go about the country, like the donkeys on the common, with a clog fastened to my hind leg.'

'I shouldn't mind your calling me a clog, if only we were fastened together.'

'But I do mind you calling me a donkey,' he replied.

'I never did. At least I didn't mean to. But it is such a comfort to know that I may be as rude as I like.'

'Is that what you've learnt from the grand company you've been keeping today?'

'Oh, I do hope I shall never be a lord or a lady. I should lose myself every time I had to fetch my bonnet, or else get tired of long passages and great staircases long before I could go out walking. I shall never forget the morning in that garden. But I was never so unhappy as I have been this afternoon.'

Mr Gibson thought it his duty to ride round by the Towers, and pay a visit of apology and thanks to the family, before they left for London. No one was sufficiently at liberty to listen to his grateful civilities but Mrs Kirkpatrick, who made leisure enough to receive Mr Gibson on behalf of the family, and assured him of her remembrance of his great professional attention to her in former days in the most winning manner.

## CHAPTER 3

# Molly Gibson's Childhood

Sixteen years before this time, all Hollingford had been disturbed to its foundations by the intelligence that Mr Hall, the doctor, who had attended them all their days, was going to take a partner. Deaf and rheumatic as he might be, he was still Mr Hall the doctor who could heal all their ailments – unless they died meanwhile – and he had no right to speak of growing old, and taking a partner. And, just when the elderly maiden ladies of Hollingford thought that they had convinced their contemporary that he was as young as ever, he startled them by bringing his new partner, Mr Gibson, to call upon them. And 'Who was this Mr Gibson?' they asked, and echo might answer the question, if she liked, for no one else did. No one ever in all his life knew anything more of his antecedents than the Hollingford people might have found out the first day they saw him: that he was tall, grave, rather handsome; thin enough to be called 'a very genteel figure'; speaking with a slight Scotch accent; and, as one good lady observed, 'so very trite in his conversation', by which she meant sarcastic. As to his birth, parentage, and education, the favourite conjecture was that he was the illegitimate son of a Scotch Duke by a Frenchwoman; and the grounds for this conjecture were these: – He spoke with a Scotch accent; therefore, he must be Scotch. He had a very genteel appearance, an elegant figure, and was apt – so his ill-wishers said – to give himself airs; therefore, his father must have been some person of quality.

Then his mother must have been a Frenchwoman, because his hair was so black; and he was so sallow; and because he had been in Paris. All this might be true, or might not; nobody ever knew, or found out anything more about him than what Mr Hall told them, namely, that his professional qualifications were as high as his moral character, and that both were far above the average. The popularity of this world is as transient as its glory. Mr Gibson was received, at the end of a twelvemonth, with as much welcome respect for his professional skill as Mr Hall himself had ever been. Nay – and this was a little too much for even the kind old doctor's good temper – Mr Gibson had even been invited once to dinner at the Towers; to dine with the great Sir Astley, the head of the profession! To be sure, Mr Hall had been asked as well; but he was laid up just then with his gout and he had not been able to go. Poor Mr Hall never quite got over this mortification and kept pretty closely to the house during the two winters that remained of his life. He sent for an orphan grand-niece, to keep him company in his old age; he, the woman-contemning old bachelor, became thankful for the cheerful presence of the pretty, bonny Mary Pearson, who was good and sensible, and nothing more. She formed a close friendship with the daughters of the vicar, Mr Browning; and Mr Gibson found time to become very intimate with all three. Hollingford speculated much on which young lady would become Mrs Gibson, and was rather sorry when the talk about possibilities with regard to the handsome young surgeon's marriage, ended by his marrying his predecessor's niece. The two Miss Brownings showed no signs of going into a consumption on the occasion. On the contrary, they were boisterously merry at the wedding; and poor Mrs Gibson died of consumption, four or five years after her marriage and when her only child, Molly, was just three years old.

Several years before the opening of this story, Mr Gibson's position seemed settled for life, both socially and professionally. He was a widower, and likely to remain so; his domestic affections were centred on little Molly, but even to her, in their most private moments, he did not give way to much expression of his feelings; his most caressing appellation for her was 'Goosey', and he took a pleasure in bewildering her infant mind with his badinage. The child grew to understand her father well, and the two had the most delightful intercourse together – half banter, half seriousness, but altogether confidential friendship. Mr Gibson kept three servants: Betty, a cook, and a girl who was supposed to be housemaid. Three servants would not have been required if it had not been Mr Gibson's habit to take two 'pupils', as they were called in the genteel language of Hollingford – 'apprentices' as they were in fact, being bound by indentures, and paying a handsome premium to learn their business. They lived in the house, and had their meals with Mr Gibson and Molly, and were felt to be terribly in the way; Mr Gibson not being a man who could make conversation, and hating the duty of talking under restraint.

Beyond direct professional instruction, he did not know what to do with the succession of pairs of young men, whose mission seemed to be to be plagued by their master consciously, and to plague him unconsciously. As Molly grew to be a little girl, when she was about eight years old, her father perceived the awkwardness of her having her breakfasts and dinners so often alone with the pupils, without his uncertain presence. To do away with this evil, he engaged the daughter of a shop-keeper in the town, who had left a destitute family, to come every morning before breakfast, and stay with Molly till he came home at night; or, if he was detained, until the child's bed-time.

'Now, Miss Eyre,' said he, the day before she entered on her office, 'remember this: you are to make good tea for the young men, and see that they have their meals comfortably; and – you are five-and-thirty, I think you said? – try and make them talk – rationally, I am afraid is beyond your or any body's power; but make them talk without stammering or giggling. Don't teach Molly too much: she must sew, and read, and write, and do her sums; but I want to keep her a child; and, if I find more learning desirable for her, I'll see about giving it to her myself. After all, I'm not sure that reading or writing is necessary. Many a good woman gets married with only a cross instead of her name; it's rather a diluting of mother-wit, to my fancy; but, however, we must yield to the prejudices of society, Miss Eyre, and so you may teach the child to read.'

Miss Eyre listened in silence, perplexed but determined to be obedient to the directions of the doctor, whose kindness she and her family had good cause to know. She taught Molly to read and write, but tried honestly to keep her back in every other branch of education. It was only by fighting and struggling hard, that, bit by bit, Molly persuaded her father to let her have French and drawing-lessons. Once a week she joined a dancing-class in the assembly-room at the principal inn in the town, the 'Cumnor Arms'; and, being daunted by her father in every intellectual attempt, she read every book that came in her way, almost with as much delight as if it had been forbidden.

CHAPTER 4

# Mr Gibson's Neighbours

Molly grew up without any greater event than that which has been recorded – the being left behind at the Towers – until she was nearly seventeen. She had become a visitor at the school, but she had never gone again to the annual festival at the great house; it was easy to find some excuse for keeping away.

Lady Agnes was married; there was only Lady Harriet remaining at home; Lord Hollingford, the eldest son, had lost his wife, and was a good deal more at the Towers since he had become a widower. He was a tall, ungainly man, shy, and slow at making commonplace speeches. He often envied the fluency of his garrulous father, who delighted in talking to everybody, and was perfectly unconscious of the incoherence of his conversation. But, owing to his constitutional reserve and shyness, Lord Hollingford was not a popular man, although his kindness of heart was very great, and his scientific acquirements considerable enough to entitle him to much reputation in the European republic of learned men. In this respect Hollingford was proud of him. The inhabitants knew that the clumsy heir to its fealty was highly esteemed and that he had made one or two discoveries, though in what they were not quite sure.

He was left a widower with two or three boys. They were at a public school, so he consequently spent much of his time at the Towers. His friends were always welcomed by Lord and Lady Cumnor; it was a proof of Lady Cumnor's real affection for her distinguished son, that she allowed him to ask what she called 'all sorts of people' to the Towers. 'All sorts of people' meant really those who were distinguished for science and learning, without regard to rank; and, it must be confessed, without much regard to polished manners likewise.

Mr Hall, Mr Gibson's predecessor, had always been received with friendly condescension by my lady, who had found him established as the family medical man, when first she came to the Towers on her marriage; but she never thought of interfering with his custom of taking his meals, if he needed refreshment, in the housekeeper's room, not *with* the housekeeper, *bien entendu*. Of course, if some great surgical gun (like Sir Astley) was brought down from London, it was due to him, as well as to the local medical attendant, to ask Mr Hall to dinner, in a formal ceremonious manner. But things had changed since Mr Gibson had become 'the doctor' at Hollingford. Although he might frequently ask Mrs Brown to give him something to eat in the housekeeper's room – he had no time for all the fuss and ceremony of luncheon with my lady – he was always welcome to the grandest circle of visitors in the house. He might lunch with a duke any day that he chose. His accent was Scotch, not provincial. He had not an ounce of superfluous flesh on his bones; and leanness goes a great way to gentility. He was not jovial (as my lord remarked with a sigh), sparing of his words, intelligent, and slightly sarcastic. Therefore he was perfectly presentable.

The grandeur of being from time to time an invited guest to dinner at the Towers gave him but little pleasure for many years; but, when Lord Hollingford returned to make the Towers his home, Mr Gibson really heard and learnt things that interested him seriously, and that gave fresh flavour to his reading. From time to time he met the leaders of the scientific world; odd-looking, simple-hearted men, very much in earnest about their own particular subjects, and not having much to say on any other. Mr Gibson found himself capable of appreciating such persons, and also perceived that they valued his appreciation, as it was honestly and intelligently given. Indeed, by-and-by, he began to send contributions of his own to the more scientific of the medical journals, and thus a new zest was added to his life. There was not much intercourse between Lord Hollingford and himself;

the one was too silent and shy, the other too busy, to seek each other's society with the perseverance required to do away with the social distinction of rank that prevented their frequent meetings. But each was thoroughly pleased to come into contact with the other. Each could rely on the other's respect and sympathy with a security unknown to many who call themselves friends, and this was a source of happiness to both; to Mr Gibson the most so, of course; for his range of intelligent and cultivated society was the smaller. Indeed, there was no one equal to himself among the men with whom he associated. There was Mr Ashton, the vicar, who had succeeded Mr Browning, a thoroughly good and kind-hearted man, but one without an original thought in him. He had some private fortune, and was not married, and lived the life of an indolent and refined bachelor; but, though he himself was no very active visitor among his poorer parishioners, he was always willing to relieve their wants in the most liberal, and, occasionally, in the most self-denying manner, whenever Mr Gibson, or anyone else, made them known to him. 'Use my purse as freely as if it was your own, Gibson,' he was wont to say. 'I'm such a bad one at going about and making talk to poor folk but I am most willing to give you anything for anyone you may consider in want.'

Perhaps the man of all others to whom Mr Gibson took the most kindly – at least, until Lord Hollingford came into the neighbourhood – was Squire Hamley. There was many a greater landowner in the county, for Squire Hamley's estate was not more than eight hundred acres or so. But his family had been in possession of it long before the Earls of Cumnor had been heard of; no one in Hollingford knew the time when the Hamleys had not lived at Hamley. The Hamleys had not increased their estate for centuries; they had held their own, and had not sold a rood of it for the last hundred years or so. But they were not an adventurous race. They never traded, or speculated, or tried agricultural improvements of any kind. They had no capital in any bank; nor, what perhaps would have been more in character, hoards of gold in any stocking. Their mode of life was simple, and more like that of yeomen than squires. There was a dignity in this quiet conservatism that gained Squire Hamley an immense amount of respect both from high and low; and he might have visited at every house in the county, had he so chosen. But he was very indifferent to the charms of society; and perhaps this was owing to the fact that the Squire, Roger Hamley, who at present reigned at Hamley, had not received so good an education as he ought to have done. His father, Squire Stephen, had been plucked at Oxford, and, with stubborn pride, he had refused to go up again. Nay more: he had sworn a great oath, that none of his children to come should ever know either university by becoming a member of it. The present Squire was sent to a petty provincial school and then turned loose upon the estate as its heir. He was ignorant on many points; but he was aware of his deficiency, and regretted it in theory. He was ungainly in society, and so kept out of it as much as possible; and he was obstinate, violent-tempered, and dictatorial in his own immediate circle. On the other side, he was generous, and the very soul of honour. He had so much natural shrewdness, that his conversation was always worth listening to, although he was apt to start by assuming entirely false premises, which he considered incontrovertible; but, given the correctness of his premises, nobody could bring more natural wit and sense to bear upon the arguments based upon them. He had married a delicate fine London lady; it was one of those perplexing marriages of which one cannot understand the reasons. Yet they were very happy, though possibly Mrs Hamley would not have sunk into the condition of a chronic invalid, if her husband had cared a little more for her various tastes. After his marriage, he was wont to say he had got all that was worth having out of the crowd of houses they called London. It was a compliment to his wife which pleased her up to the last time of her hearing it; but, for all that, she used sometimes to wish that he would recognise the fact that there might still be something worth hearing and seeing in the great city. But he never went there again; and, though he did not prohibit her going; yet he showed so little sympathy with her, when she came back full of what she had done, that she ceased caring to go. Not but what he was willing in giving his consent, and in furnishing her amply with money.

Mrs Hamley was a great reader, and had considerable literary taste. She was gentle and sentimental; tender and good. She gave up her visits to London; she gave up her sociable pleasure in the company of her fellows in education and position. Her husband loved his wife all the more dearly for her sacrifices for him; but she sank into ill-health; nothing definite; only she never was well. Perhaps, if she had had a daughter, it would have been better for her; but her two children were boys, and their father, anxious to give them the advantages of which he himself had suffered the deprivation, sent the lads very early to a preparatory school. They were to go on to Rugby and Cambridge. Osborne, the eldest – so called after his mother's maiden name – was full of taste, and had some talent. His appearance had all the grace and refinement of his mother's. He did well at school, and was the pride and delight of both father and mother. Roger was two years younger than Osborne; clumsy and heavily built, like his father. He was good, but dull, his schoolmasters said. He won no prizes, but brought home a favourable report of his conduct. When he caressed his mother, she used laughingly to allude to the fable of the lap-dog and the donkey; so he left off all personal demonstration of affection. Roger followed his brother Osborne to Trinity, and Mrs Hamley was again left alone. She had not been able for many years to walk beyond her garden; the greater part of her life was spent on a sofa, wheeled to the window in summer, to the fireside in winter. The room which she inhabited was large and pleasant; four tall windows looked out upon a lawn dotted over with flower-beds, and melting away into a small wood, in the centre of which there was a pond, filled with water-lilies. About this unseen pond in the deep shade Mrs Hamley had written many a pretty four-versed poem since she lay on her sofa. She had a small table by her side on which there were the newest works of poetry and fiction; a pencil and blotting-book, with loose sheets of blank paper; a vase of flowers always of her husband's gathering; winter and summer, she had a sweet fresh nosegay every day. Her maid brought her a draught of medicine every three hours, with a glass of clear water and a biscuit; her husband came to her as often as his love for the open air and his labours out-of-doors permitted; but the event of her day, when her boys were absent, was Mr Gibson's professional visit.

He knew there was real secret harm going on, all this time that people spoke of her as a merely fanciful invalid, and he felt that his visits were a real pleasure and lightening of her growing and indescribable discomfort; he knew that Squire Hamley would have been only too glad, if he had come every day; and he was conscious that by careful watching of her symptoms he might mitigate her bodily pain. Besides all these reasons, he took great pleasure in the Squire's society. Mr Gibson enjoyed the other's unreasonableness; his quaintness; his strong conservatism in religion, politics, and morals. Mrs Hamley tried sometimes to soften away opinions which she fancied were offensive to the doctor; but at such times her husband would lay his great hand almost caressingly on Mr Gibson's shoulder, and soothe his wife's anxiety by saying, 'Let us alone, little woman. We understand each other, don't we, doctor? Why, he gives me better than he gets many a time; only, you see, he sugars it over, and says a sharp thing, and pretends it's all civility and humility; but I can tell when he's giving me a pill.'

One of Mrs Hamley's often-expressed wishes had been, that Molly might come and pay her a visit. Mr Gibson always refused this request of hers, though he could hardly have given his reasons for these refusals. He thought the life in Mrs Hamley's heated and scented room would not be good for the girl. But at length the day came when Mr Gibson rode over, and volunteered a visit from Molly; an offer which Mrs Hamley received with the 'open arms of her heart', as she expressed it, and of which the duration was unspecified.

## CHAPTER 5

# Calf-Love

The cause for the change in Mr Gibson's wishes just referred to was as follows. It has been mentioned that he took pupils; a Mr Wynne and a Mr Coxe. Mr Wynne was the elder, and Mr Gibson used to try and elicit his opinions in the vain hope that, some day or another, Mr Wynne might start an original thought. The young man was cautious and slow; he would never do any harm by his rashness. Mr Coxe was a boy of nineteen or so, with brilliant red hair, and a tolerably red face. He was the son of an Indian officer, an old acquaintance of Mr Gibson's. Besides this claim upon his regard, there was something about the young man himself that pleased Mr Gibson. He was rash and impulsive, apt to speak, hitting the nail on the head sometimes with unconscious cleverness, at other times making gross and startling blunders. Mr Gibson used to tell him that his motto would always be 'kill or cure', and to this Mr Coxe once made answer that he thought it was the best motto a doctor could have; for if he could not cure the patient, it was surely best to get him out of his misery quietly, and at once.

One day, Mr Gibson came home unexpectedly. He was crossing the hall, having come in by the garden-door, when the kitchen-door opened, and the girl who was underling in the establishment, came quickly into the hall with a note in her hand, and made as if she was taking it upstairs; but on seeing her master she gave a little start, and turned back as if to hide herself in the kitchen. Mr Gibson stepped quickly forwards, opened the kitchen-door, and called out 'Bethia' so sharply that she could not delay coming forwards.

'Give me that note,' he said. She hesitated a little.

'It's for Miss Molly,' she stammered out.

'Give it to me!' he repeated more quickly than before.

'He said as I was to give it into her own hands; and I promised as I would, faithful.'

'Cook, go and find Miss Molly. Tell her to come here at once.' He fixed Bethia with his eyes.

'Molly, my dear!'

'Papa! I did not know you were at home,' said innocent, wondering Molly.

'Bethia, here is Miss Molly; give her the note.'

'Indeed, miss, I couldn't help it!'

Molly took the note, but, before she could open it, her father said – 'That's all, my dear; you needn't read it. Give it to me. Tell those who sent you, Bethia, that all letters for Miss Molly must pass through my hands. Now be off with you, goosey, and go back to where you came from.'

'Papa, I shall make you tell me who my correspondent is.'

'We'll see about that, by-and-by.'

She went a little reluctantly, with ungratified curiosity, upstairs to Miss Eyre. He turned into the empty dining-room, shut the door, broke the seal of the note, and began to read it. It was a flaming love-letter from Mr Coxe; who professed himself unable to go on seeing her day after day without speaking to her of the passion she had inspired.

Mr Gibson finished reading it; and began to think about it in his own mind. 'Who would have thought the lad had been so poetical? One comfort is the conviction of her perfect innocence – ignorance, I should rather say – for it's easy to see it's the first "confession of his love", as he calls it. But it's an awful worry – to begin with lovers so early. Why, she's not seventeen till July; not for six weeks yet. I'll not be hard upon him. I'll give him a hint; he's quite sharp enough to take it.'

Mr Gibson sat down at the writing-table.

He smiled a little sadly as he re-read his words. And then he chose out an envelope and sealed it with his seal-ring.

Then Mr Gibson applied himself to the professional business which had brought him home, and afterwards he went back through the garden to the stables; and just as he had mounted his horse, he said to the stable-man – 'Oh! by the way, here's a letter for Mr Coxe. Take it to the surgery-door, at once.'

Mr Gibson made a long round that afternoon, and came back to his home imagining that the worst was over. All that would be needed was to find a safe place for the unfortunate Bethia, who had displayed such a daring aptitude for intrigue. It was the habit of the young men to come in to tea with the family in the dining-room, to swallow two cups, munch their toast, and then disappear. This night Mr Gibson watched their countenances furtively from under his long eyelashes. He saw that Mr Wynne was on the point of breaking out into laughter, and that red-haired, red-faced Mr Coxe was redder than ever, while his whole aspect and ways betrayed indignation and anger.

'He will have it, will he?' thought Mr Gibson to himself; and he girded up his loins for the battle. He did not follow Molly and Miss Eyre into the drawing-room as he usually did. He remained where he was, pretending to read the newspaper, and not five minutes after the room was cleared, came the expected tap at the door.

'May I speak to you, sir?' said Mr Coxe.

'To be sure. Come in, Mr Coxe. Pray sit down.'

'No, thank you, I would rather not.' He, accordingly, stood in offended dignity. 'It is about that letter, sir – it was not the conduct of a gentleman, sir, to intercept it, and to open it, and to read words never addressed to you, sir. It was not the conduct of a gentleman, sir,' repeated Mr Coxe – he was going on to say something more, when Mr Gibson broke in –

'And let me tell you, young man,' replied Mr Gibson, with a sudden sternness in his voice, 'that what you have done is only excusable in consideration of your youth and extreme ignorance of what are considered the laws of domestic honour. I receive you into my house as a member of the family – you induced one of my servants – corrupting her with a bribe, I have no doubt –'

'Indeed, sir! I never gave her a penny.'

'Then you ought to have done. You should always pay those who do your dirty work.'

'Just now, sir, you called it corrupting with a bribe,' muttered Mr Coxe.

Mr Gibson took no notice, but went on – 'Inducing one of my servants to risk her place, without offering her the slightest equivalent, by begging her to convey a letter clandestinely to my daughter – a mere child.'

'Miss Gibson, sir, is nearly seventeen!' said Mr Coxe, aged twenty. Again Mr Gibson ignored the remark.

'A letter which you were unwilling to have seen by her father, who had tacitly trusted to your honour, by receiving you as an inmate of his house. Your father's son ought to have come to me, and have said out openly, "Mr Gibson, I love – or I fancy that I love – your daughter; I do not think it right to conceal this from you, although unable to earn a penny; and with no prospect of an unassisted livelihood, even for myself, for several years, I shall not say a word about my feelings – or fancied feelings – to the very young lady herself." That is what your father's son ought to have said.'

'And if I had said it, sir, what would have been your answer? Would you have sanctioned my passion, sir?'

'I would have said, most probably, that you were a young fool; and I should have told you not to let your thoughts run upon a calf-love until you had magnified it into a passion. And I daresay I might have prescribed your joining the Hollingford Cricket Club, and set you at liberty, as often as I could, on the Saturday afternoons. As it is, I must write to your father's agent in London, and ask him to remove you out of my household, repaying the premium, of course, which will enable you to start afresh in some other doctor's surgery.'

'It will so grieve my father,' said Mr Coxe, startled into dismay, if not repentance.

'I see no other course open; for I trusted you, Edward!' There was something in Mr Gibson's voice when he referred to any feeling of his own – he who so rarely betrayed what was passing in his heart – that was irresistible to most people.

Mr Coxe hung his head a little, and meditated.

'I do love Miss Gibson,' said he, at length. 'Who could help it?'

'Mr Wynne, I hope!' said Mr Gibson.

'His heart is pre-engaged,' replied Mr Coxe. 'Mine was free as air till I saw her.'

'Come, Mr Coxe, let us see if we can't make a bargain,' said Mr Gibson, after a minute or so of silence. 'You have done a really wrong thing. But I won't lose all respect for your father's son. If you will give me your word that, as long as you remain my pupil, apprentice, what you will – you won't again try to disclose your passion by word or writing, looks or acts, in any manner whatever, to my daughter, or to talk about your feelings to any one else, you shall remain here. If you cannot give me your word, I must write to your father's agent.'

Mr Coxe stood irresolute.

'Remember how soon a young girl's name may be breathed upon, and sullied. Molly has no mother, and for that very reason she ought to move among you all, as unharmed as Una herself.'

'Mr Gibson, if you wish it, I'll swear it on the Bible!'

'Nonsense. As if your word, if it's worth anything, wasn't enough! We'll shake hands upon it, if you like.'

Mr Coxe came forward eagerly, and almost squeezed Mr Gibson's ring into his finger.

As he was leaving the room, he said, a little uneasily, 'May I give Bethia a crown-piece?'

'No, indeed! Leave Bethia to me. I hope you won't say another word to her, while she's here. I shall see that she gets a respectable place, when she goes away.'

Then Mr Gibson rang for his horse, and went out on the last visits of the day. There were not many surgeons in the county who had so wide a range of practice as he. He was, of necessity, a great deal from home, and on this soft and pleasant summer evening he felt the absence as a great evil. He was startled at discovering that his little one was already the object of some of the strong interests that affect a woman's life; and he so much away that he could not guard her as he would wish. The end of his cogitations was that ride to Hamley the next morning, when he proposed to allow his daughter to accept Mrs Hamley's last invitation.

Mrs Hamley was charmed with the prospect of having a young girl for a visitor.

'I only wish Osborne and Roger had been at home,' said Mrs Hamley. 'She may find it dull, being with old people, like the Squire and me. When can she come? the darling – I am beginning to love her already.'

Mr Gibson was very glad in his heart that the young men of the house were out of the way; he did not want his little Molly to be passing from Scylla to Charybdis.

When the Squire heard from his wife of Mr Gibson's proposal, he was as much pleased as she at the prospect of their youthful visitor; for he was a man of hearty hospitality, when his pride did not interfere with its gratification. After a while, he said – 'It's as well the lads are at Cambridge; we might have been having a love-affair if they had been at home.'

'Well – and if we had?' asked his more romantic wife.

'It wouldn't have done,' said the Squire decidedly. 'Osborne will have had a first-rate education; he'll have this property, and he's a Hamley of Hamley. If Lord Hollingford had a daughter, Osborne would have been as good a match as she could have required. It would never do for him to fall in love with Gibson's daughter – I shouldn't allow it. So it's as well he's out of the way.'

CHAPTER 6

# A Visit to the Hamleys

Molly had got her keys, and her purse; and her little box was put up on the seat by the coachman; and her father handed her in; the door was shut, and she drove away in solitary grandeur, looking back and kissing her hand to her father.

Molly cried a little, but checked her tears, as soon as she remembered how annoyed her father would have been at the sight of them. It was very pleasant driving quickly along in the luxurious carriage, through the pretty green lanes, with dog-roses and honeysuckles so plentiful and fresh in the hedges. At length they came to a village; Molly had long passed the limit of her rides, but she knew this must be the village of Hamley, and that they must be very near to the Hall. They swung in at the gates of the park in a few minutes, and drove up through meadow-grass, ripening for hay – it was no grand aristocratic deer-park this – to the old red-brick hall. A respectable servant stood at the door, ready to receive the expected visitor, and take her into the drawing-room where his mistress lay awaiting her.

Mrs Hamley rose from her sofa to give Molly a gentle welcome; she kept the girl's hand in hers after she had finished speaking, looking into her face, as if studying it.

'I think we shall be great friends,' said she, at length. 'I like your face, and I am always guided by first impressions. Give me a kiss, dear.'

Molly willingly kissed the sweet pale face held up to her.

'And now I'll take you to your room; I have had you put close to me; I thought you would like it better, even though it was a smaller room than the other.'

She rose languidly and led the way upstairs. Molly's bed-room opened out of Mrs Hamley's private sitting-room; on the other side of which was her own bed-room. She showed Molly this easy means of communication; and then, telling her visitor she would await her in the sitting-room, she closed the door, and Molly was left to make acquaintance with her surroundings.

First of all, she went to the window to see what was to be seen. A flower-garden right below; a meadow of ripe grass just beyond, changing colour in long sweeps, as the soft wind blew over it; great old forest-trees a little on one side; and, beyond them, the silver shimmer of a mere. The deliciousness of the early summer silence was only broken by the song of the birds, and the nearer hum of bees. Listening to these sounds, and puzzling out objects obscured by distance or shadow, Molly forgot herself, and was suddenly startled into a sense of the present by a sound of voices in the next room – some servant or other speaking to Mrs Hamley. Molly hurried to unpack her box, and arrange her few clothes in the pretty old-fashioned chest of drawers. In one corner of the walls was a bracket, holding an Indian jar filled with potpourri; and that and the climbing honeysuckle outside the open window scented the room more exquisitely than any toilette perfumes. Molly, having arranged her hair and dress, and taken out her company worsted-work, opened the door softly, and saw Mrs Hamley lying on the sofa.

'Shall we stay up here, dear? It is pleasanter than down below; and then I shall not have to come upstairs again at dressing-time.'

'I should like it very much,' replied Molly.

'Ah! you've got your sewing, like a good girl,' said Mrs Hamley. 'Now, I don't sew much. I read a great deal. Do you like reading?'

'It depends upon the kind of book,' said Molly. 'I'm afraid I don't like "steady reading", as papa calls it.'

'But you like poetry!' said Mrs Hamley. 'I was sure you did, from your face. Have you read this last poem of Mrs Hemans'? Shall I read it aloud to you?'

So she began. Molly was not so much absorbed in listening but that she could glance round the room. The character of the furniture was much the same as in her own. Old-fashioned, of handsome material, and faultlessly clean. On the walls there hung some crayon sketches – portraits. She thought she could make out that one of them was a likeness of Mrs Hamley, in her beautiful youth. And then she became interested in the poem, and listened in a manner that was after Mrs Hamley's own heart. When the reading was ended, Mrs Hamley replied to some of Molly's words of admiration, by saying –

'Ah! I think I must read you some of Osborne's poetry some day; under seal of secrecy; but I really fancy it is almost as good as Mrs Hemans.'

'Mr Osborne Hamley? Does your son write poetry?'

'Yes. He is a very brilliant, clever young man, and he quite hopes to get a fellowship at Trinity. He says he is sure to be high up among the wranglers. That is his likeness hanging against the wall behind you.'

Molly turned round, and saw one of the crayon sketches representing two boys. The elder was sitting down, reading intently. The younger was standing by him, and evidently trying to call the attention of the reader off to some object out-of-doors – out of the window of the very room in which they were sitting.

'I like their faces!' said Molly. 'I suppose it is so long ago now, that I may speak of their likenesses to you as if they were somebody else; may not I?'

'Certainly. Tell me what you think of them; it will amuse me to compare your impressions with what they really are.'

'Oh! but I did not mean to guess at their characters. I can only speak about their faces as I see them in the picture.'

'Well! tell me what you think of them!'

'The eldest – the reading boy – is very beautiful; but I can't quite make out his face yet, because his head is down, and I can't quite see the eyes. That is the Mr Osborne Hamley who writes poetry?'

'Yes. He was a beautiful boy. Roger was never to be compared with him.'

'No; he is not handsome. And yet I like his face. His eyes are grave and solemn-looking; but all the rest of his face is rather merry than otherwise. It looks too steady and sober, too good a face, to go tempting his brother to leave his lesson.'

'Ah! but it was not a lesson. The painter, Mr Green, once saw Osborne reading some poetry, while Roger was trying to persuade him to come out and have a ride in the hay-cart – that was the "motive" of the picture. Roger is not much of a reader; at least, he doesn't care for poetry, and books of romance. He is so fond of natural history; and that takes him, like the Squire, a great deal out-of-doors; and, when he is in, he is always reading scientific books that bear upon his pursuits. He is a good, steady fellow, though, and gives us great satisfaction; but he is not likely to have such a brilliant career as Osborne.'

Molly tried to find out in the picture the characteristics of the two boys, as they were now explained to her by their mother; and in questions and answers about the various drawings hung round the room the time passed away, until the dressing-bell rang for the six o'clock dinner.

Molly was rather dismayed by the offers of the maid whom Mrs Hamley had sent to assist her. 'I am afraid they expect me to be very smart,' she kept thinking to herself. 'If they do, they'll be disappointed; that's all.'

She looked at herself in the glass with some anxiety, for the first time in her life. She saw a slight, lean figure, promising to be tall, a complexion browner than cream-coloured; plentiful curly black hair, tied up in a bunch behind with a rose-coloured ribbon; long, almond-shaped, soft grey eyes, shaded both above and below by curling black eyelashes.

'I don't think I am pretty,' thought Molly, 'and yet I'm not sure.' She would have been sure, if she had smiled her own sweet, merry smile, and called out the gleam of her teeth, and the charm of her dimples.

She found her way downstairs into the drawing-room in good time. The room was forty feet long or so and stands of plants, great jars of flowers, old Indian china and cabinets gave the room the pleasant aspect it certainly had. And to add to it there were five high, long windows on one side of the room, all opening to the prettiest bit of flower-garden in the grounds. The Squire came in abruptly and stood at the door, as if surprised at the white-robed stranger in possession of his hearth.

'Why, I'd quite forgotten you; you're Gibson's daughter, aren't you? I'm sure I'm very glad to see you, my dear.'

By this time, they had met in the middle of the room, and he was shaking Molly's hand with vehement friendliness.

'I must go and dress, though,' said he, looking at his soiled gaiters. 'Madam likes it. It's one of her fine London ways, and she's broken me into it at last. Does your father dress for dinner, Miss Gibson?' He did not stay to wait for her answer, but hastened away to perform his toilette.

They dined at a small table in a room so vast that Molly longed for the snugness of the home dining-room. Mrs Hamley seemed tired out. She ate less than Molly, and sent for fan and smelling-bottle to amuse herself with, until the tablecloth was cleared away, and the dessert was put upon a mahogany table, polished like a looking-glass. The Squire had hitherto been too busy to talk. Now, peeling his orange, he turned to Molly –

'Tomorrow, you'll have to do this for me, Miss Gibson.'

'Shall I? I'll do it today, if you like, sir.'

'No; today I shall treat you as a visitor, with all proper ceremony. Tomorrow I shall send you errands, and call you by your Christian name.'

'I shall like that,' said Molly.

'I was wanting to call you something less formal than Miss Gibson,' said Mrs Hamley.

'My name's Molly. I was christened Mary. But papa likes Molly. I think it was because mamma was Mary, and I was called Molly while she lived.'

'Ah, poor thing!' said the Squire, 'I remember how sorry everyone was when she died; no one thought she was delicate, she had such a fresh colour, till all at once she popped off, as one may say.'

'It must have been a terrible blow to your father,' said Mrs Hamley, seeing that Molly did not know what to answer.

'Ay, ay. It came so sudden, so soon after they were married.'

'I thought it was nearly four years,' said Molly.

'And four years is soon – is a short time to a couple who look to spending their lifetime together. Everyone thought Gibson would have married again.'

'Hush,' said Mrs Hamley. But the Squire was not so easily stopped.

'Well – it's the truth. He's not likely to marry now; so one may say it out. Why, your father is past forty, isn't he?'

'Forty-three. I don't believe he ever thought of marrying again,' said Molly, recurring to the idea, as one does to that of danger which has passed by, without one's being aware of it.

'No! I don't believe he did, my dear. He looks to me just like a man who would be constant to the memory of his wife.'

Molly went into the drawing-room with Mrs Hamley; but her thoughts did not change with the room. She was astonished at her own stupidity at never having imagined such a possibility as her father's second marriage.

'There is papa, with the Squire!' she suddenly exclaimed. There they were coming across the flower-garden from the stable-yard and seeing him in the flesh was the most efficacious way of dispelling the phantom fears of a second wedding; and the pleasant conviction that he could not rest, till he had come over to see how she was going on in her new home, stole into her heart, although he spoke but little to her, and that little was all in a joking tone. After he had gone away, the Squire undertook to teach her cribbage, and she was happy enough now to give him all her attention. He kept on prattling while they played, till the butler came in with a solemn look, placed a large prayer-book before his master, and then the maids and men trooped in to prayers – the windows were still open, and the sounds of the solitary corncrake, and of the owl hooting in the trees, mingled with the words spoken. Then to bed; and so ended the day.

Molly looked out of her chamber-window – leaning on the sill, and snuffing up the night-odours of the honeysuckle. The soft velvet darkness hid all the things that were at any distance from her; although she was as conscious of their presence as if she had seen them.

'I think I shall be very happy here,' was in Molly's thoughts, as she turned away at length, and began to prepare for bed. Before long the Squire's words spoilt the sweet peace of her final thoughts. The one great question, 'Who was it that people thought papa might marry?' kept popping up, like a troublesome Jack-in-the-box.

Books, the greater part of them, were kept in a large, musty-smelling room, in an unfrequented part of the house; but those in the drawing-room were quite enough to employ Molly; indeed, she was so deep in one of Sir Walter Scott's novels next morning that she jumped as if she had been shot, when, an hour or so after breakfast, the Squire came to the gravel-path outside one of the windows, and called to ask her if she would like to go about the garden and home fields with him.

'It must be a little dull for you, my girl, all by yourself, with nothing but books to look at, in the mornings here; but, you see, madam has a fancy for being quiet in the mornings.'

Molly had been in the very middle of the 'Bride of Lammermoor', and would gladly have stayed indoors to finish it; but she felt the Squire's kindness all the same. They went in and out of old-fashioned greenhouses, over trim lawns; the Squire unlocked the great walled kitchen-garden, and went about giving directions to gardeners; and all the time Molly followed him like a little dog, her mind quite full of Ravenswood and Lucy Ashton. Presently, every place near the house had been inspected and regulated, and the Squire was more at liberty to give his attention to his companion. Molly plucked away her thoughts from the seventeenth century; and that question which had haunted her came out of her lips –

'Who did people think papa would marry? That time – long ago – soon after mamma died?'

The Squire turned round upon her, and looked at her face. It was very grave, a little pale.

'Whew,' said he. 'His name was never coupled with any lady's

– 'twas only in the nature of things that he should marry again; he may do it yet, for aught I know, and I don't think it would be a bad move either. I told him so, the last time but one he was here.'

'And what did he say?' asked breathless Molly.

'Oh: he only smiled and said nothing. You shouldn't take up words so seriously, my dear. Very likely he may never think of marrying again; and, if he did, it would be a very good thing both for him and for you!'

Molly muttered something, as if to herself, but the Squire might have heard it if he had chosen. As it was, he wisely turned the current of the conversation.

'Look at that!' he said, as they suddenly came upon the mere, or large pond. There was a small island in the middle of the glassy water, on which grew silvery shimmering willows. 'We must get you punted over there, some of these days. I'm not fond of using the boat at this time of the year, because the young birds are still in the nests among the reeds and water-plants; but we'll go. There are coots and grebes.'

'Oh, look, there's a swan!'

'Yes; there are two pair of them here. And in those trees there's both a rookery and a heronry; the herons and the rooks are always at war, which doesn't do for such near neighbours. Once Roger showed me a long straggling fellow of a heron, with a flight of rooks after him. Roger knows a deal of natural history, and finds out queer things sometimes. If we came upon such a thing as this,' touching a delicate film of cobweb upon a leaf with his stick, 'he could tell you what insect or spider made it, and if it lived in rotten fir-wood, or in a cranny of sound timber. It's a pity they don't take honours in Natural History at Cambridge. Roger would be safe enough, if they did.'

'Mr Osborne Hamley is very clever, is he not?' Molly asked.

'Oh, yes. Osborne's a bit of a genius. He'll get a Trinity fellowship, if they play him fair. Now, isn't it a queer quip of Nature,' continued the Squire, 'that I, a Hamley of Hamley, of as good and as old a descent as any man in England, and I doubt if a stranger, to look at me, would take me for a gentleman, with my red face, great hands and feet, and thick figure; and there's Osborne, who takes after his mother, who couldn't tell her great-grandfather from Adam, bless her. Now, Roger is like me, a Hamley of Hamley, and no one who sees him in the street will ever think that big-boned, clumsy chap is of gentle blood. I was talking to madam the other day about Osborne's marrying a daughter of Lord Hollingford's – that's to say, if he had a daughter; but I'm not sure if I should consent to it; for, you see, Osborne will have had a first-rate education, and his family dates from the Heptarchy, while I should be glad to know where the Cumnor folk were in the time of Queen Anne?'

## CHAPTER 7

# Foreshadows of Love Perils

If Squire Hamley had been unable to tell Molly who had ever been thought of as her father's second wife, fate was all this time preparing an answer of a pretty positive kind to her wondering curiosity. But fate is a cunning hussy, and builds up her plans with unconsidered trifles. The first 'trifle' of an event was the disturbance which Jenny (Mr Gibson's cook) chose to make at Bethia's being dismissed. Bethia was a distant relation of Jenny's, and she chose to say it was Mr Coxe the tempter who ought to have 'been sent packing'. In this view there was quite enough plausibility to make Mr Gibson feel that he had been rather unjust. He had, however, taken care to provide Bethia with another situation. Jenny, nevertheless, chose to give warning; and, though Mr Gibson knew full well from former experience that her warnings were words, not deeds, he hated the discomfort, the entire disagreeableness, of meeting a woman at any time in his house, who wore a grievance and an injury upon her face as legibly as Jenny took care to do.

Down into the middle of this small domestic trouble came another, and one of greater consequence. Miss Eyre had gone with her old mother, and her orphan nephews and nieces, to the seaside, during Molly's absence. After about ten days had elapsed, Mr Gibson received a beautifully written letter from Miss Eyre. Her eldest nephew had fallen ill of scarlet fever, and Miss Eyre apologised with humble sincerity for her inability to return at the appointed time to her charge, for Molly had never had the scarlet fever, and, even if Miss Eyre had been able to leave the orphan children to return to her employments, it might not have been a safe or a prudent step.

'To be sure not,' said Mr Gibson. 'Molly must stay at Hamley. I'll ride round today, and see how the land lies.'

He found Mrs Hamley lying on a sofa placed under the shadow of the great cedar-tree on the lawn. Molly was gardening under her directions; tying up the long sea-green stalks of bright budded carnations, snipping off dead roses.

'Oh! here's papa!' she cried out joyfully.

Mr Gibson rather disliked asking for Molly to prolong her visit; so he determined to swallow his bitter first, and then take the pleasure of the delicious day.

'I've come here today to ask a favour,' he began.

'Granted before you name it. Am not I a bold woman?'

He smiled and bowed, but went straight on with his speech.

'Miss Eyre writes today to say that one of the little nephews has caught the scarlet fever.'

'I guess your request. I make it before you do. I beg for dear little Molly to stay on here. Of course Miss Eyre can't come back to you; and of course Molly must stay here! She's a darling. I cannot tell you how fond the Squire and I are of her; I am so delighted to think she isn't to go away for a long time.'

Mrs Hamley was quite right in speaking of her husband's fondness for Molly. But he received the news in anything but a gracious frame of mind.

'Stay longer! And to be in the house with Osborne! Roger, too, will be at home.'

'Oh, she's not at all the sort of girl young men of their age would take to. Lads of one and two and twenty want all the accessories of a young woman.'

'Want what?' growled the Squire.

'Such things as becoming dress, style of manner.'

'All I know is, that it's a very dangerous thing to shut two young men up in a country-house like this with a girl of seventeen – choose what her gowns may be like.'

However, the next morning at breakfast, a letter was passed from the Squire to his wife, and back again, without a word as to its contents; but –

'Fortunate!'

'Yes! very!'

Little did Molly apply these expressions to the piece of news Mrs Hamley told her in the course of the day; namely, that her son Osborne had received an invitation to stay with a friend and that he would not accompany his brother home.

Molly was very sympathetic.

'Oh, dear! I am so sorry! You have been thinking so long of his coming home. I am afraid it is a great disappointment.'

Mrs Hamley smiled.

'Yes! it is a disappointment certainly, but we must think of Osborne's pleasure. Only – I should like to have seen him, my own dear boy. But it is best as it is.'

Molly was a little puzzled by this speech, but soon put it out of her head. Her days at Hamley were well filled up with the small duties that would have belonged to a daughter of the house. She made breakfast for the lonely Squire, and would willingly have carried up Madam's; but that daily piece of work belonged to the Squire, and was jealously guarded by him. She read the smaller print of the newspapers aloud to him. She strolled about the gardens with him, gathering fresh flowers, meanwhile, to deck the drawing-room against Mrs Hamley should come down. She was her companion when she took her drives in the close carriage; they read poetry and mild literature together in Mrs Hamley's sitting-room upstairs. Besides these things, she used to try to practise daily on the grand-piano in the drawing-room, because she had promised Miss Eyre she would do so. And she had found her way into the library. The summer days were very short to this happy girl of seventeen.

## CHAPTER 8

# Drifting into Danger

On Thursday, the quiet country-household was stirred through all its fibres with the thought of Roger's coming home. Mrs Hamley had not seemed quite in such good spirits for two or three days before; and the Squire appeared to be put out. They had not chosen to tell Molly that Osborne's name had only appeared very low down in the mathematical tripos.

On Thursday, after luncheon, Mrs Hamley went to rest, in preparation for Roger's return; and Molly also retired to her own room, feeling that it would be better for her to remain there until dinner-time, and so to leave the father and mother to receive their boy in privacy. She took a book of MS. poems with her; they were all of Osborne Hamley's composition. Molly had asked permission to copy one or two of those which were her greatest favourites; and this quiet summer-afternoon she took this copying for her employment, sitting at the pleasant open window.

Suddenly, there was the snap of a shutting gate; wheels crackling on the dry gravel; horses' feet on the drive; a loud cheerful voice in the house. Molly heard the Squire's glad 'Hallo! here he is!' and Madam's softer, more plaintive voice; and then the loud, full, strange tone, which she knew must be Roger's. Then there was an opening and shutting of doors, and only a distant buzz of talking.

She had nearly finished learning the poem, when she heard Mrs Hamley come hastily into her sitting-room and burst out into an irrepressible, half-hysterical fit of sobbing. In an instant, Molly was kneeling at Mrs Hamley's feet, holding the poor lady's hands, kissing them, murmuring soft words.

'It's only Osborne,' said Mrs Hamley, at last. 'Roger has been telling us about him. I knew on Monday; we had a letter – he said he had not done so well as we had hoped! He said he had just passed, only low down and the Squire has been asking Roger all about it; and it has made him so angry. Roger is so good. All he said was that Osborne was nervous. But after failing like this, he is not very likely to get a fellowship, which the Squire had placed his hopes on. Osborne himself seemed so sure of it, that the Squire can't understand it, and is seriously angry. Poor, poor Osborne!'

So, talking out what was in her heart, Mrs Hamley became more composed; and at length she dismissed Molly to dress for dinner, with a kiss, saying –

'You're a real "blessing to mothers", child! And now your being a fourth at dinner will keep us off that sore subject; there are times when a stranger in the household is a wonderful help.'

Molly thought over all that she had heard. Her unconscious fealty to Osborne was not in the least shaken by his having come to grief at Cambridge. Only she was indignant against Roger, who seemed to have brought the reality of bad news as an offering of first-fruits on his return home.

She went down into the drawing-room with anything but a welcome to him in her heart. He was standing by his mother; the Squire had not yet made his appearance. Mrs Hamley introduced her to her son. He was a tall, powerfully-made young man, giving the impression of strength rather than elegance. His face was rather square, ruddy-coloured, hair and eyes brown – and he had a trick of wrinkling up his eyelids when he wanted particularly to observe anything, which made his eyes look smaller. He had a large mouth, with excessively mobile lips; and another trick of his was, that when he was amused at anything, he resisted the impulse to laugh, by a droll manner of twitching and puckering up his mouth, till at length the sense of humour had its way, and his features relaxed, and he broke into a broad, sunny smile; his beautiful teeth – his only beautiful feature – breaking out with a white gleam upon the red-brown countenance. To Molly, this first night, he simply appeared 'heavy-looking, clumsy', and 'a person she was sure she should never get on with.' He certainly did not seem to care much what impression he made upon his mother's visitor. He was at that age when young men admire a formed beauty more than a face with any amount of future capability of loveliness, and besides, his thoughts were full of other subjects, which he did not intend to allow to ooze out in words. He only looked upon Molly as a rather awkward girl, with black hair and an intelligent face, who might help him in the task he had set himself of keeping up a bright general conversation during the rest of the evening; might help him – but she would not. She thought him unfeeling in his talkativeness. Had Mr Roger Hamley no sympathy in him?

And so, in mute opposition on Molly's side, in polite indifference, scarcely verging upon kindliness on his, Roger and she steered clear of each other. He had many occupations in which he needed no companionship, even if she had been qualified to give it. The worst was, that she found he was in the habit of occupying the library, her favourite retreat, in the mornings before Mrs Hamley came down.

Altogether it was pleasanter before he came home.

Her father rode over pretty frequently, it was true, but during this absence of hers, Mr Gibson was drifting into matrimony. He was more passive than active in the affair; though if he had not believed that a second marriage was the very best way of cutting the Gordian knot of domestic difficulties, he could have extricated himself without pain from the mesh of circumstances. It happened in this manner. Lady Cumnor, having married her two eldest daughters, found her labours as a chaperon to Lady Harriet, the youngest, considerably lightened by co-operation; and had leisure to be an invalid. Leaving Lady Harriet with either Lady Cuxhaven or Lady Agnes Manners, she betook herself to the comparative quiet of the Towers. This particular summer she believed that her state of health was more serious than previously; but she did not say a word of this to her husband or daughters, reserving her confidence for Mr Gibson's ears. She did not wish to take Lady Harriet away from the gaieties of town, and yet she did not quite like being without a companion in the three weeks or a month that might intervene before her family would join her at the Towers.

'Thursday the 19th, Harriet,' said Lady Cumnor meditatively; 'what do you say to coming down to the Towers on the 18th, and helping me over that long day. You could stay in the country till Monday, and return a great deal fresher to the remainder of your gaieties. Your father would bring you down, I know; indeed, he is coming naturally.'

'Oh, mamma!' said Lady Harriet; 'I cannot go; there's the water-party up to Maidenhead on the 20th! Besides, I can't make provincial small-talk; I'm not up in the local politics of Hollingford. I should be making mischief, I know I should.'

'Well,' said Lady Cuxhaven, 'mamma, why shouldn't you have Clare to stay with you?'

'Yes, Clare would do very well,' said Lady Cumnor; 'but we must not interfere with her school so as to injure her, for I am afraid she is not doing too well as it is; she has been so very unlucky – first her husband died, and then she lost Lady Davies' situation, and then Mrs Maude's, and now Mr Preston told your father it was all she could do to pay her way in Ashcombe, though Lord Cumnor lets her have the house rent-free.'

'I can't think how it is,' said Lady Harriet. 'She's not very wise, certainly; but she has such pleasant manners, I should have thought anyone who wasn't particular about education would have been charmed to keep her as a governess.'

'What do you mean by not being particular about education? Most people who keep governesses for their children are supposed to be particular,' said Lady Cuxhaven.

'Well, they think themselves so; but I call you particular, Mary, and I don't think mamma was.'

'I can't think what you mean, Harriet,' said Lady Cumnor.

'Oh dear, mamma, you gave us the best of masters in every department, and Clare to keep us up to our preparation for them; but some of the masters admired our very pretty governess, and there was a kind of respectable veiled flirtation going on, which never came to anything, to be sure; and then you were often so overwhelmed with your business as a great lady – fashionable and benevolent, and all that sort of thing – that you used to call Clare away from us at the most critical times of our lessons, to write your notes, and the consequence is, that I'm about the most ill-informed girl in London. Only Mary was so capitally trained by good awkward Miss Benson, that she is always full to overflowing with accurate knowledge.'

'Do you think what Harriet says is true, Mary?'

'I was so little with Clare in the school-room. I used to read French with her; she had a beautiful accent, I remember. Both Agnes and Harriet were very fond of her. I used to be jealous for Miss Benson's sake, and perhaps that made me fancy that she had a way of flattering and indulging them. But girls are severe judges, and certainly she had had an anxious enough lifetime. I am always glad when we can have her, and give her a little pleasure. The only thing that makes me uneasy is the way in which she seems to send her daughter away from her; we never can persuade her to bring Cynthia with her. Well, we are not discussing Clare and her affairs, but trying to plan for mamma's comfort. I don't see that she can do better than ask Mrs Kirkpatrick to come to the Towers – as soon as her holidays begin, I mean.'

'Here is her last letter,' said Lady Cumnor, who had been searching for it in her escritoire. '"My wonted misfortunes appear to have followed me to Ashcombe" – um, um, um; that's not it – oh, here it is! "The vacation begins on the 11th, and I must then try and obtain some change of air in order to fit myself for the resumption of my duties on the 10th of August." You see, girls, she would be at liberty, if she has not made any other arrangement for spending her holidays. Today is the fifteenth.'

'I'll write to her at once, mamma,' Lady Harriet said. 'Clare and I are great friends: I was her confidant in her loves with Mr Kirkpatrick, and we've kept up our intimacy ever since.'

'I sincerely hope Miss Bowes is not telling her love-affairs to Grace or Lily. Why, Harriet, you could not have been older than Grace, when Clare was married!' said Lady Cuxhaven, in maternal alarm.

'No; but I was well versed in the tender passion, thanks to novels. Now, I daresay you don't admit novels into your school-room, Mary; so your daughters wouldn't be able to administer discreet sympathy to their governess, in case she was the heroine of a love-affair.'

'My dear Harriet, don't let me hear you talking of love in that way; it is not pretty. Love is a serious thing.'

'My dear mamma, your exhortations are just eighteen years too late. I've talked all the freshness off love, and that's the reason I'm tired of the subject.'

This last speech referred to a recent refusal of Lady Harriet's, which had displeased Lady Cumnor. Lady Cuxhaven did not want to have the subject brought up, so hastened to say –

'Do ask the poor little daughter to come with her mother to the Towers; why, she must be seventeen or more; she would really be a companion to you, mamma, if her mother was unable to come.'

'I was not ten when Clare married, and I'm nearly nine-and-twenty,' added Lady Harriet. 'I think she can't be far from eighteen.'

'She is at school at Boulogne, I know; and so I don't think she can be as old as that. Clare says something about her in this letter: "Under these circumstances" (the ill-success of her school), "I cannot think myself justified in allowing myself the pleasure of having darling Cynthia at home for the holidays." So, you see, Clare would be quite at liberty to come to me, and I daresay it would be a very nice change for her.'

So the plan was told to Lord Cumnor, who highly approved of it; as he always did of every project of his wife's.

'Very good – very good, indeed! Clare to join you at the Towers! Capital! I shall go down with you on Wednesday in time for the jollification on Thursday. I always enjoy that day; they are such nice people, those good Hollingford ladies. Then I'll have a day with Sheepshanks, and perhaps I may ride over to Ashcombe and see Preston. Preston's a clever, sharp fellow.'

'I don't like him,' said my lady.

'He's such a good-looking man, I wonder you don't like him;

and what should make you like him is the interest he takes in Clare and her prospects. He's constantly suggesting something that can be done to her house, and I know he sends her fruit, and flowers, and game just as regularly as we should ourselves, if we lived at Ashcombe.'

'How old is he?' said Lady Cumnor.

'About twenty-seven. Ah! I see what is in your ladyship's head. No! no! he's too young for that. You must look out for some middle-aged man, if you want to get poor Clare married; Preston won't do. I say, my lady, what do you think of Gibson? He would be just the right age.'

'I am no match-maker, my lord. I suppose we had better go by the old road – the people at those inns know us?'

And so they passed on to speaking about other things than Mrs Kirkpatrick and her prospects.

## CHAPTER 9

# The Widower and the Widow

Mrs Kirkpatrick was only too happy to accept Lady Cumnor's invitation. It was what she had been hoping for, but hardly daring to expect. Her wardrobe did not require much arrangement; if it had done, the poor lady would not have had much money to appropriate to the purpose. She was very pretty and graceful, and that goes a great way towards carrying off shabby clothes; and it was her taste that had made her persevere in wearing all the delicate tints – the violets and greys – which, with a certain admixture of black, constitute half-mourning. This style of becoming dress she was supposed to wear in memory of Mr Kirkpatrick; in reality, because it was both lady-like and economical. Her beautiful hair was of that rich auburn that hardly ever turns grey; and her complexion had the vivid tints that often accompany the kind of hair which has once been red. Her eyes were soft, large, and china-blue in colour; they had not much expression or shadow about them, which was perhaps owing to the flaxen colour of her eyelashes. Her figure was a little fuller than it used to be, but her movements were as soft and sinuous as ever. Altogether, she looked much younger than her age, which was not far short of forty. She had a very pleasant voice, and read aloud well and distinctly, which Lady Cumnor liked. About novels and poetry, travels and gossip, personal details, or anecdotes of any kind, she always made exactly the remarks which are expected from an agreeable listener; and she had sense enough to confine herself to those short expressions of wonder, admiration, and astonishment, which may mean anything, when more recondite things were talked about.

It was a very pleasant change to a poor unsuccessful schoolmistress to pass up the deep-piled carpets of the broad shallow stairs into my lady's own room, cool and deliciously fresh, even on this sultry day, and fragrant with great bowls of freshly gathered roses of every shade of colour.

Lady Cumnor, in spite of her languor and fatigue, had gone through the day when the school-visitors came to the Towers, in full dignity, dictating clearly all that was to be done, what walks were to be taken, what hothouses to be seen, and when the party were to return to the 'collation'. She herself remained indoors, with one or two ladies who had ventured to think that the fatigue or the heat might be too much for them, but the exertion tired her; and, when everyone had left, the probability is that she would have gone to lie down and rest, had not her husband made an unlucky remark in the kindness of his heart. He came up to her and put his hand on her shoulder.

'I'm afraid you're sadly tired, my lady?' he said.

She braced her muscles, and drew herself up, saying coldly –

'When I am tired, Lord Cumnor, I will tell you so.' And her fatigue showed itself during the rest of the evening in her sitting particularly upright, and declining all offers of easy-chairs or footstools. She went on in something of this kind of manner, as long as Lord Cumnor remained at the Towers. Mrs Kirkpatrick was quite deceived by it, but Lord Cumnor had an affectionate heart, if a blundering head; and he was almost certain his wife was not well. Yet he was too much afraid of her to send for Mr Gibson without her permission. His last words to Clare were –

'Don't you be deluded by her ways. If I were you, I'd send and ask Gibson to call – you might make any kind of pretence' – and then the idea he had had in London of the fitness of a match between the two coming into his head just now, he could not help adding – 'Get him to come and see you; Lord Hollingford says there's no one like him in these parts; and he might be looking at my lady while he was talking to you, and see if he thinks her really ill. And let me know what he says about her.'

But Clare was just as great a coward about doing anything for Lady Cumnor which she had not expressly ordered, as Lord

Cumnor himself. She knew she might fall into such disgrace, if she sent for Mr Gibson without direct permission, that she might never be asked to stay at the Towers again.

But a day or two after this, Lady Cumnor startled Mrs Kirkpatrick, by saying – 'Clare, I wish you'd write a note to Mr Gibson, saying I should like to see him this afternoon.'

Mr Gibson's domestic 'rows' had not healed over in the least. The final straw had been an impromptu visit of Lord Hollingford's, whom he had met in the town one forenoon. They had had a good deal to say to each other about some new scientific discovery, and Lord Hollingford said suddenly –

'Gibson, I wonder if you'd give me some lunch; I've been a good deal about since breakfast, and am getting quite ravenous.'

Mr Gibson gladly took him home with him to the early family dinner. But the cook was sulking at Bethia's dismissal – and she chose to be careless. At last, dinner was ready; but the poor host saw the want of nicety in all its accompaniments: dingy plate, dull-looking glass, a tablecloth that was anything but fresh. After dinner, just as they were parting, he said –

'You see a man like me – a widower – with a daughter who cannot always be at home – has not a regulated household, which would enable me to command the small portions of time I can spend there.'

He made no allusion to the comfortless meal of which they had both partaken, though it was full in his mind. Nor was it absent from Lord Hollingford's, as he made reply –

'True, true. Yet a man like you ought to be free from any thought of household cares. Excuse me, Gibson, but we're talking like friends. Have you never thought of marrying again? If you found a sensible, agreeable woman of thirty or so, I really think you couldn't do better than take her to manage your home; and, besides, she would be able to give your daughter that kind of tender supervision which all girls of that age require. You'll excuse my having spoken frankly.'

Mr Gibson had thought of this advice several times since it was given; but it was a case of 'first catch your hare'. Where was the 'sensible and agreeable woman of thirty or so? Among his country patients there were two classes pretty distinctly marked: farmers, whose children were uneducated; squires, whose daughters would, indeed, think the world was coming to a pretty pass, if they were to marry a country surgeon.

But, the day on which Mr Gibson paid his visit to Lady Cumnor, he began to think that Mrs Kirkpatrick was his 'hare'. He remembered with a certain pleasure that five or six years ago Mrs Kirkpatrick had behaved very kindly to his little girl.

So there the matter rested for the present, as far as he was concerned.

Lady Cumnor was out of health; but not so ill as she had been fancying herself when the people about her dared not send for the doctor. It was a great relief to her and reports were duly sent up to my lord, but he and his daughters were strictly forbidden to come down. Lady Cumnor wished to be weak and languid without the family observation. Sometimes she herself wrote the daily bulletins; at other times she bade Clare do it, but she would always see the letters. Any answers she received from her daughters she used to read herself, but anybody might read my lord's letters. There was no great fear of family-secrets oozing out in his sprawling lines of affection. But once Mrs Kirkpatrick came upon a sentence in a letter from Lord Cumnor, which she was reading out loud to his wife, that if she could have skipped it and kept it for private perusal, she would gladly have done so. My lady was too sharp for her, though.

'Read on. What are you stopping for? There is no bad news, is there, about Agnes? Give me the letter.'

Lady Cumnor read, half aloud –

'How are Clare and Gibson getting on! You despised my advice to help on that affair; but a little match-making would be a very pleasant amusement now that you are shut up in the house; and I cannot conceive any marriage more suitable.'

'Oh!' said Lady Cumnor, laughing, 'I don't wonder you stopped short.'

'Lord Cumnor is so fond of joking,' said Mrs Kirkpatrick, a

little flurried, yet quite recognising the truth of his last words – 'I cannot conceive any marriage more suitable.' It was not an unpleasant idea; it brought a faint smile out upon her face, as she sat by Lady Cumnor, while the latter took her nap.

## CHAPTER 10

# A Crisis

Mrs Kirkpatrick had been reading aloud till Lady Cumnor fell asleep. She was looking out of the window, thinking how pleasant it would be to have a husband once more – some one who would work, while she sate at her elegant ease in a prettily furnished drawing-room; and she was rapidly investing this imaginary bread-winner with the form and features of the country surgeon, when there was a tap at the door, and almost before she could rise, the object of her thoughts came in. She felt herself blush, and she was not displeased at the consciousness. She advanced to meet him, making a sign towards her sleeping ladyship.

'Very good,' said he, in a low voice; 'can I speak to you for a minute or two in the library?'

'Is he going to offer?' thought she, with a sudden palpitation.

He was only going to make one or two medical inquiries; she found that out very speedily, and considered the conversation as rather flat to her. She was not aware that he finally made up his mind to propose, during the time that she was speaking; her voice was so soft, her accent so pleasant, that it struck him as particularly agreeable after the broad country accent he was perpetually hearing. Then the harmonious colours of her dress, and her slow and graceful movements, had something of the same soothing effect upon his nerves that a cat's purring has upon some people's. Yesterday he had looked upon her more as a possible stepmother for Molly; today he thought of her more as a wife for himself. A lucky shower came on. Mr Gibson did not care a jot for rain, but it gave him an excuse for lingering.

'It's very stormy weather,' said he.

'Yes, very. My daughter writes me word, that for two days last week the packet could not sail from Boulogne.'

'Miss Kirkpatrick is at Boulogne, is she?'

'Yes, poor girl. But, Mr Gibson, you must not call her Miss Kirkpatrick. Cynthia remembers you with much – affection. She was your little patient when she had the measles here four years ago, you know. Pray call her Cynthia; she would be quite hurt at such a formal name as Miss Kirkpatrick from you.'

'Cynthia seems to me such an out-of-the-way name; only fit for poetry, not for daily use.'

'It is mine,' said Mrs Kirkpatrick, in a tone of reproach. 'I was christened Hyacinth, and her poor father would have her called after me. Hyacinth Clare! Once upon a time I was quite proud of my pretty name. Perhaps I did wrong in yielding to his wish to have her called by such a romantic name. It may excite prejudice against her in some people; and, poor child! she will have enough to struggle with. A daughter is a great charge, especially when there is only one parent to look after her.'

'You are quite right,' said he, 'though I should have thought that a girl who is so fortunate as to have a mother could not feel the loss of her father so acutely as one who is motherless must suffer from her deprivation.'

'You are thinking of your own daughter. Dear child! how well I remember her sweet little face, as she lay sleeping on my bed! I suppose she is nearly grown up now. She must be near my Cynthia's age. How I should like to see her!'

'I hope you will. I should like you to see her. I should like you to love my poor little Molly – to love her as your own' – He swallowed down something that rose in his throat.

'Could you love her as your daughter? Will you try? Will you give me the right of introducing you to her as her future mother; as my wife?'

There! he had done it! but he was aware that a question as to its wisdom came into his mind the instant that the words were said past recall.

'Oh! Mr Gibson,' she said; and then, a little to his surprise, and a great deal to her own, she burst into hysterical tears: it was such a wonderful relief to feel that she need not struggle any more for a livelihood.

'My dear – my dearest,' said he, trying to soothe her with word and caress, but, just at the moment, uncertain what name he ought to use. She said, as if understanding his difficulty –

'Call me Hyacinth – your own Hyacinth! I can't bear "Clare", it does so remind me of being a governess; and those days are all past now.'

'Yes; but surely no one can have been more valued, more be-loved, than you have been in this family at least.'

'Oh, yes! they have been very good. But still one has always had to remember one's position.'

It was the next morning, before Mr Gibson arrived at the Hall, timing his visit as well as he could so as to have half-an-hour's private talk with Molly, before Mrs Hamley came down into the drawing-room. He made his way into the drawing-room, half expecting, however, that Molly would be in the garden. She had been there; but it was too hot and dazzling, and she had come in by the open window of the drawing-room. Oppressed with the heat, she had fallen asleep in an easy-chair, one arm hanging list-lessly down. She looked very soft, and child-like; and a gush of love sprang into her father's heart.

'Molly!' said he gently, taking the little brown hand that was hanging down, and holding it in his own. 'Molly!'

She opened her eyes and sprang up and threw her arms round his neck, exclaiming –

'Oh, papa, my dear, dear papa! What made you come while I was asleep? I lose the pleasure of watching for you.'

Mr Gibson turned paler. He drew her to a seat on a sofa, with-out speaking. There was no need; she was chattering away.

'Do you know, papa, I don't think you are looking well? You want me at home, to take care of you. How soon may I come home?'

'That must be all your fancy, goosey. I feel uncommonly well; and I – I have a piece of news for you. Can you guess it?'

'How should I?' said she; but her tone was changed, and she was evidently uneasy, as with the presage of an instinct.

'Why, you see, my love,' said he, 'you are in a very awkward position – a girl growing up in such a family as mine – young men – which was a piece of confounded stupidity on my part. And I am obliged to be away so much.'

'But there is Miss Eyre,' said she, sick with the strengthening indefinite presage of what was to come. 'Dear Miss Eyre, I want nothing but her and you.'

'Still, there are times like the present when Miss Eyre cannot be with you. I've been in great perplexity for some time; but at last I've taken a step which will, I hope, make us both happier.'

'You're going to be married again,' said she, drawing her hand out of his.

'Yes. To Mrs Kirkpatrick – you remember her? They call her "Clare" at the Towers. You recollect how kind she was to you that day you were left there?'

She did not answer. She was afraid of saying anything, lest the passion of anger that was boiling up in her breast should find vent in cries and screams, or worse, in raging words that could never be forgotten.

'She's a very suitable age for me. She's highly respected by Lord and Lady Cumnor and their family, which is of itself a character. She has very agreeable and polished manners and you and I, goosey, are apt to be a little brusque, or so; we must brush up our manners now.'

No remark from her on this bit of playfulness. He went on –

'She has been accustomed to house-keeping for of late years she has had a school at Ashcombe, and has had, of course, to arrange all things for a large family. And last, but not least, she has a daughter – about your age, Molly – who will come and live with us, and be a nice companion – a sister – for you.'

'So I was sent out of the house that all this might be quietly arranged in my absence?'

Out of the bitterness of her heart she spoke. Her father started up, and quickly left the room, saying something to himself – what, she could not hear, though she ran after him, followed him through dark stone-passages, into the glare of the stable-yard, into the stables –

'Oh, papa, papa – I'm not myself – I don't know what to say about this hateful – detestable – '

He led his horse out. Just as he mounted, he turned round upon her with a grey, grim face –

'I think it's better, for both of us, for me to go away now. We may say things difficult to forget. By tomorrow we shall be more composed; you will have thought it over, and seen that the one great motive was your good. You may tell Mrs Hamley. I will come again tomorrow. Good-bye, Molly.'

For many minutes after he had ridden away Molly stood there. She turned away at last, but could not forget how her father had looked and spoken – and left her. She went out through a side-door and went quickly on to the bourne which she had fixed for herself – a seat almost surrounded by the drooping leaves of a weeping-ash on the long broad terrace-walk on the other side of the wood, that overlooked the pleasant slope of the meadows beyond. It was a deserted walk. The Squire or his sons might cross it, in passing to a little gate that led to the meadow beyond; but no one loitered there. When Molly had once got to the seat, she broke out with suppressed passion of grief. Her father was going to be married again – her father was angry with her; she had done very wrong – he had gone away displeased; she had lost his love.

She did not see Roger Hamley returning from the meadows, nor hear the click of the little white gate. He had been out dredging in ponds and ditches, and had his wet sling-net, with its imprisoned treasures of nastiness, over his shoulder. He did not see Molly, when, looking among the grass and wild plants under the trees, he spied out one which he had been long wishing to find in flower. Down went his net and, in search of the treasure, his steps led him in the direction of the ash-tree seat. He stopped; he saw somebody half-lying on the seat. It was Miss Gibson crying in a broken voice –

'Oh, papa, papa! if you would but come back!'

For a minute or two, he thought it would be kinder to leave her fancying herself unobserved; but when he heard the sad voice talking in such tones of uncomforted, lonely misery, he turned back, and went to the green tent under the ash-tree.

She started up, when he came thus close to her and he looked down upon her with grave, kind sympathy.

'Is it lunch-time?' said she, trying to believe that he did not see her tears and the disturbance of her features.

'I don't know. I was going home to lunch. But I couldn't go on when I saw your distress. Has anything happened? – anything in which I can help you, I mean; for, of course, I've no right to make the inquiry, if it is any private sorrow, in which I can be of no use.'

She sate down on the seat, and sighed, and turned so pale, that he thought she was going to faint.

'Wait a moment,' said he – quite unnecessarily, for she could not have stirred – and he was off like a shot to some spring of water that he knew of in the wood; and in a minute or two he returned with careful steps, bringing a little in a broad green leaf, turned into an impromptu cup. It did her good.

'Thank you!' she said: 'I can walk back now, in a short time. Don't stop.'

'You must let me,' said he; 'my mother wouldn't like me to leave you to come home alone, while you are so faint.'

So they remained in silence for a little while.

'Papa is going to be married again,' said she at length.

He turned round, and looked at her. Her poor wistful eyes were filling with tears as they met his, with a dumb appeal for sympathy.

'You are sorry for it?'

She did not take her eyes away from his, as her quivering lips formed the word 'Yes', though her voice made no sound. He was silent again now. At last he spoke – almost as if he was reasoning out the matter with himself.

'It seems as if there might be cases where – setting the question of love entirely on one side – it must be almost a duty to find some one to be a substitute for the mother. . . . I can believe,' said he, in a different tone of voice, and looking at Molly afresh, 'that this step may be greatly for your father's happiness – it may relieve him from many cares, and may give him a pleasant companion.'

'He had me. You don't know what we were to each other – at least, what he was to me,' she added humbly.

'Still he must have thought it for the best, or he wouldn't have done it. He may have thought it the best for your sake even more than for his own.'

'That is what he tried to convince me of.'

Roger began kicking a pebble. Suddenly he looked up.

'I want to tell you of a girl I know. Her mother died when she was about sixteen – the eldest of a large family. From that time she gave herself up to her father, first as his comforter, afterwards as his companion, friend, secretary – anything you like. He was a man with a great deal of business on hand, and Harriet was always there, ready to help, to talk, or to be silent. It went on for eight or ten years in this way; and then her father married again – a woman not many years older than Harriet herself. Well – they are just the happiest set of people I know – you wouldn't have thought it likely, would you?'

'How was it?' she sighed out at last.

'Harriet thought of her father's happiness before she thought of her own,' Roger answered. Molly began to cry again a little.

'If it were for papa's happiness' –

'He must believe that it is. Whatever you fancy, give him a chance. He cannot have much comfort, I should think, if he sees you fretting or pining – you who have been so much to him. The lady herself, too – if Harriet's stepmother had been a selfish woman – but she was not: she was as anxious for Harriet to be happy as Harriet was for her father – and your father's future wife may be another of the same kind.'

'I don't think she is, though,' murmured Molly.

Roger did not want to hear Molly's reasons for this doubting speech. He felt as if he had no right to hear more of Mr Gibson's family life than was necessary for him that he might comfort and help the crying girl.

'It is right to hope for the best about everybody, and not to expect the worst. This sounds like a truism, but it has comforted me before now. One has always to try to think more of others than of oneself, and it is best not to prejudge people on the bad side. My sermons aren't long, are they? Have they given you an appetite for lunch? Sermons always make me hungry, I know.'

She rose up, too languid to say how much she should prefer being left alone. She was very weak, and stumbled over the straggling root of a tree. He saw this stumble, and, putting out his hand, held her up from falling. This little physical failure impressed on his heart how young and helpless she was.

'You will have thought me hard,' he burst out at length, as they were nearing the drawing-room windows. 'I never can manage to express what I feel – somehow I always fall to philosophising – but I am sorry for you. It's beyond my power to help you, as far as altering facts goes; but I can feel for you. Remember how sorry I am for you! I shall often be thinking of you, though I daresay it's best not to talk about it again.'

She said, 'I know you are sorry,' under her breath; and then she broke away, and ran indoors to her room. He went straight to his mother, who was sitting before the luncheon, as much annoyed by the mysterious unpunctuality of her visitor as she was capable of being with anything.

'Where have you been, Roger? Where is Molly? – Miss Gibson, I mean,' for she was careful to keep up a barrier of forms between the young man and the young woman who were thrown together in the same household.

'I've been out dredging. I found Miss Gibson crying as if her heart would break. Her father is going to be married again.'

'Married again! You don't say so!'

'Yes, he is; and she takes it very hardly, poor girl. Mother, I think if you could send some one to her with a glass of wine – she was very nearly fainting' –

'I'll go to her myself, poor child,' said Mrs Hamley, rising.

'Indeed you must not,' said he. 'We have kept you waiting already too long; you are looking quite pale. Hammond can take it,' he continued, ringing the bell. She sat down again.

'Whom is he going to marry?'

'I don't know. I didn't ask, and she didn't tell me. I was as sorry as could be for her, and yet I couldn't tell what to say.'

'What did you say?'

'I gave her the best advice in my power.'

'Advice! you ought to have comforted her. Poor little Molly! Hush! here she is.'

To their surprise, Molly came in, trying hard to look as usual. She had bathed her eyes, and arranged her hair, and was making a great struggle to keep from crying, and to bring her voice into order. She was unwilling to distress Mrs Hamley by the sight of pain and suffering. She did not know that she was following Roger's injunction to think more of others than of herself – but so she was.

'So I hear your father is going to be married, my dear? May I ask whom it is to?'

'Mrs Kirkpatrick. She was governess a long time ago at the Countess of Cumnor's. She stays with them a great deal, and they call her "Clare", and I believe they are very fond of her.' Molly tried to speak of her future stepmother in the most favourable manner she knew how.

'Then she's not very young? Has she any family?'

'One girl, I believe. But I know so little about her!'

'Never mind, my dear. That will all come in good time. Roger, where are you going?'

'To fetch my dredging-net. It's full of things I don't want to lose.' The truth was partly told. He thought he had better leave the other two alone. His mother had such sweet power of sympathy that she would draw the sting out of the girl's heart, when she had her alone. As soon as he was gone, Molly lifted up her poor eyes, and, looking at Mrs Hamley, she said – 'He was so good to me. I mean to remember all he said.'

'I'm glad to hear it, love. He has a good heart, but he isn't so tender in his manner as Osborne. Roger is a little rough some-times.'

'Then I like roughness. It made me feel how badly – oh, Mrs Hamley, I did behave so badly to papa this morning!'

She threw herself into Mrs Hamley's arms, and sobbed upon her breast. Her sorrow was now for her own ill behaviour.

If Roger was not tender in words, he was in deeds. That evening he adjusted his microscope, and put the treasures he had collected in his morning's ramble on a little table; and then he asked his mother to come and admire. Of course Molly came too, and this was what he had intended. He tried to interest her in his pursuit, cherished her first little morsel of curiosity, and nursed it into a very proper desire for further information. Then he brought out books on the subject. Molly had come down to dinner, wondering how the long hours till bed-time would ever pass away. But prayers and bed-time came long before she expected, and she was very thankful to Roger. And now there was tomorrow to come, and a confession of penitence to be made to her father.

But Mr Gibson did not want speech or words. He read her repentance in her eyes; he saw how much she had suffered; and he had a sharp pang at his heart in consequence.

'There, there, that will do. I know all you want to say. I know my little Molly – my silly little goosey – better than she knows herself. I've brought you an invitation. Lady Cumnor wants you to go and spend next Thursday at the Towers.'

'Do you wish me to go?' said she, her heart sinking.

'I wish you and Hyacinth to become better acquainted – to learn to love each other.'

'Hyacinth!' said Molly, entirely bewildered.

'Yes; Hyacinth! It's the silliest name I ever heard of; but it's hers, and I must call her by it. "Mrs Kirkpatrick" is formal and nonsensical too, as she'll change her name so soon.'

'When, papa?' asked Molly.

'Not till after Michaelmas. And the worst is, she's gone and perpetuated her own affected name by having her daughter called after her. Cynthia!'

'How old is she – Cynthia, I mean?'

'About as old as you. She's at school in France, picking up airs and graces. She's to come home for the wedding, so you'll be able to get acquainted with her then; though, I think, she's to go back again for another half-year or so.'

CHAPTER 11

# Making Friendship

Mr Gibson believed that Cynthia Kirkpatrick was to return to England to be present at her mother's wedding; but Mrs Kirkpatrick had no such intention. She felt how disagreeable it would be to her to have her young daughter flashing out her beauty by the side of the faded bride, her mother; and, as the further arrangements for the wedding became more definite, she saw further reasons in her own mind for Cynthia's remaining quietly at her school at Boulogne.

Mrs Kirkpatrick had gone to bed that first night of her engagement to Mr Gibson, fully anticipating a speedy marriage. She looked to it as a release from the thraldom of keeping school. She saw no reason for ever going back to Ashcombe, except to wind up her affairs, and to pack up her clothes.

It was rather like a douche of cold water when, the next morning at breakfast, Lady Cumnor began to decide upon the arrangements and duties of the two middle-aged lovers.

'Of course you can't give up your school all at once, Clare. The wedding can't be before Christmas, but that will do very well. We shall all be down at the Towers; and it will be a nice amusement for the children to go over to Ashcombe, and see you married.'

'I think – I don't believe Mr Gibson will like waiting.'

'Oh, nonsense! Lord Cumnor has recommended you to his tenants, and he wouldn't like them to be put to inconvenience. Mr Gibson will see that in a moment. Now, I must give you time to settle some of your affairs today. Come to a clear understanding with each other.'

So they did come to a clear understanding about one or two

things. Mrs Kirkpatrick found that Mr Gibson had no more idea than Lady Cumnor of her breaking faith with the parents of her pupils. With all her winning wiles, she could scarcely lead him to feel impatience for the wedding to take place at Michaelmas.

'I can hardly tell you what a comfort and relief it will be to me, Hyacinth, when you are once my wife; but I wouldn't interfere with your previous engagements for the world.'

'Thank you, my own love. How good you are! I'm sure the parents of my dear pupils will be quite surprised at your consideration for their interests.'

'Don't tell them, then. I hate being admired. Why shouldn't you say it is your wish to keep on your school till they've had time to look out for another?'

'Because it isn't,' said she, daring all. 'I long to be making you happy; I want to make your home a place of rest and comfort to you; and I do so wish to cherish your sweet Molly. If I have to speak for myself, I shall say, "Good people, find a school for your daughters by Michaelmas – for after that time I must go and make the happiness of others." I can't bear to think of your long rides in November – coming home wet at night, with no one to take care of you. Oh! if you leave it to me, I shall advise the parents to take their daughters away from the care of one whose heart will be absent.'

'Well, let it be Michaelmas with all my heart. What does Lady Cumnor say?'

'Oh! I told her I was afraid you wouldn't like waiting, because of your difficulties with your servants, and because of Molly – it would be so desirable to enter on the new relationship with her as soon as possible.'

'To be sure, so it would. Poor child! I'm afraid the intelligence of my engagement has rather startled her.'

'Cynthia will feel it deeply, too,' said Mrs Kirkpatrick, unwilling to let her daughter be behind Mr Gibson's in sensibility and affection.

'We will have her over to the wedding! She and Molly shall be bridesmaids,' said Mr Gibson.

This plan did not quite suit Mrs Kirkpatrick: but she thought it best not to oppose it, until she had a presentable excuse to give; so at this time she only smiled.

It is a question whether Mrs Kirkpatrick or Molly wished the most for the day to be over which they were to spend together at the Towers. Mrs Kirkpatrick was rather weary of girls as a class. All the trials of her life were connected with girls in some way. She was very young when she first became a governess, and had been worsted in her struggles with her pupils, in the first place she ever went to. And again, before Cynthia was born, she had longed for a boy, and, lo and behold it was a daughter! Nevertheless, she really meant to be as kind as she could be to her new stepdaughter. Mrs Kirkpatrick accepted Mr Gibson principally because she was tired of earning her own livelihood; but she liked him personally – nay, she even loved him in her torpid way, and she intended to be good to his daughter.

Molly was bracing herself up in her way too. 'I will be like Harriet. I will think of others. I won't think of myself,' she kept repeating all the way to the Towers. Her father was to meet her there; but he had been detained, and she had to face Mrs Kirkpatrick by herself. Mrs Kirkpatrick was as caressing as could be. She held Molly's hand in hers, as they sate together in the library. She kept stroking it from time to time, and purring out inarticulate sounds of loving satisfaction.

'What eyes! so like your dear father's! How we shall love each other – shan't we, darling? For his sake!'

'I'll try,' said Molly bravely.

'And you've just got the same beautiful black curling hair!' said Mrs Kirkpatrick, softly lifting one of Molly's curls. 'He is so fond of you, dear. You don't know how he speaks of you; "his little treasure", as he calls you. I'm almost jealous sometimes.'

Molly took her hand away, and her heart began to harden; these speeches were so discordant to her. But she set her teeth together, and 'tried to be good'.

'We must make him so happy. I'm afraid he has had a great deal to annoy him at home; but we will do away with all that now.

You must tell me what he likes and dislikes, for of course you will know. You must tell me what your dear father dislikes most, and I shall take care to avoid it. About my dress, too – what colours does he like best? I want to do everything in my power with a view to his approval.'

Molly was gratified by all this, and began to think that really, after all, perhaps her father had done well for himself.

'I think,' said she, 'papa isn't particular about many things; but, I think, our not having the dinner quite ready for him when he comes in fidgets him more than anything. You see, he has often had a long ride, and there is another long ride to come, and he has only half-an-hour to eat in. Papa doesn't care what he has, if it's only ready. He would take bread-and-cheese, if cook would only send it in instead of dinner.'

'Bread-and-cheese! Does Mr Gibson eat cheese?'

'Yes; he's very fond of it,' said Molly innocently.

'Oh! but, my dear, I shouldn't like to think of your father eating cheese; it's such a strong-smelling, coarse kind of thing. We must get him a cook who can toss him up an omelette, or something elegant. I couldn't bear the smell of cheese.'

It did not do, Molly found, to be too minute in telling about her father's likes or dislikes. She had better leave them for Mrs Kirkpatrick to find out for herself.

'Please! I should so like to know something about Cynthia – your daughter.'

'Yes, call her Cynthia. It's a pretty name, isn't it? Cynthia Kirkpatrick. Not so pretty, though, as my old name, Hyacinth Clare. People used to say it suited me so well. I must show you an acrostic that a gentleman – he was a lieutenant in the 53rd – made upon it!'

'But about Cynthia?'

'Oh, yes! What do you want to know, my dear?'

'Papa said she was to live with us! When will she come? When will she leave school?'

'I don't think I must let her leave before next summer. She teaches English as well as learning French. Next summer she shall come home, and then shan't we be a happy little quartette!'

'I hope so,' said Molly. 'But she is to come to the wedding, isn't she?'

'Your father has begged for her to come; but we must think about it a little more. The journey is a great expense!'

'Is she like you? I do so want to see her.'

'She is very handsome, people say. In the bright-coloured style – perhaps something like what I was. But I like the dark-haired, foreign kind of beauty best – just now,' touching Molly's hair.

'Does Cynthia – is she very accomplished?' asked Molly.

'She ought to be; I've paid ever so much money to have her taught by the best masters. But you will see her before long, and I'm afraid we must go now to Lady Cumnor. She was very curious to see you – my future daughter, as she calls you.'

Mrs Kirkpatrick led her into Lady Cumnor's presence by the hand, and, in presenting her, said – 'My dear little daughter, Lady Cumnor!'

'Now, Clare, don't let me have any nonsense. She is not your daughter yet, and may never be – I believe that one-third of the engagements I have heard of have never come to marriages. Miss Gibson, I am very glad to see you, for your father's sake; when I know you better, I hope it will be for your own.'

Molly very heartily hoped that she might never be known any better by the stern-looking lady who sate so upright.

'Yes, yes, I like her looks, Clare. I'll tell you what, Clare! you and she must become better acquainted; you are not to be married till Christmas, and what could be better than that she should go back with you to Ashcombe! It's a capital plan; I'm very glad I thought of it!'

Now it would be difficult to say which of Lady Cumnor's two hearers was the more dismayed at the idea which had taken possession of her. Mrs Kirkpatrick had no fancy for being encumbered with a stepdaughter before her time. But she smiled sweetly. It was a question which of the three was the most surprised by the words which burst out of Molly's lips.

'My lady, I should dislike it very much; it would be taking me away from papa just these very few last months. I will like you,' she went on, her eyes full of tears; and, turning to Mrs Kirkpatrick, she put her hand into her future stepmother's with the prettiest and most trustful action. 'I will try hard to love you, but you must not take me away from papa just this very last bit of time that I shall have him.'

Mrs Kirkpatrick was exceedingly unwilling to back up Molly by any words of her own until Lady Cumnor had spoken and given the cue. But there was something in Molly's little speech that amused instead of irritating Lady Cumnor.

'Upon my word, young lady! Why, Clare, you've got your work before you! Not but what there is a good deal of truth in what she says. It must be very disagreeable to a girl of her age to have a stepmother coming in between her father and herself, whatever may be the advantages to her in the long run.'

Molly almost felt as if she could make a friend of the stiff old countess, for her clearness of sight as to the plan proposed being a trial and Lady Cumnor was more interested in Molly, the more she looked at her. She began a sort of catechism.

'You are sixteen, are you not?'

'No; I am seventeen. My birthday was three weeks ago.'

'Very much the same thing. Have you ever been to school?'

'No, never! Miss Eyre has taught me everything I know.'

'Umph! Miss Eyre was your governess, I suppose? And I suppose you've been taught music, and the use of globes, and French, and all the usual accomplishments, since you have had a governess? I never heard of such nonsense!' she went on, lashing herself up. 'An only daughter! If there had been half-a-dozen, there might have been some sense in it.'

It was, perhaps, fortunate for the general peace that just at this moment Mr Gibson was announced. Of course, after the first greeting, my lady had to have a private interview with her doctor; and Molly and her future stepmother wandered about in the gardens, with their arms round each other's waists, or hand in hand; Mrs Kirkpatrick active in such endearments, Molly passive, and feeling within herself very shy and strange.

Molly had held up all the day bravely; but, when once more by herself in the Hamley carriage, she burst into a passion of tears, and cried her fill till she reached the village of Hamley. Then she tried in vain to smooth her face into smiles, and do away with the other signs of her grief. She only hoped she could run upstairs to her own room without notice, and bathe her eyes before she was seen. But at the Hall-door she was caught by the Squire and Roger, coming in from an after-dinner stroll. Roger saw the state of things in an instant, and, saying –

'My mother has been looking for you to come back for this last hour,' he led the way to the drawing-room. But Mrs Hamley was not there; the Squire had stopped to speak to the coachman; they two were alone. Roger said –

'I'm afraid you've had a very trying day. I have thought of you, for I know how awkward these new relations are.'

'Thank you,' said she, with her lips trembling. 'I did try to remember what you said, and to think more of others, but it is so difficult sometimes; you know it is, don't you?'

'Yes,' said he gravely. He was gratified by her simple confession of having borne his words of advice in mind, and tried to act up to them. 'It is difficult,' he went on, 'but by-and-by you will be so much happier for it.'

'No, I shan't!' said Molly. 'It will be very dull when I shall have killed myself, as it were, and live only in trying to do, and to be, as other people like. I don't see any end to it. I might as well never have lived. And as for the happiness you speak of, I shall never be happy again.'

'Nonsense: perhaps in ten years' time you will be looking back on this trial as a very light one – who knows?'

'I daresay it seems foolish; perhaps all our earthly trials will appear foolish to us after a while; perhaps they seem so now to angels. But we are ourselves, you know, and this is *now*, not some time to come, a long, long way off. And we are not angels, to be comforted by seeing the ends for which everything is sent.'

She had never spoken so long a sentence to him before; and, when she had said it, though she did not take her eyes away from his, she blushed a little; she could not have told why. Nor did he tell himself why a sudden pleasure came over him, as he gazed at her simple, expressive face – and for a moment lost the sense of what she was saying, in the sensation of pity for her sad earnestness. In an instant more he was himself again.

'I know, I understand. Yes: it is *now* we have to do with. Don't let us go into metaphysics.' Molly opened her eyes wide at this. Had she been talking metaphysics without knowing it? 'One looks forward to a mass of trials, which will only have to be encountered one by one, little by little. Oh, here is my mother! she will tell you better than I can.'

And the *tête-à-tête* was merged into a trio. Mrs Hamley lay down; she had missed Molly, she said, and now she wanted to hear of all the adventures that had occurred to the girl at the Towers. Molly sate on a stool close to the head of the sofa, and Roger, though at first he took up a book and tried to read that he might be no restraint, soon found his reading all a pretence.

And so they went on during all the remaining time of Molly's stay at Hamley. The bond between the Mentor and his Telemachus strengthened every day. He endeavoured to lead her out of morbid thought into interest in other than personal things; and she felt that he did her good, she did not know why or how; but, after a talk with him, she always fancied that she had got the clue to goodness and peace, whatever befell.

## CHAPTER 12

# Preparing for the Wedding

Meanwhile the love affairs of the middle-aged couple were prospering well, after a fashion. Lord Cumnor's first words on the subject to Lady Cumnor were –

'I told you so. Now didn't I say what a good, suitable affair this affair between Gibson and Clare would be! I don't know when I've been so much pleased. I shall give Clare something towards her rigging-out, and they shall have a breakfast at Ashcombe Manor-house. I'll write to Preston about it. When did you say they were to be married?'

'I think they'd better wait till Christmas, and I have told them so. It would amuse the children, going over to Ashcombe for the wedding; and if it's bad weather during the holidays I'm always afraid of their finding it dull at the Towers. It's very different if it's a good frost, and they can go out skating and sledging in the park. But these last two years it has been so wet for them, poor dears!'

'And will the other poor dears be content to wait to make a holiday for your grandchildren?'

'Well,' said Lady Cumnor. 'I have told Clare she had better not think of being married before Christmas.'

But Clare did not intend to wait till Christmas; and for this once she carried her point against the will of the countess, and without any open opposition. She had a harder task in setting aside Mr Gibson's desire to have Cynthia over for the wedding. At first she had said that it would be delightful, a charming plan; only she feared that she must give up her own wishes to have her child near her at such a time, on account of the expense of the double journey.

But Mr Gibson had a really generous heart. He had already shown it, in entirely relinquishing his future wife's life-interest in the very small property the late Mr Kirkpatrick had left, in favour of Cynthia; while he arranged that she should come to his home as a daughter, as soon as she left the school she was at. The life-interest was about thirty pounds a year. Now he gave Mrs Kirkpatrick three five-pounds notes, saying that he hoped they would do away with the objections to Cynthia's coming over to the wedding. If the letter could have been written and the money sent off that day while the reflected glow of affection lasted, Cynthia would have been bridesmaid to her mother. But a hundred little interruptions came in the way of letter-writing, and Mrs Kirkpatrick persuaded herself, afresh, that it would be unwise to disturb Cynthia at her studies; and she wrote a letter to Madame Lefèvre so well imbued with this persuasion, that an answer which was almost an echo of her words was returned, the sense of which being conveyed to Mr Gibson settled the vexed question, to his regret. But the fifteen pounds were not returned. Indeed, not merely that sum, but a great part of the hundred which Lord Cumnor had given her for her trousseau, was required to pay off debts at Ashcombe. It was very much to her credit that she preferred clearing herself from debt to purchasing wedding finery. Whatever other faults might arise from her superficial and flimsy character, she was always uneasy till she was out of debt. Yet she had no scruple in appropriating her future husband's money to her own use, when it was decided that it was not to be employed as he intended.

Her wedding-dress was secure. Her former pupils at the Towers were going to present her with that; they were to dress her from head to foot on the auspicious day. Lord Cumnor had sent Mr Preston a carte-blanche order for the wedding breakfast in the old hall in Ashcombe Manor-house. Lady Cumnor had nevertheless given Mrs Kirkpatrick an excellent English-made watch and chain; more clumsy but more serviceable than the little foreign elegance that had hung at her side so long, and misled her so often.

Her preparations were thus in a very considerable state of forwardness, while Mr Gibson had done nothing as yet towards any new arrangement or decoration of his house for his intended bride. He knew he ought to do something. But what? At length he came to the wise decision of asking one of the Miss Brownings, for old friendship's sake, to take the trouble of preparing what was immediately requisite; and to let Molly come and stay.

# CHAPTER 13

# Molly Gibson's New Friends

In several ways Mr Gibson's arrangements with Miss Browning had not been made too soon. The Squire had heard that Osborne might probably return home for a few days before going abroad; and, though the growing intimacy between Roger and Molly did not alarm him in the least, yet he was possessed by a very hearty panic lest the heir might take a fancy to the surgeon's daughter.

Every young girl of seventeen or so, who is at all thoughtful, is very apt to make a Pope out of the first person who presents to her a new or larger system of duty than that by which she has been unconsciously guided hitherto. Such a Pope was Roger to Molly. Still, although they were drawn together in this very pleasant relationship, each was imagining some one very different for their highest and completest love. Roger looked to find a grand woman, beautiful in person, serene in wisdom, ready for counsel. Molly's little wavering maiden-fancy dwelt on the unseen Osborne, who was now a troubadour, and now a knight, such as he wrote about in one of his own poems. The Squire was not unwise in wishing her well out of the house before Osborne came home, if he was considering her peace of mind. Yet, when she went away he missed her constantly. And Roger missed her too. She occupied his thoughts a good deal, those first few days after she left the Hall. Mrs Hamley regretted her more. She had given her the place of a daughter in her heart.

Molly, too, felt the change of atmosphere keenly. By her dear old friends the Miss Brownings she was petted and caressed so much that she became ashamed of noticing the coarser and louder tones in which they spoke, the provincialism of their pronunciation, the absence of interest in things, and their greediness of details about persons.

Mr Gibson had thought of Molly and presently a very smart dressmaker came over from the county-town to try on a dress, which was both so simple and so elegant as at once to charm Molly. When it came home, all ready to put on, Molly had a private dressing-up, for the Miss Brownings' benefit; and she was almost startled when she looked into the glass, and saw the improvement in her appearance. 'I wonder if I'm pretty,' thought she. 'I almost think I am – in this kind of dress, I mean, of course. Betty would say, "Fine feathers make fine birds".'

When she went downstairs in her bridal attire, she was greeted with a burst of admiration.

'Well, upon my word! I shouldn't have known you. You are really beautiful – isn't she, sister?' said Miss Phoebe.

'Well! and if she is, Providence made her, and not she herself. Besides, the dressmaker must go shares. What a fine India muslin it is! it'll have cost a pretty penny!'

Mr Gibson and Molly drove over to Ashcombe the night before the wedding, in the one yellow post-chaise that Hollingford possessed. They were to be Mr Preston's, or, rather, my lord's guests at the Manor-house. The Manor-house delighted Molly at first sight. It was built of stone, had many gables and mullioned windows, and was covered over with Virginian creeper and late-blowing roses. Molly did not know Mr Preston, who stood in the doorway to greet her father. She took standing with him as a young lady at once, and it was the first time she had met with the kind of behaviour – half-complimentary, half-flirting – which some men think it necessary to assume with every woman under five-and-twenty. Mr Preston was very handsome, and knew it. He was a fair man, with light-brown hair and whiskers; grey, roving, well-shaped eyes, with lashes darker than his hair; and a figure rendered easy and supple by the athletic exercises in which his excellence was famous, and which had procured him admission into much higher society than he was otherwise entitled to enter. He had his own private reasons for wishing to get up a flirtation with Molly just at this time; he had amused himself so much with the widow when she first came to Ashcombe, that he fancied that the sight of him, standing by her less polished, less handsome, middle-aged husband, might be too much of a contrast to be agreeable. Besides, he had really a strong passion for some one else; and that passion it was necessary for him to conceal. So that, altogether, he had resolved, even had 'Gibson's little girl' been less attractive than she was, to devote himself to her for the next sixteen hours.

They were taken by their host into a wainscoted parlour, where a wood fire crackled and burnt, and the crimson curtains shut out the waning day and the outer chill. And then he rang for a servant to show Molly to her room. She was taken into a most comfortable chamber; a wood fire on the hearth, dark woolen curtains surrounding a snow-white bed, great vases of china standing here and there.

'This is my Lady Harriet's room when her ladyship comes to the Manor-house with my lord the earl,' said the housemaid. 'Shall I help you to dress, miss? I always helps her ladyship.'

Molly, quite aware of the fact that she had but her white muslin gown for the wedding besides that she had on, dismissed the good woman, and was thankful to be left to herself.

'Dinner' was it called? Why, it was nearly eight o'clock; and preparations for bed seemed a more natural employment than dressing at this hour of night. All the dressing she could manage was the placing of a red damask rose or two in the band of her grey stuff gown, from a great nosegay standing on the toilette-table. Mr Preston must have heard her step, for he met her in the hall, and led her into a small drawing-room. This room reminded her a little of Hamley – yellow satin upholstery of seventy or a hundred years ago, all delicately kept and scrupulously clean; great Indian cabinets, and china jars, emitting spicy odours; a large blazing fire, before which her father stood in his morning dress, grave and thoughtful.

'This room is that which Lady Harriet uses when she comes here with her father for a day or two,' said Mr Preston.

'I should think it was a very pleasant house to stay at,' said

Molly, remembering the look of warm comfort that pervaded it. But Mr Preston seemed to take it as a compliment to himself.

'I was afraid a young lady like you might perceive all the incongruities of a bachelor's home. I'm very much obliged to you, Miss Gibson. In general, I live pretty much in the room in which we shall dine; and I've a sort of agent's office in which I keep books and papers, and receive callers on business.'

Then they went in to dinner. Molly thought everything that was served was delicious; but it did not seem to satisfy Mr Preston, who apologised several times for the bad cooking of this dish, or the omission of a particular sauce to that; always referring to bachelor's this, and bachelor's that, till Molly grew quite impatient at the word. Her father's depression, which was rendering him very silent, made her uneasy. She did not know when to leave the gentlemen, but her father made a sign to her; and she was conducted back to the yellow drawing-room by Mr Preston, who made many apologies for leaving her there alone. She enjoyed herself extremely, however, feeling at liberty to prowl about, and examine all the curiosities the room contained. Among other things was a Louis-Quinze cabinet with lovely miniatures in enamel let into the fine woodwork. She was looking intently at these faces when her father and Mr Preston came in. Her father came up and patted her on the back, looked at what she was looking at, and then went off to the fire. Mr Preston threw himself into her interests.

'That is said to be Mademoiselle de St. Quentin, a great beauty at the French Court. This is Madame du Barri. Do you see any likeness in Mademoiselle de St. Quentin to anyone you know?' He had lowered his voice a little.

'No!' said Molly. 'I never saw anyone half so beautiful.'

'But don't you see a likeness – in the eyes particularly?' he said. 'It constantly reminds me of – of Miss Kirkpatrick.'

'Does it?' said Molly eagerly. 'Oh! I've never seen her, so of course I couldn't find out the likeness. You know her, then, do you? Please tell me all about her.'

He smiled a little before replying.

'She's very beautiful; that of course is understood, when I say that this miniature does not come up to her for beauty.'

'And besides – Go on, please.'

'What do you mean by "besides"?'

'Oh! I suppose she's very clever and accomplished?'

That was not in the least what Molly wanted to ask; but it was difficult to word the vague vastness of her unspoken inquiry.

'She is clever naturally; she has picked up accomplishments. But she has such a charm about her, one forgets what she herself is in the halo that surrounds her. You ask me all this, Miss Gibson, and I answer; or else I should not entertain one young lady with my enthusiastic praises of another.'

'I don't see why not,' said Molly. 'She is coming to live with us when she leaves school, and we are very nearly the same age; so it will be almost like having a sister.'

'She is to live with you, is she?' said Mr Preston. 'And when is she to leave school?'

'I think it is to be at Easter. Is she a grave or a merry person?'

'Never very grave. "Sparkling" would be the word for her, I think. Do you ever write to her? If you do, pray remember me to her, and tell her how we have been talking about her.'

## CHAPTER 14

# Molly Finds Herself Patronised

The wedding went off much as such affairs do. Lord Cumnor came in order to officiate as the bride's father, and was in more open glee than anyone else. Lady Harriet came as a sort of amateur bridesmaid, to 'share Molly's duties', as she called it. They went from the Manor-house in two carriages to the church in the park, Mr Preston and Mr Gibson in one, and Molly, to her dismay, with Lord Cumnor and Lady Harriet in the other. Lady Harriet was very merry, and very much inclined to talk to Molly, by way of finding out what sort of a little personage Clare was to have for her future daughter.

Lady Harriet spoke, going to the point, as she always piqued herself on doing –

'I daresay it's something of a trial to you, this marriage of your father's; but you'll find Clare the most amiable of women. She always let me have my own way, and I've no doubt she'll let you have yours.'

'I mean to try and like her,' said Molly, in a low voice. 'I've seen very little of her yet.'

'Why, it's the very best thing for you that could have happened, my dear,' said Lord Cumnor. 'You're growing up into a young lady – and a very pretty young lady, too, if you'll allow an old man to say so – and who so proper as your father's wife to bring you out, and show you off, and take you to balls, and that kind of thing?'

'Poor child!' said Lady Harriet, 'the thought of balls is too much for her just now; but you'll like having Cynthia Kirkpatrick for a companion, shan't you, dear?'

'Very much,' said Molly. 'Do you know her?'

'Oh, she's the prettiest creature that you ever saw, and with eyes that mean mischief, if I'm not mistaken. But Clare kept her spirit under pretty well, when she was staying with us – afraid of her being troublesome, I fancy.'

Before Molly could shape her next question, they were at the church; and she and Lady Harriet went into a pew near the door to wait for the bride. The earl drove on alone to fetch her from her own house, not a quarter of a mile distant. It was pleasant to her to be led to the hymeneal altar by a belted earl, and pleasant to have his daughter as a volunteer bridesmaid. Mrs Kirkpatrick, on the brink of matrimony with a man whom she liked, and who would be bound to support her without any exertion of her own, looked beamingly happy and handsome. Ten minutes, and all was over. The bride and bridegroom were driving together to the Manor-house, and Molly was again in the carriage with my lord and Lady Harriet.

Molly found out, to her dismay, that the plan was for her to return with Lord Cumnor and Lady Harriet, when they went back to the Towers in the evening. In the meantime, Lord Cumnor had business to do with Mr Preston; and, after the happy couple had driven off on their week's holiday tour, she was to be left alone with the formidable Lady Harriet. When they were by themselves, Lady Harriet gazed intently at Molly, then suddenly said –

'I like you – you are a little wild creature, and I want to tame you. Come here, and sit on this stool by me. What is your name? or what do they call you? – as North-country people would express it.'

'Molly Gibson. My real name is Mary.'

'Molly is a nice, soft-sounding name. People in the last century weren't afraid of homely names; now we are all so smart and fine: no more "Lady Bettys" now. I almost wonder they haven't rechristened all the worsted and knitting-cotton that bears her name. Fancy Lady Constantia's cotton, or Lady Anna-Maria's worsted!'

'I didn't know there was a Lady Betty's cotton,' said Molly.

'That proves you don't do fancy-work! You'll find Clare will set you to it, though. She used to set me at piece after piece. I wonder how you'll get on together?'

'So do I!' sighed out Molly, under her breath.

'I used to think I managed her, till one day an uncomfortable suspicion arose that all the time she had been managing me. Still it's easy work to let oneself be managed; at any rate till one wakens up to the consciousness of the process, and then it may become amusing, if one takes it in that light.'

'I should hate to be managed,' said Molly indignantly. 'I should dislike to be trapped into anything.'

'Now I,' said Lady Harriet, 'am too lazy to avoid traps; and I rather like to remark the cleverness with which they're set. But then, of course, I know that, if I choose to exert myself, I can break through the withes of green flax with which they try to bind me. Now, perhaps, you won't be able.'

'I don't quite understand what you mean,' said Molly.

'I daresay it's as well for you that you shouldn't. The moral of all I have been saying is, "Be a good girl, and suffer yourself to be led, and you'll find your new stepmother the sweetest creature imaginable." How you'll get on with her daughter is another affair; but I daresay very well.'

Mr Preston came into the room just at this time, and Molly was a little surprised at Lady Harriet's cool manner of dismissing him, remembering Mr Preston had implied his intimacy with her ladyship, the evening before at dinner-time.

'I cannot bear that sort of person,' said Lady Harriet, almost before he was out of hearing; 'giving himself airs of gallantry towards one to whom his simple respect is all his duty. I can talk to one of my father's labourers with pleasure, while with a man like that underbred fop I am all over thorns and nettles. What is it the Irish call that style of creature? They've some capital word for it, I know. What is it?'

'I don't know – I never heard it,' said Molly.

'Oh! that shows you've never read Miss Edgeworth's tales – now, have you? If you had, you'd have recollected that there was such a word. If you've never read those stories, they would be just the thing to beguile your solitude – vastly improving and moral, and yet quite sufficiently interesting. I'll lend them to you while you're all alone.'

'I'm not alone. I'm on a visit to the Miss Brownings.'

'Then I'll bring them to you. I like the Miss Brownings; one gets enough of respect from them at any rate; and I've always wanted to see the kind of *ménage* of such people.'

Molly mustered up courage to speak what was in her mind.

'Your ladyship keeps speaking of the sort of – the class of – people to which I belong, as if it was a kind of strange animal you were talking about; yet you talk so openly to me that' –

'You think me in your heart a little impertinent – now, don't you?' said Lady Harriet almost kindly.

Molly lifted her beautiful, honest eyes to Lady Harriet's face, and said –

'Yes! – a little.'

'Don't you see, little one, I talk after my kind, just as you talk after your kind. It's only on the surface with both of us. Why, I daresay some of your good Hollingford ladies talk of the poor people in a manner which they would consider just as impertinent in their turn, if they could hear it. I ought not to have used it to you; but somehow I separate you from all these Hollingford people.'

'But why?' persevered Molly. 'I'm one of them.'

'Yes, you are. But most of them are so unnatural in their exaggerated respect and admiration when they come up to the Towers, and put on so much pretence by way of fine manners, that they only make themselves objects of ridicule. You at least are simple and truthful, and that's why I separate you in my own mind from them, and have talked unconsciously to you as I would – well! now here's another piece of impertinence – as I would to my equal – in rank, I mean; for I don't set myself up in solid things as any better than my neighbours. Here's tea, however, come in time to stop me from growing too humble.'

It was a very pleasant little tea in the fading September twilight. Then the carriage came round, and they drove back to the Towers.

'Would you rather come in and dine with us or go home straight?' asked Lady Harriet of Molly.

'I would rather go back to the Miss Brownings' at once, please,' said Molly, with a nightmare-like recollection of the last evening she had spent at the Towers.

Lady Harriet stopped to kiss Molly on the forehead.

'I shall come some day soon, and bring you a load of Miss Edgeworth's tales, and make further acquaintance with Pecksy and Flapsy.'

'No, don't, please,' said Molly, taking hold of her. 'You must not come – indeed you must not.'

'Why not?'

'Because I think that I ought not to have anyone coming to see me who laughs at the friends I am staying with, and calls them names.'

'My dear little woman!' said Lady Harriet, bending over her. 'I'm very sorry to have called them names – very, very sorry to have hurt you. If I promise you to be respectful to them in word and in deed – and in very thought, if I can – you'll let me come then, won't you?'

Molly hesitated. 'I'd better go home at once; I shall only say wrong things – and there's Lord Cumnor waiting all this time.'

'Let him alone; he's very well amused hearing all the news of the day from Brown. Then I shall come – under promise?'

So Molly drove off in solitary grandeur; and before Lady Harriet's call was paid, Molly received another visit.

Roger Hamley came riding over one day with a note from his mother, and a wasps'-nest as a present from himself. The Miss Brownings thought Mr Roger Hamley a very personable young fellow, as he came into the room. He talked pleasantly to them, while Molly read Mrs Hamley's little missive; then he turned to her, and, though the Miss Brownings listened with all their ears, they could not find out anything remarkable either in the words he said or the tone in which they were spoken.

While Molly finished reading her note, he explained its contents to Miss Browning.

'My brother and I are going with my father to an agricultural meeting at Canonbury on Thursday, and my mother desired me to say to you how very much obliged she would be, if you would spare her Miss Gibson for the day. She was very anxious to ask for the pleasure of your company, too, but she really is so poorly that we persuaded her to be content with Miss Gibson.'

'Nothing would have given us more pleasure,' said Miss Browning, drawing herself up in gratified dignity. 'Oh, yes, we fully recognise Mrs Hamley's kind intention. We will take the will for the deed, as the common people express it. I believe that there was an intermarriage between the Brownings and the Hamleys, a generation or two ago.'

'I daresay there was,' said Roger. 'My mother is very delicate, and obliged to humour her health, which has made her keep aloof from society.'

'Then I may go?' said Molly, sparkling.

'To be sure, my dear. Write a pretty note, and tell Mrs Hamley how much obliged to her we are for thinking of us.'

All the gentlemen were gone before the carriage, which came to fetch Molly on Thursday, reached Hamley Hall. But Molly was glad she had her dear Mrs Hamley the more to herself. As they were sitting at lunch, a strange man's voice and step were heard in the hall; the door was opened, and a young man came in, who could be no other than Osborne. He was beautiful and languid-looking, almost as frail in appearance as his mother, whom he strongly resembled. He came up to his mother, and stood by her, holding her hand, while his eyes sought Molly, not boldly, but as if appraising her critically.

'Yes! I'm back again. Bullocks, I find, are not in my line. The smell was insufferable on such a hot day.'

'My dear boy, I'm only too glad to have you back. Miss Gibson, this tall fellow is my son Osborne. Osborne – Miss Gibson. Now, what will you have?'

He looked round the table as he sate down.

'Nothing here. Isn't there some game-pie? I'll ring for that.'

Molly was trying to reconcile the ideal with the real. The ideal was agile, yet powerful, with Greek features and an eagle eye, capable of enduring long fasting, and indifferent as to what he ate. The real was almost effeminate in movement, though not in figure; he had the Greek features, but his blue eyes had a cold, weary expression in them. However, he was extremely attentive to his mother, which pleased Molly; yet, again, it struck the shrewd, if simple, girl, that Osborne was mentally squinting at her in the conversation which was directed to his mother. But it was flattering rather than otherwise to perceive that a very fine young man, who was a poet to boot, should think it worth while to talk on the tight-rope for her benefit. And before the afternoon was ended, without there having been any direct conversation between Osborne and Molly, she had reinstated him on his throne in her imagination. Before Molly left, the Squire and Roger returned from Canonbury.

'Osborne here!' said the Squire, red and panting. 'Why the deuce couldn't you tell us you were coming home? I looked about for you everywhere, just as we were going into the ordinary; and Roger there missed above half his dinner hunting about for you; and, all the time, you'd stole away, and were quietly sitting here with the women. I wish you'd let me know, the next time you make off. I've lost half my pleasure in looking at as fine a lot of cattle as I ever saw, with thinking you might be having one of your old attacks of faintness.'

'I should have had one, I think, if I'd stayed longer in that atmosphere. But I'm sorry if I've caused you anxiety.'

'Well! well!' said the Squire, somewhat mollified. 'And Roger, too, there – I've been sending him here and sending him there all the afternoon.'

'I didn't mind it, sir. I was only sorry you were so uneasy. I thought Osborne had gone home, for I knew it wasn't much in his way,' said Roger.

Molly intercepted a glance between the two brothers – a look of true confidence and love, which suddenly made her like them both under the aspect of relationship – new to her observation.

Roger came up to her, and sat down by her.

'Well, and how are you getting on with Huber? don't you find him very interesting?'

'I'm afraid,' said Molly penitently, 'I haven't read much. The Miss Brownings like me to talk; and, besides, there is so much to do at home before papa comes back; and Miss Browning doesn't like me to go without her. I know it sounds nothing; but it does take up a great deal of time.'

'When is your father coming back?'

'Next Tuesday, I believe. He cannot stay long away.'

'I shall ride over and pay my respects to Mrs Gibson,' said he. 'I shall come as soon as I may. And, when I come, I shall expect my pupil to have been very diligent.'

Then the carriage came round, and she had the long solitary drive back to the Miss Brownings'. Miss Phoebe was standing on the stairs, with a lighted candle in her hand.

'Oh, Molly! I thought you'd never come back! Such a piece of news! Sister has gone to bed; she's had a headache – with the excitement, I think. Who do you think has been here – drinking tea with us, too, in the most condescending manner?'

'Lady Harriet?' said Molly, suddenly enlightened by the word 'condescending'.

'Yes. Why, how did you guess it? But, after all, her call, at any rate in the first instance, was upon you. Oh dear, Molly! if you're not in a hurry to go to bed, let me sit down quietly and tell you all about it. And you may tell me your news, my dear.'

Molly told her small events; which, interesting as they might have been at other times to the gossip-loving and sympathetic Miss Phoebe, were rather pale in the stronger light reflected from the visit of an earl's daughter.

## CHAPTER 15

# The New Mamma

On Tuesday afternoon, Molly returned home – to the home which was already strange. New paint, new paper, new colours; grim servants dressed in their best, and objecting to every change from their master's marriage to the new oil-cloth in the hall, 'which tripped 'em up, and threw 'em down, and was cold to the feet, and smelt just abominable.'

The sound of their carriage-wheels was heard at last, and Molly went to the front door to meet them. Her father got out first, and took her hand and held it, while he helped his bride to alight. Then he kissed her fondly, and passed her on to his wife; but her veil was so securely (and becomingly) fastened down, that it was some time before Mrs Gibson could get her lips clear to greet her new daughter.

'Molly, my dear, show – your mamma to her room!'

Mr Gibson had hesitated, because the question of the name by which Molly was to call her new relation had never occurred to him before. The colour flashed into Molly's face. Was she to call her 'mamma'? The rebellious heart rose against it, but she said nothing. Mrs Gibson hardly spoke to Molly, till they were both in the newly-furnished bed-room, where a small fire had been lighted by Molly's orders.

'Now, my love, we can embrace each other in peace. O dear, how tired I am!' – (after the embrace had been accomplished). 'But your dear papa has been kindness itself. Dear! what an old-fashioned bed! And what a – But it doesn't signify. By-and-by we'll renovate the house – won't we, my dear? And you'll be my little maid tonight, and help me to arrange a few things; for I'm worn out with the day's journey.'

'I've ordered a sort of tea-dinner to be ready for you,' said Molly. 'Shall I go and tell them to send it in?'

'I'm not sure if I can go down again tonight. It would be very comfortable to have a little table brought in here, and sit in my dressing-gown by this cheerful fire. But, to be sure, there's your dear papa! I really don't think he would eat anything, if I were not there. Yes, I'll come down in a quarter of an hour.'

But Mr Gibson had found a note awaiting him, with an immediate summons to an old patient, dangerously ill.

As soon as Mrs Gibson found that he was not likely to miss her presence she desired to have her meal upstairs; and poor Molly, not daring to tell the servants of this whim, had to carry up, first a table, afterwards all the choice portions of the meal, which she had taken great pains to arrange on the table, as she had seen such things done at Hamley. How pretty Molly had thought her handiwork an hour or two before! How dreary it seemed as, at last released from Mrs Gibson's conversation, she sate down in solitude to cold tea and the drumsticks of the chicken! Her stepmother even now was ringing her bell to have the tray taken away, and Miss Gibson summoned to her bed-room.

Molly hastily finished her meal, and went upstairs again.

'I feel so lonely, darling; do come and be with me, and help me to unpack. I think your dear papa might have put off his visit to Mr Craven Smith for just this one evening.'

'Mr Craven Smith couldn't put off his dying,' said Molly bluntly.

'You droll girl!' said Mrs Gibson, with a faint laugh. 'But, if this Mr Smith is dying, what's the use of your father's going off to him in such a hurry? Does he expect any legacy?'

Molly bit her lips, to prevent herself from saying something disagreeable. She only answered –

'I don't quite know that he is dying. The man said so; and papa can sometimes do something to make the last struggle easier.'

'What dreary knowledge of death you have learnt, for a girl of your age! Well, don't let us talk any more of such gloomy things, tonight! I think I shall go to bed at once, I am so tired, if you will only sit by me till I get sleepy, darling.'

Molly got a book, and read her stepmother to sleep. Then she stole down to the dining-room, where the fire was gone out; purposely neglected by the servants, to mark their displeasure at their new mistress's having had her tea in her own room. Molly managed to light it, however, before her father came home, and collected some comfortable food for him. Then she knelt down on the hearthrug, gazing into the fire in a dreamy reverie, which had enough of sadness about it to cause the tear to drop unnoticed from her eyes. But she jumped up, and shook herself into brightness, at the sound of her father's step.

'How is Mr Craven Smith?' she asked.

'Dead. He just recognised me. He was one of my first patients on my coming to Hollingford.'

Mr Gibson sate down and warmed his hands at the fire, seeming neither to need food nor talk. Then he roused himself from his sadness, and said briskly enough –

'And where's the new mamma?'

'She was tired, and went to bed early. Oh, papa! must I call her "mamma"?'

'I should like it,' replied he.

Molly was silent. She put a cup of tea near him; he stirred it, and sipped it, and then he recurred to the subject.

'Why shouldn't you call her "mamma"? I'm sure she means to do the duty of a mother to you. We all may make mistakes, and her ways may not be quite all at once our ways; but at any rate let us start with a family bond between us.'

What would Roger say was right? Molly kept silence, though she knew her father was expecting an answer. At last he gave up his expectation, and told about their journey, questioned her as to the Hamleys, the Brownings, Lady Harriet, and the afternoon they had passed at the Manor-house. But there was a certain hardness and constraint in his manner, and in hers a heaviness and absence of mind. All at once she said –

'Papa, I will call her "mamma"!'

He took her hand, and grasped it tight.

'You won't be sorry for it, Molly, when you come to lie as poor Craven Smith did tonight.'

For some time the murmurs and grumblings of the two elder servants were confined to Molly's ears; then they spread to her father's, who made summary work with them.

'You don't like Mrs Gibson's ringing her bell so often, don't you? You've been spoilt; but, if you don't conform to my wife's desires, you have the remedy in your own hands, you know.'

What servant ever resisted the temptation to give warning after such a speech as that? Betty told Molly she was going to leave, in as indifferent a manner as she could possibly assume towards the girl whom she had tended and been about for the last sixteen years. But this was assumed hardness. In a week or two Betty was in a flood of tears at the prospect of leaving her nursling, and would fain have stayed and answered all the bells in the house once every quarter of an hour. Even Mr Gibson's masculine heart was touched by the sorrow of the old servant.

One day he said to Molly, 'I wish you'd ask your mamma if Betty might not stay, if she made a proper apology, and all that sort of thing.'

'I don't much think it will be of any use,' said Molly, in a mournful voice. 'I know she is writing, or has written, about some under-housemaid at the Towers.'

'Well! – all I want is peace and a decent quantity of cheerfulness when I come home. I see enough of tears at other people's houses. Do as you like about asking mamma; only, if she agrees, I shall be quite willing.'

So Molly tried her hand at making a request to that effect to Mrs Gibson. Her instinct told her she would be unsuccessful; but surely favour was never refused in so soft a tone.

'My dear girl, I should never have thought of sending an old servant away – one who has had the charge of you from your birth, or nearly so. She might have stayed for ever for me, if she had only attended to my wishes; and I am not unreasonable, am I? But, you see, she complained; and, when your papa spoke to her, she gave warning; and it is quite against my principles to take an apology from a servant who has given warning.'

'She is so sorry,' pleaded Molly; 'she says she will do anything you wish, and attend to all your orders.'

'But, sweet one, I cannot go against my principles, however much I may be sorry for Betty. Now I have all but engaged Maria, who was under-housemaid at the Towers; so don't let me hear any more of Betty's sorrow, for I'm sure, what with your dear papa's sad stories, I'm getting quite low.'

'Poor Betty!' said Molly softly.

'Poor old soul! I hope she'll profit by the lesson, I'm sure,' sighed out Mrs Gibson; 'but it's a pity we hadn't Maria before the county-families began to call.'

Mrs Gibson had been highly gratified by the circumstance of so many calls 'from county-families'. Her husband was much respected; and many ladies from various halls, courts, and houses thought it right to pay his new wife the attention of a call, when they drove into Hollingford to shop. The state of expectation into which these calls threw Mrs Gibson rather diminished Mr Gibson's domestic comfort. It was awkward to be carrying hot, savoury-smelling dishes from the kitchen to the dining-room at the very time when high-born ladies, with noses of aristo-cratic refinement, might be calling. The remedy proposed by Mrs Gibson was a late dinner. The luncheon for the young men, as she observed to her husband, might be sent into the surgery. A few el-egant cold trifles for herself and Molly would not scent the house, and she would always take care to have some little dainty ready for him. He acceded, but unwillingly; for he felt as if he should never be able to arrange his rounds aright, with this six o'clock dinner.

'Don't get any dainties for me, my dear; bread-and-cheese is the chief of my diet, as it was that of the old woman's.'

'I know nothing of your old woman,' replied his wife; 'but really I cannot allow cheese to come beyond the kitchen.'

'Then I'll eat it there,' said he.

'Really, Mr Gibson, it is astonishing to compare your appearance and manners with your tastes. You look such a gentleman, as dear Lady Cumnor used to say.'

Then the cook left. The cook did not like the trouble of late dinners; and, being a Methodist, she objected on religious grounds to trying any of Mrs Gibson's new receipts for French dishes. It was not scriptural, she said. There was a deal of mention of food in the Bible; but it was of sheep ready-dressed, which meant mutton, and of wine, and of bread-and-milk, and figs and raisins and suchlike. So the cook followed in Betty's track, and Mr Gibson had to satisfy his healthy English appetite on badly-made omelettes, rissoles, vol-au-vents, croquettes, and timbales; never being exactly sure what he was eating.

He had made up his mind before his marriage to yield in trifles, and be firm in greater things. But the differences of opinion about trifles arose every day, and were perhaps more annoying than if they had related to things of more consequence. He never allowed himself to put any regret into shape, even in his own mind; he repeatedly reminded himself of his wife's good qualities, and comforted himself by thinking they should work together better as time rolled on; but he was very angry at a bachelor great-uncle of Mr Coxe's, who, after taking no notice of his red-headed nephew for years, suddenly sent for him and appointed him his heir, on condition that his great-nephew remained with him during the rest of his life. This had happened almost directly after Mr and Mrs Gibson's return from their wedding journey, and once or twice since that time Mr Gibson had found himself wondering why the deuce old Benson could not have made up his mind sooner, and so have rid his house of the unwelcome presence of the young lover.

So Mr Coxe went away, with an oath of unalterable faithfulness in his heart; and Mr Gibson had unwillingly to fulfil an old promise made to a gentleman farmer in the neighbourhood, and to take the second son of Mr Browne in young Coxe's place. He was rather more than a year younger than Molly. Mr Gibson trusted that there would be no repetition of the Coxe romance.

CHAPTER 16

# The Bride at Home

Among the 'county-people' (as Mrs Gibson termed them) who called upon her as a bride, were the two young Mr Hamleys. The Squire, their father, had done his congratulations, as far as he ever intended to do them, to Mr Gibson himself when he came to the Hall; but Mrs Hamley, unable to go and pay visits herself, and with perhaps a little sympathetic curiosity as to how Molly and her stepmother got on together, made her sons ride over to Hollingford with her cards and apologies. They came into the newly furnished drawing-room, looking bright and fresh from their ride: Osborne first, as usual, perfectly dressed for the occasion; Roger, looking like a strong-built, cheerful, intelligent country-farmer. Mrs Gibson made the effect she always intended to produce, of a very pretty woman, no longer in her first youth, but with such soft manners and such a caressing voice that people forgot to wonder what her real age might be. Molly was better dressed than formerly; her stepmother saw after that. She disliked anything old or shabby, or out of taste about her; it hurt her eye; and she had already fidgeted Molly into a new amount of care about the manner in which she put on her clothes, arranged her hair, and was gloved and shod. Her appearance was extremely improved, even to Osborne's critical eye.

Osborne and Mrs Gibson made themselves agreeable to each other. They talked of the 'Shakspeare and musical glasses' of the day, each vieing with the other in their knowledge of London topics. Molly heard fragments of their conversation, in the pauses of silence between Roger and herself. Her hero was coming out in quite a new character; no longer literary or poetical, or romantic or critical, he was now full of the last new play, of the singers at the opera. He had the advantage over Mrs Gibson, who, in fact, only spoke of these things from hearsay, while Osborne had run up from Cambridge two or three times to hear this, or to see that, wonder of the season. But she had the advantage over him in greater boldness of invention to eke out her facts; for instance, in speaking of the mannerisms of a famous Italian singer, she would ask –

'Did you observe her constant trick of heaving her shoulders and clasping her hands together, before she took a high note?' – which was so said as to imply that Mrs Gibson herself had noticed this trick.

Roger saw Molly glancing at his brother.

'You think my brother looking ill?' said he, lowering his voice. 'That run on the Continent did him harm, instead of good; and his disappointment at his examination has told upon him, I'm afraid.'

'I was not thinking he looked ill; only changed somehow.'

'He says he must go back to Cambridge soon; and I shall be off next week. This is a farewell visit to you, as well as one of congratulation to Mrs Gibson.'

'Your mother will feel your both going away, won't she?'

'Yes,' he replied. 'And I'm not satisfied about her health either. You will go out and see her sometimes, will you? she is very fond of you.'

'If I may,' said Molly, unconsciously glancing at her step-mother.

As soon as they had left, Mrs Gibson began her usual comments on the departed visitors.

'I do like that Osborne Hamley! What a nice fellow he is! Somehow, I always do like eldest sons. He will have the estate, won't he? I shall ask your dear papa to encourage him to come about the house. He will be a very good, very pleasant acquaintance for you and Cynthia. The other is but a loutish young fellow. I suppose he takes after his mother, who is but a parvenue, I've heard them say at the Towers.'

Molly was spiteful enough to have great pleasure in saying –

'I've heard her father was a Russian merchant, and imported tallow and hemp. Mr Osborne Hamley is extremely like her.'

'Indeed! But there's no calculating these things. Anyhow, he is the perfect gentleman in appearance and manner. The estate is entailed, is it not?' Then Mrs Gibson said –

'Do you know, I almost think I must get dear papa to give a little dinner-party, and ask Mr Osborne Hamley? It would be something cheerful for him after the dulness and solitude of Hamley Hall. For the old people don't visit much, I believe?'

'He's going back to Cambridge next week,' said Molly.

'Is he? Well, then, we'll put off our little dinner till Cynthia comes home. I must get this drawing-room all new-furnished first; and then I mean to fit up her room and yours just alike.'

'Are you going to new-furnish that room?' said Molly, in astonishment at the never-ending changes.

'Yes; and yours, too, darling; so don't be jealous!'

'Oh, please, mamma, not mine,' said Molly. 'I like it as it is. Pray don't do anything to it!'

'What nonsense, child! I never heard anything more ridiculous! Most girls would be glad to get rid of furniture only fit for the lumber-room.'

'It was my own mamma's, before she was married,' said Molly, in a very low voice.

Mrs Gibson paused for a moment, before she replied –

'It's very much to your credit that you should have such feelings, I'm sure. But don't you think sentiment may be carried too far? Besides, my dear, Hollingford will seem very dull to Cynthia, after pretty, gay France, and I want to make the first impressions attractive. I want her to come in a good temper; for, between ourselves, my dear, she is a little, leetle, wilful. You need not mention this to your papa.'

'But can't you do Cynthia's room, and not mine?'

'No, indeed! I couldn't agree to that. Only think what would be said of me by everybody; petting my own child and neglecting my husband's! I couldn't bear it. Every penny I spend on Cynthia

I shall spend on you too; so it's no use talking any more about it.'

Squire Hamley came. He shook Mrs Gibson's hand heartily, as a mark of congratulation on her good fortune in having secured such a prize as his friend Gibson, but said nothing about his long neglect of duty. Molly, who by this time knew the few strong expressions of his countenance well, was sure that something was the matter, and that he was very much disturbed. He hardly attended to Mrs Gibson's fluent opening of conversation, but turned to Molly and said in a low voice, as if he was making a confidence to her that he did not intend Mrs Gibson to hear –

'Molly, we are all wrong at home! Osborne has lost the fellowship at Trinity he went back to try for. Then he has gone and failed miserably in his degree, after all that he said, and that his mother said; and I, like a fool, went and boasted about my clever son. I can't understand it. And then it has thrown madam into one of her bad fits of illness; and she seems to have a fancy for you, child! Your father came to see her this morning. Poor things, she's very poorly, I'm afraid; and she told him how she should like to have you about her, and he said I might fetch you. You'll come, won't you, my dear?'

'I'll be ready in ten minutes,' said Molly, much touched by the Squire's words and manner, never thinking of asking her stepmother's consent, now that she had heard that her father had given his. As she rose to leave the room, Mrs Gibson said –

'Stop a minute, darling. I am sure dear papa quite forgot that you were to go out with me tonight, to visit people,' continued she, addressing herself to the Squire, 'with whom I am quite unacquainted – and it is very uncertain if Mr Gibson can return in time to accompany me – so, you see, I cannot allow Molly to go with you.'

'I shouldn't have thought it would have signified. And my wife sets her heart on things, as sick people do. Well, Molly' (in a louder tone, for these foregoing sentences were spoken *sotto voce*), 'we must put it off till tomorrow; and it's our loss, not yours,' he continued. 'You'll be as gay as can be tonight, I daresay.'

'No, I shall not,' broke in Molly. 'I never wanted to go, and now I shall want it less than ever.'

'Hush, my dear,' said Mrs Gibson; and, addressing the Squire, she added, 'The visiting here is not all one could wish for so young a girl – no young people, no dances, nothing of gaiety; but it is wrong in you, Molly, to speak against such kind friends of your father's as I understand these Cockerells are. Don't give so bad an impression of yourself to the kind Squire.'

'Let her alone! let her alone!' quoth he. 'She'd rather come and be in my wife's sick-room than go out for this visit tonight. Is there no way of getting her off?'

'None whatever,' said Mrs Gibson.

The Squire was put out; at length, after a pause of silence, he started up, and said –

'Well! it's no use. Poor madam; she won't like it. She'll be disappointed! But it's but for one evening! She may come tomorrow, mayn't she? Or will the dissipation of such an evening as she describes be too much for her?'

There was a touch of savage irony in his manner which frightened Mrs Gibson into good behaviour.

'She shall be ready at any time you name. I am so sorry; my foolish shyness is in fault, I believe; but still, you must acknowledge that an engagement is an engagement.'

'Did I ever say an engagement was an elephant, madam? However, there's no use saying any more about it, or I shall forget my manners. So you'll excuse me, Mrs Gibson, and let Molly come along with me at ten tomorrow morning?'

'Certainly,' said Mrs Gibson, smiling. But, when his back was turned, she said to Molly –

'Now, my dear, I must never have you exposing me to the ill-manners of such a man again! I don't call him a squire; I call him a boor, or a yeoman at best. You must not go on accepting or rejecting invitations, as if you were an independent young lady, Molly. Pay me the respect of a reference to my wishes another time, if you please, my dear!'

'Papa had said I might go,' said Molly, on the point of crying at the thought of her friend lying ill and lonely, and looking for her arrival. Mrs Gibson, too, was sorry; she had an uncomfortable consciousness of having given way to temper before a stranger, and a stranger, too, whose good opinion she had meant to cultivate; and she was also annoyed at Molly's tearful face.

'What can I do for you, to bring you back into good temper?' she said. 'You jump at invitations without ever consulting me, or thinking of how awkward it would be for me to go stumping into a drawing-room all by myself; following my new name, too, which always makes me feel uncomfortable, it is such a sad comedown after Kirkpatrick! What can I do to please you, Molly? I, who delight in nothing more than peace in a family, to see you sitting there with despair upon your face!'

Molly could stand it no longer; she went upstairs to her own room – her own smart new room, which hardly yet seemed a familiar place; and began to cry so heartily. She thought of Mrs Hamley wearying for her; of the old Hall whose very quietness might become oppressive to an ailing person; of the trust the Squire had had in her, that she would come off directly with him. And all this oppressed her much more than the querulousness of her stepmother's words.

## CHAPTER 17

# Trouble at Hamley Hall

If Molly thought that peace dwelt perpetually at Hamley Hall, she was sorely mistaken. Something was out of tune in the whole establishment. All the servants were old in their places, and any one of them could have told Molly that the grievance which lay at the root of everything was the amount of the bills run up by Osborne at Cambridge, and which, now that all chance of his obtaining a fellowship was over, came pouring down upon the Squire. But Molly encouraged no confidences from anyone else.

She was struck with the change in 'madam's' look, as soon as she caught sight of her lying on the sofa in her dressing-room, all dressed in white, which almost rivalled the white wanness of her face. The Squire ushered Molly in with –

'Here she is at last!' and Mrs Hamley stretched out one hand to Molly, and held hers firm; with the other she shaded her eyes.

'She is not so well this morning,' said the Squire, shaking his head. 'But never fear, my dear one; here's the doctor's daughter, nearly as good as the doctor himself.' He looked at her for a minute or two, and then softly kissed her, and told Molly he would leave her in charge.

As if Mrs Hamley were afraid of Molly's remarks or questions, she began in her turn a hasty system of interrogatories.

'Now, dear child, tell me all; it's no breach of confidence, for I shan't mention it again, and I shan't be here long. How does it all go on – the new mother, the good resolutions? I didn't like what the Squire told me last night. He was very angry.'

That sore had not yet healed over; but Molly resolutely kept silence, beating her brains to think of some other subject of conversation.

'Ah! I see, Molly,' said Mrs Hamley; 'you won't tell me your sorrows, and yet, perhaps, I could have done you some good.'

'I don't like,' said Molly, in a low voice. 'I think papa wouldn't like it. And, besides, you have helped me so much – you and Mr Roger Hamley. I often think of the things he said; they come in so usefully, and are such a strength to me.'

'Ah, Roger! yes. He is to be trusted, Oh, Molly! I've a great deal to say to you myself.' And she told Molly of the family distress and disappointment.

'Osborne has so disappointed us! And the Squire was so terribly angry! I cannot think how all the money was spent – advances through money-lenders, besides bills. The Squire does not show me how angry he is now, because he's afraid of another attack; but I know how angry he is. You see, he has been spending ever so much money in reclaiming that land at Upton Common, and is very hard pressed himself. But it would have doubled the value of the estate; and so we never thought anything of economies which would benefit Osborne in the long run. And now the Squire says he must mortgage some of the land; and you can't think how it cuts him to the heart. Osborne – oh! the Squire, in his anger, told him not to show his face at home, till he had paid off the debts he had incurred out of his allowance. Out of two hundred and fifty a year to pay off more than nine hundred, one way or another! Perhaps Roger will have debts too! He had but two hundred; but, then, he was not the eldest son. The Squire has given orders that the men are to be turned off the draining-works; and I lie awake thinking of their poor families this wintry weather. But what shall we do? Oh, Molly! Osborne was such a sweet little baby, and such a loving boy: so clever, too!'

'Don't you know, at all, how the money has gone?' asked Molly.

'No! not at all. That's the sting. There are tailors' bills, and bills for book-binding and wine and pictures – those come to four or five hundred; but the money for which he will give no account – of which, indeed, we only heard through the Squire's London agents, who found out that certain disreputable attorneys were making inquiries as to the entail of the estate; oh, Molly! worse than all – as to the age and health of the Squire, his dear father' – (she began to sob almost hysterically) – 'who held him in his arms, and blessed him, even before I had kissed him; and thought always so much of him as his heir and first-born darling! How he has loved him! How I have loved him! I sometimes have thought of late, that we've almost done that good Roger injustice.'

'No! I'm sure you've not: only look at the way he loves you. Why, you are his first thought. And dear, dear Mrs Hamley,' said Molly, 'don't you think that it would be better not to misjudge Mr Osborne Hamley? We don't know what he has done with the money; he is so good (is he not?) that he may have wanted it to relieve some poor person – some tradesman, for instance, pressed by creditors – some – '

'You forget, dear,' said Mrs Hamley, smiling a little at the girl's impetuous romance, 'that all the other bills come from tradesmen, who complain piteously of being kept out of their money.'

Osborne's name was never mentioned during meals. The Squire asked Molly every day how she thought his wife was; but if Molly told the truth – that every day seemed to make her weaker and weaker – he was almost savage with the girl. He could not bear it; and he would not. Nay, once he was on the point of dismissing Mr Gibson, because he insisted on a consultation with Dr Nicholls, the great physician of the county.

'It's nonsense thinking her so ill as that – you know it's only the delicacy she's had for years.'

Mr Gibson replied very quietly –

'I shall bring Dr Nicholls with me the next time I come. I may be mistaken in my treatment; and I wish to God he may say I am mistaken in my apprehensions.'

'Don't tell me them! I cannot bear them!' cried the Squire. 'Of course we must all die; and she must too. But the cleverest doctor in England shan't go about coolly meting out the life of such as her. I daresay I shall die first. I hope I shall. But I'll knock anyone down who speaks to me of death sitting within me. And, besides, I think all doctors are ignorant quacks, pretending to knowledge they haven't got. Ay, you may smile at me. I don't care. Unless you can tell me I shall die first, neither you nor Dr Nicholls shall come prophesying and croaking about this house.'

Mr Gibson went away, heavy at heart from the thought of Mrs Hamley's approaching death, but thinking little enough of the Squire's speeches. He had almost forgotten them, in fact, when about nine o'clock that evening, a groom rode in from Hamley Hall in hot haste, with a note from the Squire.

'DEAR GIBSON,

 – For God's sake forgive me if I was rude today. She is much worse. Come and spend the night here. Write for Nicholls, and all the physicians you want. They may give her ease. I put myself in your hands. Sometimes I think it is the turning point, and she'll rally after this bout. I trust all to you.
 – Yours ever,

'R. HAMLEY.

'P.S. – Molly is a treasure. – God help me!'

Of course Mr Gibson went. He brought Mrs Hamley through this attack; and for a day or two the Squire's alarm and gratitude made him docile in Mr Gibson's hands. The day after the consultation with Dr Nicholls, Mr Gibson said to Molly –

'Molly! I've written to Osborne and Roger. Do you know Osborne's address?'

'No, papa. He's in disgrace. I don't know if the Squire knows; and she has been too ill to write.'

'Never mind. I'll enclose it to Roger; whatever those lads may be to others, there's as strong a brotherly love, as ever I saw, between the two. Roger will know. And, Molly, they are sure to come home, as soon as they hear my report of their mother's state. I wish you'd tell the Squire what I've done. It's not a pleasant piece of work; and I'll tell madam myself in my own way. I'd have told him if he'd been at home; but you say he was obliged to go to Ashcombe on business.'

'Quite obliged. But, papa, he will be so angry! You don't know how mad he is against Osborne.'

Molly dreaded the Squire's anger when she gave him her father's message. However, it had to be done, and that without delay.

The great log was placed on the after-dinner fire, the hearth swept up, the ponderous candles snuffed, and then the door was shut and Molly and the Squire were left to their dessert. The Squire got up and went to the broad fire-place, to strike into the middle of the great log, and split it up into blazing, sparkling pieces. His back was towards her.

Molly began, 'When papa was here today, he bade me tell you he had written to Mr Roger Hamley, to say that – that he thought he had better come home; and he enclosed a letter to Mr Osborne Hamley, to say the same thing.'

The Squire put down the poker; but he still kept his back to Molly.

'He sent for Osborne and Roger?' he asked at length.

Molly answered, 'Yes.' Then there was a dead silence, which Molly thought would never end. The Squire had placed his two hands on the high chimney-piece, and stood leaning over the fire.

'Roger would have been down from Cambridge on the 18th,' said he. 'And he has sent for Osborne, too! Did he know?' he continued, turning round to Molly, with something of the fierceness she had anticipated in voice and look. In another moment, he had dropped his voice. 'It's right; quite right. I understand. It has come at length. Come! Come! Osborne has brought it on, though,' with a fresh access of anger in his tones. 'She might have lingered but for that. I can't forgive him; I cannot.'

And then he suddenly left the room. While Molly sat there still, very sad in her sympathy with all, he put his head in again –

'Go to her, my dear; I cannot – not just yet. But I will soon. Just this bit; and after that I won't lose a moment. You're a good girl. God bless you!'

## CHAPTER 18

# Mr Osborne's Secret

Roger came to the Hall; Molly gathered that Osborne was coming, but very little was said about him in any way. The Squire scarcely ever left his wife's room. She was so much under the influence of opiates that she did not often rouse up; but, when she did, she almost invariably asked for Molly. On these rare occasions, she would ask after Osborne – if he was coming? Before the Squire she never mentioned Osborne's name, nor did she seem at her ease in speaking about him to Roger; while, when she was alone with Molly, she hardly spoke of anyone else. She sent her to ask Roger how soon he would come.

At length Molly came upon Roger sitting in the library, his head buried in his hands. He lifted up his face, red, and stained with tears, his hair in disorder.

She began. 'Your mother does so want some news of your brother Osborne.'

He put his head again between his hands.

'I believe he's abroad, but I'm not sure.'

'But you've sent papa's letter to him?'

'I've sent it to a friend of his, who will know better than I do where he's to be found.'

'You are sure he will come?'

'Quite sure. Molly, I don't know what we should any of us have done without you. You've been like a daughter to my mother.'

'I do so love her,' said Molly softly.

'Yes; I see. Have you ever noticed that she sometimes calls you "Fanny"? It was the name of a little sister of ours who died. I think she often takes you for her. It was partly that, and partly because, at such a time as this, one can't stand on formalities, that made me call you Molly. I hope you don't mind it?'

'No; I like it. But will you tell me something more about your brother? She really hungers for news of him.'

'I believe he's in Belgium, and that he went there about a fort-night ago, partly to avoid his creditors. You know my father has refused to pay his debts?'

'Yes: at least, I knew something like it.'

'I don't believe my father could raise the money all at once. Yet, for the time, it places Osborne in a very awkward position.'

'I think, what vexes your father a good deal is some mystery as to how the money was spent.'

'If my mother ever says anything about that part of the affair,' said Roger hastily, 'assure her from me that there's nothing of vice or wrong-doing about it. I can't say more: I'm tied. But set her mind at ease on that point! My mother would have brought us all right, if she'd been what she once was.'

He turned away, leaving Molly very sad. She knew that every member of the family she cared for so much was in trouble, out of which she saw no exit; and her small power of helping them was diminishing day by day, as Mrs Hamley sank more and more under the influence of opiates and stupefying illness. Her father had spoken to her, only this very day, of the desirableness of her returning home. But Molly had begged hard to remain two or three days longer – only that – only till Friday. If Mrs Hamley should want her (she argued, with tears in her eyes), and should hear that she had left the house, she would think her so unkind, so ungrateful!

'My dear child, she's getting past wanting anyone! The keenness of earthly feelings is deadened.'

'Papa, I cannot bear it. She may not ask for me again, but I'm sure, to the very last, she will look round for the Squire and her children. For poor Osborne most of all.'

Mr Gibson shook his head.

'I don't like to take you away while you even fancy you can be of use or comfort to one who has been so kind to you; but, if she hasn't wanted you before Friday, will you be convinced, will you come home willingly?'

'Yes, papa, I will.'

So Molly hung about the house, trying to do all she could out of the sick-room, for the comfort of those in it. The evening of the day on which she had had the above conversation with Roger, Osborne arrived. He came straight into the drawing-room, where Molly was seated on the rug, reading by the fire-light. Osborne came in, with a kind of hurry, which almost made him appear as if he would trip himself up and fall down. Molly rose. He came forwards and took hold of her hands, straining his eyes to look into her face.

'How is she? You will tell me – you must know the truth! I've travelled day and night, since I got your father's letter.'

Before she could frame her answer, he had sate down in the nearest chair, covering his eyes with his hand.

'She's very ill,' said Molly. 'But I don't think she suffers much pain. She has wanted you sadly.'

He groaned aloud. 'My father forbade me to come.'

'I know!' said Molly. 'I think no one knew how ill she was – she had been an invalid for so long.'

'God knows how I loved her. If I had not been forbidden to come home, I should have told her all.'

Just at that moment the Squire came in. He had not heard of Osborne's arrival, and was seeking Molly to ask her to write a letter for him.

Osborne did not stand up, when his father entered. He was too much exhausted, too much oppressed by his feelings. If he had come forward with any manifestation of feeling at this moment, everything might have been different. All that the Squire said was –

'You here, sir!' And, breaking off in the directions he was giving to Molly, he abruptly left the room.

The last afternoon of her stay at the Hall came. Molly had leave given to choose out any books she wished, and to take them home with her; and it was just the sort of half-dawdling employment suited to her taste this afternoon.

She mounted on the ladder to get to a particular shelf, high up in a dark corner of the room; and, finding there some volume that looked interesting, she sat down on the step to read part of it. There she sat when Osborne suddenly came in. He did not see her at first; indeed, he might not have noticed her at all, if she had not spoken.

'Am I in your way?' She came down the steps as she spoke.

'Not at all. I must just write a letter for the post, and then I shall be gone. Is not this open door too cold for you?'

'Oh, no. It is so fresh and pleasant.'

She began to read again, sitting on the lowest step of the ladder; he to write at the large old-fashioned writing-table close to the window. Then came a click of the gate, and Roger stood at the open door. His face was towards Osborne, sitting in the light; his back to Molly. He held out a letter, and said in hoarse breathlessness –

'Here's a letter from your wife, Osborne. I went past the post-office and thought –'

Osborne stood up, angry dismay upon his face –

'Roger! what have you done? Don't you see her?'

Roger looked round, and Molly stood up in her corner. All three seemed to be equally dismayed. Molly was the first to speak; she came forward and said –

'I am so sorry! I didn't wish to hear it, but I couldn't help it.' and, turning to Roger, she said to him, with tears in her eyes, 'Please say you know I shall not tell.'

'I'm as sure of you as of myself.'

'Yes; but,' said Osborne, 'you see how many chances there are that even the best-meaning persons may let out what it is of such consequence to me to keep secret.'

Molly said –

'I'm going away. Perhaps I ought not to have been here. I'm sorry – very. But I'll forget what I've heard.'

'You can't do that,' said Osborne, still ungraciously. 'But will you promise me never to speak about it to anyone – not even to me, or to Roger? From what Roger has told me about you, if you give me this promise, I may rely upon it.'

'Yes; I will promise,' said Molly. 'I think I should have done so, even without a promise. But it is, perhaps, better to bind oneself. I will go away now!'

She put down her book on the table very softly, and turned to leave the room, choking down her tears. But Roger was at the door before her, holding it open for her, and reading her face. He held out his hand for hers, and his grasp expressed sympathy and regret for what had occurred.

She could hardly keep back her sobs till she reached her bed-room. The leaving Hamley Hall had seemed so sad before; and now she was troubled with having to bear away a secret which she ought never to have known. Then there would arise a very natural wonder as to who Osborne's wife was. Osborne had spoken with such languid criticism to Mrs Gibson about various country belles – what unspeakably elegant beauty had he chosen for his wife? Who had satisfied him, and yet, satisfying him, had to have her marriage kept in concealment from his parents?

Molly dreaded seeing either of the brothers again; but they all met at dinner-time, as if nothing had happened. The Squire was taciturn, either from melancholy or from displeasure. He had never spoken to Osborne since his return, excepting about the commonest trifles. Osborne put on an indifferent manner to his father, which Molly felt sure was assumed; but it was not conciliatory for all that. Roger, quiet, steady, and natural, talked more than all the others; but he too was in distress on many accounts. Today he principally addressed himself to Molly; entering into rather long narrations of late discoveries in natural history, which kept up the current of talk without requiring much reply from anyone. Molly had always wished to come into direct contact with a love-story; here she had, and she only found it very uncomfortable; there was a sense of concealment and uncertainty about it all; and her honest, straightforward father, her quiet life at Hollingford, which, even with all its drawbacks, was above-board, and where everybody knew what everybody was doing, seemed secure and pleasant in comparison. Of course she felt great pain at quitting the Hall, and at the mute farewell she had taken of her sleeping and unconscious friend. But leaving Mrs Hamley now was a different thing to what it had been a fortnight ago. Then, she was wanted at any moment, and felt herself to be of comfort.

She was sent home in the carriage, loaded with true thanks from everyone of the family. Osborne ransacked the greenhouses for flowers for her; Roger had chosen her out books of every kind. The Squire himself kept shaking her hand, without being able to speak his gratitude, till at last he took her in his arms, and kissed her as he would have done a daughter.

## CHAPTER 19

# Cynthia's Arrival

Molly's father was not at home when she returned; and Mrs Gibson was out paying calls, the servants told Molly. She went upstairs to her own room, meaning to unpack and arrange her borrowed books. Rather to her surprise, she saw the chamber corresponding to her own being dusted.

'Is anyone coming?' she asked of the housemaid.

'Miss Kirkpatrick is coming tomorrow. Missus's daughter from France.'

Was Cynthia coming at last? Oh, what a pleasure it would be to have a companion, a girl, a sister of her own age! Molly's depressed spirits sprang up again.

She was up almost before it was light – arranging her pretty Hamley flowers in Cynthia's room. She could hardly eat her breakfast that morning. She ran upstairs and put on her things, thinking that Mrs Gibson was quite sure to go down to the 'Angel Inn', where the 'Umpire' stopped, to meet her daughter after a two years' absence. But, to her surprise, Mrs Gibson had arranged herself at her great worsted-work frame; and she, in her turn, was astonished at Molly's bonnet and cloak.

'Where are you going so early, child?'

'I thought you would go and meet Cynthia; and I wanted to go with you.'

'She will be here in half-an-hour; and dear papa has told the gardener to take the wheelbarrow down for her luggage. I'm not sure if he is not gone himself.'

'Then are not you going?' asked Molly.

'No, certainly not. You forget, I have not seen her for two years, and I hate scenes in the market-place.'

She settled herself to her work again; and Molly employed herself in looking out of the downstairs window which commanded the approach from the town.

'Here she is – here she is!' she cried out at last. Her father was walking by the side of a tall young lady; William the gardener was wheeling along a great cargo of baggage. Molly flew to the front door.

'Well! here she is. Molly, this is Cynthia. Cynthia, Molly. You're to be sisters, you know.'

Molly saw the tall, swaying figure, against the light of the open door, but could not see any of the features that were, for the moment, in shadow. A sudden gush of shyness had come over her just at the instant, but Cynthia took her in her arms, and kissed her on both cheeks.

'Here's mamma,' she said, looking beyond Molly on to the stairs, where Mrs Gibson stood, wrapped up in a shawl, and shivering in the cold. She ran past Molly and Mr Gibson, who averted their eyes from this first greeting between mother and child.

Mrs Gibson said –

'Why, how you are grown, darling! You look quite a woman.'

'And so I am,' said Cynthia. 'I was, before I went away; I've hardly grown since – except, it is to be hoped, in wisdom.'

'Yes! That we will hope,' said Mrs Gibson, in rather a meaning way. Indeed, there were evidently hidden allusions in their seemingly commonplace speeches. When they all came into the full light and repose of the drawing-room, Molly was absorbed in the contemplation of Cynthia's beauty. Perhaps her features were not regular; but the changes in her expressive countenance gave one no time to think of that. Her smile was perfect; her pouting charming; the play of the face was in the mouth. Her eyes were beautifully shaped, but their expression hardly seemed to vary. In colouring she was not unlike her mother; only she had not so much of the red-haired tints in her complexion, and her long-shaped, serious grey eyes were fringed with dark lashes, instead of her mother's insipid flaxen ones. Molly fell in love with her, so to speak, on the instant. She sate there warming her feet and hands, as much at her ease as if she had been there all her life; measuring Molly and Mr Gibson with grave observant looks.

'There's a hot breakfast ready for you in the dining-room, when you are ready for it,' said Mr Gibson. He looked round at his wife, at Cynthia's mother; but she did not seem inclined to leave the warm room again.

'Molly will take you to your room, darling,' said she; 'it is near hers, and she has got her things to take off. I'll come down and sit in the dining-room, while you are having your breakfast; but I really am afraid of the cold now.'

Cynthia rose and followed Molly upstairs.

'I'm so sorry there isn't a fire for you,' said Molly, 'but – I suppose it wasn't ordered; and, of course, I don't give any orders. Here is some hot water, though.'

'Stop a minute,' said Cynthia, getting hold of both Molly's hands, and looking steadily into her face. 'I think I shall like you. I am so glad! We're all in a very awkward position together, aren't we? I like your father's looks, though.'

Molly could not help smiling at the way this was said. Cynthia replied to her smile.

'Ah, you may laugh. But mamma and I didn't suit when we were last together. Now, please leave me for a quarter of an hour. I don't want anything more.'

Molly went into her own room, waiting to show Cynthia down to the dining-room. In the short time since they had met, Cynthia's unconscious power of fascination had been exercised upon her. Some people have this power. Of course, its effects are only manifested in the susceptible. A school-girl may be found in every school who attracts and influences all the others, not by her virtues, nor her beauty, nor her sweetness, nor her cleverness, but by something that can neither be described nor reasoned upon.

A woman will have this charm, not only over men but over her own sex; it is so delicate a mixture of many gifts and qualities that it is impossible to decide on the proportions of each. Perhaps it is incompatible with very high principle; as its essence seems to consist in the most exquisite power of adaptation to varying people and still more various moods – 'being all things to all men'. At any rate, Molly might soon have been aware that Cynthia was not remarkable for unflinching morality; but the glamour thrown over her would have prevented Molly from any attempt at penetrating into and judging her companion's character, even had such processes been the least in accordance with her own disposition.

Cynthia was very beautiful, and was so well aware of this fact that she had forgotten to care about it. Molly would watch her perpetually as she went about the room, moving almost, as it were, to the continual sound of music. Her dress, too, though now to our ideas it would be considered ugly and disfiguring, was suited to her complexion and figure, and the fashion of it subdued within fit bounds by her exquisite taste. Mrs Gibson professed herself shocked to find that Cynthia had but four gowns, when she might have stocked herself so well, and brought over so many useful French patterns. But Cynthia took no apparent notice of the frequent recurrence of these small complaints. Indeed, she received much of what her mother said with a kind of complete indifference, that made Mrs Gibson hold her rather in awe; and she was much more communicative to Molly than to her own child. With regard to dress, however, Cynthia soon showed that she was her mother's own daughter, in the manner in which she could use her deft and nimble fingers. She was a capital workwoman; and, unlike Molly, who excelled in plain-sewing, but had no notion of dress-making or millinery, she could repeat the fashions she had only seen in passing along the streets of Boulogne, with one or two pretty rapid movements as she turned and twisted the ribbons and gauze her mother furnished her with. So she refurbished Mrs Gibson's wardrobe; doing it in a sort of contemptuous manner, the source of which Molly could not quite make out.

Day after day, the course of these small frivolities was broken in upon by the news Mr Gibson brought of Mrs Hamley's nearer approach to death. Molly heard the bulletins, like the toll of a funeral bell at a marriage feast. Her father sympathised with her;

but he was so accustomed to death, that it seemed to him the natural end of all things human. To Molly, the death of some one she had known so well and loved so much was a sad and gloomy phenomenon. She loathed the small vanities with which she was surrounded, and would wander out into the frosty garden, and pace the walk, which was both sheltered and concealed by evergreens.

At length – not a fortnight since Molly had left the Hall – the end came. Mrs Hamley had sunk out of life, as gradually as she had sunk out of consciousness and her place in this world.

'They all sent their love to you, Molly,' said her father. 'Roger said he knew how you would feel it.'

Mr Gibson had come in very late, and was having a solitary dinner in the dining-room. Molly was sitting near him, to keep him company. Cynthia and her mother were upstairs.

Molly remained downstairs, after her father had gone out afresh. The fire was growing very low, and the lights were waning. Cynthia came softly in, and, taking Molly's listless hand, sat at her feet on the rug, chafing her chilly fingers without speaking. The tender action thawed the tears that had been gathering heavily at Molly's heart.

'You loved her dearly, did you not, Molly?'

'Yes,' sobbed Molly.

'Had you known her long?'

'No, not a year. But I had seen a great deal of her. I was almost like a daughter to her; she said so. Yet I never bid her good-bye or anything. Her mind became weak and confused.'

The girls were silent for some time. Cynthia spoke first –

'I wish I could love people as you do, Molly!'

'Don't you?' said the other, in surprise.

'No. A good number of people love me, I believe, or at least they think they do; but I never seem to care much for anyone. I do believe I love you, little Molly, whom I have only known for ten days, better than anyone.'

'Not than your mother?' said Molly, in grave astonishment.

'Yes, than my mother!' replied Cynthia, half-smiling. 'It's very shocking, I daresay; but it is so. Now, don't go and condemn me.

I don't think love for one's mother quite comes by nature! I loved my father, if you will, but he died when I was quite a little thing, and no one believes that I remember him. I heard mamma say to a caller, not a fortnight after his funeral, "Oh, no, Cynthia is too young; she has quite forgotten him" – and I bit my lips, to keep from crying out, "Papa! papa! have I?" But it's of no use. Well, then mamma had to go out as a governess, poor thing! But she didn't much care for parting with me. So I was sent to a school at four years old; first one, and then another; and, in the holidays, mamma went to stay at grand houses, and I was generally left with the schoolmistresses. Once I went to the Towers; and mamma lectured me continually, and so I never went again; and I was very glad of it, for it was a horrid place.'

'That it was!' said Molly.

'And once I went to London, to stay with my uncle Kirkpatrick. He is a lawyer, and getting on now; but then he was poor enough, and had six or seven children. It was winter-time, and we were all shut up in a small house in Doughty Street. But, after all, that wasn't so bad.'

'But then you lived with your mother when she began school at Ashcombe. Mr Preston told me that, when I stayed that day at the Manor-house.'

'What did he tell you?' asked Cynthia, almost fiercely.

'Nothing but that. Oh, yes! He praised your beauty, and wanted me to tell you what he had said.'

'I should have hated you if you had,' said Cynthia.

'Of course I never thought of doing such a thing,' replied Molly. 'I didn't like him; and Lady Harriet spoke of him the next day, as if he wasn't a person to be liked.'

Cynthia was quite silent. At length she said –

'I wish I was good!'

'So do I,' said Molly simply. She was thinking again of Mrs Hamley.

'Nonsense, Molly! You are good. At least, if you're not good, what am I? Perhaps I might be a heroine still, but I shall never be a good woman, I know.'

'Do you think it easier to be a heroine?'

'Yes. I'm capable of a great jerk, an effort, and then a relaxation – but steady, every-day goodness is beyond me. I must be a moral kangaroo!'

Molly could not follow Cynthia's ideas; she could not distract herself from the thoughts of the sorrowing at the Hall.

'Papa says the funeral is to be on Tuesday, and that Roger Hamley is to go back to Cambridge. I wonder how the Squire and Mr Osborne Hamley will get on together.'

'He's the eldest son, is he not? Why shouldn't he and his father get on well together?'

'Oh! I don't know. That is to say, I do know, but I think I ought not to tell.'

'Don't be so truthful, Molly. Besides, your manner shows when you speak truth and when you speak falsehood, without troubling yourself to use words. I knew exactly what your "I don't know" meant. I never consider myself bound to be truthful; so I beg we may be on equal terms.'

Cynthia might well say she did not consider herself bound to be truthful; but there was no ill-nature, and, in a general way, no attempt at procuring any advantage for herself in all her deviations; and there was often such a latent sense of fun in them that Molly could not help being amused with them in fact, though she condemned them in theory. Molly could not resist her, even when she affirmed the most startling things. The little account she made of her own beauty pleased Mr Gibson extremely; and her pretty deference to him won his heart. She was restless too, till she had attacked Molly's dress, after she had remodelled her mother's.

'Now for you, sweet one,' said she, as she began upon one of Molly's gowns. All the time she worked, she sang; she had a sweet voice in singing, as well as in speaking. Yet she rarely touched the piano, on which Molly practised with daily conscientiousness. She was a most sympathetic listener to all Molly's innocent confidences of joys and sorrows: sympathising even to the extent of wondering how she could endure Mr Gibson's second marriage.

In spite of all this agreeable companionship at home, Molly yearned after the Hamleys. If there had been a woman in that family, she would probably have received many little notes, and heard numerous details which were now lost to her, or summed up in condensed accounts of her father's visits at the Hall, which were only occasional.

'Yes! The Squire is a good deal changed; but he's better than he was. There's an unspoken estrangement between him and Osborne; but they are civil at any rate. Osborne doesn't look well. I think he feels his mother's death acutely. It's a wonder that he and his father are not drawn together by their common loss. Roger's away at Cambridge too – examination for the mathematical tripos.'

Mrs Gibson generally said, as a comment upon her husband's account of Osborne's melancholy –

'My dear! why don't you ask him to dinner here? Cook is quite up to it; and we would all of us wear blacks and lilacs; he couldn't consider that as gaiety.'

Mr Gibson took no more notice of these suggestions than by shaking his head. He had grown accustomed to his wife by this time, and regarded silence on his own part as a great preservative against long inconsequential arguments. But every time that Mrs Gibson was struck by Cynthia's beauty, she thought it more and more advisable that Mr Osborne Hamley should be cheered up by a quiet little dinner-party.

Cynthia herself appeared extremely indifferent upon the subject. Molly was almost sorry for Mrs Gibson, who seemed so unable to gain influence over her child. One day Cynthia read Molly's thought.

'I'm not good, and I told you so. Somehow, I cannot forgive her for her neglect of me as a child. Besides, I hardly ever heard from her when I was at school. And I know she put a stop to my coming over to her wedding. A child should be brought up with its parents, if it is to think them infallible when it grows up.'

'But, though it may know that there must be faults,' replied

## CHAPTER 20

# Mrs Gibson's Visitors

One day, to Molly's infinite surprise, Mr Preston was announced as a caller. Mrs Gibson and she were sitting together in the drawing-room; Cynthia was out – gone into the town a-shopping – when the door was opened, the name given, and in walked the young man. His entrance seemed to cause more confusion than Molly could well account for. He looked remarkably handsome in his riding-dress, but Mrs Gibson's reception of him was much cooler than that which she usually gave to visitors.

At length they were seated, and conversation began.

'It is the first time I have been in Hollingford since your marriage, Mrs Gibson, or I should certainly have called to pay my respects sooner.'

'I know you are very busy. Is Lord Cumnor at the Towers? I have not heard from her ladyship for more than a week!'

'No! he seems still detained at Bath. But I had a letter from him giving me certain messages for Mr Sheepshanks. Mr Gibson is not at home, I'm afraid?'

'No. He is a great deal out – almost constantly, I may say. A doctor's wife leads a very solitary life, Mr Preston!'

'You can hardly call it solitary, I should think, when you have such a companion as Miss Gibson always at hand,' said he, bowing to Molly.

'Oh, but I call it solitude for a wife when her husband is away. Poor Mr Kirkpatrick was never happy, unless I always went with him. But, somehow, Mr Gibson feels as if I should be rather in his way.'

'I don't think you could ride pillion behind him on Black Bess, mamma,' said Molly. 'And unless you could do that, you could hardly go with him in his rounds.'

'Oh! but he might keep a brougham! I've often said so. And then I could use it for visiting in the evenings. Really it was one reason why I didn't go to the Hollingford Charity Ball. I couldn't bring myself to use the dirty fly from the Angel. We really must stir papa up against next winter, Molly; it will never do for you and – '

She pulled herself up, and looked furtively at Mr Preston, to see if he had taken any notice of her abruptness. He had; but he was not going to show it. He turned to Molly.

'Have you ever been to a public ball yet, Miss Gibson?'

'No!' said Molly.

'It will be a great pleasure to you, when the time comes.'

'I shall like it, if I have plenty of partners; but I'm afraid I shan't know many people.'

'And you suppose that young men haven't their own ways and means of being introduced to pretty girls?'

It was exactly one of the speeches Molly had disliked him for before, and delivered, too, in that kind of under-bred manner which showed that it was meant to convey a personal compliment.

'I only hope I may be one of your partners at the first ball you go to. Pray remember my early application for that honour, when you are overwhelmed with requests for dances.'

'I don't choose to engage myself beforehand,' said Molly, perceiving, from under her dropped eyelids, that he was leaning forward and looking at her as though he was determined to have an answer.

'Young ladies are always very cautious in fact, however modest they may be in profession,' he replied, addressing himself in a nonchalant manner to Mrs Gibson. 'In spite of Miss Gibson's apprehension of not having many partners, she declines the certainty of having one. I suppose Miss Kirkpatrick will have returned from France before then?'

He said these last words exactly in the same tone as he had used before; but Molly's instinct told her that he was making an effort to do so. She looked up.

Mrs Gibson reddened a little.

'Yes; certainly. My daughter will be with us next winter, I believe; and I daresay she will go out with us.'

'Why can't she say at once that Cynthia is here now?' asked Molly of herself, yet glad that his curiosity was baffled.

'You have good news from her, I hope?'

'Yes; very. By the way, how are our old friends the Robinsons? How often I think of their kindness to me at Ashcombe! Dear good people, I wish I could see them again.'

'I will certainly tell them of your kind inquiries. They are very well, I believe.'

Just at this moment, Cynthia opened the drawing-room door, and stood in it, looking at her mother, at Molly, at Mr Preston, but not advancing one step. Her eyes – her beautiful eyes – usually so soft and grave, seemed to fill with fire, and her brows to contract, as she took the resolution to come forward and take her place among the three. Mr Preston went a step or two to meet her, his hand held out, and the whole expression of his face that of eager delight.

But she took no notice of the outstretched hand, nor of the chair that he offered her. She sate down on a little sofa in one of the windows, and called Molly to her.

'Look at my purchases!' said she. 'This green ribbon was fourteen-pence a yard, this silk three shillings,' and so she went on, as if she had no attention to throw away on her mother and her mother's visitor.

Mr Preston took his cue from her. He, too, talked of the news of the day, the local gossip – but Molly was almost alarmed by the suppressed anger, nearly amounting to vindictiveness, which entirely marred his handsome looks. She did not wish to look again, and tried rather to back up Cynthia's efforts at maintaining a separate conversation. Yet she could not help overhearing Mrs Gibson's strain after increased civility, as if to make up for Cynthia's rudeness, and, if possible, to deprecate his anger.

In the course of the conversation between them, the Hamleys came up. Mrs Gibson was never unwilling to dwell upon Molly's intimacy with this county-family.

'Poor Mrs Hamley could hardly do without Molly; she quite looked upon her as a daughter. Mr Osborne Hamley did not do so well at college, and they had expected so much – parents will, you know; but what did it signify? for he has not to earn his living!'

'Well, the Squire must be satisfied now. I saw this morning's "Times", with the Cambridge examination lists in it. Isn't the second son called after his father, Roger?'

'Yes,' said Molly, starting up, and coming nearer.

'He's senior wrangler, that's all.' said Mr Preston, almost as though he were vexed with himself for having anything to say that could give her pleasure.

Molly went back to her seat by Cynthia. 'Poor Mrs Hamley,' said she, as if to herself. Cynthia took her hand, in sympathy with Molly's sad and tender look, rather than because she understood all that was passing in her mind.

Mr Preston was saying all the unpleasant things he could think of about the Hamleys, in a tone of false sympathy.

'The poor old Squire – not the wisest of men – has woefully mismanaged his estate. Of course, Osborne will try and marry some one with money; the family is old and well-established, and he mustn't object to commercial descent, though I daresay the Squire will for him; but then the young fellow himself is not the man for the work. No! the family's going down fast; even the senior wrangler will have spent all his brains in one effort. You never hear of a senior wrangler being worth anything afterwards. He'll be a Fellow of his college, of course – that will be a livelihood for him, at any rate.'

'I believe in senior wranglers,' said Cynthia, her clear high voice ringing through the room. 'And from all I've ever heard of Mr Roger Hamley, I believe he will keep up the distinction he has earned. And I don't believe that the house of Hamley is so near extinction in wealth and fame, and good name.'

'They are fortunate in having Miss Kirkpatrick's good word,' said Mr Preston, rising to take his leave.

'Dear Molly,' said Cynthia, in a whisper, 'I know nothing about your friends the Hamleys, except that they are your friends, but I won't have that man speaking of them so – and your eyes filling with tears all the time. I'd sooner swear to their having all the talents and good fortune under the sun.'

The only person of whom Cynthia appeared to be wholesomely afraid was Mr Gibson. Her evident respect for him, and desire to win his good opinion, made her curb herself before him; and in this manner she earned his favour as a lively, sensible girl, with just so much knowledge of the world as made her a very desirable companion for Molly. Indeed, she made something of the same kind of impression on all men.

If Molly had not had the sweetest disposition in the world, she might have become jealous of all the allegiance laid at Cynthia's feet; but she never thought of comparing the amount of admiration and love which they each received. Yet, once, she did feel a little as if Cynthia were poaching on her manor. The invitation to the quiet dinner had been sent to Osborne Hamley, and declined by him. But he thought it right to call soon afterwards. Molly tried to wait patiently till Mrs Gibson had exhausted the first gush of her infinite nothings; and then Molly came in with her modest questions. How was the Squire? Had he returned to his old habits? Had his health suffered? – putting each inquiry with as light and delicate a touch as if she had been dressing a wound. She hesitated a little, a very little, before speaking of Roger; and had just entered upon the subject, when Cynthia came into the room, and took up her work. No one could have been quieter – but Osborne seemed to fall under her power at once; and, by-and-by, without Molly's rightly understanding how it was, he had turned towards Cynthia, and was addressing himself to her. Molly saw the look of content on Mrs Gibson's face; and all at once she perceived that Mrs Gibson would not dislike a marriage between Osborne and Cynthia, and considered the present occasion as an auspicious beginning. Remembering the secret which she had been let into so unwillingly, Molly watched his behaviour, thinking as much of the possibility of his attracting Cynthia as of the unknown and mysterious Mrs Osborne Hamley. His manner was expressive of great interest and of strong prepossession in favour of the beautiful girl to whom he was talking. But there was nothing of flirting, as far as Molly understood the meaning of the word, in either looks or words. As soon as he was gone, Mrs Gibson began in his praise.

'Well, really, I begin to have some faith in long descent. What a gentleman he is! So different from that forward Mr Preston,' she continued, looking anxiously at Cynthia. Cynthia, quite aware that her reply was being watched for, said coolly –

'There was a time, mamma, when I think both you and I thought Mr Preston very agreeable.'

'I don't remember. But we were talking of this delightful Mr Osborne Hamley. Did you hear him say that, though he did not like to leave his father alone just at present, yet, when his brother Roger came back from Cambridge, he should feel more at liberty! It was quite as much as to say, "If you will ask me to dinner then, I shall be delighted to come."'

## CHAPTER 21

# The Half-Sisters

It appeared as if Mrs Gibson's predictions were likely to be verified; for Osborne Hamley found his way to her drawing-room pretty frequently.

Molly was altogether puzzled by his manners and ways. He spoke of occasional absences from the Hall, without exactly saying where he had been. But that was not her idea of the conduct of a married man. Who this mysterious wife might be, faded into insignificance before the wonder of where she was. London, Cambridge, Dover, nay, even France, were mentioned by him as places to which he had been on these different little journeys.

Osborne had lost the slight touch of cynicism which he had affected when he was expected to do wonders at college; and that was one good result of his failure. His conversation was not so amply sprinkled with critical pepper. He was more absent, not so agreeable, Mrs Gibson thought, but did not say. He looked ill in health; but that might be the consequence of the real depression of spirits which Molly occasionally saw peeping out through all his pleasant surface-talk. Probably Molly would have been rendered much more uncomfortable, if Osborne had struck her as particularly attentive in his devotion to Cynthia. She evidently amused and attracted him, but not in any lively or passionate kind of way. He would leave her side, and come to sit near Molly, if anything reminded him of his mother, about which he could talk to her, and to her alone. Yet he came so often to the Gibsons', that Mrs Gibson might be excused for the fancy she had taken into her head, that it was for Cynthia's sake.

Roger had not come home since he had obtained his high place in the mathematical lists; that Molly knew; and she knew, too, that he was working hard for something – she supposed a fellowship – and that was all. Osborne's tone in speaking of him was always the same: every word, every inflection of the voice breathed out affection and respect – nay, even admiration!

'Ah, Roger!' he said one day. Molly caught the name in an instant, though she had not heard what had gone before. 'He is a fellow in a thousand – in a thousand! I don't believe there is his match anywhere, for goodness and real solid power combined.'

'Molly,' said Cynthia, after Mr Osborne Hamley had gone, 'what sort of a man is this Roger Hamley?'

While Molly hesitated on which point of the large round to begin her description, Mrs Gibson struck in –

'It just shows what a sweet disposition Osborne Hamley is of – that he should praise his brother as he does. I daresay he is a senior wrangler, and much good may it do him – I don't deny that; but, as for conversation, he's as heavy as heavy can be. A great awkward fellow, to boot. You would hardly believe he was Osborne Hamley's brother, to see him!'

'What do you think of him, Molly?' said the persevering Cynthia.

'I like him,' said Molly. 'He has been very kind to me. I know he isn't handsome like Osborne.' It was rather difficult to say all this quietly; but Molly managed to do it.

'I suppose he will come home at Easter,' said Cynthia, 'and then I shall see him for myself.'

Miss Browning – that old friend of the Gibson family – came in one morning to ask the two girls to come to a friendly tea and a round game afterwards; this mild piece of gaiety being designed as an attention to three of Mrs Goodenough's grandchildren – two young ladies and their school-boy brother – who were staying on a visit to their grandmamma.

Mr Osborne Hamley had been named as one of the probable visitors, but, though he was not there, his brother Roger was. Molly saw him in a minute, when she entered the little drawing-room; but Cynthia did not.

'And see, my dears,' said Miss Phoebe Browning, turning them round to the side where Roger stood, waiting for his turn of speaking to Molly; 'we've got a gentleman for you!'

The moment Roger had done his cordial greeting to Molly, he asked her to introduce him to Cynthia.

'I want to know her – your new sister,' he added, with the kind smile that Molly remembered so well. Molly had always felt that she should have a right to a good long talk with Roger, when she next saw him, and that she should gather from him all the details she so longed to hear about the Squire – about the Hall – about Osborne – about himself. If Cynthia had not been there, all would have gone on as she had anticipated; but of all the victims to Cynthia's charms he fell most prone and abject. Molly saw it all, as she was sitting next to Miss Phoebe at the tea-table, acting right-hand, and passing cake, cream, sugar, with such assiduity that everyone besides herself thought that her mind, as well as her hands, was fully occupied so that she could not ever have joined in the animated conversation going on between Roger and Cynthia. Or, rather, it would be more correct to say that Roger was talking in a most animated manner to Cynthia, whose sweet eyes were fixed upon his face with a look of great interest in all he was saying, while it was only now and then that she made her low replies. Molly caught a few words occasionally.

Cynthia was hearing all about Cambridge, and the very ex-amination about which Molly had felt such keen interest, without having ever been able to have her questions answered by a com-petent person. And when everyone sate in their places round the table, Roger and Cynthia had to be called twice before they came. They stood up, it is true, at the first sound of their names; but they did not move – Roger went on talking, Cynthia listening, till the second call; when they hurried to the table and tried to appear, all on a sudden, quite interested in the great questions of the game.

When they got home, Mr and Mrs Gibson were sitting in the drawing-room, ready to be amused by details of the evening.

'Oh! it wasn't very entertaining. One didn't expect that,' and Cynthia yawned wearily.

'Who were there?' asked Mr Gibson. 'Quite a young party – wasn't it?'

'They'd only asked Lizzie and Fanny Orford, and their brother; but Mr Roger Hamley had ridden over and called on the Miss Brownings, and they kept him to tea. No one else.'

'Roger Hamley there!' said Mr Gibson. 'He's come home then. I must make time to ride over and see him. And what did you think of my favourite, Cynthia? You hadn't seen him before, I think?'

'Oh! he's nothing like so handsome as his brother; nor so easy to talk to. He entertained me for more than an hour with a long account of some examination or other; but there's something one likes about him.'

'Well – and Molly,' said Mrs Gibson, who piqued herself on being an impartial stepmother, 'what sort of an evening have you had?'

'Very pleasant, thank you.' Her heart a little belied her, as she said this.

'We've had our unexpected visitor, too,' said Mr Gibson. 'Just after dinner, who should come in but Mr Preston! I fancy he's having more of the management of the Hollingford property than formerly. Sheepshanks is getting an old man. And, if so, I suspect we shall see a good deal of Preston.'

'Do you like Mr Preston, papa?' asked Molly.

'About as much as I do half the men I meet. I know very little of him, though; except that he's my lord's steward. You must know about Mr Preston, my dear. I suppose you saw a good deal of him at Ashcombe?'

Mrs Gibson coloured, and looked at Cynthia before she replied.

'We saw a good deal of him – at one time. He's changeable, I think. But he always sent us game, and sometimes fruit. There were stories against him, but I never believed them.'

'What kind of stories?' said Mr Gibson quickly.

'Oh, vague stories, you know. No one ever believed them. He could be so agreeable, if he chose; and my lord, who is so very particular, would never have kept him as agent, if they were true;

not that I ever knew what they were, for I consider all scandal as abominable gossip.'

The very next day, Roger came to call. Molly was in the garden with Williams, planning the arrangement of some new flower-beds, when her eye was caught by the figure of a gentleman, sitting with his back to the light, leaning forwards, and talking, or listening. Molly knew the shape of the head perfectly, and hastily began to put off her gardening apron, as she spoke to Williams.

'You can finish it now, I think,' said she. 'You know about the bright-coloured flowers being against the privet-hedge, and where the new rose-bed is to be?'

'I can't justly say as I do,' said he. 'Mebbe, you'll just go o'er it all once again, Miss Molly! I'd be loath to make mistakes, when you're so set upon your plans.'

Molly saw that the old gardener was really perplexed, so she went over the ground again, till the wrinkled brow was smooth again, and he kept saying, 'I see, miss. All right, Miss Molly; I'se getten it in my head as clear as patch-work now.'

So she could leave him, and go in. But, just as she was close to the garden-door, Roger came out. It really was for once a case of virtue its own reward, for it was far pleasanter to her to have him in a *tête-à-tête*, however short, than in the restraint of Mrs Gibson's and Cynthia's presence.

'I only just found out where you were, Molly. Mrs Gibson said you had gone out, and it was the greatest chance that I turned round and saw you.'

'I saw you some time ago, but I couldn't leave Williams. He couldn't understand my plans for the new flower-beds.'

'Is that the paper you've got in your hand? Let me look at it, will you? Ah, I see! you've borrowed some of your ideas from our garden at home, haven't you? This bed of scarlet geraniums, with the border of young oaks, pegged down? That was a fancy of my dear mother's.'

They were both silent for a minute or two. Then –

'How is the Squire? I've never seen him since.'

'No; he told me how much he wanted to see you, but he couldn't make up his mind to come and call. I suppose it would never do now for you to come and stay at the Hall, would it? It would give my father so much pleasure – he looks upon you as a daughter; and I'm sure both Osborne and I shall always consider you are like a sister to us, after all my mother's love for you, and your tender care of her at the last. But I suppose it wouldn't do?'

'No! certainly not,' said Molly hastily.

'I fancy, if you could come, it would put us a little to rights. Osborne has behaved differently to what I should have done, though not wrongly – only what I call an error of judgment. But my father holds Osborne still in tacit disgrace, and is miserable himself all the time. It is just what my mother would have put right very soon, and perhaps you could have done it – unconsciously, I mean – for this wretched mystery that Osborne preserves about his affairs is at the root of it all. But there's no use talking about it; I don't know why I began.' Then, with a wrench, changing the subject, he broke out –

'I can't tell you how much I like Miss Kirkpatrick, Molly. It must be a great pleasure to you, having such a companion!'

'Yes,' said Molly, half smiling. 'I'm very fond of her. But how quickly you have found out her virtues!'

'I didn't say "virtues", did I?' asked he, reddening. 'Yet I don't think one could be deceived in that face. And Mrs Gibson appears to be a very friendly person – she has asked Osborne and me to dine here on Friday.'

'And are you coming?'

'Certainly, I am, unless my father wants me; and I've given Mrs Gibson a conditional promise for Osborne, too. So I shall see you all very soon again. But I must go now. Good luck to your flower-garden, Molly!'

## CHAPTER 22

# Osborne Hamley
# Reviews His Position

Osborne had his solitary cup of coffee in the drawing-room. He was very unhappy, after his fashion. Every now and then the Squire threw him a ten-pound note or so; but the sort of suppressed growl with which it was given, and the entire uncertainty as to when he might receive such gifts, rendered any calculation based upon their receipt exceeding vague and uncertain.

'What in the world can I do to secure an income?' thought Osborne. 'What can I do to be sure of a present income? Things cannot go on as they are. I should need support for two or three years, even if I entered myself at the Temple or Lincoln's Inn. It would be impossible to live on my pay in the army; besides, I should hate that profession. In fact, there are evils attending all professions – I couldn't bring myself to become a member of any I've ever heard of. Yet poor Aimée must have money! I can't bear to compare our dinners here, overloaded with joints and game and sweets, with Aimée's two little mutton-chops. If my mother had been in good health – if she could have heard my story, and known Aimée! As it is, I must keep it secret; but where to get money? Where to get money?'

Then he bethought him of his poems – would they sell, and bring him in money? He thought they might; and he went to fetch his MSS. out of his room. He sate down near the fire, trying to study them with a critical eye, to represent public opinion as far as he could. They were almost equivalent to an autobiographical passage in his life. Arranging them in their order, they came as follows:

'To Aimée, Walking with a Little Child.'
'To Aimée, Singing at her Work.'
'To Aimée, Turning away from me while I told my Love.'
'Aimée's Confession.'
'Aimée in Despair.'
'The Foreign Land in which my Aimée dwells.'
'The Wedding-Ring.'
'The Wife.'

When he came to this last sonnet, he put down his bundle of papers. 'The wife'. Yes, and a French wife; and a Roman Catholic wife – and a wife who might be said to have been in service! And his father's hatred of the French, both collectively and individually – collectively, as tumultuous brutal ruffians, who had murdered their king – individually, as represented by 'Boney', and the various caricatures of 'Johnny Crapaud' that had been in full circulation about five-and-twenty years before this time, when the Squire had been young and capable of receiving impressions. As for the form of religion in which Mrs Osborne Hamley had been brought up, it is enough to say that Catholic emancipation had begun to be talked about by some politicians, and that the sullen roar of the majority of Englishmen, at the bare idea of it, was surging in the distance with ominous threatenings; the very mention of such a measure before the Squire was, as Osborne well knew, like shaking a red flag before a bull.

And if Aimée had had the incomparable blessing of being born of English parents in the very heart of England and had never heard of priests, or mass, or confession, or the Pope, or Guy Fawkes – even with all these advantages, her having been a nursery-maid would be a shock to his father's ancestral pride that he would hardly ever get over.

'She would make such a loving, sweet, docile little daughter to my father – she would go as near as anyone could towards filling up the blank void in this house, if he could but have her; but he won't. Yet if I called her "Lucy" in these sonnets; and if they made a great effect and all the world was agog to find out the author;

and I told him my secret – I could if I were successful – I think then he would ask who Lucy was, and I could tell him all then. If – how I hate "ifs"!'

## CHAPTER 23

# Mrs Gibson's Little Dinner

The little dinner on Friday, Mrs Gibson intended the Hamleys to find pleasant; and they did. Mr Gibson was fond of the two young men, and to those whom he liked Mr Gibson could be remarkably agreeable. Cynthia and Molly looked their best, which was all the duty Mrs Gibson absolutely required of them, as she was willing enough to take her full share in the conversation. Osborne fell to her lot, of course, and for some time he and she prattled on with all the ease of manner and commonplaceness of meaning which go far to make the 'art of polite conversation'. Roger was exceedingly interested in what Mr Gibson was telling him of a paper on comparative osteology. Yet, every now and then while he listened, he caught his attention wandering to the face of Cynthia, who was placed between his brother and Mr Gibson. Her eyelids were carelessly dropped, as she crumbled her bread on the tablecloth, and her beautiful long eyelashes were seen on the clear tint of her oval cheek. Suddenly Cynthia looked up, and caught Roger's gaze of intent admiration. She coloured a little; but, after the first moment of rosy confusion at his evident admiration of her, she flew to the attack, diverting his confusion at thus being caught, to the defence of himself from her accusation.

'It is quite true!' she said to him. 'I was not attending: you see I don't know even the ABC of science. But please don't look so severely at me, even if I am a dunce!'

'I didn't know – I didn't mean to look severely, I am sure,' replied he, not knowing well what to say.

'Cynthia is not a dunce either,' said Mrs Gibson. 'But Cynthia's talents are not for science and the severer studies. Do you remember, love, what trouble I had to teach you the use of the globes? Yet, I do assure you,' her mother continued, rather addressing herself to Osborne, 'that her memory for poetry is prodigious. I have heard her repeat the "Prisoner of Chillon" from beginning to end.'

'It would be rather a bore to have to hear her, I think,' said Mr Gibson, smiling at Cynthia, who gave him back one of her bright looks of mutual understanding.

'Ah, Mr Gibson, I have found out before now that you have no soul for poetry; and Molly there is your own child. She reads such deep books – all about facts and figures; she'll be quite a blue-stocking by-and-by.'

'Mamma,' said Molly, reddening, 'you think it was a deep book, because there were the shapes of the different cells of bees in it! but it was not at all deep. It was very interesting.'

'Never mind, Molly,' said Osborne. 'I stand up for blue-stockings.'

'And I object to the distinction implied in what you say,' said Roger. 'It was not deep, *ergo*, it was very interesting. Now, a book may be both deep and interesting.'

'Oh, if you are going to chop logic and use Latin words, I think it is time for us to leave the room,' said Mrs Gibson.

'Don't let us run away as if we were beaten, mamma,' said Cynthia. 'I read some of Molly's books; and I found it very interesting – more so than I should think the "Prisoner of Chillon" now-a-days. I've displaced the Prisoner to make room for Johnnie Gilpin as my favourite poem.'

'How could you talk such nonsense, Cynthia!' said Mrs Gibson, as the girls followed her upstairs. 'It is all very well not to be a blue-stocking, because gentle-people don't like that kind of woman; but running yourself down – to Osborne Hamley of all men too!'

Mrs Gibson spoke quite crossly for her.

'But, mamma,' Cynthia replied, 'I am either a dunce, or I am not. If I am, I did right to own it; if I am not, he's a dunce if he doesn't find out I was joking.'

'Well,' said Mrs Gibson, a little puzzled by this speech.

'Only that, if he's a dunce, his opinion of me is worth nothing. So, any way, it doesn't signify.'

'You really bewilder me with your nonsense, child. Molly is worth twenty of you.'

'I quite agree with you, mamma,' said Cynthia, turning round to take Molly's hand.

'But she ought not to be. Think of the advantages you've had!'

'I'm afraid I'd rather be a dunce than a blue-stocking,' said Molly.

'Hush; here they are coming: I hear the dining-room door! I never meant you were a blue-stocking, dear; so don't look vexed! – Cynthia, my love, where did you get those lovely flowers – anemones, are they? They suit your complexion so exactly.'

'Come, Molly, don't look so grave and thoughtful,' exclaimed Cynthia. 'Don't you perceive mamma wants us to be smiling and amiable?'

Mr Gibson had had to go out to his evening-round; and the young men were all too glad to come up into the pretty drawing-room; the bright little wood-fire; the comfortable easy-chairs; the good-natured hostess; the pretty, agreeable girls. Roger sauntered up to the corner where Cynthia was standing.

'There is a charity ball in Hollingford soon, isn't there? Are you going? I suppose you are?'

'Yes; mamma is going to take Molly and me.'

'You will enjoy it very much – going together?'

For the first time during this little conversation she glanced up at him – real honest pleasure shining out of her eyes.

'Yes; going together will make the enjoyment of the thing. It would be dull without her.'

'You are great friends, then?' he asked.

'I never thought I should like anyone so much – any girl, I mean.'

She put in the final reservation in all simplicity of heart; and in all simplicity did he understand it. He came ever so little nearer; and dropped his voice a little.

'I was so anxious to know. I am so glad. I have often wondered how you two were getting on.'

'Have you?' said she. 'You must be very fond of Molly!'

'Yes, I am. I look upon her almost as a sister.'

'And she is very fond of all of you. I seem to know you all, from hearing her talk about you so much.'

'Cynthia,' said Mrs Gibson, who thought that the younger son had had quite his share of confidential conversation, 'come here, and sing that little French ballad to Mr Osborne Hamley.'

## CHAPTER 24

# Hollingford in a Bustle

All Hollingford felt as if there was a great deal to be done before Easter this year. There was Easter proper, which always required new clothing of some kind, for fear of certain consequences from little birds, who were supposed to resent the impiety of those that did not wear some new article of dress on Easter-day. So piety demanded a new bonnet, or a new gown, and was barely satisfied with a pair of gloves. Then this year there was the ball. Ashcombe, Hollingford, and Coreham were three neighbouring towns. In imitation of greater cities with their festivals, these three towns had agreed to have an annual ball for the benefit of the county-hospital, to be held in turn at each place; and Hollingford was to be the place this year.

Another cause of unusual bustle at Hollingford this Easter was the expected return of the family to the Towers, after their unusually long absence. Mr Sheepshanks might be seen trotting up and down on his stout old cob, speaking to attentive masons, plasterers, and glaziers about putting everything – on the outside at least – about the cottages belonging to 'my lord', in perfect repair. Lord Cumnor owned the greater part of the town; and so the ladders of white-washers and painters were sadly in the way of the ladies tripping daintily along to make their purchases.

Lady Harriet came to call on her old governess, the day after the arrival of the family at the Towers. Molly and Cynthia were out walking when she came, and Mrs Gibson did not give Molly the message of remembrance that Lady Harriet had left for her; but she imparted various pieces of news relating to the Towers with great animation and interest. The Duchess of Menteith and her daughter, Lady Alice, were coming to the Towers; would come to the ball; and the Menteith diamonds were famous. That was piece of news the first. The second was that ever so many gentlemen were coming to the Towers – some English, some French. This piece of news would have come first had there been much probability of their being dancing men. But Lady Harriet had spoken of them as Lord Hollingford's friends, useless scientific men in all probability. Then, finally, Mrs Gibson was to go to the Towers next day to lunch; if Mrs Gibson could manage to find her way to the Towers, one of the carriages in use should bring her back to her own home in the course of the afternoon.

'The dear countess!' said Mrs Gibson, with soft affection.

And all the rest of that day her conversation had an aristocratic perfume hanging about it. Mr Gibson made his mouth up into a droll whistle when he came home at night, and found himself in a Towers atmosphere. Molly saw the shade of annoyance through the drollery; she was beginning to see it oftener than she liked.

The afternoon of the day on which the ball was to take place, a servant rode over from Hamley with two lovely nosegays, 'with the Mr Hamleys' compliments to Miss Gibson and Miss Kirkpatrick.' Cynthia was the first to receive them. She came dancing into the drawing-room, flourishing the flowers about in either hand, and danced up to Molly.

'Look, Molly, look! Here are bouquets for us? Long life to the givers!'

'Who are they from?' asked Molly, taking hold of one, and examining it with tender delight at its beauty.

'Who from? Why, the two paragons of Hamleys to be sure. Isn't it a pretty attention?'

'How kind of them!' said Molly.

'I'm sure it is Osborne who thought of it. He has been so much abroad, where it is such a common compliment to send bouquets to young ladies.'

'I don't see why you should think it is Osborne's thought!' said Molly, reddening a little. 'Mr Roger Hamley used to gather nosegays constantly for his mother, and sometimes for me.'

'Well, never mind whose thought it was; we've got the flowers, and that's enough. Molly, I'm sure these red flowers will just match your coral necklace and bracelets,' said Cynthia, pulling out some camellias, then a rare kind of flower.

'Oh, please, don't!' exclaimed Molly. 'Don't you see how carefully the colours are arranged – they have taken such pains; please don't.'

'Nonsense!' said Cynthia, continuing to pull them out; 'see, I'll make you a little coronet of them – sewn on black velvet, which will never be seen – just as they do in France.'

'Oh, I am so sorry! It is quite spoilt,' said Molly.

'Never mind! I'll take this spoilt bouquet; I can make it up again just as prettily as ever; and you shall have this, which has never been touched.' Cynthia went on arranging the crimson buds and flowers to her taste.

'There!' said Cynthia at last; 'when that is sewn on black velvet, to keep the flowers from dying, you'll see how pretty it will look. And there are enough red flowers in this untouched nosegay to carry out the idea!'

'Thank you' (very slowly). 'But sha'n't you mind having only the wrecks of the other?'

'Not I; red flowers would not go with my pink dress.'

'But – I daresay they arranged each nosegay so carefully!'

'Perhaps they did. But I never would allow sentiment to interfere with my choice of colours; and pink does tie one down. Now you, in white muslin, just tipped with crimson, like a daisy, may wear anything.'

Cynthia took the utmost pains in dressing Molly. Molly wanted her appearance to be correct and unnoticed; and Cynthia was desirous of setting off Molly's rather peculiar charms – her cream-coloured skin, her profusion of curly black hair, her beautiful long-shaped eyes, with their shy, loving expression. Cynthia took up so much time in dressing Molly to her mind, that she herself had to perform her toilet in a hurry.

The two girls were dressed, and standing over the fire waiting for the carriage in Cynthia's room, when Maria (Betty's successor) came hurrying into the room with a nosegay still more beautiful than the two previous ones.

'Here, Miss Kirkpatrick, it's for you, miss! And there's a note besides!'

Cynthia said nothing, but took the note and the flowers. She held the note so that Molly could read it at the same time she did.

'I send you some flowers; and you must allow me to claim the first dance after nine o'clock, before which time I fear I cannot arrive.

C.P.'

'Who is it?' asked Molly.

Cynthia looked extremely irritated.

'It is Mr Preston. I shall not dance with him; and here go his flowers' –

Into the very middle of the embers, which she immediately stirred down upon the beautiful shining petals as if she wished to annihilate them as soon as possible.

'Oh!' said Molly, 'those beautiful flowers! We might have put them in water.'

'No,' said Cynthia; 'it's best to destroy them. We don't want them; and I can't bear to be reminded of that man.'

'It was an impertinent, familiar note,' said Molly. 'Did you know him well, when you were at Ashcombe, Cynthia?'

'Oh, don't let us think any more about him,' replied Cynthia. 'It is quite enough to spoil my pleasure at the ball to think that he will be there. But I hope I shall get engaged before he comes, so that I can't dance with him – and don't you, either!'

'There! they are calling for us,' exclaimed Molly, and with quick step they made their way downstairs to the place where Mr and Mrs Gibson awaited them. Yes; Mr Gibson was going – even if he had to leave them afterwards to attend to any professional call. And Molly suddenly began to admire her father as a handsome man, when she saw him now, in full evening attire. Mrs Gibson, too – how pretty she was! In short, it was true that no better-looking a party than these four people entered the Hollingford ball-room that evening.

## CHAPTER 25

# A Charity Ball

At the present time there are few people at a public ball besides the dancers and their chaperons, or relations in some degree interested in them. But in the days when Molly and Cynthia were young, going to an annual charity-ball, even though all thought of dancing had passed by years ago, was a very allowable piece of dissipation to all the kindly old maids who thronged the country towns of England. They aired their old lace and their best dresses; they saw the aristocratic magnates of the country side; they gossipped with their coevals, and speculated on the romances of the young around them in a curious, yet friendly, spirit. The Miss Brownings would have thought themselves sadly defrauded if anything had prevented their attending the charity-ball. They had come in one of the two sedan-chairs that yet lingered in use at Hollingford. There were some post-chaises, and some 'flys' but, after mature deliberation, Miss Browning had decided to keep to the more comfortable custom of the sedan-chair. Of course, only one could go at a time; but here a little of Miss Browning's good management arranged everything so very nicely, as Miss Hornblower remarked. She went first, and remained in the warm cloak-room until her hostess followed; and then the two ladies went arm-in-arm into the ball-room, finding out convenient seats whence they could watch the arrivals and speak to their passing friends, until Miss Phoebe and Miss Piper entered, and came to take possession of the seats reserved for them by Miss Browning's care. When all four were once more assembled together, they took breath, and began to converse.

'Upon my word, I really do think this is a better room than our Ashcombe Court-house!'

'And how prettily it is decorated!' piped out Miss Piper. 'But you all have such taste at Hollingford.'

'There's Mrs Dempster,' cried Miss Hornblower; 'she said she and her two daughters were asked to stay at Mr Sheepshanks'. Mr Preston was to be there, too; but I suppose they could not all come at once. Look! and there is young Roscoe, our new doctor. Mr Roscoe! Mr Roscoe! come here and let me introduce you to Miss Browning, the friend we are staying with. We think very highly of our young doctor, I can assure you, Miss Browning.'

But Miss Browning had no notion of having any doctor praised who had come to settle on the very verge of Mr Gibson's practice; so she said to Miss Hornblower –

'You must be glad, I am sure, to have somebody you can call in, if you are in a sudden hurry, or for things that are too trifling to trouble Mr Gibson about; and I should think Mr Roscoe would feel it a great advantage to profit, as he will naturally have the opportunity of doing, by witnessing Mr Gibson's skill!'

Probably, Mr Roscoe would have felt more aggrieved by this speech than he really was, if his attention had not been called off, just then, by the entrance of the very Mr Gibson who was being spoken of. Almost before Miss Browning had ended her depreciatory remark, she had asked Miss Hornblower –

'Who is that lovely girl in pink, just come in?'

'Why, that's Cynthia Kirkpatrick!' said Miss Hornblower, taking up a ponderous gold eyeglass to make sure of her fact. 'How she has grown! To be sure, it is two or three years since she left Ashcombe – she was very pretty then – people did say Mr Preston admired her very much; but she was so young!'

'Can you introduce me?' asked the impatient young surgeon. 'I should like to ask her to dance.'

When Miss Hornblower returned from her greeting to her former acquaintance, Mrs Gibson, and had accomplished the introduction which Mr Roscoe had requested, she began her little confidences to Miss Browning.

'Well, to be sure! How condescending we are! I remember the time when Mrs Kirkpatrick wore old black silks, and was thankful and civil as became her place as a schoolmistress. And now she is in a satin; and she speaks to me as if she just could recollect who I was! It isn't so long ago since she would have been glad enough to marry Mr Preston.'

'I thought you said he admired her daughter,' put in Miss Browning.

'Well! perhaps I did; he was a great deal at the house. Miss Dixon keeps a school in the same house now, and I'm sure she does it a great deal better.'

Meanwhile Miss Piper and Miss Phoebe talked of the dresses of the people present, beginning by complimenting each other.

'What a lovely turban you have got on, Miss Piper, if I may be allowed to say so: so becoming to your complexion!'

'Do you think so?' said Miss Piper, with ill-concealed gratification; it was something to have a 'complexion' at forty-five. 'I thought I must have something to set off my gown, which isn't quite so new as it once was; and I have no handsome jewellery like you' – looking with admiring eyes at a large miniature, set round with pearls, which served as a shield to Miss Phoebe's breast.

'It is handsome,' that lady replied. 'It is a likeness of my dear mother; Dorothy has got my father on. The miniatures were both taken at the same time; and just about then my uncle died and left us each a legacy of fifty pounds, which we agreed to spend on the setting of our miniatures. But, because they are so valuable, Dorothy always keeps them locked up with the best silver, and hides the box somewhere; she never will tell me where, because, she says, I've such weak nerves, and that if a burglar, with a loaded pistol at my head, were to ask me where we kept our plate and jewels, I should be sure to tell him. It's only the second time I've had it on; and I can't even get at it, and look at it, which I should like to do. I shouldn't have had it on tonight, but that Dorothy gave it out to me, saying it was but a proper compliment to pay to the Duchess of Menteith, who is to be here in her diamonds.'

'Dear-ah-me! Do you know I never saw a duchess before! Look, look! that's our Mr Cholmley, the magistrate' (he was the great man of Coreham); 'and that's Mrs Cholmley in red satin, and

Mr George and Mr Harry from Oxford, I do declare; and Miss Cholmley; and pretty Miss Sophy. And there is Coxe the butcher and his wife! Why, all Coreham seems to be here! And how Mrs Coxe can afford such a gown I can't make out, for I know Coxe had some difficulty in paying for the last sheep he bought of my brother.'

Just at this moment the band, consisting of two violins, a harp, and an occasional clarionet, having finished their tuning, struck up a brisk country-dance, and partners quickly took their places. Mrs Gibson was secretly a little annoyed at Cynthia's being one of those to stand up in this early dance, the performers in which were principally the punctual plebeians of Hollingford.

This was to be a very good ball, people said. Every great house in the district was expected to be full of guests on these occasions; but, at this early hour, the townspeople had the floor almost entirely to themselves; the county-magnates came dropping in later; and chiefest among them all was the lord-lieutenant from the Towers. But tonight they were unusually late; and, the aristocratic ozone being absent from the atmosphere, there was a flatness about the dancing of all those who considered themselves above the plebeian ranks of the trades-people. They, however, enjoyed themselves thoroughly, and sprang and bounded, till their eyes sparkled and their cheeks glowed with exercise and excitement. Mr Gibson had had to leave the ball-room for a time, as he had anticipated; and, in his absence, Mrs Gibson kept herself a little aloof from the Miss Brownings and those of her acquaintance who would willingly have entered into conversation with her, with the view of attaching herself to the skirts of the Towers party, when they should make their appearance. If Cynthia would not be so very ready in engaging herself to every possible partner who asked her to dance, there were sure to be young men staying at the Towers who would be on the look-out for pretty girls; and who could tell to what a dance might lead? Molly, too, though not so good a dancer as Cynthia, was becoming engaged pretty deeply; and, it must be confessed, she was longing to dance every dance, no matter with whom. Even she might not be available for the more aristocratic partners Mrs Gibson anticipated. She was feeling very much annoyed with the whole proceedings of the evening, when she was aware of some one standing by her; and, turning a little to one side, she saw Mr Preston. He was looking so black that, if their eyes had not met, Mrs Gibson would have preferred not speaking to him; as it was, she thought it unavoidable.

'The rooms are not well lighted tonight; are they, Mr Preston?'

'No,' said he; 'but who could light such dingy old paint as this, loaded with evergreens, too, which always darken a room?'

Mr Preston had put his glass in his eye, apparently for the purpose of watching the dancers. If its exact direction could have been ascertained, it would have been found that he was looking intently and angrily at a flying figure in pink muslin; many a one was gazing at Cynthia with intentness besides himself, but no one in anger. Mrs Gibson was not so fine an observer as to read all this; so she went on with her small remarks.

'You are not dancing, Mr Preston!'

'No! The partner I had engaged has made some mistake. I am waiting to have an explanation with her.'

Mrs Gibson was silent. An uncomfortable tide of recollections appeared to come over her; she, like Mr Preston, watched Cynthia; the dance was ended, and presently, her partner, Mr Harry Cholmley, brought her back to her seat. She took the one vacant next to Mr Preston, leaving that by her mother for Molly's occupation. The latter returned a moment afterwards. Cynthia seemed entirely unconscious of Mr Preston's neighbourhood. Mrs Gibson leaned forwards, and said to her daughter –

'Your last partner was a gentleman, my dear. You are improving in your selection. I really was ashamed of you before, figuring away with that attorney's clerk. Molly, do you know whom you have been dancing with? I have found out he is the Coreham bookseller.'

'That accounts for his being so well-up in all the books I've been wanting to hear about,' said Molly eagerly, but with a spice of malice in her mind.

'Very well. But remember, if you go on in this way, you will have to shake hands over the counter tomorrow morning with some of your partners of tonight,' said Mrs Gibson coldly.

'But I really don't know how to refuse when people are introduced to me and ask me, and I am longing to dance.' What reply Mrs Gibson would have made cannot now be ascertained; for, before she could answer, Mr Preston stepped a little forwards, and said, in a tone which trembled with anger –

'If Miss Gibson finds any difficulty in refusing a partner, she has only to apply to Miss Kirkpatrick for instructions.'

Cynthia lifted up her beautiful eyes, and said, very quietly –

'You forget, Mr Preston; Miss Gibson implied that she wished to dance with the person who asked her – I can't instruct her how to act in that difficulty.'

And to the rest of this little conversation Cynthia appeared to lend no ear; and she was almost directly claimed by her next partner. Mr Preston took the seat now left empty, much to Molly's annoyance. He put out his hand for Cynthia's nosegay, which she had entrusted to Molly. It was not the one Mr Preston had sent.

'Miss Kirkpatrick has not done me the honour of wearing the bouquet I sent her, I see. She received it, I suppose?'

'Yes,' said Molly, rather intimidated by the tone in which this was said. 'But we had already accepted these nosegays.'

Mrs Gibson was just the person to come to the rescue with her honeyed words, on such an occasion as the present.

'Oh, yes, we were so sorry! Of course, I don't mean to say we could be sorry for anyone's kindness; but two such lovely nosegays had been sent from Hamley Hall and they had come before yours, Mr Preston.'

'I should have felt honoured if you had accepted of mine, since the young ladies were so well provided for. I was at some pains in selecting the flowers at Green's; I think I may say it was rather more *recherché* than that of Miss Kirkpatrick's.'

'Oh, because Cynthia would take out the most effective flowers to put in my hair!' exclaimed Molly eagerly.

'Did she?' said Mr Preston, with a certain accent of pleasure in his voice, as though he were glad she set so little store by the nosegay; and he walked off to stand behind Cynthia in the quadrille that was being danced; and Molly saw him making her reply to him – against her will, Molly was sure. But, somehow, his face and manner implied power over her. She looked grave, deaf, indifferent, indignant, defiant; but, after a half-whispered speech to Cynthia, at the conclusion of the dance, she evidently threw him an impatient consent to what he was asking, for he walked off with a smile of satisfaction on his handsome face.

All this time, the murmurs were spreading at the lateness of the party from the Towers, and person after person came up to Mrs Gibson, as if she were the accredited authority as to the earl and countess's plans. In one sense this was flattering; but then the acknowledgment of common ignorance and wonder reduced her to the level of the inquirers.

At last, there was a rumbling, and a rushing, and a whispering, and the music stopped; so the dancers were obliged to do so too; and in came Lord Cumnor in his state dress, with a fat, middle-aged woman on his arm; she was dressed almost like a girl – in a sprigged muslin, with natural flowers in her hair, but not a vestige of a jewel or a diamond. Yet it must be the duchess; but what was a duchess without diamonds? After the duchess came Lady Cumnor, looking like Lady Macbeth in black velvet – a cloud upon her brow; and Lady Harriet, and other ladies, amongst whom there was one dressed so like the duchess as to suggest the idea of a sister rather than a daughter. There was Lord Hollingford, plain in face, awkward in person, gentlemanly in manner; and half-a-dozen younger men, Lord Albert Monson, Captain James, and others of their age and standing, who came in looking nothing if not critical. This long-expected party swept up to the seats reserved for them at the head of the room, apparently regardless of the interruption they caused; and, when 'Monymusk' struck up again, not half the former set of people stood up to finish the dance.

Lady Harriet spied the Gibson party pretty quickly out, and came across to them.

'Here we are at last. How d'ye do, dear? Why, little one' (to Molly), 'how nice you're looking! Aren't we shamefully late?'

'Oh! it's only just past twelve,' said Mrs Gibson, 'and I daresay you dined very late.'

'It wasn't that; it was that ill-mannered woman, who went to her own room after we came out from dinner; and she and Lady Alice stayed there invisible, till we thought they were putting on some splendid attire – as they ought to have done – and at half-past ten, when mamma sent up to them to say the carriages were at the door, the duchess sent down for some beef-tea, and at last appeared *à l'enfant* as you see her. Mamma is so angry with her, and some of the others are so annoyed at not coming earlier, and one or two are giving themselves airs about coming at all. Papa is the only one who is not affected by it.' Then, turning to Molly, Lady Harriet asked –

'Have you been dancing much, Miss Gibson?'

'Yes; not every dance, but nearly all.'

Mrs Gibson contrived to baffle any endeavours at further conversation between the two, by placing herself betwixt Lady Harriet and Molly, when the former asked to sit down in the absent Cynthia's room.

'I won't go back to those people, I am so mad with them; and, besides, I must have some gossip with you.' So she sat down by Mrs Gibson, and, as Mrs Goodenough afterwards expressed it, 'looked like anybody else'. Mrs Goodenough said this to excuse herself for a little misadventure she fell into. On her way to departure, she stopped opposite to Mrs Gibson, and thus addressed her –

'Such a shabby thing for a duchess I never saw; not a bit of a diamond near her! They're none of 'em worth looking at except the countess, and she's not so lusty as she was. But they're not worth waiting up for till this time o' night.'

There was a moment's pause. Then Lady Harriet put her hand out, and said –

'You don't remember me, but I know you from having seen you at the Towers. Lady Cumnor is a good deal thinner than she was, but we hope her health is better for it.'

'It's Lady Harriet,' said Mrs Gibson to Mrs Goodenough, in reproachful dismay.

'Deary me, your ladyship! I hope I've given no offence! But, you see – it's late hours for such folks as me, and I only stayed to see the duchess, and I thought she'd come in diamonds and a coronet; and it puts one out, at my age, to be disappointed in the only chance I'm likely to have of so fine a sight.'

'I'm put out too,' said Lady Harriet. 'I wanted to have come early, and I'm so cross and ill-tempered, I should be glad to hide myself in bed as soon as you will do.'

She said this so sweetly that Mrs Goodenough relaxed into a smile.

'I don't believe as ever your ladyship can be cross and ill-tempered with that pretty face. I'm an old woman, so you must let me say so.' Lady Harriet stood up, and made a low curtsey. Then holding out her hand, she said –

'I won't keep you up any longer; but I'll promise one thing in return for your pretty speech; if ever I am a duchess, I'll come and show myself to you in all my robes and gewgaws. Good-night, madam!'

'There! I knew how it would be!' said she, not resuming her seat. 'And on the eve of a county election too!'

'Oh! you must not take old Mrs Goodenough as a specimen, dear Lady Harriet. I am sure no one else would complain of your all being as late as you liked,' said Mrs Gibson.

'What do you say, Molly?' said Lady Harriet, suddenly turning her eyes on Molly's face. 'Don't you think we've lost some of our popularity – which at this time means votes – by coming so late?'

'I don't know about popularity or votes,' said Molly, rather un-willingly. 'But I think many people were sorry you did not come sooner; and isn't that rather a proof of popularity?'

'That's a very neat and diplomatic answer,' said Lady Harriet, smiling, and tapping Molly's cheek with her fan.

'Molly knows nothing about it,' said Mrs Gibson. 'It would be very impertinent if she or anyone else questioned Lady Cumnor's perfect right to come when she chose.'

'Well, all I know is, I must go back to mamma now; but I shall make another raid into these regions by-and-by, and you must keep a place for me. Ah! there are – the Miss Brownings; you see I don't forget my lesson, Miss Gibson.'

'Molly, I cannot have you speaking so to Lady Harriet,' said Mrs Gibson, as soon as she was left alone with her stepdaughter. 'You would never have known her at all, if it had not been for me, and don't be always putting yourself into our conversation.'

'But I must speak if she asks me questions,' pleaded Molly.

'Well! if you must, you must, I acknowledge. But there's no need for you to set up to have an opinion at your age.'

'I don't know how to help it,' said Molly.

'She's such a whimsical person; look there, if she's not talking to Miss Phoebe; and Miss Phoebe is so weak she'll be easily led away into fancying she's hand and glove with Lady Harriet. If there is one thing I hate more than another, it is the trying to make out an intimacy with great people.'

Molly made no reply. Indeed, she was more occupied in watching Cynthia. She was dancing, it was true, with the same lightness and grace as before; but the smooth, bounding motion, as of a feather blown onwards by the wind, was gone. And, when she was brought back to her seat, Molly noticed her changed colour, and her dreamily abstracted eyes.

'What is the matter, Cynthia?' asked she, in a low voice.

'Nothing,' said Cynthia, in an accent of what, in her, was sharpness. 'Why should there be?'

'I don't know; but you look different to what you did – tired or something.'

'There's nothing the matter; or, if there is, don't talk about it! It's all your fancy.'

This was a rather contradictory speech, to be interpreted by intuition rather than by logic. But what was Molly's surprise, after the speeches that had passed before, and the implication of Cynthia's whole manner to Mr Preston, to see him come up to her, and, without a word, offer his arm and lead her away to dance! It appeared to strike Mrs Gibson as something remarkable; for she asked, wonderingly –

'Is Cynthia going to dance with Mr Preston?'

Molly had scarcely time to answer, before she herself was led off by her partner. She could hardly attend to him or to the figures of the quadrille, for watching for Cynthia among the moving forms.

Once she caught a glimpse of her standing still – downcast – listening to Mr Preston's eager speech. When she and Molly joined each other again, the shade on Cynthia's face had deepened to gloom. But, at the same time, if a physiognomist had studied her expression, he would have read in it defiance and anger, and perhaps also a little perplexity. While this quadrille was going on, Lady Harriet had been speaking to her brother.

'Hollingford!' she said, drawing him a little apart from the well-born crowd amid which he stood silent and abstracted, 'you don't know how these good people here have been hurt and disappointed with our being so late, and with the duchess's ridiculous simplicity of dress.'

'Why should they mind it?' asked he.

'Oh, don't be so wise and stupid; don't you see, we're a show and a spectacle – it's like having a pantomime with harlequin and columbine in plain clothes. They really are a little disappointed, whether they are logical or not in being so, and we must try and make it up to them; for one thing, because I can't bear our vassals to look dissatisfied and disloyal, and then there's the election in June.'

'I really would as soon be out of the House as in it.'

'Nonsense; it would grieve papa beyond measure. You must go and dance with some of the townspeople, and I'll ask Sheepshanks to introduce me to a respectable young farmer. Can't you get Captain James to make himself useful? There he goes with Lady Alice! If I don't get him introduced to the ugliest tailor's daughter I can find for the next dance!' She put her arm in her brother's as she spoke, as if to lead him to some partner. He resisted, however – resisted piteously.

'Pray don't, Harriet. You know I can't dance. I hate it; I always did. I don't know how to get through a quadrille.'

'It's a country-dance!' said she resolutely.

'And what shall I say to my partner? I haven't a notion. Speak of being disappointed – they'll be ten times more disappointed, when they find I can neither dance nor talk!'

'In their eyes a lord may dance like a bear if he likes, and they'll take it for grace. And you shall begin with Molly Gibson. She's a good, simple, intelligent little girl, which you'll think a great deal more of, I suppose, than of the frivolous fact of her being very pretty. Clare! will you allow me to introduce my brother to Miss Gibson? He hopes to engage her for this dance. Lord Hollingford, Miss Gibson!'

Molly found Lord Hollingford, the wise and learned Lord Hollingford, strangely stupid in understanding the mystery of 'Cross hands and back again, down the middle and up again.' He was constantly getting hold of the wrong hands, and as constantly stopping when he had returned to his place, quite unaware that the laws of the game required that he should go on capering till he had arrived at the bottom of the room. He apologised to Molly, when once they had arrived at that haven of comparative peace; and he expressed his regret so simply and heartily that she felt at her ease with him at once, and by-and-by they got into very pleasant conversation. She learnt from him that Roger Hamley had just been publishing a paper in some scientific periodical, which had excited considerable attention. This piece of news was of great interest to Molly; and, in her questions, she herself evinced so much intelligence, and a mind so well prepared for the reception of information, that Lord Hollingford would have felt his quest of popularity a very easy affair indeed, if he might have gone on talking quietly to Molly during the rest of the evening. When he took her back to her place, he found Mr Gibson there, and fell into talk with him, until Lady Harriet once more came to stir him up to his duties. Before very long, however, he returned to Mr Gibson's side, and began telling him of this paper of Roger Hamley's. In the midst of their conversation, Lord Hollingford saw Molly in the distance, and interrupted himself to say –

'What a charming little lady that daughter of yours is! Most girls of her age are so difficult to talk to; but she is intelligent and full of interest in all sorts of sensible things; well read, too – she was up in the *Règne Animal* – and very pretty!'

Mr Gibson bowed, much pleased at such a compliment from such a man, were he lord or not. When she next returned to her place, Mrs Gibson greeted her with soft words and a gracious smile. She only wished that the happy chance had fallen to Cynthia's instead of to Molly's lot. It was a pity that Cynthia preferred making millinery to reading; but perhaps that could be rectified. And there was Lord Cumnor coming to speak to her, and Lady Cumnor nodding to her, and indicating a place by her side.

It was not an unsatisfactory ball upon the whole to Mrs Gibson.

## CHAPTER 26

# Rivalry

For some days after the ball Cynthia seemed languid, and was very silent. Molly was disappointed when she found that all conversation on the subject was rather evaded than encouraged. Mrs Gibson, it is true, was ready to go over the ground as many times as anyone liked; but her words were always like ready-made clothes, and never fitted individual thoughts. Anybody might have used them, and, with a change of proper names, they might have served to describe any ball. Molly knew the sentences and their sequence, even to irritation.

'Ah! Mr Osborne, you should have been there! I said to myself, many a time, how you really should have been there – you and your brother, of course.'

'I thought of you very often during the evening!'

'Did you? Now, that I call very kind of you. Cynthia, darling! Do you hear what Mr Osborne Hamley was saying?' as Cynthia came into the room just then. 'He thought of us all on the evening of the ball.'

'He did better than merely remember us,' said Cynthia, with her slow smile. 'We owe him thanks for those beautiful flowers, mamma.'

'Oh!' said Osborne, 'you must not thank me exclusively. I believe it was my thought, but Roger took all the trouble of it.'

'I consider the thought as everything,' said Mrs Gibson. 'Thought is spiritual, while action is merely material.'

'I'm afraid the flowers were too late to be of much use, though,' continued Osborne. 'I met Preston the next morning, and I was sorry to find he had been beforehand with us.'

'He only sent one nosegay, and that was for Cynthia,' said Molly, looking up from her work. 'And it did not come till after we had received the flowers from Hamley.' Molly caught a sight of Cynthia's face, before she bent down again to her sewing. It was scarlet in colour, and there was a flash of anger in her eyes.

'Mr Preston had no business to speak as if he had forestalled you,' said Cynthia. 'It came just as we were ready to go, and I put it into the fire directly.'

'Cynthia, my dear love!' said Mrs Gibson (who had never heard of the fate of the flowers until now), 'what an idea of yourself you will give to Mr Osborne Hamley; but, to be sure, I can quite understand it. You inherit my feeling – my prejudice – sentimental I grant, against bought flowers.'

Cynthia said, 'I used some of your flowers, Mr Hamley, to dress Molly's hair. It was a great temptation, for the colour so exactly matched her coral ornaments; but I believe she thought it treacherous to disturb the arrangement, so I ought to take all the blame on myself.'

'The arrangement was my brother's; but I am sure he would have preferred seeing them in Miss Gibson's hair rather than in the blazing fire. Mr Preston comes off far the worst.' Osborne was rather amused at the whole affair, and would have liked to probe Cynthia's motives a little farther. He did not hear Molly saying in as soft a voice as if she were talking to herself, 'I wore mine just as they were sent,' for Mrs Gibson came in with a total change of subject.

'Speaking of lilies of the valley, is it true that they grow wild in Hurstwood? It is not the season for them to be in flower yet; but, when it is, I think we must take a walk there – with a little picnic, in fact. You'll join us, won't you?' turning to Osborne. 'You could ride to Hollingford and put up your horse here, and we could have a long day in the woods, and all come home to dinner – dinner with a basket of lilies in the middle of the table!'

'I should like it very much,' said Osborne; 'but I may not be at home. Roger is more likely to be here, I believe, at that time – a month hence.' He was thinking of the visit to London to sell his poems, and the run down to Winchester which he anticipated afterwards.

'Oh, but you must be with us! We must wait for Mr Osborne Hamley, must not we, Cynthia?'

'I'm afraid the lilies won't wait,' replied Cynthia.

'Well, then, we must put it off till dog-rose and honey-suckle time. You will be at home then, won't you? Or does the London season present too many attractions?'

'I don't exactly know when dog-roses are in flower; and I believe my movements are guided more by the lunar calendar than the floral. You had better take my brother for your companion; he is practical in his love of flowers. I am only theoretical.'

'Does that fine word "theoretical" imply that you are ignorant?' asked Cynthia. 'Of course we shall be happy to see your brother; but why can't we have you too? I confess to a little timidity in the presence of one so learned as your brother is. Give me a little charming ignorance, if we must call it by that hard word.'

Osborne bowed. It was very pleasant to him to be petted and flattered. It was an agreeable contrast to the home that was so dismal to him, to come to this house, where the society of two agreeable girls, and the soothing syrup of their mother's speeches, awaited him whenever he liked to come. The fact of his marriage was constantly present to his mind, and Aimée too securely enthroned in his heart, for him to remember that he might be looked upon by others in the light of a possible husband; but the reflection forced itself upon him occasionally, whether he was not trespassing too often on hospitality which he had at present no means of returning?

But Mrs Gibson, in her ignorance of the true state of affairs, was secretly exultant in the attraction which made him come so often and lounge away the hours in her house and garden. She had no doubt that it was Cynthia who drew him thither. But Cynthia had come across too many varieties of flirtation, admiration, and even passionate love, to be for a moment at fault as to the quiet, friendly nature of Osborne's attentions. She received him always as a sister might a brother. It was different when Roger returned from his election as a Fellow of Trinity. The hardly suppressed ardour of his manner made Cynthia understand before long with what kind of love she had now to deal. She recognised the difference between Roger's relation to her and Osborne's long before Mrs Gibson found it out. Molly was, however, the first to discover the nature of Roger's attentions. The first time they saw him after the ball, it came out to her observant eyes. Cynthia had not been looking well since that evening. Molly watched with tender anxiety; once, Molly touched on Mr Preston's name, and found that this was a subject on which Cynthia was raw; she said a few sharp words, expressive of anything but kindly feeling towards the gentleman, and then bade Molly never name his name to her again.

Now, the first person out of the house to notice Cynthia's change of look and manner was Roger Hamley. His eyes were scarcely off her during the first five minutes he was in the room. All the time he was trying to talk to Mrs Gibson in reply to her civil platitudes, he was studying Cynthia; and at the first convenient pause he came and stood before Molly, so as to interpose his person between her and the rest of the room; for some visitors had come in subsequently to his entrance.

'Molly, how ill your sister is looking! What is it? Has she had advice?'

Now, Molly's love for Cynthia was fast and unwavering; but, if anything tried it, it was the habit Roger had fallen into of always calling Cynthia Molly's sister. It vexed both ear and heart when Roger used the expression; and there was a curtness of manner as well as of words in her reply.

'Oh! she was over-tired by the ball. Papa has seen her, and says she will be all right very soon.'

'Is there anything I could do? We have plenty of books, as you know, if she cares for reading. Or flowers? she likes flowers. Oh! and our forced strawberries are just ready – I will bring some over tomorrow.'

'I am sure she will like them,' said Molly.

For some reason or other, unknown to the Gibsons, a longer interval than usual occurred between Osborne's visits, while Roger came nearly every day, always with some fresh offering by which he openly sought to relieve Cynthia's indisposition. Her manner to him was so gentle and gracious that Mrs Gibson became alarmed lest he might come to be preferred to Osborne. In her quiet way, she contrived to pass many slights upon Roger; but the darts rebounded from his generous nature, which could not have imagined her motives. What seemed neither to hurt Roger nor annoy Cynthia made Molly's blood boil; and, now she had discovered Mrs Gibson's wish to make Roger's visits shorter and less frequent, she was on the watch for indications of this desire.

'Mr Gibson and I should be so delighted, if you could have stopped to dinner; but, of course, we cannot be so selfish as to ask you to stay when we remember how your father would be left alone.'

Or, as soon as Roger came with his bunch of early roses, it was desirable for Cynthia to go and rest in her own room, while Molly had to accompany Mrs Gibson on some improvised errand or call. Still, Roger was slow to perceive that he was not wanted. At last there came a day when Mrs Gibson went beyond her usual negative snubbiness, and when, in some unwonted fit of cross-ness, she was guilty of positive rudeness.

Cynthia was very much better. Her pretty bloom and much of her light-heartedness had come back, and Mrs Gibson was sitting at her embroidery in the drawing-room, and the two girls were at the window, Cynthia laughing at Molly's earnest endeavour to imitate the French accent in which the former had been reading a page of Voltaire. It was as yet early morning; a delicious, fresh, lovely June day, the air redolent with the scents of flower-growth and bloom; and, half the time the girls had been ostensibly em-ployed in the French reading, they had been leaning out of the open window, trying to reach a cluster of climbing roses. They had secured them at last, and the buds lay on Cynthia's lap, but many of the petals had fallen off.

'Mr Roger Hamley,' was announced.

'So tiresome!' said Mrs Gibson, as she pushed away her embroidery-frame. She put out her cold, motionless hand to him, with a half-murmured word of welcome, still eyeing her lost embroidery. He took no apparent notice, and passed on to the window.

'How delicious!' said he. 'No need for any more Hamley roses, now yours are out!'

'I agree with you,' said Mrs Gibson. 'You have been very kind in bringing us flowers so long; but, now our own are out, we need not trouble you any more.'

He looked at her, with a little surprise clouding his honest face. Molly would perhaps have been more pained, if she had not seen Cynthia's colour rise. She waited for her to speak, if need were; for she knew that Roger's defence might be safely entrusted to Cynthia's ready wit.

He put out his hand for the shattered cluster of roses that lay in Cynthia's lap.

'At any rate,' said he, 'my trouble – if Mrs Gibson considers it has been a trouble to me – will be overpaid, if I may have this.'

'Old lamps for new,' said Cynthia, smiling as she gave it to him. 'I wish one could always buy nosegays such as you have brought us, as cheaply.'

'You forget the waste of time that, I think, we must reckon as part of the payment,' said her mother. 'Really, Mr Hamley, we must learn to shut our doors on you if you come so often, and at such early hours! I settle myself to my own employment regularly after breakfast till lunchtime; and it is my wish to keep Cynthia and Molly to a course of improving reading and study – but with early visitors it is quite impossible to observe any regularity of habits.'

All this was said in that sweet, false tone which of late had gone through Molly like the scraping of a slate-pencil on a slate. Roger's ruddy colour grew paler for a moment, and he looked grave. In another moment, the wonted frankness of expression returned.

'I believe I have been very thoughtless – I'll not come so early again; but I had some excuse today: my brother told me you had made a plan for going to see Hurstwood when the roses were out, and they are earlier than usual this year. He spoke of a long day there, going before lunch –'

'The plan was made with Mr Osborne Hamley. I could not think of going without him!' said Mrs Gibson coldly.

'I had a letter from him this morning, in which he named your wish, and he says he fears he cannot be at home till they are out of flower. I daresay they are not much to see in reality; but the day is so lovely I thought that the plan of going to Hurstwood would be a charming excuse for being out-of-doors.'

'How kind you are! and so good, too, in sacrificing your natural desire to be with your father as much as possible.'

'I'm glad to say my father is so much better than he was in the winter, that he spends much of his time out-of-doors in his fields. He has been accustomed to go about alone, and I – we think that as great a return to his former habits as he can be induced to make is the best for him.'

'And when do you return to Cambridge?'

'It is uncertain. You probably know that I am a Fellow of Trinity now. I hardly yet know what my future plans may be; I am thinking of going up to London soon.'

'Ah! London is the true place for a young man,' said Mrs Gibson, with decision, as if she had reflected a good deal on the question. 'If it were not that we really are so busy this morning, I should have been tempted to make an exception to our general rule; one more exception, for your early visits have made us make too many already. Perhaps, however, we may see you again before you go?'

'Certainly I shall come,' replied he, rising to take his leave. Then, addressing himself more especially to Cynthia, he added, 'My stay in London will not exceed a fortnight or so – is there anything I can do for you – or you?' turning a little to Molly.

'No, thank you very much,' said Cynthia, very sweetly; and then, acting on a sudden impulse, she leant out of the window, and gathered him some half-opened roses. 'You deserve these; do throw that poor shabby bunch away!'

His eyes brightened, his cheeks glowed. He took the offered buds, but did not throw away the other bunch.

'At any rate, I may come after lunch is over, and the afternoons and evenings will be the most delicious time of day a month hence.' He said this to both Molly and Cynthia, but in his heart he addressed it to the latter.

Mrs Gibson affected not to hear what he was saying, but held out her limp hand once more to him.

'I suppose we shall see you when you return; and pray tell your brother how we are longing to have a visit from him.'

When he had left the room, Molly's heart was quite full.

'I can't think why he will come at such untimely hours,' said Mrs Gibson, as soon as she heard him fairly out of the house. 'It's different from Osborne; we are so much more intimate with him. Fellow of Trinity, indeed! I wish he would learn to stay there, and not come intruding here, and assuming that, because I asked Osborne to join in a picnic, it was all the same to me which brother came.'

'In short, mamma, one man may steal a horse, but another must not look over the hedge,' said Cynthia, pouting a little.

'And the two brothers have always been treated so exactly alike by their friends, and there has been such a strong friendship between them, that it is no wonder Roger thinks he may be welcome where Osborne is allowed to come at all hours,' continued Molly, in high dudgeon.

'Oh, very well, my dears! When I was young, it wouldn't have been thought becoming for girls of your age to fly out, because a little restraint was exercised as to the hours at which they should receive the calls of young men. And they would have supposed that there might be good reasons why their parents disapproved of the visits of certain gentlemen, while they were pleased to see some members of the same family.'

'But that was what I said, mamma,' said Cynthia, looking at her mother with an expression of innocent bewilderment on her face. 'One man may –'

'Be quiet, child! All proverbs are vulgar, and, I do believe, that is the vulgarest of all. You are really catching Roger Hamley's coarseness, Cynthia!'

'Mamma,' said Cynthia, roused to anger, 'I don't mind your abusing me, but Mr Roger Hamley has been very kind to me while I've not been well: I can't bear to hear him disparaged. If he's coarse, I've no objection to be coarse as well; for it seems to me it must mean kindliness and pleasantness, and the bringing of pretty flowers and presents.'

Molly's tears were brimming over at these words; she could have kissed Cynthia for her warm partisanship; but, afraid of betraying emotion, she laid down her book hastily, and ran upstairs to her room, and locked the door, in order to breathe freely.

## CHAPTER 27

# Bush-Fighting

Osborne came home, in fact, not long after Roger had gone away; but he was languid and unwell and felt unequal to any exertion. Thus a week or more elapsed before any of the Gibsons knew he was at the Hall; and then it was only by chance that they became aware of it. Mr Gibson met him in one of the lanes near Hamley. When he overtook him he said –

'Why, Osborne, is it you? I thought it was an old man of fifty loitering before me! I didn't know you had come back.'

'Yes,' said Osborne, 'I've been at home nearly ten days. I daresay I ought to have called on your people, but the fact is, I'm feeling very good-for-nothing; I could hardly breathe in the house, and yet I'm already tired with this short walk.'

'You'd better get home at once; and I'll call and see you, as I come back from Rowe's.'

'No, you mustn't on any account!' said Osborne hastily; 'my father is annoyed enough about my going from home so often. He puts down all my languor to my having been away.'

'May I ask where you do spend your time when you are not at Hamley Hall?' asked Mr Gibson.

'No!' replied Osborne reluctantly. 'I will tell you this: – I stay with friends in the country. I lead a life which ought to be conducive to health, because it is thoroughly simple, rational, and happy. And now I've told you more about it than my father himself knows. He never asks me where I've been; and I shouldn't tell him if he did – at least, I think not.'

Mr Gibson rode on by Osborne's side, not speaking for a moment or two.

'Osborne, whatever scrapes you may have got into, I should advise your telling your father boldly out. I know him; he'll be angry enough at first, but he'll come round, take my word for it; and, somehow or another, he'll find money to pay your debts and set you free, if it's that kind of difficulty; and if it's any other kind of entanglement, why, still he's your best friend. It's this estrangement from your father that's telling on your health, I'll be bound.'

'No,' said Osborne, 'I beg your pardon; but I am really out of order. My instinct tells me there is something really the matter with me.'

'Come, don't be setting up your instinct against the profession!' said Mr Gibson cheerily.

He dismounted, and throwing the reins of his horse round his arm, he looked at Osborne's tongue and felt his pulse, asking him various questions. At the end he said –

'We'll soon bring you about; though I should like a little more quiet talk with you, without this tugging brute for a third. If you'll manage to ride over and lunch with us tomorrow, Dr Nicholls will be with us and you shall have the benefit of the advice of two doctors instead of one. Go home now; you've had enough exercise for the middle of a day as hot as this is. And don't mope in the house, listening to the maunderings of your stupid instinct.'

'What else have I to do?' said Osborne. 'My father and I are not companions; one can't read and write for ever, especially when there's no end to be gained by it. I don't mind telling you – in confidence, recollect – that I've been trying to get some of my poems published; but there's no one like a publisher for taking the conceit out of one. Not a man among them would have them as a gift.'

'I wouldn't trouble my head about it, if I were you; though that's always very easily said, I know. Try your hand at prose; but, at any rate, don't go on fretting over spilt milk. But I mustn't lose my time here. Come over to us tomorrow, and, what with the wisdom of two doctors, and the wit and folly of three women, I think we shall cheer you up a bit.'

So saying, Mr Gibson remounted, and rode away.

'I don't like his looks,' thought Mr Gibson to himself at night, as he reviewed the events of the day. 'And then his pulse! But how often we're all mistaken!'

Osborne made his appearance a considerable time before luncheon the next morning; and no one objected to the earliness of his call. He was feeling better. There were few signs of the invalid about him; and what few there were disappeared under the bright pleasant influence of such a welcome as he received from all. Presently, Dr Nicholls and Mr Gibson came in; the former had had some conference with the latter on the subject of Osborne's health; and, from time to time, the skilful old physician's sharp and observant eyes gave a comprehensive look at Osborne. Then there was lunch, when everyone was merry.

When luncheon was over, presently, Osborne came upstairs, and, after his old fashion, began to take up new books, and to question the girls as to their music. After a while they adjourned into the garden, Osborne lounging on a chair, while Molly employed herself busily in tying up carnations, and Cynthia gathered flowers in her careless, graceful way.

'I hope you notice the difference in our occupations, Mr Hamley? Molly, you see, devotes herself to the useful and I to the ornamental. I think you might help one of us, instead of looking on like the *Grand Seigneur.*'

'I don't know what I can do,' said he rather plaintively. 'I'm rather exhausted by being pulled about by those good doctors.'

'Why, you don't mean to say they have been attacking you since lunch!' exclaimed Molly.

'Yes; indeed, they have; and they might have gone on till now, if Mrs Gibson had not come in opportunely.'

'I thought mamma had gone out some time ago!' said Cynthia.

'She came into the dining-room not five minutes ago. Do you want her?' and Osborne half rose.

'Oh, not at all!' said Cynthia. 'Only she seemed to be in such a hurry to go out, I fancied she had set off long ago. She had some errand to do for Lady Cumnor.'

'Are the family coming to the Towers this autumn?'

'I believe so. But they don't take kindly to me,' continued Cynthia, 'and I'm not generous enough to take kindly to them.'

'I should have thought that such a very unusual blot in their discrimination would have interested you in them as extraordinary people,' said Osborne, with a little air of conscious gallantry.

'Isn't that a compliment?' said Cynthia, after a pause of mock meditation. 'If anyone pays me a compliment, please let it be short and clear! I'm very stupid at finding out hidden meanings.'

'Then such speeches as "you are very pretty", or "you have charming manners", are what you prefer. Now, I pique myself on wrapping up my sugar-plums delicately.'

'What are you two talking about?' said Molly, resting on her light spade.

'It's only a discussion on the best way of administering compliments,' said Cynthia.

'I don't like them at all in any way,' said Molly. 'But, perhaps, it's rather sour grapes with me,' she added.

'Nonsense!' said Osborne. 'Shall I tell you what I heard of you at the ball?'

'Or shall I provoke Mr Preston,' said Cynthia, 'to begin upon you? It's like turning a tap, such a stream of pretty speeches flows out at the moment.' Her lip curled with scorn.

'For you, perhaps,' said Molly; 'but not for me.'

'For any woman. It's his notion of making himself agreeable. If you dare me, Molly, I'll try the experiment, and you'll see with what success.'

'No, don't, pray!' said Molly, in a hurry. 'I do so dislike him!'

'Why?' said Osborne.

'Oh! I don't know. He never seems to know what one is feeling.'

'He wouldn't care, if he did know,' said Cynthia. 'And he might know he is not wanted.'

'If he chooses to stay, he cares little whether he is wanted or not. And he's coming to take Mr Sheepshanks' place; then he'll live here altogether,' said Molly.

'Molly! who told you that?' said Cynthia, in quite a different tone of voice.

'Papa met Mr Sheepshanks yesterday, and he told him it was all settled.'

Cynthia was very silent after this. Presently, she said that she had gathered all the flowers she wanted, and that the heat was so great she would go indoors. And then Osborne went away. But Molly had set herself a task and tired and heated as she was, she finished it, and then went upstairs to rest. According to her wont, she sought for Cynthia; there was no reply to her soft knock at the bed-room door; and, thinking that Cynthia might have fallen asleep, and be lying uncovered in the draught of the open window, she went in softly. Cynthia was lying upon the bed, as if she had thrown herself down without caring for the comfort of her position. She was very still; and Molly took a shawl, and was going to place it over her, when she opened her eyes, and spoke –

'Is that you, dear? Don't go.' She started up into a sitting posture, pushed her hair away from her forehead and burning eyes, and gazed intently at Molly.

'Do you know what I've been thinking, dear?' said she. 'I think I've been long enough here, and that I had better go out as a governess.'

'Cynthia! what do you mean?' asked Molly, aghast. 'You've been asleep – you've been dreaming. You're over-tired,' continued she, sitting down on the bed, and taking Cynthia's passive hand, and stroking it softly.

'Oh, how good you are, Molly! I wonder, if I had been brought up like you, whether I should have been as good. But I've been tossed about so.'

'Then, don't go and be tossed about any more,' said Molly softly.

'Oh, dear! I had better go. But, you see, no one ever loved me like you, and, I think, your father – doesn't he, Molly? And it's hard to be driven out.'

'Cynthia, I am sure you're not well, or else you're not half awake.'

Cynthia sate with her arms encircling her knees.

'Well!' said she, at last. 'I suppose there's no escaping one's doom; and anywhere else I should be much more forlorn and unprotected.'

'What do you mean by your doom?'

'Ah, that's telling, little one,' said Cynthia, who seemed now to have recovered her usual manner. 'I don't mean to have one, though. I think that I can show fight.'

'With whom?' asked Molly, really anxious to probe the mystery to the bottom.

'Why, my doom, to be sure. Am not I a grand young lady to have a doom? Why, Molly, child, how pale and grave you look!' said she, kissing her all of a sudden. 'You ought not to care so much for me; I'm not good enough for you to worry yourself about me. I've given myself up a long time ago as a heartless baggage!'

'Nonsense! I wish you wouldn't talk so, Cynthia!'

'My child! what dirty hands you've got, and face too; and I've been kissing you – I daresay I'm dirty with it, too. Now, isn't that like one of mamma's speeches?' This had the effect that Cynthia intended; the daintily clean Molly became conscious of her soiled condition, and she hastily withdrew to her own room. When she had gone, Cynthia noiselessly locked the door; and, taking her purse out of her desk, she began to count over her money. The end of it all was a sigh.

'What a fool! – what a fool I was!' said she, at length. 'But, even if I don't go out as a governess, I shall make it up in time.'

Some weeks after the time he had anticipated when he spoke of his departure to the Gibsons, Roger returned back to the Hall. One morning when he called, Osborne told them that his brother had been at home for two or three days.

'And why has he not come here, then?' said Mrs Gibson. 'It is not kind of him not to come and see us as soon as he can. Tell him I say so – pray do.'

Osborne had gained one or two ideas as to her treatment of Roger the last time he had called. Neither of them let out the suspicion which had entered both their minds – the well-grounded suspicion arising from the fact that Osborne's visits, be they paid early or late, had never yet been met with a repulse. Osborne now reproached himself with having done Mrs Gibson injustice. She was evidently a weak, but probably a disinterested, woman; and it was only a bit of ill-temper on her part which had caused her to speak to Roger as she had done.

'I daresay it was rather impertinent of me to call at such an untimely hour,' said Roger.

'Not at all. It was just because she was put out that morning. I'll answer for it she's sorry now, and I'm sure you may go there at any time you like in future.'

Still, Roger did not choose to go again for two or three weeks, and the next time he called, the ladies were out. Once again he had the same ill-luck; and then he received a little pretty three-cornered note from Mrs Gibson: –

'MY DEAR SIR,
   – How is it that you are become so formal all of a sudden,
leaving cards, instead of awaiting our return? Fie for shame!
If you had seen the faces of disappointment that I did when
the horrid little bits of pasteboard were displayed to our view,
you would not have borne malice against me so long; for it is
really punishing others as well as my naughty self. If you will
come tomorrow – as early as you like – and lunch with us, I'll
own I was cross, and acknowledge myself a penitent. – Yours
ever,

                                    'HYACINTH C. F. GIBSON.'

There was no resisting this. Roger went, and Mrs Gibson caressed and petted him in her sweetest, silkiest manner. Cynthia looked lovelier than ever to him. She might be gay and sparkling with Osborne; with Roger she was soft and grave. Instinctively she knew her men. She saw that Osborne was only interested in her because of her position in a family with whom he was intimate, and that his admiration was only the warm criticism of an artist for unusual beauty. But she felt how different Roger's relation to her was. Her personal loveliness was only one of the many charms that made him tremble into passion. Cynthia was not capable of returning such feelings; but she appreciated this honest ardour. Such appreciation, and such respect for his true and affectionate nature, gave a serious tenderness to her manner to Roger, which allured him with a fresh and separate grace. Molly sate by, and wondered how soon it would all end, for she thought that no girl could resist such reverent passion. An older spectator might have looked far ahead, and thought of the question of pounds, shillings, and pence. Roger had his fellowship now, it is true; but the income of that would be lost, if he married; he had no profession, a life-interest in the two or three thousand pounds that he inherited from his mother, belonging to his father. This older spectator might have been a little surprised at the *empressement* of Mrs Gibson's manner to a younger son and he was too glad to avail himself of this privilege, to examine over-closely into what might be her motives for her change of manner.

## CHAPTER 28

# Old Ways and New Ways

Mr Preston was now installed in his new house at Hollingford; Mr Sheepshanks having entered into dignified idleness at the house of his married daughter, who lived in the county town. All Hollingford came forward to do the earl's new agent honour. He accepted every civility right and left, and won golden opinions accordingly.

'What's the man after?' said Mr Sheepshanks to himself, when he heard of his successor's affability. 'Preston's not a man to put himself out for nothing. He'll be after something solider than popularity.'

The sagacious old bachelor was right. Mr Preston went wherever he had a chance of meeting Cynthia Kirkpatrick.

Molly was dejected. The cause was certainly this. As long as Roger was drawn to Cynthia, and sought her of his own accord, it had been a sore pain and bewilderment to Molly's heart; but it was a straightforward attraction, and one which Molly acknowledged, in her great power of loving, to be the most natural thing in the world. And she would have been willing to cut off her right hand, if need were, to forward his attachment to Cynthia. But when she became aware that Mrs Gibson had totally changed her behaviour to Roger, for some cause unknown to Molly and was constantly making projects for throwing Roger and Cynthia together, with so evident a betrayal of her wish to bring about an engagement, Molly chafed at the net spread so evidently, and at Roger's blindness in coming so willingly to be entrapped. She forgot his former evidences of manly fondness for the beautiful Cynthia; she only saw plots of which he was the victim, and Cynthia the conscious

181

if passive bait. Cynthia heard and saw as much of the domestic background as she did, and yet she submitted to the role assigned to her! At last – for she could not help loving Cynthia – she determined to believe that Cynthia was unaware of all.

Roger knew that he could not marry and retain his fellowship; his intention was to hold himself loose from any employment or profession, until he had found one to his mind; so there was no prospect for many years that he would be able to marry. Yet he went on seeking Cynthia's sweet company, feeding his passion in every possible way. He knew that it was folly – and yet he did it; and it was perhaps this that made him so sympathetic with Osborne. Roger racked his brains about Osborne's affairs much more frequently than Osborne troubled himself. Indeed, he had become so ailing and languid of late, that even the Squire made only very faint objections to his desire for frequent change of scene.

'After all, it doesn't cost much,' the Squire said to Roger one day. 'Choose how he does it, he does it cheaply; he used to come and ask me for twenty, where now he does it for five. But he and I have lost each other's language, that's what we have! and my dictionary has all got wrong because of those confounded debts – which he will never explain to me, or talk about – me, his old dad, as was his primest favourite of all, when he was a little bit of a chap!'

The Squire felt the dismissal of his work-people very keenly; it fell in with the reproaches of his own conscience, though, as he would repeat to Roger over and over again –

'I couldn't help it – how could I? – I was drained dry of ready money – I wish the land was drained as dry as I am!' said he, with a touch of humour that came out before he was aware, and at which he smiled sadly enough.

'Look here, father!' said Roger suddenly, 'I'll manage somehow about the money for the works. You trust to me; give me two months to turn myself in, and you shall have some money, at any rate, to begin with.'

'But how will you get it? It's hard enough work.'

'Never mind; I'll get it – a hundred or so at first – I don't yet know how – but remember, father, I'm a senior wrangler, and a "very promising young writer", as that review called me. Oh, you don't know what a fine fellow you've got for a son! You should have read that review to know all my wonderful merits.'

'I did, Roger. I heard Gibson speaking of it, and I made him get it for me. I should have understood it better, if they could have called the animals by their English names, and not put so much of their French jingo into it.'

'But it was an answer to an article by a French writer,' pleaded Roger.

'I'd ha' let him alone!' said the Squire earnestly. 'We had to beat 'em, and we did it at Waterloo; but I'd not demean myself by answering any of their lies, if I was you. But I got through the review, and if you doubt me, you just look at the end of the great ledger, turn it upside down, and you'll find I've copied out all the fine words they said of you: "careful observer", "strong nervous English", "rising philosopher". Oh! I can nearly say it all off by heart; for, many a time when I'm frabbed by bad debts, or Osborne's bills, or moidered with accounts, I turn the ledger wrong way up, and smoke a pipe over it, while I read those pieces out of the review which speak about you, lad!'

## CHAPTER 29

# Coming Events

Roger had turned over many plans in his mind, by which he thought that he could obtain sufficient money for the purpose he desired to accomplish. Another distress at this time weighed upon Roger. Osborne, heir to the estate, was going to have a child. The Hamley property was entailed on 'heirs-male born in lawful wedlock'. Was the 'wedlock' lawful? One evening, Roger began to question Osborne as to the details of the marriage.

'My marriage is *bonâ fide* in intention and I believe it to be legal in fact. We went over to Strasbourg! Aimée picked up a friend who served half as bridesmaid, half as chaperon, and then we went before the mayor. I signed all manner of papers in the *préfecture*; I did not read them over, for fear lest I could not sign them conscientiously. Aimée kept trembling so, I thought she would faint; and then we went off to the nearest English chaplaincy, Carlsruhe, and we were married the next day.'

'You must be married again,' said Roger, 'and that before the child is born. Aimée goes to the Roman Catholic chapel at Prestham, doesn't she? Then you shall be married both there and at the church of the parish in which she lives, as well. I'll go down to Aimée next week when I'm in town, and I'll make all necessary arrangements before you come. I think you'll be happier, if it is all done.'

'I shall be happier if I've a chance of seeing the little woman; that I grant you. But what is taking you up to town?'

'Lord Hollingford knows my great wish for employment, and has heard of something which he considers suitable; there's his letter if you care to read it. But it does not tell anything definitely.'

Osborne read the letter and returned it to Roger.

'Why do you want money? Are we taking too much from you? It's a great shame of me; but what can I do? Only suggest a career for me, and I'll follow it tomorrow.'

'My dear fellow, don't get those notions into your head! I must do something for myself some time, and I've been on the look-out. Besides, I want my father to go on with his drainage; it would do good both to his health and his spirits. If I can advance any part of the money requisite, he and you shall pay me interest until you can return the capital.'

So Roger went up to London, and Osborne followed him; and for two or three weeks the Gibsons saw nothing of the brothers. But 'the family', as they were called, came down for their autumn sojourn at the Towers, and again the house was full of visitors.

Mrs Gibson found the chances of intercourse with the Towers rather more personally exciting than Roger's visits, or the rarer calls of Osborne Hamley. Cynthia had an old antipathy to the great family, who had made so much of her mother and so little of her. Moreover, Cynthia missed her slave. The earl and the countess, Lord Hollingford and Lady Harriet, lords and ladies in general, were as nothing to her, compared with Roger's absence. And yet she did not love him. No, she did not love him. Molly knew that Cynthia did not love him. Molly could have cried with passionate regret at the thought of the unvalued treasure lying at Cynthia's feet; and it would have been a merely unselfish regret. Cynthia's love was the moon Roger yearned for; and Molly saw that it was far away and out of reach, else would she have strained her heart-cords to give it to Roger.

'I am his sister,' she would say to herself. 'I must wait and watch, and see if I can do anything for my brother.'

One day Lady Harriet came to call on the Gibsons, or rather on Mrs Gibson; for the latter was jealous of the fancy Lady Harriet had evidently taken for her stepdaughter, and she contrived to place quiet obstacles in the way of a too frequent intercourse between them.

To Lady Harriet it was 'Molly is gone out; she will be sorry to miss you, but she was obliged to go and see some old friends of her mother's whom she ought not to neglect; and I said to her, constancy is everything. But, dear Lady Harriet, you'll stop till she comes home, won't you? I know how fond you are of her.'

To Molly it had previously been –

'Lady Harriet is coming here this morning. I can't have anyone else coming in. Tell Maria to say I'm not at home. Lady Harriet has always so much to tell me; dear Lady Harriet! I've known all her secrets since she was twelve years old. You two girls must keep out of the way. Of course she'll ask for you, out of common civility; but you would only interrupt us if you came in, as you did the other day;' – now addressing Molly – 'I hardly like to say so, but I thought it was very forward.'

'Maria told me she had asked for me,' put in Molly simply.

'Very forward indeed!' continued Mrs Gibson, taking no notice. 'I think, this time, I must secure her ladyship from the chances of such an intrusion, by taking care that you are out of the house, Molly. You had better go to the Holly Farm, and speak about those damsons I ordered.'

'I'll go,' said Cynthia. 'It's far too long a walk for Molly; she's had a bad cold, and isn't as strong as she was. If you want Molly out of the way, mamma, send her to the Miss Brownings; they are always glad to see her.'

'I never said I wanted Molly out of the way, Cynthia,' replied Mrs Gibson. 'You always put things in such an exaggerated – I might almost say, so coarse a manner. I am sure, Molly, my love, you could never have so misunderstood me. Suppose you do go and see Miss Browning; you can pay her a nice long call, you know she likes that; and ask after Miss Phoebe's cold from me, you know.'

'Now, mamma, where am I to go?' asked Cynthia. 'Though Lady Harriet doesn't care for me as much as she does for Molly, yet she might ask after me, and I had better be safely out of the way.'

'True!' said Mrs Gibson, unconscious of any satire in Cynthia's speech. 'She is much less likely to ask after you, my dear: I almost think you might remain in the house, so as to be ready to arrange lunch prettily, if she does take a fancy to stay for it. I would not like her to think we made any difference in our meals because she stayed. "Simple elegance," as I tell her, "always is what we aim at." But still you could put out the best service, and arrange some flowers, and ask cook what there is for dinner that she could send us for lunch, and make it all look pretty, and impromptu, and natural. I think you had better stay at home, and then you could fetch Molly in the afternoon, and you two could take a walk together.'

'After Lady Harriet was fairly gone! I understand, mamma. Off with you, Molly! Make haste, or Lady Harriet may come and ask for you as well as mamma! I'll take care and forget where you are going to, so that no one shall learn from me where you are, and I'll answer for mamma's loss of memory.'

'Child! what nonsense you talk; you quite confuse me with being so silly,' said Mrs Gibson, fluttered and annoyed as she usually was with the Lilliputian darts Cynthia flung at her.

Lady Harriet was sorry to miss Molly, as she was fond of the girl; but sat down in a little low chair with her feet on the fender. This fender was made of bright steel, and was strictly tabooed to all household and plebeian feet; indeed the position, if they assumed it, was considered low-bred and vulgar.

'That's right, dear Lady Harriet! you can't think what a pleasure it is to me to welcome you at my own fireside, into my humble home.'

'Humble! now, Clare, that's a little bit of nonsense. I don't call this pretty little drawing-room a bit of a "humble home". It's as full of comforts, and of pretty things too, as any room of its size can be.'

'Ah! how small you must feel it! even I had to reconcile myself to it at first.'

'Well! perhaps your school-room was larger, but remember how bare it was, how empty of anything but deal tables, and forms, and mats. Oh, indeed, Clare, I quite agree with mamma, who always says you have done very well for yourself; and Mr Gibson too! What an agreeable, well-informed man!'

'Yes, he is,' said his wife slowly, as if she did not like to relinquish her role of a victim to circumstances quite immediately. 'He is very agreeable, very; only we see so little of him; and of course he comes home tired and hungry, and not inclined to talk to his own family, and apt to go to sleep.'

'Come, come!' said Lady Harriet, 'We've had the complaint of a doctor's wife; now hear the moans of a peer's daughter! Our house is so overrun with visitors! and literally today I have come to you for a little solitude.'

'Solitude! Would you rather be alone?' slightly aggrieved.

'No, you dear silly woman; my solitude requires a listener, to whom I may say, "how sweet is solitude!" But I am tired of the responsibility of entertaining. Papa asks every friend he meets with to come and pay us a visit. Mamma is really a great invalid; but she does not choose to give up her reputation for good health, having always considered illness a want of self-control. So she gets wearied and worried by a crowd of people who are all of them open-mouthed for amusement of some kind; just like a brood of fledglings in a nest; so I have to be parent-bird, and pop morsels into their yellow leathery bills, to find them swallowed down before I can think of where to find the next. So I have told a few lies this morning, and come off here for quietness and the comfort of complaining!'

Lady Harriet threw herself back in her chair, and yawned; Mrs Gibson took one of her ladyship's hands in a soft sympathising manner, and murmured –

'Poor Lady Harriet!' and then she purred affectionately.

After a pause Lady Harriet started up and said –

'Can you give me some lunch, Clare? I don't mean to go home till three.'

'Certainly. I shall be delighted! but you know we are very simple in our habits.'

'Oh, I only want a little bread-and-butter, and perhaps a slice of cold meat – perhaps you dine now? let me sit down just like one of your family.'

'Yes, you shall; I won't make any alteration; – it will be so pleasant to have you sharing our family-meal, dear Lady Harriet. But we dine late; we only lunch now. How low the fire is getting; I really am forgetting everything in the pleasure of this *tête-à-tête*!'

So she rang twice; with great distinctness, and with a long pause between the rings. Maria brought in coals.

But the signal was as well understood by Cynthia. The brace of partridges that were to have been for the late dinner were instantly put down to the fire; and the prettiest china brought out, and the table decked with flowers and fruit, arranged with all Cynthia's usual dexterity and taste. So that, when the meal was announced, and Lady Harriet entered the room, she could not but think her hostess's apologies had been quite unnecessary, and be more and more convinced that Clare had done very well for herself. Cynthia now joined the party, pretty and elegant as she always was; but, somehow, she did not take Lady Harriet's fancy. Her presence made the conversation more general, and Lady Harriet gave out several pieces of news, none of them of any great importance to her, but as what had been talked about by the circle of visitors assembled at the Towers.

'Lord Hollingford ought to have been with us,' she said, amongst other things; 'but he is obliged, or fancies himself obliged, to stay in town about this Crichton legacy!'

'A legacy? To Lord Hollingford? I am so glad!'

'Don't be in a hurry to be glad! It's nothing for him but trouble. Didn't you hear of that rich eccentric Mr Crichton, who died some time ago, and left a sum of money in the hands of trustees, of whom my brother is one, to send out a man with a thousand fine qualifications, to make a scientific voyage, with a view to bringing back specimens of the fauna of distant lands, and so forming the nucleus of a museum which is to be called the Crichton Museum. Such forms does man's vanity take! Hollingford thinks he is going to be very successful in the choice of his man – and he belongs to this county, too – young Hamley of Hamley, if he can only get his college to let him go, for he is a Fellow of Trinity; and they're not so foolish as to send their crack man to be eaten up by lions and tigers!'

'It must be Roger Hamley!' exclaimed Cynthia, her cheeks flushing. 'What news for Molly when she comes home!'

Lady Harriet said –

'And where is Molly all this time? I should like to see my little mentor. I hear she is very much grown since those days.'

'Oh! when she gets gossiping with the Miss Brownings, she never knows when to come home,' said Mrs Gibson.

'The Miss Brownings? Oh! I'm so glad you named them! I'm very fond of them. Pecksy and Flapsy. I'll go and see them before I go home, and then perhaps I shall see my dear Molly too. Do you know, Clare, I've quite taken a fancy to that girl!'

So Mrs Gibson, after all her precautions, had to submit to Lady Harriet's leaving her half-an-hour earlier than she otherwise would have done in order to 'make herself common' (as Mrs Gibson expressed it) by calling on the Miss Brownings.

That night at dinner, Mrs Gibson repeated the conversation between herself and Lady Harriet, giving it a very strong individual colouring, as was her wont, and telling nearly the whole of what had passed, although implying that there was a great deal said which was so purely confidential, that she was bound in honour not to repeat it. Her three auditors listened without bestowing extreme attention on what she was saying, until she came to the fact of Lord Hollingford's absence in London, and the reason for it.

'Roger Hamley going off on a scientific expedition!' exclaimed Mr Gibson.

'Yes. It is next to certain.'

'How long will he be away?' asked Cynthia. 'We shall miss him sadly.'

Molly's lips formed an acquiescing 'yes' to this remark, but no sound was heard. There was a buzzing in her ears as if the others were going on with the conversation; but the words they uttered seemed indistinct and blurred; they were merely conjectures, and did not interfere with the one great piece of news.

## CHAPTER 30

# Brightening Prospects

It was a day or two afterwards that Mr Gibson made time to ride round by Hamley, desirous to learn more exact particulars of this scheme for Roger, and rather puzzled to know whether he should interfere in the project or not. The state of the case was this. Osborne's symptoms were, in Mr Gibson's opinion, signs of his having a fatal disease. Dr Nicholls had differed from him on this head; still, Mr Gibson believed that he himself was right, and, if so, the complaint was one which might continue for years in the same state as at present, or might end the young man's life in an hour – a minute. Supposing that Mr Gibson was right, would it be well for Roger to be away where no sudden calls for his presence could reach him – away for two years? Yet, if the affair was concluded, the interference of a medical man might accelerate the very evil to be feared; and, after all, Dr Nicholls might be right, and the symptoms might proceed from some other cause. Mr Gibson rode on, meditating. It was one of those still and lovely autumn days, when the red and yellow leaves are hanging-pegs to dewy, brilliant gossamer-webs; when the hedges are full of trailing brambles, loaded with ripe blackberries; when the air is full of the farewell whistles and pipes of birds, clear and short, and there a leaf floats and flutters down to the ground, although there is not a single breath of wind. The country surgeon felt the beauty of the seasons, perhaps more than most men. He saw more of it by day, by night, in storm and sunshine, or in the still, soft cloudy weather. He never spoke about what he felt on the subject; indeed, he did not put his feelings into words, even to himself. But, if his mood ever approached to the sentimental, it was on such days as this. He rode into the stable-yard, gave his horse to a man, and went into the house by a side-entrance. In the passage he met the Squire.

'That's capital, Gibson! What good wind blew you here? You'll have some lunch? I only just this minute left the room.' And he kept shaking Mr Gibson's hand all the time till he had placed him at the well-covered dining-table.

'What's this I hear about Roger?' said Mr Gibson, plunging at once into the subject.

'Aha! It's famous, isn't it? He's a boy to be proud of, is old Roger! We used to think him slow, but it seems to me that slow and sure wins the race. But tell me; what have you heard? There's a deal to hear, and all good news; though I shall miss the lad, I know that.'

'I did not know that it was settled; I only heard that it was in progress.'

'Well, it was only in progress, as you call it, till last Tuesday. He thought I might be fidgety with thinking of the *pros* and *cons*. So I never knew a word on't till I had a letter from my Lord Hollingford – where is it? Here it is. Now, read that letter!' handing it to Mr Gibson.

It was a manly, feeling, sensible letter, explaining to the old father in very simple language the services which were demanded by the terms of the will to which the writer and two or three others were trustees; the liberal allowance for expenses; the still more liberal reward for performance, which had tempted several men of considerable renown to offer themselves as candidates for the appointment. Lord Hollingford then went on to say that, having seen a good deal of Roger lately, since the publication of his article in reply to the French osteologist, he had had reason to think that in him the trustees would find united the various qualities required, in a greater measure than in any of the applicants who had at that time presented themselves. The remuneration offered was liberal; and then he read with attention the high praise bestowed on the son in this letter to the father.

'Ay! you've come to it at last. It's the best part of the whole, isn't it. God bless the boy! And there's more to come still. I say, Gibson,

I think my luck is turning at last,' passing him on yet another letter to read. 'That only came this morning; but I've acted on it already, I sent for the foreman of the drainage works at once, and tomorrow, please God, they'll be at work again.'

Mr Gibson read the second letter, from Roger. To a certain degree it was a modest repetition of what Lord Hollingford had said, with an explanation of how he had come to take so decided a step in life without consulting his father. He felt that, by accepting this offer, he entered upon the kind of life for which he knew himself to be most fitted. And he said that he knew well the suffering his father had gone through, when he had to give up his drainage works for want of money; that he, Roger, had been enabled at once to raise money upon the remuneration he was to receive on the accomplishment of two years' work; and that he had also insured his life, in order to provide for the repayment of the money he had raised, in case he did not live to return to England. He said that the sum he had borrowed on this security would at once be forwarded to his father.

'I wish I could tell his mother,' said the Squire in an undertone.

'It seems all settled now,' said Mr Gibson, more in reply to his own thoughts than to the Squire's remark.

'Yes!' said the Squire; 'he's to be off as soon as he can get his scientific traps ready. I almost wish he wasn't to go. You don't seem quite to like it, doctor?'

'Yes, I do,' said Mr Gibson, in a more cheerful tone than before. 'It can't be helped now, without doing a mischief,' thought he to himself. 'Why, Squire, I think it a great honour to have such a son. I envy you, that's what I do!'

'Ay, ay; he's twice as much a son to me as Osborne, who has been all his life set up on nothing at all, as one may say.'

'Come, Squire, I mustn't hear anything against Osborne. Osborne hasn't had the strong health which has enabled Roger to work as he has done. I met a man who knew his tutor at Trinity the other day, and of course we began cracking about Roger. This Mr Mason told me, the tutor said that only half of Roger's success was owing to his mental powers; the other half was owing to his perfect health, which enabled him to work harder and more continuously than most men without suffering. Now I, being a doctor, trace a good deal of his superiority to the material cause of a thoroughly good constitution, which Osborne hasn't got.'

'Osborne might have, if he got out o' doors more,' said the Squire moodily; 'but, except when he can loaf into Hollingford, he doesn't care to go out at all. I hope,' he continued, 'he's not after one of your girls? I don't mean any offence, you know; but he'll have the estate, and it won't be free, and he must marry money.'

Mr Gibson spoke quietly, if shortly.

'I don't believe there's anything of the kind going on. I'm not much at home, you know; but I've never heard or seen anything that should make me suppose that there is. When I do, I'll let you know.'

'Now, Gibson, don't go and be offended! I'm glad for the boys to have a pleasant house to go to, and I thank you and Mrs Gibson for making it pleasant. Only keep off love; it can come to no good. That's all. I don't believe Osborne will ever earn a farthing to keep a wife during my life; and, if I were to die tomorrow, she would have to bring some money to clear the estate. And, if I do speak as I shouldn't have done formerly – a little sharp or so – why, it's because I've been worried by many a care no one knows anything of.'

'I'm not going to take offence,' said Mr Gibson; 'but let us understand each other clearly. If you don't want your sons to come as much to my house as they do, tell them so yourself. But, if they do come, you must take the consequences, whatever they are, and not blame me, or them either, for what may happen from the frequent intercourse between two young men and two young women. If there's an attachment at any future time, I won't interfere.'

'I shouldn't so much mind if Roger fell in love with your Molly. He can fight for himself, you see, and she's an uncommon nice girl. It's Osborne and the estate I'm thinking of!'

'Well, then, tell him not to come near us! I shall be sorry, but you will be safe. As I said, there's no harm done as yet, as far as I know. Speak out, but speak gently to Osborne, and do it at once! If you speak gently to him, he'll take the advice as from a friend.'

It was all very fine giving the Squire this good advice; but, as Osborne had already formed the very kind of marriage his father most deprecated, it did not act quite as well as Mr Gibson had hoped. The Squire began the conversation with unusual self-control; but he grew irritated, when Osborne denied his father's right to interfere in any marriage he might contemplate. Each had said bitter things to the other, and the end to poor Osborne was that he became moody and depressed in mind and body. Both father and son, however, concealed their feelings in Roger's presence. When he came home just before sailing, busy and happy, the Squire caught his infectious energy, and Osborne looked up and was cheerful.

The last day he rode into Hollingford earlier than he needed to have done to catch the London coach, in order to bid the Gibsons good-bye. He had been too actively busy for some time to have leisure to bestow much thought on Cynthia; but there was no need for fresh meditation on that subject. Her image as a prize to be worked for, to be served for seven years, and seven years more, was safe and sacred in his heart.

CHAPTER 31

# A Lover's Mistake

It was afternoon. Molly had gone out for a walk. Mrs Gibson had been paying some calls. Lazy Cynthia had declined accompanying either. Indeed, not one of the ladies would have left the house, had they been aware that Roger was in the neighbourhood; for they were all anxious to wish him good-bye before his long absence.

Molly chose a walk that had been a favourite with her ever since she was a child and her eye was caught by the sight of some fine ripe blackberries flourishing away, high up on the hedge-bank among scarlet hips and green and russet leaves. She did not care much for blackberries herself; but she had heard Cynthia say that she liked them, so she went climbing up the banks, and clutching at her almost inaccessible prizes, and slipping down again triumphant, to carry them back to the large leaf which was to serve her as a basket. The skirt of her pretty print gown was torn out of the gathers when she set off home, hoping to escape into her room and mend her gown, before it had offended Mrs Gibson's neat eye. The front-door was easily opened and Molly was in the shadow of the hall when she saw a face peep out of the dining-room; then Mrs Gibson came softly out, sufficiently at least to beckon her into the room. When Molly had entered, Mrs Gibson closed the door. Poor Molly expected a reprimand, but was soon relieved by the expression of Mrs Gibson's face – mysterious and radiant.

'I've been watching for you, dear. Don't go upstairs into the drawing-room, love! Roger Hamley is there with Cynthia; and I've reason to think – Isn't it charming? Young love, you know, ah, how sweet it is!'

'Do you mean that Roger has proposed to Cynthia?'

'I don't know; all I wanted was, to let him come to a crisis without interruption. So I've been watching for you.'

'But I may go to my own room, mayn't I?' pleaded Molly.

'Of course,' said Mrs Gibson, a little testily.

Molly escaped upstairs, and shut the door. Instinctively she had carried her leaf full of blackberries – what would blackberries be to Cynthia now? For a few minutes, her brain seemed in too great a whirl to comprehend anything. Then the room grew stifling, and instinctively she went to the open casement window, and leant out, gasping for breath. Gradually, the consciousness of the soft peaceful landscape stole into her mind, and stilled the buzzing confusion. Then she heard an opened door, steps on the lower flight of stairs. He could not have gone without even seeing her. He never, never would have done so cruel a thing! No! there were steps and voices, and the drawing-room door was opened and shut once more. She laid down her head on her arms that rested upon the window-sill, and cried – she had been so distrustful as to have let the idea enter her mind that he could go without wishing her good-bye. Suddenly, the drawing-room door opened, and some one was heard coming upstairs; it was Cynthia's step. Molly hastily wiped her eyes, and stood up and tried to look unconcerned; it was all she had time to do, before Cynthia had knocked and, on answer being given, had said, without opening the door – 'Molly! Mr Roger Hamley is here, and wants to wish you good-bye before he goes.' Then she went downstairs again, as if anxious to avoid even so short a *tête-à-tête* with Molly. With a gulp and a fit of resolution, as when a child makes up its mind to swallow a nauseous dose of medicine, Molly went instantly down to the drawing-room.

Roger was talking earnestly to Mrs Gibson in the bow of the window when Molly entered; Cynthia was standing near, listening, but taking no part in the conversation. Her eyes were downcast. Roger was saying – 'I could never forgive myself, if I had accepted a pledge from her. She shall be free till my return; but the hope, the words, her sweet goodness, have made me happy beyond description. Oh, Molly!' suddenly becoming aware of her presence, and turning to her, and taking her hand in both of his. 'I have told Cynthia how fondly I love her, as far as words can tell; and she says –' then he looked at Cynthia with passionate delight, and seemed to forget in that gaze that he had left his sentence to Molly half-finished.

Cynthia did not seem inclined to repeat her saying, whatever it was, but her mother spoke for her.

'My dear, sweet girl values your love as it ought to be valued, I am sure. And I believe I could tell tales as to the cause of her indisposition in the spring.'

'Mother,' said Cynthia suddenly, 'pray don't invent stories about me! I have engaged myself to Mr Roger Hamley, and that is enough.'

'Enough! more than enough!' said Roger. 'I will not accept your pledge. I am bound, but you are free. I like to feel bound; but, with all the chances involved in the next two years, you must not shackle yourself by promises.'

Mrs Gibson took up the word.

'You are very generous, I am sure. Perhaps it will be better not to mention it.'

'I would much rather have it kept a secret,' said Cynthia, interrupting. 'Please, Roger! Please, Molly! Mamma, I must especially beg it of you!'

Roger took her hand in silent pledge of his reply. Molly felt as if she could never bring herself to name the affair as a common piece of news. So it was only Mrs Gibson that answered aloud –

'My dear child! why "especially" of poor me? You know I'm the most trustworthy person alive!'

The little pendule on the chimney-piece struck the half-hour.

'I must go!' said Roger, in dismay. 'I had no idea it was so late. I shall write from Paris. The coach will be at the George by this time, and will only stay five minutes. Dearest Cynthia –' he took her hand; and then, as if the temptation was irresistible, he drew her to him and kissed her. 'Only remember you are free!' said he, as he released her and passed on to Mrs Gibson.

'If I had considered myself free,' said Cynthia, blushing a little, 'if I thought myself free, do you think I would have allowed that?'

Then Molly's turn came, and the old brotherly tenderness came back into his look, his voice, his bearing.

'Molly! you won't forget me, I know; I shall never forget you, nor your goodness to – her.' His voice began to quiver, and it was best to be gone. Mrs Gibson was pouring out unheard and unheeded words of farewell; Cynthia was re-arranging some flowers in a vase on the table. Molly stood, numb to the heart. She felt the slackened touch of the warm grasping hand; she looked up – for till now her eyes had been downcast, as if there were heavy weights to their lids – and the place was empty where he had been. Quick as lightning, Molly ran up to the front attic, whose window commanded the street down which he must pass.

'I must see him again; I must! I must!' she wailed. There he was, running hard to catch the London coach. In all his hurry, Molly saw him turn round and shade his eyes from the westering sun, and rake the house with his glances – in hopes, she knew, of catching one more glimpse of Cynthia. But apparently he saw no one, not even Molly at the attic casement; for she had drawn back when he turned, and kept herself in shadow; for she had no right to put herself forward as the one to watch and yearn for farewell signs. None came – another moment – he was out of sight for years!

## CHAPTER 32

# The Mother's Manoeuvre

Mrs Gibson took a seat by the fire in the dining-room, and patiently waited for the auspicious moment when Mr Gibson, having satisfied his healthy appetite, turned from the table, and took his place by her side.

'There, now! are you comfortable? for I have a great piece of news to tell you!' said she.

'I thought there was something on hand,' said he, smiling. 'Now for it!'

'Roger Hamley has been here this afternoon to bid us goodbye. Yes, yes. He felt love and regret, and all that sort of thing for you – and he found Cynthia alone, proposed to her, and was accepted.'

'Cynthia? Roger proposed to her, and she accepted him?'

'Yes, to be sure. Why not? you speak as if it was something so very surprising.'

'Did I? But I am surprised. And I wish Cynthia joy; but do you like it? It will have to be a very long engagement.'

'Perhaps,' said she, in a knowing manner.

'At any rate, he will be away for two years,' said Mr Gibson.

'A great deal may happen in two years,' she replied.

'Yes! he will have to run many risks, and go into many dangers, and will come back no nearer to the power of maintaining a wife than when he went out.'

'I don't know that,' she replied. 'A little bird did tell me that Osborne's life is not so very secure; and then – what will Roger be? Heir to the estate.'

'Who told you that about Osborne?' said he, frightening her by his sternness of voice and manner. '*Who* told you, I say?'

She made a faint rally back into her former playfulness.

'Why? can you deny it? Is it not the truth?'

'I ask you again, Hyacinth: who told you that Osborne Hamley's life is in more danger than mine – or yours?'

'Well, if you will know, and will make such a fuss about it,' said she, 'it was you yourself – you or Dr Nicholls.'

'I never spoke to you on the subject, and I don't believe Nicholls did. You'd better tell me at once what you're alluding to, for I'm resolved I'll have it out before we leave this room.'

'I wish I'd never married again!' she said, now fairly crying, and looking round the room, as if in vain search for a mouse-hole in which to hide herself. Then, as if the sight of the door into the store-room gave her courage, she turned and faced him.

'You should not talk your medical secrets so loud then, if you don't want people to hear them. I had to go into the store-room that day Dr Nicholls was here; cook wanted a jar of preserve.'

'Well! you overheard our conversation, I suppose?'

'Not much,' she answered eagerly. 'Only a sentence or two.'

'What were they?' he asked.

'Why, you had just been saying something, and Dr Nicholls said, "If he has got aneurism of the aorta, his days are numbered."'

'Well. Anything more?'

'Yes; you said, "I hope to God I may be mistaken; but there is a pretty clear indication of symptoms, in my opinion."'

'How do you know we were speaking of Osborne Hamley?' he asked.

'Oh! I heard his name mentioned before I began to listen.'

'Then you own you did listen?'

'Yes,' said she, hesitating a little now.

'And pray how do you come to remember so exactly the name of the disease spoken of?'

'Because I went – now don't be angry – I went into the surgery, and looked it out. Why might not I?'

Mr Gibson did not look at her. His face was very pale. At length he roused himself, sighed, and said –

'Well! I suppose as one brews one must bake. You overheard – I will own that it was Osborne about whom we were speaking – and then you changed your behaviour to Roger, and made him more welcome to this house than you had ever done before, regarding him as proximate heir to the Hamley estates?'

'I don't know what you mean by "proximate".'

'Go into the surgery, and look in the dictionary, then,' said he, losing his temper.

'I knew', said she through sobs and tears, 'that Roger had taken a fancy to Cynthia; and as long as Roger was only a younger son, with nothing but his fellowship, I thought it right to discourage him, as anyone would who had a grain of common sense in them; for a clumsier, more common, awkward, stupid fellow I never saw.'

'Take care; you'll have to eat your words presently, when you come to fancy he'll have Hamley some day.'

'No, I shan't,' said she. 'You are vexed now because it is not Molly he's in love with; and I call it very unjust and unfair to my poor fatherless girl. I am sure I have always tried to further Molly's interests as if she was my own daughter.'

Mr Gibson was too indifferent to this accusation to take any notice of it.

'The point I want to be clear about is this. Did you or did you not alter your behaviour to Roger, in consequence of what you overheard of my professional conversation with Dr Nicholls? Have you not favoured his suit to Cynthia since then, on the understanding gathered from that conversation that he stood a good chance of inheriting Hamley?'

'I suppose I have,' said she sulkily. 'And I can't see any harm in it, that I should be questioned as if I were in a witness-box.'

'Don't you know that all professional conversations are confidential? That it would be the most dishonourable thing possible for me to betray secrets which I learn in the exercise of my profession?'

'Yes, of course, you.'

'Well! and are not you and I one in all these respects? If it would be a deep disgrace for me to betray a professional secret, what would it be for me to trade on that knowledge?'

'I don't know what you mean by trading. Trading in a daughter's affections is the last thing I should do; and I should have thought you would be rather glad than otherwise to get Cynthia well-married, and off your hands.'

Mr Gibson got up, and walked about the room, his hands in his pockets.

'I don't know what to say to you,' he said at length. 'You either can't or won't see what I mean. I'm glad enough to have Cynthia here. But for the future I must look outside my doors, and double-lock the approaches, if I am so foolish as to – However, that's past and gone; and it remains with me to prevent its recurrence, as far as I can, for the future. Now let us hear the present state of affairs.'

'I don't think I ought to tell you anything about it. It is a secret, just as much as your mysteries are.'

'Very well; you have told me enough for me to act upon, which I most certainly shall do. It was only the other day I promised the Squire to let him know if I suspected anything – any love-affair, or entanglement, much less an engagement, between either of his sons and our girls.'

'But this is not an engagement; he would not let it be so. Only, I do hope you won't go and tell the Squire. Cynthia did so beg that it might not be known. It is only my unfortunate frankness that has led me into this scrape. I never could keep a secret from those whom I love.'

'I must tell the Squire. I shall not mention it to anyone else. And do you quite think it was consistent with your general frankness to have overheard what you did, and never to have mentioned it to me? I could have told you then that Dr Nicholls' believed that the disturbance about which I consulted him on Osborne's behalf was merely temporary. Dr Nicholls would tell you that Osborne is as likely as any man to live and marry and beget children.'

If there was any skill used by Mr Gibson so to word this speech as to conceal his own opinion, Mrs Gibson was not sharp enough to find it out. She was dismayed, and Mr Gibson enjoyed her dismay.

'Let us review this misfortune, for I see you consider it as such,' said he.

'No, not quite a misfortune,' said she. 'But certainly, if I had known Dr Nicholls' opinion' – she hesitated.

'You see the advantage of always consulting me,' he continued gravely. 'Here is Cynthia engaged'–

'Not engaged, I told you before. He would not allow it to be considered an engagement on her part.'

'Well, entangled in a love-affair with a lad of three-and-twenty, with nothing beyond his fellowship and a chance of inheriting an encumbered estate; no profession even, abroad for two years, and I must go and tell his father all about it.'

'Oh dear, pray say that, if he dislikes it, he has only to express his opinion.'

'I don't think you can act without Cynthia in the affair. And, if I am not mistaken, Cynthia will have a pretty stout will of her own on the subject.'

'Oh, I don't think she cares for him very much; she does not take things very deeply to heart. But, of course, one would not do anything abruptly; two years' absence gives one plenty of time to turn oneself in.'

'Then I'm quite at liberty to give up the affair, acting as Cynthia's proxy, if the Squire disapproves of it?'

Poor Mrs Gibson was in a strait at this question.

'No!' she said at last. 'We cannot give it up. I am sure Cynthia would not; especially if she thought others were acting for her. And he really is very much in love. I wish he were in Osborne's place!'

'Shall I tell you what I should do?' said Mr Gibson, in real earnest. 'However it may have been brought about, here are two young people in love with each other. One is as fine a young fellow as ever breathed; the other a very pretty, lively, agreeable girl. The father of the young man must be told, and it is most likely he will bluster and oppose. But let them be steady and patient, and a better lot need await no young woman. I only wish it were Molly's good fortune to meet with such another!'

'I will try for her; I will indeed,' said Mrs Gibson, relieved by his change of tone.

'No, don't! That's one thing I forbid. I'll have no "trying" for Molly.'

'Well, don't be angry, dear! Do you know I was quite afraid you were going to lose your temper at one time.'

'It would have been of no use!' said he gloomily. The conjugal interview had not been satisfactory to either. Mr Gibson had been compelled to face and acknowledge the fact, that the wife he had chosen had a very different standard of conduct from that which he had upheld all his life, and had hoped to have seen inculcated in his daughter. He followed his wife up to the drawing-room, and gravely congratulated the astonished Cynthia.

'Has mamma told you?' said she, shooting an indignant glance at her mother. 'It is hardly an engagement; and we all pledged ourselves to keep it a secret, mamma among the rest!'

'But my dearest Cynthia, you could not expect – you could not have wished me to keep a secret from my husband?' pleaded Mrs Gibson.

'No, perhaps not. At any rate, sir,' said Cynthia, 'I am glad you should know it. You have always been a most kind friend to me, and I daresay I should have told you myself, but I did not want it named; if you please, it must still be a secret. In fact, it is hardly an engagement – he would not allow me to bind myself by any promise until his return!'

Mr Gibson looked gravely at her, irresponsive to her winning looks, which at the moment reminded him too forcibly of her mother's ways. Then he took her hand, and said, seriously enough – 'I hope you are worthy of him, Cynthia; for you have indeed drawn a prize. I have never known a truer or warmer heart than Roger's; and I have known him boy and man.'

Molly felt as if she could have thanked her father aloud for this testimony to the value of him who was gone away.

'I hope you will not consider it a breach of confidence, Cynthia; but I must tell the Squire of – of what has taken place today between you and his son. I have bound myself by a promise to him. He was afraid – it's as well to tell you the truth – he was afraid of something of this kind between his sons and one of you two girls. It was only the other day I assured him there was nothing of the kind on foot; and I told him then I would inform him at once, if I saw any symptoms.'

Cynthia looked extremely annoyed.

'It was the one thing I stipulated for – secrecy.'

'But why?' said Mr Gibson. 'I can understand your not wishing to have it made public under the present circumstances. But the nearest friends on both sides! Surely you can have no objection to that?'

'Yes, I have,' said Cynthia; 'I would not have had anyone know, if I could have helped it.'

'I'm almost certain Roger will tell his father.'

'No, he won't,' said Cynthia; 'I made him promise, and I think he is one to respect a promise' – with a glance at her mother, who, feeling herself in disgrace with both husband and child, was keeping a judicious silence.

'Will you trust in my reasons when I tell you it will cause me a great deal of distress if it gets known?' Cynthia said this in so pleading a voice that, if Mr Gibson had not been thoroughly displeased by his previous conversation with her mother, he must have yielded to her. As it was, he said coldly – 'Telling Roger's father is not making it public. I don't like this exaggerated desire for such secrecy. It seems to me as if something more than is apparent was concealed behind it.'

'Come, Molly,' said Cynthia suddenly; 'let us sing that duet I've been teaching you; it's better than talking as we are doing.'

It was a little lively French duet. Molly sang it carelessly, with heaviness at her heart; but Cynthia sang it with spirit and apparent merriment; only she broke down in hysterics at last, and flew upstairs to her own room. Molly followed her, and found the door of her bed-room locked; and Cynthia crying.

It was more than a week after the incidents just recorded, before Mr Gibson found himself at liberty to call on the Squire; and he heartily hoped that, long before then, Roger's letter might have arrived from Paris, telling his father the whole story. But he saw at the first glance that the Squire had heard nothing unusual to disturb his equanimity. He was looking better than he had done for months past. The first greetings over, Mr Gibson plunged into his subject.

'Any news from Roger yet?'

'Oh, yes; here's his letter,' said the Squire.

Mr Gibson read it, hardly seeing by one rapid glance that there was no mention of Cynthia in it.

'Hum! I see he doesn't name one very important event that has befallen him since he left you,' said Mr Gibson. 'I believe I'm committing a breach of confidence on one side; but I'm going to keep the promise I made the last time I was here. I find there is something between him and my stepdaughter, Cynthia Kirkpatrick. He called at our house to wish us good-bye, while waiting for the London coach, found her alone, and spoke to her. They don't call it an engagement; but of course it is one.'

'No!' the Squire said with a sigh. 'Lads may play at confidences with their fathers, but they keep a deal back.'

The Squire appeared more disappointed at not having heard of this straight from Roger than displeased at the fact itself, Mr Gibson thought.

'He's not the eldest son,' continued the Squire. 'But it's not the match I should have planned for him. How came you, sir,' said he, firing round on Mr Gibson suddenly – 'to say when you were last here, that there was nothing between my sons and either of your girls? Why, this must have been going on all the time!'

'I'm afraid it was. But I was ignorant about it. I only heard of it on the evening of the day of Roger's departure.'

'That's a week ago, sir. What's kept you quiet ever since?'

'I thought that Roger would tell you himself.'

'That shows you've no sons. Is it a folly, or is it not? I ask you, for you know this girl. She hasn't money, I suppose?'

'About thirty pounds a year, at my pleasure, during her mother's life.'

'Whew! It's well he's not Osborne. They'll have to wait. What family is she of?'

'I believe her father was grandson of a certain Sir Gerald Kirkpatrick. Her mother tells me it is an old baronetcy. I know nothing of such things.'

'That's something. I do know something of such things, as you are pleased to call them. I like honourable blood. How old is she?'

'Eighteen or nineteen.'

'Pretty?'

'Yes, I think so; but it's all a matter of taste. Come, Squire, ride over and take lunch with us any day you like, and make acquaintance with your son's future wife.'

This was going too fast. Mr Hamley drew back within his shell, and spoke in a surly manner –

'Roger's "future wife"! But you said it was no engagement. If he thinks better of it, you won't keep him to it, will you?'

'If he wishes to break it off, I shall certainly advise Cynthia to be equally willing.' And he took up his hat to go.

'Don't go, Gibson! Don't take offence at what I've said, though I'm sure I don't know why you should. What's the girl like in herself?'

'I don't know what you mean,' said Mr Gibson. But he did; only he was vexed, and did not choose to understand.

'Is she – well, is she like your Molly? – sweet-tempered and sensible – with her gloves always mended, and neat about the feet, and ready to do anything one asks her, just as if doing it was the very thing she liked best in the world?'

Mr Gibson's face relaxed now, and he could understand all the Squire's meanings.

'She's much prettier than Molly, and has very winning ways. She's always well-dressed and smart-looking, and I know she hasn't much to spend on her clothes, and always does what she's asked to do, and is ready enough with her pretty, lively answers.

I don't think I ever saw her out of temper; but then I'm not sure if she takes things keenly to heart, and a certain obtuseness of feeling goes a great way towards a character for good temper, I've noticed. Altogether I think Cynthia is one in a hundred.'

The Squire meditated a little.

'Your Molly is one in a thousand, to my mind. But then, you see, she comes of no family at all – and I don't suppose she'll have a chance of much money.' This he said as if he were thinking aloud, and without reference to Mr Gibson; but it nettled the latter, and he replied somewhat impatiently –

'Well, but, as there's no question of Molly in this business, I don't see the use of bringing her name in, and considering either her family or her fortune.'

'No, to be sure not,' said the Squire. 'My wits had gone far afield, and I'll own I was only thinking what a pity it was she wouldn't do for Osborne. But, of course, it's out of the question – out of the question.'

'Yes,' said Mr Gibson, 'and if you will excuse me, Squire, I really must go now, and then you'll be at liberty to send your wits afield uninterrupted.' This time he was at the door, before the Squire called him back.

'I say, Gibson, we're old friends, and you're a fool if you take anything I say as an offence. Madam your wife and I didn't hit it off, the only time I ever saw her. I won't say she was silly; but I think one of us was silly, and it wasn't me. However, we'll pass that over. Suppose you bring her and this girl Cynthia (which is as outlandish a Christian name as I'd wish to hear), and little Molly, out here to lunch some day – I'm more at my ease in my own house – and I'm more sure to be civil, too. We need say nothing about Roger and you keep your wife's tongue quiet, if you can. Osborne will be here too; and he's always in his element talking to women.'

The next Thursday was soon fixed upon as the day on which Mr Gibson was to bring his womenkind out to the Hall. He thought that, on the whole, the interview had gone off a good deal better than he expected.

They went on the day appointed and Mr Gibson was very curious to know how the visit had gone off, taking the first opportunity of being alone with Molly to question her.

'And so you went to Hamley?'

'Yes; I thought you would have come. The Squire seemed quite to expect you.'

'I thought of going there at first; but I changed my mind. Well! how did it go off?'

'The dear old Squire was in his best dress and on his best behaviour, and was so prettily attentive to Cynthia; and she looked so lovely, walking about with him, and listening to all his talk about the garden and farm. Mamma was tired, and stopped indoors.'

'And my little girl trotted behind?'

'Oh, yes. You know I was almost at home.'

'Do you think she's worthy of him?' asked her father.

'Of Roger, papa? oh, who is? But she's very sweet, and very, very charming.'

'Very charming if you will; but somehow I don't quite understand her.'

'I believe I don't quite understand her either, but I love her dearly all the same.'

'Umph; I like to understand people thoroughly. D'ye really think she's worthy of him?'

'Oh, papa' – said Molly, and then she stopped; she wanted to speak in favour of Cynthia, but somehow she could form no reply that pleased her to this repeated inquiry.

CHAPTER 33

# Mr Kirkpatrick, Q.C.

Mr Kirkpatrick had been, like many other men, struggling on in his profession, and encumbered with a large family; he was ready to do a good turn for his connections, if it occasioned him no loss of time, and if he remembered their existence. Cynthia's visit to Doughty Street, nine or ten years ago, had not made much impression upon him after he had once suggested its feasibility to his good-natured wife. Probably the next time he remembered her existence was when Mrs Kirkpatrick wrote to him to beg him to receive Cynthia for a night on her way to school at Boulogne. The same request was repeated on her return; but it so happened that he had not seen her either time and he thought no more about her, until he received an invitation to attend Mrs Kirkpatrick's wedding with Mr Gibson – an attention which irritated instead of pleasing him.

'Does the woman think I have nothing to do but run about in search of brides and bridegrooms, when this great case of Houghton v. Houghton is coming on?' he asked of his wife.

'Perhaps she never heard of it,' suggested Mrs Kirkpatrick.

'Nonsense! the case has been in the paper for days.'

'But she mayn't know you are engaged in it.'

'She mayn't,' said he meditatively. But now the great case of Houghton v. Houghton was a thing of the past; the hard struggle was over, the comparative table-land of Q.C.-dom gained, and Mr Kirkpatrick had leisure for family feeling and recollection. One day in the Easter vacation he found himself near Hollingford, and he wrote to offer himself as a visitor to the Gibsons from Friday till Monday; expressing strongly his wish to make Mr Gibson's acquaintance. Mr Gibson was ready to give a cordial reception to his unknown relation. Mrs Gibson was in a flutter of sentimental delight, which might not have been quite so effervescent if Mr Kirkpatrick had remained in his former position of struggling lawyer, with seven children.

When the two gentlemen met, they were attracted towards each other by a similarity of character, with just enough difference in their opinions to make the experience of each, on which such opinions were based, valuable to the other. To Mrs Gibson, although the bond between them counted for very little in their intercourse, Mr Kirkpatrick paid very polite attention; and he was, in fact, very glad that she had done so well for herself as to marry a sensible and agreeable man, who was able to keep her in comfort, and to behave to her daughter in so liberal a manner. Molly struck him as a delicate-looking girl, who might be very pretty if she had a greater look of health and animation; there was a languor over all, a slow depression of manner, which contrasted unfavourably with the brightly coloured Cynthia, sparkling, quick, graceful, and witty. As Mr Kirkpatrick expressed it afterwards to his wife, he was quite in love with that girl; and Cynthia, as ready to captivate strangers as any little girl of three or four, rose to the occasion and listened eagerly and made soft replies, intermixed with naïve sallies and droll humour, till Mr Kirkpatrick was quite captivated. He left Hollingford, almost surprised to have performed a duty, and found it a pleasure. For Mr Gibson he had a warm respect, a strong personal liking, which he would be glad to have ripen into a friendship, if there was time for it in this bustling world. And he fully resolved to see more of Cynthia; they must have her up to stay with them in London, and show her something of the world. The result was that a letter was sent off to Mrs Gibson, inviting Cynthia to pay a visit to her cousins in London.

## CHAPTER 34

# Secret Thoughts Ooze Out

It is possible that Osborne might have been induced to tell his father of his marriage during their long solitary intercourse, if the Squire, in an unlucky moment, had not given him his confidence about Roger's engagement with Cynthia. It was on one wet Sunday afternoon, when the father and son were sitting together in the large empty drawing-room. The poor father wanted the son to put down his book, and talk to him: it was so wet, so dull, and a little conversation would so wile away the time! But Osborne, with his back to his father, saw nothing of all this, and went on reading. The recollection of the affair between Roger and Cynthia came into the Squire's head, and, without giving it a moment's consideration, he began –

'Osborne! Do you know anything about this – this attachment of Roger's?'

Quite successful. Osborne laid down his book in a moment, and turned round to his father.

'Roger! an attachment! No! I never heard of it – '

And then he stopped; for he thought he had no right to betray his own conjecture, that the object was Cynthia Kirkpatrick.

'Yes. He is, though. Nobody that I particularly like, yet she's a very pretty girl. It's Miss Kirkpatrick, Gibson's step-daughter. But it's not an engagement, mind you'–

'I'm very glad – I hope she likes Roger back again' –

'"Like"! It's only too good a connection for her not to like it: if Roger is of the same mind when he comes home, I'll be bound she'll be only too happy!'

'I wonder Roger never told me,' said Osborne, a little hurt.

'He never told me either,' said the Squire. 'It was Gibson who made a clean breast of it, like a man of honour. I'd been saying to him, I couldn't have either of you two lads taking up with his lasses. I'll own it was you I was afraid of – it's bad enough with Roger, but, if it had been you, I'd ha' broken with Gibson and every mother's son of 'em, sooner than have let it go on; and so I told Gibson.'

'I beg your pardon for interrupting you; but, once for all, I claim the right of choosing my wife for myself, subject to no man's interference,' said Osborne, hotly.

'Then you'll keep your wife with no man's interference; for ne'er a penny will you get from me, my lad, unless you marry to please me a little, as well as yourself a great deal. Go against me in what I've set my heart on, and you'll find there's the devil to pay, that's all.'

After his father had left the room, Osborne leant back in his chair, and covered his eyes with his hand. The long concealment of his marriage from his father made the disclosure of it far, far more difficult than it would have been at first. He saw no way out of it all, excepting by the one strong stroke of which he felt himself incapable. He was not strong enough in character to overcome obstacles. The only overt step he took, in consequence of what he had heard from his father, was to ride over to Hollingford the first fine day, and go to see Cynthia and the Gibsons. He found them full of preparations and discussions about Cynthia's visit to London, and Cynthia herself not at all in the sentimental mood proper to respond to his delicate intimations of how glad he was in his brother's joy. With her head a little on one side, she was contemplating the effect of a knot of ribbons, when he began, in a low whisper, and leaning forward towards her as he spoke – 'Cynthia – I may call you Cynthia now, mayn't I? – I'm so glad of this news; I've only just heard of it, but I'm so glad.'

'What news do you mean?' She had her suspicions; but she was annoyed to think that from one person her secret was passing to another and another, till, in fact, it was becoming no secret at all. Still, Cynthia could always conceal her annoyance when she chose. 'Why are you to begin calling me Cynthia now?' she went on, smiling. 'The terrible word has slipped out from between your lips before, do you know?'

This light way of taking his tender congratulation did not quite please Osborne, who was in a sentimental mood. Then, having finished making her bow of ribbon, she turned to him, and continued in a quick low voice –

'I think I can guess why you made that pretty little speech just now. But do you know you ought not to have been told? Things are not quite arrived at the solemnity of – of – well – an engagement. He would not have it so. Now, I shan't say any more; and you must not. Pray remember, it is my own secret, and I particularly wished it not to be spoken about; and I don't like its being so talked about. Oh, the leaking of water through one small hole!'

And then she plunged into the talk of the other two, making the conversation general. Osborne was rather discomfited at the non-success of his congratulations; he leant back in his chair, weary and a little dispirited.

'You poor dear young man,' said Mrs Gibson, coming up to him with her soft, soothing manner; 'how tired you look! Do take some of that eau-de-cologne and bathe your forehead. This spring weather overcomes me too. It is very trying for delicate constitutions, its variableness of temperature makes me sigh perpetually; but then I am so sensitive. Dear Lady Cumnor always used to say I was like a thermometer. You've heard how ill she has been?'

'No,' said Osborne, not very much caring either.

'Oh, yes, she is better now; but the anxiety about her has tried me so: detained here by what are, of course, my duties, but far away from all intelligence, and not knowing what the next post might bring.'

'Where was she, then?' asked Osborne.

'At Spa. Such a distance off! Can't you conceive the trial? Living with her as I did; bound up in the family as I was!'

'But Lady Harriet said, in her last letter, that they hoped she would be stronger than she had been for years,' said Molly innocently.

'Yes – Lady Harriet – of course – everyone who knows Lady Harriet knows that she is of too sanguine a temperament for her statements to be perfectly relied on. Lady Harriet does not mean half she says.'

'We will hope she does in this instance,' said Cynthia shortly. 'They're in London now, and Lady Cumnor hasn't suffered from the journey.'

'They say so,' said Mrs Gibson, shaking her head. 'I am perhaps over-anxious, but I wish – I wish I could see and judge for myself. I almost think I shall go up with you, Cynthia, for a day or two. I don't quite like your travelling alone either. We will think about it, and you shall write to Mr Kirkpatrick, and propose it, if we determine upon it. You can tell him of my anxiety; and it will be only sharing your bed for a couple of nights.'

## CHAPTER 35

# Molly Gibson Breathes Freely

That was the way in which Mrs Gibson first broached her intention of accompanying Cynthia up to London.

As Molly walked home with her father from seeing Mrs Gibson and Cynthia off to London by the 'Umpire' coach, she almost danced along the street.

'Now, papa!' said she, 'I'm going to have you all to myself for a whole week. You must be very obedient.'

'Don't be tyrannical, then! You're walking me out of breath, and we're cutting Mrs Goodenough, in our hurry.'

So they crossed over the street, to speak to Mrs Goodenough.

'We've just been seeing my wife and her daughter off to London. Mrs Gibson has gone up for a week!'

'Deary, deary, Mr Gibson; why, it'll be like being a widower once again! You must come and drink tea with me some evening. We must try and cheer you up a bit amongst us. Shall it be Tuesday?'

In spite of the sharp pinch which Molly gave his arm, Mr Gibson accepted the invitation.

'Papa, how could you go and waste one of our evenings! We have but six in all, and now but five; and I had so reckoned on our doing all sorts of things together.'

'What sort of things?'

'Oh, I don't know: everything that is unrefined and ungenteel,' added she, slily looking up into her father's face. His eyes twinkled, but the rest of his face was perfectly grave.

'I'm not going to be corrupted. With toil and labour I've reached a very fair height of refinement. I won't be pulled down again.'

'Yes, you will, papa. We'll have bread-and-cheese for lunch this very day. And you shall wear your slippers in the drawing-room every evening; and oh, papa, think of riding together down the lanes – why, the dog-roses must be all out in flower, and the honeysuckles, and I should like to see Merriman's farm again! Papa, do let me have one ride with you! Please do! I'm sure we can manage it somehow.'

And 'somehow' it was managed. There was only one little drawback to this week of holiday and happy intercourse with her father. Everybody would ask them out to tea; for the fact was, that the late dinners which Mrs Gibson had introduced into her own house were a great inconvenience in the calculations of the small tea-drinkings at Hollingford. How ask people to tea at six, who dined at that hour? How, when they refused cake and sandwiches at half-past eight, how induce other people who were really hungry to commit a vulgarity before those calm and scornful eyes? So there had been a great lull of invitations for the Gibsons to Hollingford tea-parties and Molly missed the kind homeliness of the parties to which she had gone as long as she could remember; and though she grumbled a little over the loss of another charming evening with her father, she really was glad to go again in the old way among old friends. Miss Browning and Miss Phoebe were especially compassionate towards her in her loneliness. If they had had their will, she would have dined there every day; and she had to call upon them very frequently, in order to prevent their being hurt at her declining the dinners. Mrs Gibson wrote twice during her week's absence to her husband. That piece of news was quite satisfactory to the Miss Brownings. Sister looked to sister with an approving nod, as Molly named the second letter, which arrived in Hollingford the very day before Mrs Gibson was to return. They had settled between themselves that two letters would show the right amount of good feeling and proper understanding in the Gibson family.

'You've had another letter, you say, my dear?' asked Miss Browning. 'I daresay Mrs Gibson has written to you this time?'

'It is a large sheet, and Cynthia has written on one half to me, and all the rest is to papa.'

'A very nice arrangement, I'm sure. And what does Cynthia say? Is she enjoying herself?'

'Oh, yes. They've had a dinner-party; and one night, when mamma was at Lady Cumnor's, Cynthia went to the play with her cousins.'

'Upon my word! and all in one week? Well! I hope Cynthia won't find Hollingford dull, that's all, when she comes back.'

'I don't think it's likely,' said Miss Phoebe, with a knowing look, which sate oddly on her kindly innocent face. 'You see a great deal of Mr Preston, don't you, Molly?'

'Mr Preston!' said Molly. 'No! not much. What should make you think so?'

'Oh! a little bird told us,' said Miss Browning. Molly knew that little bird from her childhood, and had always hated it. Why could not people speak out and say that they did not mean to give up the name of their informant?

'The little bird was flying about one day in Heath Lane, and it saw Mr Preston and a young lady walking together in a very friendly manner; that is to say, he was on horseback, but the path is raised above the road, just where there is the little wooden bridge over the brook –'

'Perhaps Molly is in the secret, and we ought not to ask her about it,' said Miss Phoebe, seeing Molly's discomfiture.

'It can be no great secret,' said Miss Browning, 'for Miss Hornblower says Mr Preston owns to being engaged –'

'At any rate it isn't to Cynthia, that I know positively,' said Molly. 'And pray put a stop to any such reports; you don't know what mischief they may do. I do so hate that kind of chatter!'

'Heighty-teighty! Miss Molly! don't you remember that I am old enough to be your mother, and that it is not pretty behaviour to speak so to us – to me! "Chatter" to be sure. Really, Molly –'

'I beg your pardon,' said Molly, only half-penitent. 'But don't you see how bad it is to talk of such things in such a way? Supposing one of them cared for some one else; Mr Preston, for instance, may be engaged to some one else.'

'Molly! I pity the woman! Indeed I do. I have a very poor

opinion of Mr Preston,' said Miss Browning, in a warning tone of voice; for a new idea had come into her head.

'Well, but the woman, or young lady, would not like to hear such reports about Mr Preston.'

'Perhaps not. But take my word for it, he's a great flirt, and young ladies had better not have much to do with him.'

'I daresay it was all accident, their meeting in Heath Lane,' said Miss Phoebe.

'I know nothing about it,' said Molly, 'and I daresay I have been impertinent; only please don't talk about it any more. I have my reasons for asking you.' She got up, for by the striking of the church-clock she knew that her father would be at home. She bent and kissed Miss Browning's grave and passive face.

As soon as she was fairly gone, Miss Browning said, in a low voice –

'Phoebe, it was Molly herself that was with Mr Preston in Heath Lane, that day when Mrs Goodenough saw them together!'

'Gracious goodness me!' exclaimed Miss Phoebe, receiving it at once as gospel. 'How do you know?'

'By putting two and two together. Didn't you notice how red Molly went, and then pale, and how she said she knew for a fact that Mr Preston and Cynthia Kirkpatrick were not engaged?'

'Perhaps not engaged; but Mrs Goodenough saw them loitering together, all by their own two selves –'

'Mrs Goodenough was riding in her phaeton,' said Miss Browning. 'We all know her eyes are none of the best when she is standing steady on the ground. Molly and Cynthia have got their new plaid shawls just alike, and they trim their bonnets alike, and Molly is grown as tall as Cynthia since Christmas. I'll answer for it, Mrs Goodenough saw Molly.'

'It wouldn't be such a very bad match after all, sister.' She spoke very meekly, awaiting her sister's sanction to her opinion.

'Phoebe, it would be a bad match for Mary Pearson's daughter. If I had known what I know now, we'd never have had him to tea last September. Miss Hornblower told me many things; some that I don't think you ought to hear, Phoebe. He was engaged to a very pretty Miss Gregson, at Henwick, where he comes from; and her father made inquiries, and heard so much that was bad about him that he made his daughter break off the match, and she's dead since!'

'How shocking!' said Miss Phoebe, duly impressed.

'Besides, he plays at billiards, and he bets at races, and some people do say he keeps race-horses.'

'But isn't it strange that the earl keeps him on as his agent?'

'No! He's very clever about land, and very sharp in all law affairs; and my lord isn't bound to take notice – if indeed he knows – of the manner in which Mr Preston talks, when he has taken too much wine.'

Miss Phoebe was silent for a time. Presently she said, 'I do hope it wasn't Molly Gibson!'

'You may hope as much as you like; but I'm pretty sure it was. Mr Preston might do for Cynthia, who's been brought up in France. He must not, and he shall not, have Molly, if I go into church and forbid the banns myself. We must keep on the look-out, Phoebe. I'll be her guardian angel, in spite of herself.'

## CHAPTER 36

# Gathering Clouds

Mrs Gibson came back full of rose-coloured accounts of London. Lady Cumnor had been gracious and affectionate, and, as for the Kirkpatricks, no Lord Chancellor's house was ever grander than theirs. Cynthia was so much admired; and Mrs Kirkpatrick had showered down ball-dresses and pretty bonnets, like a fairy-godmother.

'And they're so fond of her, I don't know when we shall have her back! And now, what have you and papa been doing?'

'I sent Cynthia an African letter,' said Molly timidly. 'Did you hear anything of what was in it?'

'Oh, yes, poor child! It made her very uneasy; she said she did not feel inclined to go to Mr Rawson's ball that night, and for which Mrs Kirkpatrick had given her the ball-dress. But there was really nothing for her to fidget herself about. Roger only said he had had another touch of fever, but was better when he wrote. He says every European has to be acclimatised by fever, in that part of Abyssinia where he is.'

'And did she go?' asked Molly.

'Yes, to be sure. It is not an engagement; and, if it were, it is not acknowledged. Fancy her going and saying, "A young man that I know has been ill for a few days in Africa, two months ago, therefore I don't want to go to the ball tonight!" It would have seemed like affectation of sentiment; and, if there's one thing I hate, it is that.'

'She would hardly enjoy herself,' said Molly.

'Oh, yes, but she did! Her dress was white gauze, trimmed with lilacs, and she danced every dance, although she was quite a

222

stranger.' And she went out of the room, to finish her unpacking.

Molly let her work fall. 'Oh, Roger, Roger! I wish – I pray that you were safe home again! How could we all bear it, if – '

She covered her face with her hands, and tried to stop thinking. She found the long suspense as to his health hard to endure.

No more news of Roger, until some time after Cynthia had returned from London. She came back, looking fresher and prettier than ever, full of amusing details of the gay life she had been enjoying, yet not at all out of spirits at having left it behind her. She brought home all sorts of pretty and dainty devices for Molly. Yet somehow Molly felt that Cynthia was changed in her relation to her. Molly was aware that she had never had Cynthia's full confidence, that Cynthia withheld from her more than thoughts and feelings – that she withheld facts. So it was not now by any want of confidence that Molly felt distanced, as it were. It was because Cynthia rather avoided than sought her companionship; because there were certain subjects on which she evidently disliked speaking. One morning in the first week after Cynthia's return home, Mr Gibson ran up into the drawing-room, booted and spurred, and hastily laid an open pamphlet down before her; pointing out a particular passage with his finger, but not speaking a word before he rapidly quitted the room. His eyes were sparkling, and had an amused as well as pleased expression. All this Molly noticed, as well as Cynthia's flush of colour, as she read what was thus pointed out to her. Then she pushed it a little on one side.

'What is it? may I see it?' asked Molly –

'Certainly; I don't suppose there are any great secrets in a scientific journal, full of reports of meetings.' And she gave the book a little push towards Molly.

'Oh, Cynthia!' said Molly, catching her breath as she read, 'are you not proud?' For it was an account of an annual gathering of the Geographical Society, and Lord Hollingford had read a letter he had received from Roger Hamley, dated from Arracuoba, a district in Africa, hitherto unvisited by any intelligent European traveller, and about which Mr Hamley sent many curious particulars. The reading of this letter had been received with the greatest interest, and several subsequent speakers had paid the writer very high compliments.

But Molly might have known Cynthia better than to expect an answer responsive to the feelings that prompted her question.

'I'm afraid I'm not as much struck by the wonder of the thing as you are, Molly. Besides, I heard of the meeting before I left London; it was a good deal talked about in my uncle's set.' Cynthia did not lift up her head from her sewing.

Molly began to read the report over again.

'Why, Cynthia!' she said, 'you might have been there. It says "many ladies were present". Oh, couldn't you have managed to go? If your uncle's set cared about these things, wouldn't some of them have taken you?'

'Perhaps, if I had asked them. But I think they would have been rather astonished at my sudden turn for science.'

'You might have told your uncle how matters really stood.'

'Once for all, Molly,' said Cynthia, now laying down her work, 'do learn to understand that it is, and always has been my wish, not to have the relation which Roger and I bear to each other, mentioned or talked about. When the right time comes, I will make it known to my uncle, and to everybody whom it may concern; but I am not going to make mischief, and get myself into trouble – even for the sake of hearing compliments paid to him – by letting it out before the time. If I'm pushed to it, I'd sooner break it off altogether at once, and have done with it. I can't be worse off than I am now.'

Molly looked at her with dismay.

'I can't understand you, Cynthia,' she said at length.

'No, I daresay you can't,' said Cynthia, looking at her with tears in her eyes, and very tenderly, as if in atonement for her late vehemence. 'I am afraid – I hope – you never will.'

In a moment, Molly's arms were round her. 'Oh, Cynthia,' she murmured, 'have I been plaguing you? Don't say you're afraid of my knowing you! Of course you've your faults, everybody has; but I think I love you the better for them.'

'I don't know that I am so very bad,' said Cynthia, smiling a little through the tears that Molly's words and caresses had forced to overflow from her eyes. 'But I've got into scrapes. I'm in a scrape now. I do sometimes believe I shall always be in scrapes; and, if they ever come to light, I shall seem to be worse than I really am, and I know your father will throw me off, and I – no, I won't be afraid that you will, Molly.'

'I'm sure I shan't. Are they – how would Roger take it?' asked Molly, very timidly.

'I don't know. I hope he will never hear of it. I don't see why he should, for in a little while I shall be quite clear again. It all came about without my ever thinking I was doing wrong. I've a great mind to tell you all about it, Molly.'

Molly longed to know, and to see if she could not offer help; but, while Cynthia was hesitating, Mrs Gibson came in, full of some manner of altering a gown. Cynthia seemed to forget her tears and her troubles, and to throw her soul into millinery.

## CHAPTER 37

# The Storm Bursts

The autumn drifted away through all its seasons. The golden corn harvest; the walks through the stubble-fields, and rambles into hazel-copses in search of nuts; the stripping of the apple-orchards of their ruddy fruit, amid the joyous cries and shouts of watching children, and the gorgeous tulip-like colouring of the later time, had now come on with the shortening days.

In the Gibsons' house, Cynthia seemed to keep every one out at (mental) arms'-length, and particularly avoided any private talks with Molly. It was a very heavy time for Molly – zest and life had fled. She thought it was that her youth had fled – at nineteen! Cynthia was no longer the same: and perhaps Cynthia's change would injure her in the distant Roger's opinion. Her stepmother seemed almost kind, in comparison with Cynthia's withdrawal of her heart. Yet Cynthia herself seemed anxious and careworn, though she would not speak of her anxieties to Molly. And then the poor girl, in her goodness, would blame herself for feeling Cynthia's change of manner; for, as Molly said to herself, 'If it is hard work for me to help always fretting after Roger, and wondering where he is, and how he is, what must it be for her?'

One day Mr Gibson came in, bright and swift.

'Molly,' said he, 'where's Cynthia?'

'Gone out to do some errands –'

'Well, it's a pity – but never mind! Put on your bonnet and cloak as fast as you can! I've had to borrow old Simpson's dogcart – there would have been room both for you and Cynthia; but, as it is, you must walk back alone. I'll drive you as far on the Barford road as I can, and then you must jump down. I can't take you on to Broadhurst's; I may be kept there for hours.'

Molly's bonnet and cloak were on in two minutes, and she was sitting by her father's side, the light-weight going merrily bumping over the stone-paved lanes.

'Oh, this is charming!' said Molly, after a toss-up on her seat from a tremendous bump.

'For youth, but not for crabbed age,' said Mr Gibson. 'My bones would rather go smoothly over macadamised streets.'

'That's treason to this lovely view and this fine pure air, papa! Only I don't believe you!'

'Thank you. As you are so complimentary, I think I shall put you down at the foot of this hill; we've passed the second milestone from Hollingford.'

'Oh, let me just go up to the top! I know we can see the blue range of the Malverns from it, and Dorrimer Hall among the woods; the horse will want a minute's rest, and then I will get down without a word.'

She went up to the top of the hill; and there they sate still a minute or two, enjoying the view, without much speaking. The woods were golden; the old house of purple-red brick, with its twisted chimneys, rose up from among them facing on to green lawns, and a placid lake; beyond again were the Malvern Hills.

'Now jump down, lassie, and make the best of your way home before it gets dark! You'll find the cut over Croston Heath shorter than the road we've come by.'

To reach Croston Heath, Molly had to go down a narrow lane overshadowed by trees, with picturesque old cottages dotted here and there; and then there came a small wood, and then there was a brook to be crossed on a plank bridge, and up the steeper fields on the opposite side were cut steps in the turfy path; these ended, she was on Croston Heath, a wide-stretching common, past which a near road to Hollingford lay.

The loneliest part of the road was the first; past the last cottage and Molly entered the wood. As she turned a corner, she heard a passionate voice of distress; and in an instant she recognised Cynthia's tones. She looked around. There were some thick holly bushes shining out dark-green in the midst of the amber and scarlet foliage. If anyone was there, it must be behind these. So Molly left the path, and went plunging through the brown tangled ferns, and turned the holly-bushes. There stood Mr Preston and Cynthia; he holding her hands tight.

For an instant no one spoke. Then Cynthia said –

'Oh, Molly, Molly, come and judge between us!'

Mr Preston let go Cynthia's hands slowly, with a look that was more of a sneer than a smile. Molly came forward and took Cynthia's arm, her eyes steadily fixed on Mr Preston's face. He said to Cynthia –

'The subject of our conversation does not well admit of a third person's presence. As Miss Gibson seems to wish for your company now, I must beg you to fix some other time and place where we can finish our discussion.'

'I will go, if Cynthia wishes me,' said Molly.

'No, no; stay – I want you to stay – I want you to hear it all – I wish I had told you sooner.'

'You mean that you regret that she has not been made aware of our engagement – that you promised long ago to be my wife. Pray remember that it was you who made me promise secrecy, not I you!'

'I don't believe him, Cynthia. Don't, don't cry.'

'Cynthia,' said he, suddenly changing his tone to fervid tenderness, 'pray, pray do not go on so; you can't think how it distresses me!' He stepped forward, to try and take her hand and soothe her; but she shrank away from him, and sobbed the more irrepressibly. She felt Molly's presence so much to be a protection that now she dared to let herself go, and weaken herself by giving way to her emotion.

'Go away!' said Molly, vehemently, 'if it distresses you to see her cry. Don't you see it's you who are the cause of it?'

'I will go, if Cynthia tells me,' said he.

'Oh, Molly, I don't know what to do,' said Cynthia, sobbing worse than ever; and, though she tried to speak coherently, no intelligible words would come.

'Run to that cottage in the trees, and fetch her a cup of water,' said Molly. He hesitated a little.

'I have not done speaking to her; you will not leave before I come back?'

'No. Don't you see she can't move in this state?'

He went quickly, if reluctantly.

Cynthia was some time before she could check her sobs enough to speak. At length she said –

'Molly, I do hate him!'

'But what did he mean by saying you were engaged to him?'

'It's too long a story to tell now, and I'm not strong enough. Look! he's coming back. As soon as I can, let us get home!'

'With all my heart,' said Molly.

Cynthia drank, and was restored to calmness.

'Now,' said Molly, 'we had better go home; it's getting dark quickly.'

If she hoped to carry Cynthia off so easily, she was mistaken. Mr Preston said –

'I think, since Miss Gibson has made herself acquainted with this much, we had better let her know the whole truth – that you are engaged to marry me as soon as you are twenty; otherwise your being here with me may appear strange to her.'

'As I know that Cynthia is engaged to another man, you can hardly expect me to believe what you say, Mr Preston.'

'Oh, Molly,' said Cynthia, trembling all over, 'I am not engaged – neither to the person you mean, nor to Mr Preston.'

Mr Preston forced a smile. 'I think I have some letters that would convince Miss Gibson of the truth of what I have said; and which will convince Mr Osborne Hamley, if necessary – I conclude it is to him she is alluding.'

'I am quite puzzled by you both,' said Molly. 'The only thing I do know is that Cynthia and I must go home directly. If you want to talk to Miss Kirkpatrick, Mr Preston, why don't you come to my father's house, and ask to see her openly?'

'I shall only be too glad to explain to Mr Gibson on what terms I stand in relation to her. If I have not done it sooner, it is because

I have yielded to her wishes.'

'Pray, pray don't, Molly – you don't know all; you mean well and kindly, but you are only making mischief. Do let us go; I will tell you all about it, when we are at home.' She took Molly's arm and tried to hasten her away; but Mr Preston followed, talking as he walked by their side.

'Can you deny that you are my promised wife?' Cynthia stopped, and turned at bay.

'Since you will have it out – I own that when I was a neglected girl of sixteen, you lent me money at my need, and made me give you a promise of marriage.'

'"Made you"!' said he.

Cynthia turned scarlet. '"Made" is not the right word, I confess. I liked you then, and, if it had been a question of immediate marriage, I daresay I should never have objected. But I know you better now; and you have persecuted me so of late, that I tell you once for all (as I have told you before, till I am sick of the very words), that nothing shall ever make me marry you. Nothing! I see there's no chance of escaping exposure and, I daresay, losing my character and, I know, losing all the few friends I have.'

'Never me,' said Molly.

'It is hard,' said Mr Preston. 'You may believe all the bad things you like about me, Cynthia, but I don't think you can doubt my real, passionate, disinterested love for you.'

'I do doubt it,' said Cynthia. 'Ah! when I think of the self-denying affection I have seen – I have known – affection that thought of others before itself –'

Mr Preston broke in at the pause she made. She was afraid of revealing too much to him.

'You do not call it love which has been willing to wait for years – to be silent while silence was desired – to suffer jealousy and to bear neglect! Cynthia, I have loved you, and I do love you. If you will but keep your word, and marry me, I'll swear I'll make you love me in return.'

'Oh, I wish – I wish I'd never borrowed that unlucky money. Oh, Molly, I have saved and scrimped to repay it, and he won't take it now; I thought, if I could repay it, it would set me free.'

'You seem to imply you sold yourself for twenty pounds,' he said. They were nearly on the common now, close to the protection of the cottages.

'I did not "sell" myself; I liked you then. But oh, how I do hate you now!' cried Cynthia.

He bowed and turned back, vanishing rapidly down the field staircase. Yet the two girls hastened on, as if he was still pursuing them. Once, when Molly said something to Cynthia, the latter replied –

'Molly, if you pity me – if you love me – don't say anything more just now! We shall have to look as if nothing had happened when we get home. Come to my room, when we go upstairs to bed, and I'll tell you all.'

So each of the girls went up into their separate rooms, to calm themselves before dressing for dinner. Molly felt as if she were so miserably shaken that she could not have gone down at all, if her own interests only had been at stake.

When she went into the drawing-room before dinner, she found Cynthia and her mother by themselves. Mrs Gibson was telling some of her day's adventures – whom she had found at home; and the small pieces of news she had heard. To Molly's quick sympathy Cynthia's voice sounded languid and weary; but she made all the proper replies, and Mrs Gibson was not one to notice slight differences in manner. When Mr Gibson returned, Cynthia raised herself into liveliness, partly from a consciousness that he would have noticed any depression, and partly because Cynthia was one of those natural coquettes, who, from their cradle to their grave, instinctively bring out all their prettiest airs and graces, in order to stand well with any man, young or old, who may happen to be present. She listened to his remarks and stories with all the sweet intentness of happier days, till Molly, silent and wondering, could hardly believe that the Cynthia before her was the same girl as she who was sobbing and crying as if her heart would break, but two hours before. At length came bed-time, and Molly and Cynthia went to their own rooms without exchanging a word.

Molly took off her gown and put on her dressing-gown, and went and knocked at the opposite door. When she entered the room, Cynthia sate by her dressing-table, just as she had come up from the drawing-room. She had been leaning her head on her arms, and she looked up, her face full of worry and distress.

## CHAPTER 38

# Cynthia's Confession

'You said I might come,' said Molly, 'and that you would tell me all.'

'You know all, I think. Perhaps you don't know what excuses I have, but you know what a scrape I am in.'

'I've been thinking a great deal,' said Molly, doubtfully. 'And I can't help fancying if you told papa – '

Before she could go on, Cynthia had stood up.

'No! That I won't. Unless I'm to leave here at once. And you know I have not another place to go to – without warning, I mean. I daresay my uncle would take me in, and would be bound to stand by me, in whatever disgrace I might be; or perhaps I might get a governess's situation – a pretty governess I should be!'

'Pray, please, Cynthia, don't go off into such wild talking. That horrid man has managed to get you involved in some way; but I am sure papa could set it to rights, if you would only tell him all.'

'No, Molly,' said Cynthia, 'I can't, and there's an end of it. You may if you like; only, let me leave the house first; give me that much time.'

'You know I would never tell anything you wished me not to tell, Cynthia,' said Molly, deeply hurt.

'Would you not, darling?' said Cynthia, taking her hand. 'Will you promise me that? quite a sacred promise? – for it would be such a comfort to me to tell you all.'

'Yes! I'll promise not to tell. You should not have doubted me,' said Molly, still a little sorrowfully.

'Very well. I trust to you.'

'But do think of telling papa,' persevered Molly.

'Never,' said Cynthia resolutely. 'I am one of those people, as mamma says sometimes – I cannot live with persons who don't think well of me. I really cannot be happy in the same house with anyone who knows my faults, and thinks they are greater than my merits. Now, you know your father would do that. He (and you too, Molly,) have a higher standard than I had ever known. Oh, he would be so angry with me – he would never get over it, and I have so liked him! I do so like him!'

'Well, never mind, dear; he shall not know,' said Molly, for Cynthia was again becoming hysterical. 'Now lie down on the bed, and I'll sit by you, and let us talk it over.'

But Cynthia sat down again by the dressing-table.

'When did it all begin?' said Molly.

'Long ago – four or five years. It was the holidays, and mamma was away visiting, and the Donaldsons asked me to go with them to the Worcester Festival. You can't fancy how pleasant it all sounded. I had been shut up in that great dreary house at Ashcombe, where mamma had her school; Mr Preston had to see it all painted and papered; but, besides that, he was very intimate with us; I believe mamma thought – no, I have enough blame to lay at her door, to prevent my telling you anything that may be only fancy.

'Well! he came a great deal about the house, and knew as much as anyone of mamma's affairs. I'm telling you this, in order that you may understand how natural it was for me to answer his questions, when he came one day and found me, fretting and fuming because, though mamma had written word I might go with the Donaldsons, she had never said how I was to get any money for the journey, much less for anything of dress, and I had outgrown all my last year's frocks.'

'Why didn't you write and tell her all this?' said Molly.

'I wish I had her letter to show you; she descanted largely on the enjoyment she was having, and the kindness she was receiving, and her gladness that I too was going to have some pleasure; but the only thing that would have been of real use to me she left out, and that was where she was going to next. She mentioned that she was leaving the house she was stopping at the day after she wrote, and that she should be at home by a certain date; but I got the letter on a Saturday, and the festival began the next Tuesday –'

'Poor Cynthia!' said Molly. 'Still, if you had written, your letter might have been forwarded. I don't mean to be hard, only I do so dislike the thought of your ever having made a friend of that man.'

'Ah!' said Cynthia, sighing. 'How easy it is to judge rightly, after one sees what evil comes from judging wrongly! I was only a young girl, hardly more than a child, and he was a friend to us then – excepting mamma, the only friend I knew; the Donaldsons were only kind and good-natured acquaintances.'

'I am sorry,' said Molly humbly, 'I have been so happy with papa. I hardly can understand how different it must have been with you.'

'Different! I should think so! The worry about money made me sick of my life. But I would have stinted and starved if mamma and I had got on as happily together as you and Mr Gibson do. It was not the poverty; it was that she never seemed to care to have me with her. As soon as the holidays came round, she was off to some great house or another. I was very much in mamma's way, and I felt it. Mr Preston seemed to feel it too for me; and I was very grateful to him for kind words and sympathetic looks. So this day, when he came to see how the workmen were getting on, he found me in the deserted school-room, looking at my faded summer-bonnet and some old ribbons I had been sponging, and half-worn-out gloves – a sort of rag-fair spread out on the deal table. I was in a regular passion with only looking at that shabbiness. He said he was so glad to hear I was going to this festival with the Donaldsons; old Sally, our servant, had told him the news. But I was so perplexed about money that I said I shouldn't go. Little by little he made me tell him all my troubles. He was very nice in those days. Somehow, I never felt as if it was wrong or foolish or anything to accept his offer of money at the time. He had twenty pounds in his pocket, he said, and shouldn't want it for months; I could repay it, or rather mamma could, when it suited her. I knew

– at least I thought I knew – that I should never spend twenty pounds; but I thought I could give him back what I didn't want, and so – well, that was the beginning! It doesn't sound so very wrong, does it, Molly?'

'No,' said Molly hesitatingly.

'Well, what with boots and gloves, and a bonnet and a mantle, and a white muslin gown, which was made for me before I left on Tuesday, and a silk gown that followed to the Donaldsons', and my journeys, there was very little left of the twenty pounds, especially when I found I must get a ball-dress in Worcester, for we were to go to the Ball. Mrs Donaldson gave me my ticket, but she looked grave at my idea of going to the Ball in my white muslin, which I had already worn two evenings at their house. You know,' continued Cynthia, smiling a very little, 'I can't help being aware that I'm pretty, and that people admire me very much. I found it out first at the Donaldsons'. I was the belle of the house, and it was very pleasant to feel my power. The last day or two of that gay week Mr Preston joined our party. The last time he had seen me was when I was dressed in shabby clothes too small for me, neglected and penniless. At the Donaldsons' I was a little queen; and at that Ball, which was the first night he came, I had more partners than I knew what to do with. I suppose he really did fall in love with me then. And then I began to feel how awkward it was to be in his debt. But I liked him, and felt him as a friend all the time. The last day, I was walking in the garden along with the others, and I thought I could tell him how much I had enjoyed myself, and how happy I had been, all thanks to his twenty pounds, and could tell him it should be repaid to him as soon as possible; though I turned sick at the thought of telling mamma. The end of our talk came very soon; for, almost to my terror, he began to talk violent love to me, and to beg me to promise to marry him. I was so frightened, that I ran away to the others. But that night I got a letter from him, apologising for startling me, renewing his offer, his entreaties for a promise of marriage, to be fulfilled at any date I would please to name – and in it a reference to my unlucky debt, which was to be a debt no longer, only an advance of the money to be hereafter mine if only – You can fancy it all, Molly, better than I can remember it to tell it you.'

'And what did you say?' asked Molly, breathless.

'I did not answer it at all, until another letter came, entreating for a reply. By that time mamma had returned home, and the old daily pressure and plaint of poverty had come on. Mary Donaldson wrote to me often, singing the praises of Mr Preston as enthusiastically as if she had been bribed to do it, and I liked him well enough, and felt grateful to him. So I wrote and gave him my promise to marry him when I was twenty, but it was to be a secret till then. But somehow, as soon as I felt pledged to him, I began to hate him. I couldn't endure his eagerness of greeting, if ever he found me alone; I never ventured to name the hateful twenty pounds to mamma, but went on trying to think that, if I was to marry Mr Preston, it need never be paid. Oh Molly! He made me feel as if I was in his power. There was an insolence in his manner to mamma, too. Ah! you're thinking that I'm not too respectful a daughter – and perhaps not; but I couldn't bear his covert sneers at her faults, and I hated his way of showing what he called his "love" for me. Then, after I had been a *semestre* at Mdme. Lefèbre's, a new English girl came – a cousin of his. Now, Molly, you must forget as soon as I've told you what I'm going to say; and she used to talk so much and perpetually about her cousin Robert and how he was so handsome, and every lady of the land in love with him – a lady of title into the bargain –'

'Lady Harriet! I daresay,' said Molly indignantly.

'I don't know,' said Cynthia wearily. 'She went on to say there was a very pretty widow too, who made desperate love to him. He had often laughed with them at all her little advances, which she thought he didn't see through. And, oh! and this was the man I had promised to marry, and gone into debt to, and written love-letters to! So now you understand it all, Molly.'

'No, I don't yet. What did you do, on hearing how he had spoken about your mother?'

'I wrote and told him I hated him, and would never, never

marry him, and would pay him back his money and the interest on it as soon as ever I could.'

'Well?'

'And Mdme. Lefèbre brought me back my letter, unopened; and told me that she didn't allow letters to gentlemen to be sent by the pupils of her establishment unless she had previously seen their contents. I had to see her burn it, and to give her my promise I wouldn't write again before she would consent not to tell mamma. So I had to calm down and wait till I came home.'

'But you didn't see him then?'

'No, but I could write; and I began to try and save up my money to pay him.'

'What did he say to your letter?'

'Oh, at first he pretended not to believe I could be in earnest; he thought it was only pique, or a temporary offence, to be apologised for and covered over with passionate protestations.'

'And afterwards?'

'He condescended to threats; and then I turned coward. I couldn't bear to have it all known and talked about, and my silly letters shown – oh, such letters! I cannot bear to think of them, beginning, "My dearest Robert", to that man' –

'But, oh, Cynthia, how could you go and engage yourself to Roger?' asked Molly.

'Why not?' said Cynthia, sharply. 'I was free – I am free; and I did like Roger; and I was not a stone that I could fail to be touched by his tender, unselfish love. I know you don't think me good enough for him; and, of course, if all this comes out, he won't think me good enough either' (falling into a plaintive tone, very touching to hear); 'and sometimes I think I'll give him up, and go off to some fresh life amongst strangers; and once or twice I've thought I would marry Mr Preston out of pure revenge, and have him for ever in my power – only I think I should have the worst of it; for he is cruel in his very soul. I have so begged and begged him to let me go without exposure.'

'Never mind the exposure,' said Molly. 'It will recoil far more on him than harm you.'

Cynthia went a little paler. 'But I said things in those letters about mamma; and he says he will show those letters to your father, unless I consent to acknowledge our engagement.'

'He shall not!' said Molly, rising up and standing before Cynthia almost as resolutely fierce as if she were in the very presence of Mr Preston himself. 'I am not afraid of him. I will ask him for those letters, and see if he will dare to refuse me.'

'You don't know him,' said Cynthia, shaking her head. 'Poor, poor Roger! When I want to write words of love to him, I pull myself up; for I have written words as affectionate to that other man. Those unlucky letters – written when I was not sixteen, Molly – only seven of them! They are like a mine under my feet, which may blow up any day; and down will come father and mother and all.'

'How can I get them?' said Molly, thinking: 'for get them I will. With papa to back me, he dare not refuse.'

'Ah! But that's just the thing. He knows I'm afraid of your father's hearing of it all, more than of anyone else.'

'And yet he thinks he loves you!'

'It is his way of loving. He says he doesn't care what he does so he gets me to be his wife; and that, after that, he is sure he can make me love him.' Cynthia began to cry, out of weariness of body and despair of mind. Molly's arms were round her in a minute, and she hushed her up with lulling words, just as if she were a little child.

'Oh, it is such a comfort to have told you all!' murmured Cynthia. And Molly made reply –

'I am sure we have right on our side; and that makes me certain he must and shall give up the letters.'

'And take the money?' added Cynthia, lifting her head. 'He must take the money. Oh, Molly, you can never manage it all without its coming out to your father! And I would far rather go out to Russia as a governess. I almost think I would rather – no, not that,' said she, shuddering away from what she was going to say. 'But he must not know – please, Molly, he must not know. You'll promise me never to tell him – or mamma?'

'I never will. You do not think I would for anything short of saving –' She was going to have said, 'saving you and Roger from pain.' But Cynthia broke in –

'For nothing! No reason whatever must make you tell your father. Promise me not to tell Mr Gibson.'

'I have promised once,' said Molly, 'but I promise again; so now do go to bed. You'll be ill, if you don't get some rest; and it's past two o'clock, and you're shivering with cold.'

So they wished each other good-night. But when Molly got into her room, all her spirit left her; and she threw herself down on her bed. If Roger ever heard of it all by any chance, she felt how it would disturb his love for Cynthia. And yet was it right to conceal it from him? She must try and persuade Cynthia to tell it all straight out to him, as soon as he returned to England. And she suddenly recollected what she herself had promised to do. Now that the first *furor* was over, she saw the difficulties clearly; and the foremost of all was how she was to manage to have an interview with Mr Preston. How had Cynthia managed? and the letters that had passed between them, too? Unwillingly, Molly was compelled to perceive that there must have been a good deal of underhand work going on beneath Cynthia's apparent openness of behaviour; and still more unwillingly she began to be afraid that she herself might be led into the practice.

CHAPTER 39

# Molly Gibson to the Rescue

It seemed strange enough, after the storms of the night, to meet in smooth tranquillity at breakfast. Cynthia was pale; but she talked as quietly as usual about all manner of different things, while Molly sate silent, watching and wondering, and becoming convinced that Cynthia must have gone through a long experience of concealing her real thoughts and secret troubles, before she could have been able to put on such a semblance of composure. Among the letters that came in that morning was one from the London Kirkpatricks; but not from Helen, Cynthia's own particular correspondent. Her sister wrote to apologise for Helen, who was not well, she said.

Whether it was from Helen's illness, or some other cause, after breakfast Cynthia became very flat and absent, and this lasted all day long. Molly understood now why her moods had been so changeable for many months, and was tender and forbearing with her accordingly. Towards evening, when the two girls were left alone, Cynthia came and stood over Molly, so that her face could not be seen.

'Molly,' said she, 'will you do it? Will you do what you said last night? I've been thinking of it all day, and sometimes I believe he would give you back the letters if you asked him.'

Now it so happened that Molly disliked the idea of the proposed interview with Mr Preston more and more; but it was her own offer, so she gave her consent, and tried to conceal her distaste, which grew upon her even more as Cynthia hastily arranged the details.

'You shall meet him in the avenue leading from the park lodge up to the Towers. He can come in one way from the Towers, where he has often business – you can go in, as we have often done, by the lodge.'

Molly ventured to ask how he was to be informed of all this. Cynthia only reddened and replied, 'Oh! never mind! He will only be too glad to come; it is the first time the appointment has come from my side. If I can but once be free – oh, Molly, I will love you, and be grateful to you all my life!'

Molly thought of Roger, and that prompted her next speech.

'It must be horrible – I think I'm very brave – but I don't think I could have – could have accepted even Roger, with a half-cancelled engagement hanging over me.'

'You forget how I detest Mr Preston!' said Cynthia. 'It was that, more than any excess of love for Roger, that made me thankful to be at least as securely pledged to some one else. He did not want to call it an engagement; but I did; because it gave me the feeling of assurance that I was free from Mr Preston. And so I am! all but these letters. Oh! if you can but make him take back his abominable money, and get me my letters! Then I would marry Roger, and no one would be the wiser. After all, it was only what people call "youthful folly". And you may tell Mr Preston that, as soon as he makes my letters public, shows them to your father or anything, I'll go away from Hollingford, and never come back.'

Loaded with many such messages, not really knowing what she should say, hating the errand, not satisfied with Cynthia's manner of speaking about her relations to Roger, yet willing to bear all and brave all, if she could once set Cynthia in a straight path: Molly set out on her walk towards the appointed place. She did not like going quite out of sight of the lodge, and she stood facing it, close by the trunk of one of the trees. Presently, she heard a step coming on the grass. It was Mr Preston. He saw a woman's figure half-behind the trunk of a tree, and made no doubt that it was Cynthia. But when he came near, the figure turned round, and he met the pale, resolved look of Molly. Her steady grey eyes met his with courageous innocence.

'Is Cynthia unable to come?' asked he.

'I did not know you thought that you should meet her,' said Molly, surprised. In her simplicity she believed that Cynthia had named that it was she, Molly Gibson, who would meet Mr Preston; but Cynthia had been too worldly-wise for that, and had decoyed him thither by a vaguely worded note, which led him to suppose that she herself would give him the meeting.

'At any rate, she sent me here to meet you,' said Molly. 'She has told me exactly how matters stand between you.'

'Has she?' sneered he. 'She is not always the most open or reliable person in the world!'

Molly reddened; and her temper was none of the coolest. But she mastered herself and gained courage by so doing.

'You should not speak so of the person you profess to wish to have for your wife. But, putting all that aside, you have some letters of hers that she wishes to have back again. And that you have no right to keep.'

'No legal, or no moral right? which do you mean?'

'I do not know; simply you have no right at all, as a gentleman, to keep a girl's letters when she asks for them back again, much less to hold them over her as a threat.'

'I see you do know all, Miss Gibson,' said he, changing his manner to one of more respect. 'She has told you her story from her side; now you must hear mine. She promised me as solemnly as ever woman'–

'She was only a girl, barely sixteen.'

'Old enough to know what she was doing. She promised me solemnly to be my wife, making the one stipulation of secrecy, and a certain period of waiting; she wrote me letters repeating this promise, and confidential enough to prove that she considered herself bound to me by such an implied relation. It was as sincere and unworldly a passion as ever man felt; she must say so herself. I might have married two or three girls with plenty of money; one of them was handsome enough, and not at all reluctant.'

Molly was chafed at the conceit of his manner. 'I beg your pardon, but I don't want to hear accounts of young ladies whom you might have married; I come here simply on behalf of

Cynthia, who does not like you, and who does not wish to marry you.'

'Well, then, I must make her "like" me, as you call it. She did "like" me once, and made promises which she will find it requires the consent of two people to break. I don't despair of making her love me when we are married.'

'She will never marry you,' said Molly firmly.

'Then, if she ever honours anyone else with her preference, he shall be allowed the perusal of her letters to me. You said the other day that Cynthia was engaged. May I ask whom to?'

'No,' said Molly, 'you may not. You heard her say it was not an engagement. And if it were a full engagement, do you think, after what you last said, I should tell you to whom? But you may be sure of this, he would never read a line of your letters.'

'It seems to me that this mysterious "he" is a very fortunate person to have such a warm defender in Miss Gibson, to whom he is not at all engaged,' said Mr Preston, with so disagreeable a look on his face that Molly suddenly found herself on the point of bursting into tears. But she rallied herself.

'No honourable man or woman will read your letters; and, if any people do read them, they will be so much ashamed of it that they won't dare to speak of them. What use can they be of to you?'

'They contain Cynthia's reiterated promises of marriage.'

'She says she would rather leave Hollingford for ever, and go out to earn her bread, than marry you.'

He looked so bitterly mortified, that Molly was almost sorry for him.

'Does she say that to you in cold blood? Do you know you are telling me very hard truths, Miss Gibson? If they are truths, that is to say. Young ladies are very fond of the words "hate" and "detest". I've known many who have applied them to men whom they were hoping all the time to marry.'

'I cannot tell about other people,' said Molly; 'I only know that Cynthia does as nearly hate you as anybody like her ever does hate.'

'Like her?' said he.

'I mean I should hate worse,' said Molly in a low voice.

But he did not attend much to her answer. He was working the point of his stick into the turf, and his eyes were bent on it.

'So now would you mind sending her back the letters by me? I do assure you that you cannot make her marry you.'

'You are very simple, Miss Gibson,' said he, suddenly lifting up his head. 'Have you never heard of revenge? Cynthia has cajoled me with promises, and I don't mean to let her go unpunished. You may tell her that. I shall keep the letters, and make use of them as I see fit when the occasion arises.'

Molly was miserably angry with herself for her mismanagement of the affair. She had hoped to succeed; she had only made matters worse.

'Mr Osborne Hamley may hear of their contents, though he may be too honourable to read them. Nay, even your father may hear whispers; and if I remember them rightly, Miss Cynthia Kirkpatrick does not always speak in the most respectful terms of the lady who is now Mrs Gibson. There are –'

'Stop,' said Molly. 'I won't hear anything out of these letters, written, when she was almost without friends, to you, whom she looked upon as a friend! But I have thought of what I will do next. If I had not been foolish, I should have told my father; but Cynthia made me promise that I would not. So I will tell it all, from beginning to end, to Lady Harriet, and ask her to speak to her father. I feel sure that she will do it; and I don't think you will dare to refuse Lord Cumnor.'

He felt at once that he should not dare; the conduct of which he had been guilty in regard to the letters and the threats which he had held out respecting them, were just what no gentleman, no honourable man could put up with in anyone about him. He knew that much, and he wondered how she, the girl standing before him, had been clever enough to find it out. He forgot himself for an instant in admiration of her. There she stood, frightened, yet brave, not letting go her hold on what she meant to do; there was something that struck him most of all perhaps, and which shows the kind of man he was – he perceived that Molly was as unconscious that he was a young man, and she a young woman, as if she had been a pure angel from heaven. Though he felt that he would have to yield, and give up the letters, he was thinking what to say, he, with his quick senses all about him, heard the trotting of a horse crunching quickly along over the gravel of the drive. A moment afterwards, Molly's perception overtook his. He could see the startled look overspread her face; and in an instant she would have run away; but Mr Preston laid his hand firmly on her arm.

'Keep quiet. You must be seen. You, at any rate, have done nothing to be ashamed of.'

As he spoke, Mr Sheepshanks came round the bend of the road and was close upon them. Mr Preston saw, if Molly did not, the sudden look of intelligence that dawned upon the shrewd ruddy face of the old gentleman – saw, but did not much heed. He went forwards and spoke to Mr Sheepshanks, who made a halt right before them.

'Miss Gibson! your servant. Rather a blustering day for a young lady to be out – and cold, I should say, for standing still too long; eh, Preston?' poking his whip at the latter in a knowing manner.

'Yes,' said Mr Preston; 'and I'm afraid I've kept Miss Gibson too long standing.'

Molly did not know what to say; so she only bowed a silent farewell, and turned away to go home, feeling very heavy at heart at the non-success of her undertaking. For she did not know she had conquered.

Cynthia was on the watch for her return, and, rushing downstairs, dragged Molly into the dining-room.

'Well, Molly? Oh! I see you haven't got them. After all, I never expected it.' She sate down, as if she could get over her disappointment better in that position.

'I am so sorry; I did all I could; we were interrupted at last –Mr Sheepshanks rode up.'

'Provoking old man! Do you think you should have persuaded him to give up the letters, if you had had more time?'

'I don't know. I wish Mr Sheepshanks hadn't come up just then. I didn't like his finding me standing talking to Mr Preston.'

'Oh! I daresay he'd never think anything about it. What did he – Mr Preston – say?'

'He seemed to think you were fully engaged to him, and that these letters were the only proof he had. I think he loves you in his way.'

'His way, indeed!' said Cynthia scornfully.

'The more I think of it, the more I see it would be better for papa to speak to him. I did say I would tell it all to Lady Harriet, and get Lord Cumnor to make him give up the letters. But it would be very awkward.'

'Very!' said Cynthia gloomily. 'But he would see it was only a threat.'

'But I will do it in a moment, if you like. I meant what I said; only I feel that papa would manage it best of all.'

'I'll tell you what, Molly – you're bound by promise, you know, and cannot tell Mr Gibson without breaking your solemn word – but it's just this: I'll leave Hollingford and never come back again, if ever your father hears of this affair; there!'

Cynthia stood up now, and began to fold up Molly's shawl, in her nervous excitement.

'Oh, Cynthia – Roger!' was all that Molly said.

'Yes, I know! you need not remind me of him. But I'm not going to live in the house with anyone who may be always casting up in his mind the things he has heard against me. I was so happy, when I first came here; you all liked me, and admired me, and thought well of me, and now – Why, Molly, I can see the difference in you already. You've been thinking, "How Cynthia must have deceived me; keeping up a correspondence all this time – having half-engagements to two men!" You've been more full of that, than of pity for me as a girl who has always been obliged to manage for herself, without any friend to help her and protect her.'

Molly was silent. There was a great deal of truth in what Cynthia was saying: and yet a great deal of falsehood. For, through all this long forty-eight hours, Molly had loved Cynthia dearly. She also knew – but this was a second thought following on the other – that she had suffered much pain in trying to do her best in this interview with Mr Preston. The great tears welled up into her eyes, and fell slowly down her cheeks.

'Oh! what a brute I am!' said Cynthia, kissing them away. 'I know it is the truth, and I deserve it – but I need not reproach you.'

'You did not reproach me!' said Molly, trying to smile. 'I have thought something of what you said – but I do love you dearly, Cynthia – I should have done just the same as you did.'

'No, you would not. Your grain is different, somehow.'

## CHAPTER 40

# Confidences

All the rest of that day, Molly was depressed and not well. Having anything to conceal was almost so unprecedented a circumstance with her that it preyed upon her in every way.

The next morning's post brought several letters; one from Roger for Cynthia. It appeared to Molly as though Cynthia should have no satisfaction in these letters, until she had told him what was her exact position with Mr Preston; yet Cynthia was colouring and dimpling up, as she always did at any pretty words of praise, or admiration, or love. But Molly's thoughts and Cynthia's reading were both interrupted by a little triumphant sound from Mrs Gibson, as she pushed a letter she had just received to her husband, with a –

'There! I must say I expected that!' Then, turning to Cynthia, she explained, 'It is a letter from uncle Kirkpatrick, love. So kind, wishing you to go and stay with them, and help them to cheer up Helen.'

Cynthia's eyes sparkled. 'I shall like going,' said she – 'all but leaving you, Molly,' she added, in a lower tone.

'Can you be ready to go by the Bang-up tonight?' said Mr Gibson; 'for, curiously enough, after more than twenty years of quiet practice at Hollingford, I am summoned up today for the first time to a consultation in London tomorrow. I am afraid Lady Cumnor is worse, my dear.'

'You don't say so? Poor dear lady! I'm so glad I've had some breakfast. I could not have eaten anything.'

'Nay, with her complaint, being worse may only be a preliminary to being better. Don't take my words for more than their literal meaning.'

'Thank you. How kind and reassuring dear papa always is! About your gowns, Cynthia?'

'Oh, they're all right, mamma, thank you. I shall be quite ready by four o'clock. Molly, will you come with me and help me to pack? I wanted to speak to you, dear,' said she, as soon as they had gone upstairs. 'It is such a relief to get away from a place haunted by that man; but I'm afraid you thought I was glad to leave you; and indeed I am not.' There was a little flavour of 'protesting too much' about this; but Molly did not perceive it. She only said, 'Indeed I did not. I know from my own feelings how you must dislike meeting a man in public in a different manner from what you have done in private. I shall try not to see Mr Preston again for a long, long time, I'm sure. But, Cynthia, you haven't told me one word out of Roger's letter. Please, how is he?'

'He writes in very good spirits. A great deal about birds and beasts, as usual, habits of natives, and things of that kind. You may read from there' (indicating a place in the letter) 'to there. And I'll tell you what, I'll trust you with it, Molly, while I pack; and that shows my sense of your honour – not but what you might read it all, only you'd find the lovemaking dull; but make a little account of where he is, and what he is doing, date, and that sort of thing, and send it to his father.'

Molly took the letter down without a word, and began to copy it at the writing-table; often pausing, her cheek on her hand, her eyes on the letter, and letting her imagination rove to the writer, and all the scenes in which she had either seen him herself, or in which her fancy had painted him. She was startled from her meditations by Cynthia's sudden entrance into the drawing-room, looking the picture of glowing delight.

'No one here? What a blessing! Ah, Miss Molly, you're more eloquent than you believe yourself. Look here!' holding up a large full envelope, and then quickly replacing it in her pocket, as if she was afraid of being seen. 'What's the matter, sweet one?' coming up and caressing Molly. 'Is it worrying itself over that letter? Why, don't you see these are my very own horrible letters, that I am going to burn directly, that Mr Preston has had the grace to send me, thanks to you, little Molly – cuishla ma chree, pulse of my heart – the letters that have been hanging over my head like somebody's sword for these two years?'

'Oh, I am so glad!' said Molly. 'I never thought he would have sent them. And now it is all over. I am so glad!'

'It is the most charming relief; and I owe it all to you, you precious little lady! Now there's only one thing more to be done; and, if you would but do it for me –' (coaxing and caressing while she asked the question). 'It is only a very little thing. I won't burden your conscience with telling you how I got my letters, but it is not through a person I can trust with money; and I must force him to take back his twenty-three pounds odd shillings. I have put it together at the rate of five per cent, and it's sealed up. Oh, Molly, I should go off with such a light heart, if you would only try to get it safely to him. You might meet him by chance in a shop, in the street, even at a party – and, if you only had it with you in your pocket, there would be nothing so easy.'

Molly was silent. 'Papa would give it to him. There would be no harm in that. I would tell him he must ask no questions as to what it was.'

'Very well,' said Cynthia, 'have it your own way. I think my way is the best: but you've done a great deal for me already, and I won't blame you now for declining to do any more!'

'I do so dislike having these underhand dealings with him,' pleaded Molly.

'Underhand! just simply giving him a letter from me! If I left a note for Miss Browning, should you dislike giving it to her?'

'You know that's very different. I could do it openly.'

'And yet there might be writing in that; and there wouldn't be a line with the money. It would only be the winding-up – the honourable, honest winding-up of an affair which has worried me for years. But do as you like!'

'Give it me!' said Molly. 'I will try.'

'There's a darling!'

Molly looked forward to her two days alone with Mrs Gibson with very different anticipations from those with which she had welcomed the similar intercourse with her father. It was a gloomy, rainy evening, and candles had to be brought in at an unusually early hour. There would be no break for six hours – no music, no reading; but the two ladies would sit at their worsted work, pattering away at small-talk, with not even the usual break of dinner; for, to suit the requirements of those who were leaving, they had already dined early.

'You and I must go on the next journey, I think, my dear,' said Mrs Gibson, almost chiming in with Molly's wish that she could get away from Hollingford into some new air and life, for a week or two. 'We have been stay-at-homes for a long time! But I think the travellers will be wishing themselves at home by this nice bright fireside. "There's no place like home", as the poet says. "Mid pleasures and palaces though I may roam", it begins, and it's both very pretty and very true. It's a great blessing to have such a dear little home as this, is not it, Molly?'

'Yes,' said Molly, rather drearily.

'To be sure, love, it would be very nice for you and me to go on a little journey all by ourselves. If it were not such miserable weather, we would have gone off on a little impromptu tour. We live such a restricted kind of life here! And one misses the others, too! It seems so flat and deserted without them!'

'Yes! We are very forlorn tonight; but I think it's partly owing to the weather!'

'Nonsense, dear! I can't have you giving in to the silly fancy of being affected by weather. Poor dear Mr Kirkpatrick used to say, "a cheerful heart makes its own sunshine." He would say it to me, in his pretty way, whenever I was a little low – for I am a complete barometer – you may really judge of the state of the weather by my spirits, I have always been such a sensitive creature! It is well for Cynthia that she does not inherit it; I don't think her easily affected in any way, do you?'

Molly thought for a minute or two, and then replied –

'No, she certainly is not easily affected – not deeply affected, perhaps I should say.'

'Many girls, for instance, would have been touched by the

admiration she excited – I may say the attentions she received – when she was at her uncle's.'

'At Mr Kirkpatrick's?'

'Yes. There was Mr Henderson, that young lawyer; that's to say, he is studying law, but he has a good private fortune and is likely to have more. Mr Henderson was over head and ears in love with her. In one of Mrs Kirkpatrick's letters, she said that poor Mr Henderson was going into Switzerland for the long vacation, doubtless to try and forget Cynthia; but she really believed he would find it only "dragging at each remove a lengthening chain." I thought it such a refined quotation. You must know aunt Kirkpatrick some day, Molly, my love; she is what I call a woman of a truly elegant mind.'

'I can't help thinking it was a pity that Cynthia did not tell them of her engagement.'

'It is not an engagement, my dear! How often must I tell you that?'

'But there is something between Cynthia and Roger; they are more to each other than I am to Osborne, for instance. What am I to call it?'

'You should not couple your name with that of any unmarried young man; it is so difficult to teach you delicacy, child. Perhaps one may say there is a peculiar relation between dear Cynthia and Roger, but it is very difficult to characterise it; between ourselves, Molly, I sometimes think it will come to nothing. He is so long away, and, privately speaking, Cynthia is not very constant. I once knew her very much taken before – that little affair is quite gone by; and she was very civil to Mr Henderson, in her way; I fancy she inherits it, for when I was a girl I was beset by lovers, and could never find in my heart to shake them off. You have not heard dear papa say anything of the old Squire, or dear Osborne, have you? It seems so long since we have heard or seen anything of Osborne. But he must be quite well, I think, or we should have heard of it.'

'I believe he is quite well. Some one said the other day that they had met him riding ... it was Mrs Goodenough, now I remember – and that he was looking stronger than he had done for years.'

'Indeed! I am truly glad to hear it. I always was fond of Osborne; and, do you know, I never really took to Roger? I respected him and all that, of course; but to compare him with Mr Henderson! Mr Henderson is so handsome and well-bred, and gets all his gloves from Houbigant!'

It was true that they had not seen anything of Osborne Hamley for a long time; but, as it often happens, just after they had been speaking about him he appeared. It was on the day following Mr Gibson's departure that Mrs Gibson received one of the notes from the family in town, asking her to go over to the Towers, and find a book that Lady Cumnor wanted with all an invalid's impatience. It was just the kind of employment she required for an amusement on a gloomy day, and it put her into a good humour immediately. She asked Molly to accompany her, but was not sorry when Molly preferred stopping at home.

Molly enjoyed the house to herself; she ventured on having her lunch brought up on a tray into the drawing-room, so that she might eat her sandwiches while she went on with her book. In the middle, Mr Osborne Hamley was announced. He came in, looking wretchedly ill.

'This call is not on you, Molly,' said he. 'I was in hopes I might have found your father at home.'

'He was summoned up to London. Lady Cumnor is worse. I fancy there is some operation going on; but I don't know. He will be back tomorrow night.'

'Very well. Then I must wait. Perhaps I shall be better by that time. I think it's half fancy; but I should like your father to tell me so. He always is severe on fanciful patients, isn't he, Molly?'

Molly thought that, if he saw Osborne's looks just then, he would hardly think him fanciful, or be inclined to be severe. But she only said –

'Papa enjoys a joke at everything, you know. It is a relief after all the sorrow he sees.'

'Very true. There is a great deal of sorrow in the world. So

Cynthia is gone to London?' he added, after a pause. 'I think I should like to have seen her again. Poor old Roger! He loves her very dearly, Molly.'

Molly hardly knew how to answer him in all this; she was so struck by the change in both voice and manner.

'Mamma has gone to the Towers,' she began at length. 'Lady Cumnor wanted several things that mamma only can find. She will be sorry to miss you. We were speaking of you yesterday, and she said how long it was since we had seen you.'

'I've grown careless; I've often felt so weary and ill that it was all I could do to keep up a brave face before my father.'

'Why did you not come and see papa?' said Molly; 'or write to him?'

'I cannot tell. I drifted on, till today I mustered up pluck, and came to hear what your father has got to tell me.' He was silent for some time. Then, as if he had taken a sudden resolution, he spoke again. 'You see, there are others depending upon me – upon my health. You haven't forgotten what you heard that day in the library at home. I didn't know you at that time. I think I do now.'

'Don't go on talking so fast,' said Molly. 'Rest.' For she was alarmed at the pallor that had come over his face.

'Thank you.'

After a time he roused himself, and began to speak.

'The name of my wife is Aimée. Aimée Hamley. She lives at Bishopfield, a village near Winchester. Write it down, but keep it to yourself. She is a French-woman, a Roman Catholic, and was a servant. She is a thoroughly good woman. I must not say how dear she is to me. It is a relief to think that some one else has my secret; and you are like one of us, Molly. I can trust you almost as I can trust Roger. I feel better already, now I feel that some one else knows the whereabouts of my wife and child.'

'Child!' said Molly, surprised. But before he could reply, Maria had announced, 'Miss Phoebe Browning.'

'Fold up that paper,' said he quickly, putting something into her hands. 'It is only for yourself.'

CHAPTER 41

# Hollingford Gossips

'My dear Molly, why didn't you come and dine with us? I said to sister I would come and scold you well. Oh, Mr Osborne Hamley, is that you?' and a look of mistaken intelligence at the *tête-à-tête* she had disturbed came so perceptibly over Miss Phoebe's face, that Molly caught Osborne's sympathetic eye, and both smiled at the notion.

'We only just heard of Mrs Gibson's having a fly from the George, because sister sent our Betty to pay for a couple of rabbits Tom Ostler had snared, and she heard he was gone off with the fly to the Towers with your dear mamma; for Coxe, who drives the fly in general, has sprained his ankle. When Betty said Tom Ostler would not be back till night, I said, "Why, there's that poor dear girl left all alone by herself."'

Osborne said, 'I came to speak to Mr Gibson, not knowing he had gone to London. I must go now.'

'Oh dear! I am so sorry,' fluttered out Miss Phoebe, 'I disturbed you.' But Osborne was gone, before she had finished her apologies. As he left, his eyes met Molly's with a strange look of yearning farewell that she remembered strongly afterwards. 'Such a nice suitable thing, and I came in the midst, and spoilt it all.'

'My dear Miss Phoebe, if you are conjecturing a love-affair between Mr Osborne Hamley and me, you never were more mistaken in your life. Please do believe me,' said Molly, smiling, and trying to look perfectly indifferent.

It was very difficult for her to keep up any conversation, for her heart was full of Osborne – his changed appearance, his melancholy words of foreboding, and his confidences about his wife.

Molly found it very hard work to attend to kind Miss Phoebe's unceasing patter. She came up to the point, however, when the voice ceased. The last words, Molly perceived to be a question. Miss Phoebe was asking her if she would go out with her to Grinstead's, the bookseller of Hollingford; who, in addition to his regular business, was the agent for the Hollingford Book Society. It was the centre of news, and the club, as it were, of the little town. Everybody who pretended to gentility in the place belonged to it. It was a test of gentility, indeed, rather than of education or a love of literature.

Molly went upstairs to get ready to accompany Miss Phoebe; and, on opening one of her drawers, she saw Cynthia's envelope, containing the money she owed to Mr Preston. Molly took it up, hating it. She put it into her pocket for the chances of the walk and the day, and fortune for once seemed to befriend her; for, on their entering Grinstead's shop, there was Mr Preston. He bowed as they came in. He could not help that; but, at the sight of Molly, he looked as ill-tempered and out of humour as a man well could do. If Miss Phoebe had seen the scowl upon his handsome face, she might have undeceived her sister in her suppositions about him and Molly. But Miss Phoebe found herself an errand at the other end of the shop, and occupied herself in buying writing-paper. Molly fingered her valuable letter; did she dare to cross over to Mr Preston, and give it to him, or not? While she was still undecided, Miss Phoebe, having finished her purchase, and after looking a little pathetically at Mr Preston's back, said to Molly in a whisper –

'I think we'll go to Johnson's now, and come back for the books in a little while.' So across the street to Johnson's they went; but, no sooner had they entered the draper's shop, than Molly's conscience smote her for her cowardice.

'I'll be back directly,' said she, as soon as Miss Phoebe was engaged with her purchases; and ran across to Grinstead's; she had been watching the door, and she knew that no Mr Preston had issued forth. She ran in; he was at the counter now, talking to Grinstead himself; Molly put the letter into his hand, to his surprise, and turned round to go back to Miss Phoebe. At the door of the shop stood Mrs Goodenough, arrested in the act of entering, staring, with her round eyes, made still rounder and more owl-like by spectacles, to see Molly Gibson giving Mr Preston a letter, which he, conscious of being watched, put quickly into his pocket, unopened.

Scandal sleeps in the summer, comparatively speaking. Its nature is the reverse of that of the dormouse. Warm ambient air, loiterings abroad, gardenings, flowers to talk about, and preserves to make, soothed the wicked imp to slumber in the parish of Hollingford in summer-time. But when evenings grew short, and people gathered round the fires, then was the time for confidential conversation! Small crumbs and scraps of daily news came up to the surface, such as 'Martindale has raised the price of his best joints a halfpenny in the pound;' or 'Mr Preston and Miss Gibson, my uncle Sheepshanks came upon them in the Park Avenue – he startled 'em a good deal, he said; and, when he taxed Mr Preston with being with her sweetheart, he didn't deny it.'

'Well! Now so much has come out, I'll tell you what I know. Only, ladies, I wouldn't wish to do the girl an unkind turn, – so you must keep what I've got to tell you a secret.'

CHAPTER 42

# Scandal and Its Victims

When Mr Gibson returned to Hollingford, he found an accumulation of business waiting for him, and had immediately to rush off to pressing cases of illness. But Molly managed to arrest him in the hall, whispering as she did so –

'Papa! Mr Osborne Hamley was here to see you yesterday. He looks very ill, and he's evidently frightened about himself.'

Mr Gibson faced about, but all he said was –

'I'll go and see him; I can't today – but I will go.'

Mrs Gibson was busy reading a letter from Cynthia which Mr Gibson had brought from London; for Cynthia had forgotten so many things in her hurried packing, that she now sent a list of the clothes which she required. Molly almost wondered that it had not come to her; but she did not understand the sort of reserve that was springing up in Cynthia's mind towards her. The truth was, she believed that she no longer held her former high place in Molly's estimation, and she could not help turning away from one who knew things to her discredit.

The operation on Lady Cumnor had been successfully performed, and in a few days they hoped to bring her down to the Towers to recruit her strength in the fresh country air. The case was one which interested Mr Gibson extremely, and in which his opinion had been proved to be right, in opposition to that of one or two great names in London. The consequence was that he was frequently consulted and referred to during the progress of her recovery; and he found it difficult to spare the three or four hours necessary to go over to Hamley to see Osborne. He wrote to him, however, begging him to reply immediately and detail his symptoms; and from the answer he received he did not imagine that the case was immediately pressing. So the visit was deferred.

All these days the buzzing gossip about Molly's meetings with Mr Preston, her clandestine correspondence, the secret interviews in lonely places, had been gathering strength, and assuming the positive form of scandal. The simple, innocent girl became for a time the unconscious black sheep of the town. Servants heard part of what was said in their mistresses' drawing-rooms, and exaggerated the sayings amongst themselves with the coarse strengthening of expression common with uneducated people. Mr Preston himself became aware that her name was being coupled with his; he chuckled over the mistake, but took no pains to correct it.

'It serves her right,' said he to himself, 'for meddling with other folk's business,' and he felt himself avenged for the discomfiture which her menace of appealing to Lady Harriet had caused him, and the mortification he had experienced in learning from her plain-speaking lips, how he had been talked over by Cynthia and herself, with personal dislike on the one side, and evident contempt on the other.

There came a time when Molly felt that people looked askance at her. Mrs Goodenough pulled her grand-daughter away, when the young girl stopped to speak to Molly in the street, and an engagement which the two had made for a long walk together was cut very short by a very trumpery excuse.

For a good while, the Miss Brownings were kept in ignorance of the evil tongues that whispered hard words about Molly. Miss Browning was known to 'have a temper', and by instinct every one who came in contact with her shrank from irritating that temper by uttering the slightest syllable against the smallest of those creatures over whom she spread the aegis of her love. Miss Phoebe inspired no such terror but she was of so tender a nature that even thick-skinned Mrs Goodenough was unwilling to say what would give her pain; it was the new-comer, Mrs Dawes, who in all ignorance alluded to the town's talk, as to something of which Miss Phoebe must be aware. Then Miss Phoebe poured down her questions, although she protested, even with tears, her total disbelief in all the answers she received. It was a small act of heroism on her part to keep all that she then learnt a secret from her sister Dorothy, as she did for four or five days; till Miss Browning attacked her one evening with the following speech –

'Phoebe! either you've some reason for puffing yourself out with sighs, or you've not. If you have a reason, it's your duty to tell it me directly; and if you haven't a reason, you must break yourself of a bad habit that is growing upon you.'

'Oh, sister! do you think it is really my duty to tell you? it would be such a comfort; but it will distress you so.'

'Nonsense. I am so well prepared for misfortune by the frequent contemplation of its possibility, that I believe I can receive any ill news with apparent equanimity and real resignation.'

'Oh!' said Miss Phoebe, moving to a seat close to her sister's on the sofa. 'I hardly know how to tell you, Dorothy. I really don't.'

Miss Phoebe began to cry; Miss Browning gave her a little sharp shake.

'Cry as much as you like, when you've told me; but don't cry now, child, when you're keeping me on the tenter-hooks.'

'Molly Gibson has lost her character, sister. That's it.'

'Molly Gibson has done no such thing,' said Miss Browning indignantly. 'Never let me hear you say such things again.'

'I can't help it: Mrs Dawes told me; and she says it's all over the town. Oh, sister! what are you going to do?'

For Miss Browning had risen without speaking a word, and was leaving the room in a stately and determined fashion.

'I'm going to put on my bonnet and things, and then I shall call upon Mrs Dawes, and confront her with her lies.'

Miss Browning went to Mrs Dawes's and began, civilly enough, to make inquiries concerning the reports current in Hollingford about Molly and Mr Preston. Then Miss Browning went home, and said but a few words to Phoebe, who indeed saw well enough that her sister had heard the reports confirmed. Presently, Miss Browning sate down and wrote a short note. Then she rang the bell, and told the little maiden who answered it to take it to Mr Gibson. And then she went and put on her Sunday-cap; and Miss

Phoebe knew that her sister had written to ask Mr Gibson to come and be told of the rumours affecting his daughter. When the knock at the door was heard – the well-known doctor's knock – Miss Browning took off her spectacles, and dropped them on the carpet, breaking them as she did so; and then she bade Miss Phoebe leave the room, as if her presence had cast the evil-eye, and caused the misfortune.

'Well!' said he, coming in cheerfully, 'and what is the matter with us? It's Phoebe, I suppose? I hope none of those old spasms? But, after all, a dose or two will set that to rights.'

'Oh! Mr Gibson, I wish it was Phoebe, or me either!' said Miss Browning, trembling.

He sate down by her patiently, when he saw her agitation, and took her hand in a kind, friendly manner.

'Don't hurry yourself – take your time. I daresay it's not so bad as you fancy; but we'll see about it. There's a great deal of help in the world, much as we abuse it.'

'Mr Gibson,' said she, 'it's your Molly I'm so grieved about. It's out now, and God help us both, and the poor child too; for I'm sure she's been led astray, and not gone wrong by her own free will!'

'Molly!' said he. 'What's my Molly been doing or saying?'

'Oh! Mr Gibson, I don't know how to tell you. I never would have named it, if I had not been convinced, sorely, sorely against my will.'

'At any rate, you can let me hear what you've heard,' said he. 'Not that I'm a bit afraid of anything you can hear about my girl. Only, in this little nest of gossip, it's as well to know what people are talking about.'

'They say she's been carrying on a clandestine correspondence with Mr Preston' –

'Mr Preston!' exclaimed he.

'And meeting him at all sorts of unseemly places and hours, out-of-doors. All the town is talking of it.' Mr Gibson's hand was over his eyes, and he made no sign; so Miss Browning went on. 'Mr Sheepshanks saw them together. They have exchanged notes in Grinstead's shop; she ran after him there.'

'Be quiet, can't you?' said Mr Gibson, taking his hand away, and showing his grim, set face. 'Don't go on. I said I shouldn't believe it, and I don't. I suppose I must thank you for telling me; but I can't yet.'

'I don't want your thanks,' said Miss Browning, almost crying. 'I thought you ought to know; for, though you're married again, I can't forget you were dear Mary's husband once upon a time; and Molly's her child.'

'I'd rather not speak any more about it, just at present,' said he, not at all replying to Miss Browning's last speech. 'I wish I'd the doctoring of these slanderous gossips – I'd make their tongues lie still for a while! My little girl! What harm has she done them all, that they should go and foul her fair name?'

'Indeed, Mr Gibson, I'm afraid it's all true. I would not have sent for you if I hadn't examined into it. Do ascertain the truth before you do anything violent, such as horse-whipping or poisoning.'

With all the *inconséquence* of a man in a passion, Mr Gibson laughed out, 'What have I said about horse-whipping or poisoning? Do you think I'd have Molly's name dragged about the streets in connection with any act of violence on my part? Let the report die away as it arose! Time will prove its falsehood.'

'But I don't think it will,' said Miss Browning.

'I shall go home and ask Molly herself what's the meaning of it all; that's all I shall do. Knowing Molly as I do, it's perfectly ridiculous.' He got up and walked about the room with hasty steps, laughing short unnatural laughs from time to time. 'Really, what will they say next? "Satan finds some mischief still for idle tongues to do."'

Suddenly he stopped close to Miss Browning's chair: 'I'm thoroughly ungrateful to you, for as true a mark of friendship as you've ever shown me. True or false, it was right I should know the wretched scandal that is being circulated; and it couldn't have been pleasant for you to tell it me. Thank you from the bottom of my heart!'

'Indeed, Mr Gibson, if it was false, I would never have named it, but let it die away.'

'It's not true, though!' said he doggedly.

She shook her head. 'I shall always love Molly for her mother's sake,' she said. And it was a great concession from the correct Miss Browning. But her father did not understand it as such.

'You ought to love her for her own. She has done nothing to disgrace herself. I shall go straight home, and probe into the truth.'

## CHAPTER 43

# An Innocent Culprit

With his head bent down, Mr Gibson went swiftly to his own home. He rang at the door-bell; an unusual proceeding on his part. Maria opened the door. 'Go and tell Miss Molly she's wanted in the dining-room. Don't say who it is that wants her.' There was something in Mr Gibson's manner that made Maria obey him to the letter.

Mr Gibson went into the dining-room, and shut the door, for an instant's solitude. He went up to the chimney-piece, took hold of it, and laid his head on his hands, and tried to still the beating of his heart.

The door opened. He knew that Molly stood there, before he heard her tone of astonishment.

'Papa!'

'Hush!' said he, turning round sharply. 'Shut the door. Come here.'

She came to him wondering what was amiss. 'Is it Osborne?' she asked, breathless. If Mr Gibson had not been too much agitated to judge calmly, he might have deduced comfort from these three words.

But, instead of allowing himself to seek for comfort from collateral evidence, he said –

'Molly, what is this I hear? That you have been keeping up a clandestine intercourse with Mr Preston – meeting him in out-of-the-way places; exchanging letters with him in a stealthy way?'

Though he did disbelieve it at the bottom of his soul, his face was white and grim, and his eyes fixed Molly's with the terrible keenness of their search. Molly trembled all over, but she did not attempt to evade his penetration. If she was silent for a moment, it was because she was rapidly reviewing her relation with regard to Cynthia in the matter. It was but a moment's pause of silence, but it seemed long minutes to one who was craving for a burst of indignant denial. He had taken hold of her two arms just above her wrists, as she had advanced towards him; he was unconscious of this action; but, as his impatience for her words grew upon him, he grasped her more and more tightly in his vice-like hands, till she made a little involuntary sound of pain. And then he let go; and she looked at her soft bruised flesh, with tears gathering fast to her eyes, to think that he, her father, should have hurt her so. At the instant, it appeared to her stranger that he should inflict bodily pain upon his child, than that he should have heard the truth – even in an exaggerated form. With a childish gesture, she held out her arm to him; but, if she expected pity, she received none.

'Pooh!' said he, as he just glanced at the mark, 'that is nothing. Answer my question. Have you – have you met that man in private?'

'Yes, papa, I have; but I don't think it was wrong.'

He sate down now. 'Wrong!' he echoed bitterly. 'Not wrong? Well! I must bear it somehow. Your mother is dead. That's one comfort. It is true, then, is it? Why, I didn't believe it – not I! I laughed in my sleeve at their credulity; and I was the dupe all the time!'

'Papa, I cannot tell you all. It is not my secret, or you should know it directly. Indeed, you will be sorry some time – I have never deceived you, have I? Papa! have I ever deceived you?'

'How can I tell? I hear of this from the town's talk. I don't know what next may come out!'

'The town's talk!' said Molly in dismay. 'What business is it of theirs?'

'Every one makes it their business to cast dirt on a girl's name, who has disregarded the commonest rules of propriety.'

'Papa, I will tell you exactly what I have done. I met Mr Preston once – that evening when you put me down to walk over Croston

Heath – and there was another person with him. I met him a second time – and that time by appointment – nobody but our two selves – in the Towers Park. That is all, papa. You must trust me. I cannot explain more. You must trust me indeed.'

He could not help relenting at her words; there was such truth in the tone in which they were spoken. He raised his eyes to hers, for the first time since she had acknowledged the external truth of what he charged her with. Her face was very white, but it bore the impress of the final sincerity of death, when the true expression prevails without the disguises of time.

'The letters?' he said.

'I gave him one letter – of which I did not write a word – which, in fact, I believe to have been merely an envelope, without any writing whatever inside. The giving that letter – the two interviews I have named – make all the private intercourse I have had with Mr Preston. Oh! papa, what have they been saying that has shocked you so much?'

'Never mind. As the world goes, what you say you have done, Molly, is ground enough. You must tell me all. I must be sure to refute these rumours point by point.'

'How are they to be refuted, when you say that the truth which I have acknowledged is ground enough for what people are saying?'

'You say you were not acting for yourself, but for another. If you tell me who the other was I will do my utmost to screen her – for I guess it was Cynthia – while I am exonerating you.'

'No, papa!' said Molly. 'I have told you all I can tell; all that concerns myself; I have promised not to say one word more.'

'Then your character will be impugned. It must be, unless the fullest explanation of these secret meetings is given. I've a great mind to force the whole truth out of Preston himself.'

'Papa! if you ask Mr Preston, you will be very likely to hear the whole truth; but that is just what I have been trying so hard to conceal, for it will only make several people very unhappy, if it is known, and the whole affair is over and done with now.'

'Not your share in it. Miss Browning sent for me this evening, to tell me how people were talking about you. She implied that it was a complete loss of your good name. You don't know, Molly, how slight a thing may blacken a girl's reputation for life. I'd hard work to stand all she said, even though I didn't believe a word of it. And now you've told me that much of it is true.'

'But I think you are a brave man, papa. And you believe me, don't you? We shall outlive these rumours, never fear.'

'You don't know the power of ill-natured tongues, child,' said he.

'Oh, now you've called me "child" again, I don't care for anything. Dear, dear papa, I'm sure it is best and wisest to take no notice of these speeches. After all, they may not mean them ill-naturedly. I am sure Miss Browning would not. By-and-by they'll quite forget how much they made out of so little – and even if they don't, you would not have me break my solemn word, would you?'

'Perhaps not. But I cannot easily forgive the person who, by practising on your generosity, led you into this scrape.'

'Perhaps I've been foolish; but, what I did, I did of my own self. And I'm sure it was not wrong in morals, whatever it might be in judgment. As I said, it's all over now; what I did ended the affair, and it was with that object I did it. If people choose to talk about me, I must submit; and so must you, dear papa.'

'Does your mother – does Mrs Gibson – know anything about it?' asked he, with sudden anxiety.

'No; not a word. Pray don't name it to her. That might lead to more mischief than anything else. I have really told you everything I am at liberty to tell.'

'Then, what is to be done?' said he. 'Am I to go about smiling and content with all this talk about you passing from one idle gossip to another?'

'I'm afraid so. I can see how it must distress you. But surely, when nothing comes of what has happened, the wonder and the gossip must die away. I know you believe every word I have said, and you must trust me, papa. Please, for my sake, be patient with all this gossip and cackle!'

'I don't see what else I can do,' replied he moodily, 'unless I get hold of Preston.'

'That would be the worst of all. That would make a talk. And he behaved well to me, as far as that goes,' said she, suddenly recollecting his speech, when Mr Sheepshanks came up in the Towers Park – 'Don't stir, you have done nothing to be ashamed of.'

'That's true. A quarrel between men which drags a woman's name into notice is to be avoided at any cost. But, sooner or later, I must have it out with Preston. He shall find it not so pleasant to have placed my daughter in equivocal circumstances.'

'He didn't place me. He didn't expect to meet me either time; and would far rather not have taken the letter I gave him, if he could have helped himself.'

'I hate to have you mixed-up in mysteries.'

'I hate to be mixed-up. But what can I do? I know of another mystery which I'm pledged not to speak about. I cannot help myself.'

'Well, all I can say is, never be the heroine of a mystery that you can avoid, if you can't help being an accessory. Then, I suppose I must yield to your wishes and let this scandal wear itself out without any notice from me?'

'What else can you do, under the circumstances?'

'Ay; what else, indeed? How shall you bear it?'

For an instant the quick hot tears sprang into her eyes: to have all her world thinking evil of her, did seem hard to the girl who had never thought or said an unkind thing of them. But she smiled as she made answer –

'It's like tooth-drawing; it will be over some time. It would be much worse, if I really had been doing wrong.'

'Cynthia shall beware' – he began; but Molly put her hand before his mouth.

'Papa, Cynthia must not be accused, or suspected; you will drive her out of your house if you do; she is so proud, and so unprotected, except by you. And Roger – for Roger's sake, you will never do or say anything to send Cynthia away, when he has trusted us all to take care of her, and love her in his absence. Oh!

I think, if she were really wicked, and I did not love her at all, I should feel bound to watch over her, he loves her so dearly. And she is really good at heart, and I do love her dearly. You must not vex or hurt Cynthia, papa – remember she is dependent upon you!'

'I think the world would get on tolerably well, if there were no women in it. They plague the life out of one. You've made me forget, amongst you – poor old Job Houghton, that I ought to have gone to see an hour ago.'

Molly put up her mouth to be kissed. 'You're not angry with me now, papa, are you?'

'Get out of my way' (kissing her all the same), 'If I'm not angry with you, I ought to be; for you've caused a great deal of worry, which won't be over yet awhile, I can tell you.'

For all Molly's bravery at the time of this conversation, it was she that suffered more than her father. She was perpetually thrown into the small society of the place. Mr Preston did not accept the invitations to Hollingford tea-drinkings with the same eager gratitude as he had done a year before: or else the shadow which hung over Molly would not have extended to him, her co-partner in the clandestine meetings which gave such umbrage to the feminine virtue in the town. Molly herself was invited, because it would not do to pass any apparent slight on either Mr or Mrs Gibson; but there was a tacit and underhand protest against her being received on the old terms. Everyone was civil to her, but no one was cordial. Molly, for all her clear conscience and her brave heart, felt acutely that she was only tolerated, not welcomed. Miss Browning herself, that true old friend, spoke to her with chilling dignity, and much reserve; for she had never heard a word from Mr Gibson, since the evening when she had put herself to so much pain to tell him of the disagreeable rumours affecting his daughter.

Only Miss Phoebe would seek out Molly with even more than her former tenderness; and this tried Molly's calmness more than all the slights put together. The soft hand, pressing hers under the table – the continual appeals to her, so as to bring her back into the conversation – touched Molly almost to shedding tears. She never told her father how she felt these perpetual small slights: she had chosen to bear the burden of her own free will; nay, more, she had insisted on being allowed to do so; and it was not for her to grieve him now, by showing that she shrank from the consequences of her own act.

## CHAPTER 44

# Molly Gibson Finds a Champion

Lady Cumnor had so far recovered from her operation as to be able to be removed to the Towers for change of air; and accordingly she was brought thither by her whole family, with all the pomp and state becoming an invalid peeress. Somehow, it was very pleasant and restful to come to the old ancestral home, and every member of the family enjoyed it in his or her own way; Lord Cumnor most especially. His talent for gossip and his love of small details had scarcely fair play in the hurry of a London life, and were much nipped in the bud during his Continental sojournings. Besides, he was a great proprietor, and liked to know how his land was going on; how his tenants were faring in the world. He liked to hear of their births, marriages, and deaths, and had something of a royal memory for faces. In short, if ever a peer was an old woman, Lord Cumnor was that peer; but he was a very good-natured old woman, and rode about on his stout old cob, with his pockets full of halfpence for the children, and little packets of snuff for the old people. Like an old woman, too, he enjoyed an afternoon cup of tea in his wife's sitting-room, and over his gossip's beverage he would repeat all that he had learnt in the day. Lady Cumnor was exactly in that state of convalescence when such talk as her lord's was extremely agreeable to her; but she had condemned the habit of listening to gossip so severely all her life, that she thought it due to consistency to listen first, and enter a supercilious protest afterwards. It had, however, come to be a family habit for all of them to gather together in Lady Cumnor's room on their return from their daily walks, or drives, or rides, and, over the fire, sipping their tea at her early meal, to recount the morsels of local intelligence they had heard during the morning. On one of these November evenings they were all assembled in Lady Cumnor's room. She was lying on a sofa near the fire. Lady Harriet sate on the rug, close before the wood fire, picking up fallen embers with a pair of dwarf tongs. Lady Cuxhaven, a notable from girlhood, was using the blind man's holiday to net fruit-nets for the walls at Cuxhaven Park. Lady Cumnor's woman was trying to see to pour out tea by the light of one small wax-candle in the background (for Lady Cumnor could not bear much light to her weakened eyes); and the great leafless branches of the trees outside the house kept sweeping against the windows, moved by the wind that was gathering.

It was always Lady Cumnor's habit to snub those she loved best. Her husband was perpetually snubbed by her, yet she missed him now that he was later than usual, and professed not to want her tea; but they all knew that it was only because he was not there to hand it to her, and be found fault with for his invariable stupidity in forgetting that she liked to put sugar in, before she took any cream. At length he burst in –

'I beg your pardon, my lady – I'm later than I should have been, I know. Why! haven't you had your tea yet?' he exclaimed, bustling about to get the cup for his wife.

'You know I never take cream before I've sweetened it,' said she, with even more emphasis on the 'never' than usual.

'Oh, dear! What a simpleton I am! I think I might have remembered it by this time! You see I met old Sheepshanks, and that's the reason of it. Sheepshanks is such an eternal talker, there's no getting away from him!'

'Well, I think the least you can do is to tell us something of Mr Sheepshanks's conversation.'

'Conversation! did I call it conversation? I don't think I said much. I listened. He was telling me something about Preston; – old Sheepshanks thinks he'll be married before long – he says there's a great deal of gossip going on about him and Gibson's daughter. They've been caught meeting in the park, and corresponding, and all that kind of thing.'

'I shall be very sorry,' said Lady Harriet. 'I always liked that girl; and I can't bear papa's model land-agent.'

'I daresay it's not true,' said Lady Cumnor. 'Papa picks up stories one day, to contradict them the next.'

'Ah, but this did sound like truth. Sheepshanks said all the old ladies in the town had got hold of it, and were making a great scandal out of it.'

'I don't think it does sound quite a nice story. I wonder what Clare could be doing to allow such goings-on,' said Lady Cuxhaven.

'I think it's much more likely that Clare's own daughter – that pretty Miss Kirkpatrick – is the real heroine of this story,' said Lady Harriet. 'She always looks like a heroine of genteel comedy; and those young ladies were capable of a good deal of innocent intriguing. Now, little Molly Gibson has a certain *gaucherie* about her which would disqualify her at once from any clandestine proceedings. Why, the child is truth itself.'

'Really, Harriet, I can't think what always makes you take such an interest in all these petty Hollingford affairs.'

'Mamma, I'm quite of papa's faction. I like to hear all the local gossip.'

The next day Lady Harriet rode over to Hollingford, and called on the Miss Brownings, and introduced the subject. She began abruptly to Miss Browning –

'What is all this I hear about my little friend Molly Gibson and Mr Preston?'

'Oh, Lady Harriet! have you heard of it? We are so sorry! People do say such things!'

'But I don't believe them; indeed I don't,' burst in Miss Phoebe, half-crying.

'No more will I, then,' said Lady Harriet, taking the good lady's hand.

'It's all very fine, Phoebe, but I should like to know who it was that convinced me – sadly against my will, I am sure.'

'I only told you the facts as Mrs Goodenough told them me, sister; but I'm sure, if you had seen poor patient Molly as I have done, sitting up in a corner of a room, looking at the "Beauties of England and Wales" till she must have been sick of them, and no one speaking to her; and she as gentle and sweet as ever at the end of the evening, though maybe a bit pale – facts or no facts, I won't believe anything against her!'

So there sate Miss Phoebe, in tearful defiance of facts.

'And, as I said before, I'm quite of your opinion,' said Lady Harriet.

'But how does your ladyship explain away her meetings with Mr Preston in all sorts of unlikely and open-air places?' asked Miss Browning. 'I went so far as to send for her father and tell him all about it. I thought he would have horsewhipped Mr Preston; but he seems to have taken no notice of it.'

'Then we may be quite sure he knows some way of explaining matters that we don't,' said Lady Harriet decisively. 'I choose to have faith in Molly Gibson. I've a great mind to go and call on her – Mrs Gibson is confined to her room with this horrid influenza – and take her with me on a round of calls through the little gossiping town. But I've not time today. Only remember, Miss Phoebe, it's you and I against the world, in defence of a distressed damsel.' And she ran lightly down the Miss Brownings' old-fashioned staircase.

Lady Harriet was riding homewards by her father's side, turning over the possibilities that might account for these strange interviews between Molly and Mr Preston, when they saw Mr Preston coming towards them on his good horse, point device, in his riding attire. The earl, in his threadbare coat, and on his old brown cob, called out cheerfully –

'Aha! here's Preston. Good-day to you! I was just wanting to ask you about that slip of pasture-land on the Home Farm.'

While they were talking, Lady Harriet came to her resolution. As soon as her father had finished, she said –

'Mr Preston, perhaps you will allow me to ask you one or two questions, to relieve my mind.'

'Certainly; I shall only be too happy to give you any information in my power.'

'There are reports about Miss Gibson and you current among the gossips of Hollingford. Are we to congratulate you on your engagement to that young lady?'

'I am not so fortunate,' replied he.

'Then I may contradict that report?' asked Lady Harriet quickly. 'Or is there any reason for believing that in time it may come true? I ask, because such reports, if unfounded, do harm to young ladies.'

'Keep other sweethearts off,' put in Lord Cumnor, looking a good deal pleased at his own discernment.

Lady Harriet went on –

'And I take a great interest in Miss Gibson.'

Mr Preston saw from her manner that he was 'in for it'. The question was, how much or how little did she know?

'I have no expectation or hope of ever having a nearer interest in Miss Gibson than I have at present. I shall be glad if this straightforward answer relieves your ladyship from your perplexity.' He could not help the touch of insolence that accompanied these last words.

'Then, sir! are you aware of the injury you may do to a young lady's reputation, if you meet her, and detain her in long conversations, when she is walking unaccompanied? You give rise – you have given rise to reports.'

'My dear Harriet, are not you going too far? You don't know – Mr Preston may have intentions.'

'No, my lord. I have no intentions with regard to Miss Gibson. I am, in fact, a jilted man; jilted by Miss Kirkpatrick, after a tolerably long engagement. My interviews with Miss Gibson were not of the most agreeable kind – she was the agent in this last step of Miss Kirkpatrick's. Is your ladyship's curiosity satisfied with this mortifying confession of mine?'

'Harriet, my dear, you've gone too far – we had no right to pry into Mr Preston's private affairs.'

'No more I had,' said Lady Harriet, with a smile of winning frankness. 'But he will excuse me, I hope,' continued she, still in that gracious manner which made him feel that he now held a much higher place in her esteem than he had had at the beginning of their interview, 'when he learns that the busy tongues of the Hollingford ladies have been speaking of my friend, Miss Gibson, in the most unwarrantable manner; drawing unjustifiable inferences from the facts of that intercourse with Mr Preston, the nature of which he has just conferred such a real obligation on me by explaining.'

'I think I need hardly request Lady Harriet to consider this explanation of mine as confidential,' said Mr Preston.

'Of course, of course!' said the earl. And he rode home, and told his wife and Lady Cuxhaven the whole conversation; in the strictest confidence, of course.

Lady Harriet called on the Gibsons; and, finding that Mrs Gibson (who was still an invalid) was asleep at the time, she experienced no difficulty in carrying off the unconscious Molly for a walk, which Lady Harriet so contrived that they twice passed along the whole length of the principal street of the town, loitered at Grinstead's for half-an-hour, and wound up by Lady Harriet's calling on the Miss Brownings, who, to her regret, were not at home.

'Perhaps it's as well,' said she. 'I'll leave my card, and put your name down underneath it, Molly.'

Molly was a little puzzled and exclaimed –

'Please, Lady Harriet – I never leave cards; I have not got any; and on the Miss Brownings, of all people! why, I am in and out whenever I like.'

'Never mind, little one. Today you shall do everything properly, and according to full etiquette. And now tell Mrs Gibson to come out to the Towers for a long day; we will send the carriage for her, whenever she will let us know that she is strong enough to come. Indeed, she had better come for a few days.' So spoke Lady Harriet, holding Molly's hand while she wished her good-bye. 'You'll tell her, dear, that I came partly to see her – but that, finding her asleep, I ran off with you. And now good-bye, we've done a good day's work! And better than you're aware of,' continued she, still addressing Molly, though the latter was quite out of

## CHAPTER 45

# Cynthia at Bay

Mrs Gibson was slow in recovering her strength after the influenza; and, before she was well enough to accept Lady Harriet's invitation to the Towers, Cynthia came home from London. Cynthia's whole manner was more quiet than it had been, when the weight of her unpleasant secret rested on her mind. Molly was puzzled to account for it; and all the more perplexed, because from time to time Cynthia kept calling upon her for praise for some unknown and mysterious virtue that she had practised. She sometimes said such things as these, when she had been particularly inert and desponding:

'Ah, Molly, you must let my goodness lie fallow for a while! It has borne such a wonderful crop this year. I have been so pretty-behaved – if you knew all!' Or, 'Really, Molly, my virtue must come down from the clouds! It was strained to the utmost in London.'

One day the mystery burst its shell, and Molly could not appreciate the heroic goodness so often alluded to. The revelation of the secret took place in this way. Mrs Gibson came into the drawing-room with an open letter in her hand.

'I've had a letter from Aunt Kirkpatrick, Cynthia. What does she mean by this?' (holding out the letter to her). Cynthia put her netting on one side, and looked at the writing. Suddenly her face turned scarlet, and then became of a deadly white.

'It means, mamma, Mr Henderson offered to me while I was in London, and I refused him.'

'Refused him – and you never told me, but let me hear it by chance! Really, Cynthia. And pray, what made you refuse Mr

Henderson? Such a fine young man! Your uncle told me he had a very good private fortune besides.'

'Mamma, do you forget that I have promised to marry Roger Hamley?' said Cynthia quietly.

'No! of course I don't – how can I, with Molly always dinning the word "engagement" into my ears? But after all it was not a distinct promise – he seemed almost as if he might have looked forward to something of this sort.'

'Of what sort, mamma?' said Cynthia sharply.

'Why, of a more eligible offer. He must have known you might change your mind, and meet with some one you liked better: so little as you had seen of the world.'

Cynthia made an impatient movement.

'I never said I liked him better. I'm going to marry Roger, and there's an end of it. I will not be spoken to about it again.' She got up and left the room.

'Going to marry Roger! That's all very fine. But who is to guarantee his coming back alive? And if he does, what have they to marry upon, I should like to know? Such an invalid as I am too! It has given me quite a palpitation at the heart. I do call it quite unfeeling of Cynthia.'

'Certainly' – began Molly; but then she remembered that her stepmother was far from strong. So she changed her speech into a suggestion of remedies for palpitation; but, when they were alone, and Cynthia began upon the subject, Molly was less merciful. Cynthia said –

'Well, Molly, and now you know all! I've been longing to tell you – and yet somehow I could not.'

'I suppose you were agreeable – and he took it for something more.'

'I don't know,' sighed Cynthia. 'I mean, I don't know if I was agreeable or not. He was very kind – but I didn't expect it all to end as it did. However, it's of no use thinking of it.'

'No!' said Molly simply; for in her mind the pleasantest and kindest person in the world, put in comparison with Roger, was as nothing; he stood by himself.

In a little while, Mrs Gibson was able to accept the invitation from the Towers to go and stay for a day or two. Lady Cumnor's bodily strength was not yet sufficient to be an agent to her energetic mind, and the difficulty of driving the ill-matched pair of body and will – the one weak and languid, the other strong and stern – made her ladyship often very irritable. Mrs Gibson herself was not quite strong enough for a '*souffre-douleur*'; and the visit to the Towers was not, on the whole, quite so happy a one as she had anticipated. The second and the last day of her stay at the Towers, Lady Harriet came in, and found her mother haranguing in an excited tone of voice, and Clare looking submissive and miserable and oppressed.

'What's the matter, dear mamma? Are not you tiring yourself with talking?'

'No, not at all! I was only speaking of the folly of people dressing above their station. I began by telling Clare of the fashions of my grandmother's days, when every class had a sort of costume of its own – and servants did not ape trades-people, nor trades-people professional men, and so on – and what must the foolish woman do but begin to justify her own dress; as if I had been accusing her, or even thinking about her at all! Really, Clare, your husband has spoilt you sadly, if you can't listen to anyone without thinking they are alluding to you. People may flatter themselves just as much by thinking that their faults are always present to other people's minds, as if they believe that the world is always contemplating their charms and virtues.'

'I was told, Lady Cumnor, that this silk was reduced in price. I bought it at Waterloo House after the season was over,' said Mrs Gibson, touching the very handsome gown she wore, in deprecation of Lady Cumnor's angry voice, and blundering on to the very source of irritation.

'And very pretty it is,' said Lady Harriet, hoping to soothe the poor aggrieved woman. But Lady Cumnor went on.

'No! you ought to have known me better by this time. When I think a thing, I say it out. I will tell you where I think you have been in fault, Clare, if you like to know.' Like it or not, the plain speaking was coming now. 'You have spoilt that girl of yours till she does not know her own mind. She has behaved abominably to Mr Preston; and it is all in consequence of the faults in her education. You have much to answer for.'

'Mamma, mamma!' said Lady Harriet, 'Mr Preston did not wish it spoken about.' And at the same moment Mrs Gibson exclaimed, 'Cynthia – Mr Preston!'

'As for Mr Preston's wishes, I do not suppose I am bound to regard them when I feel it my duty to reprove error,' said Lady Cumnor loftily. 'And, Clare, do you mean to say that you are not aware that your daughter has been engaged to Mr Preston for some time and has at last chosen to break it off – and has used the Gibson girl as a cat's-paw, and made her the butt for all the gossip of Hollingford? I remember, when I was young, there was a girl called Jilting Jessie. You'll have to watch over your young lady, or she will get some such name. I speak to you like a friend, Clare, when I tell you it's my opinion that girl of yours will get herself into some more mischief yet, before she's safely married. Not that I care one straw for Mr Preston's feelings. I don't even know if he's got feelings or not; but I know what is becoming in a young woman, and jilting is not. And now you may both go away and send Dawson to me, for I'm tired, and want to have a little sleep.'

'Indeed, Lady Cumnor – will you believe me? – I do not think Cynthia was ever engaged to Mr Preston. There was an old flirtation. I was afraid' –

Lady Harriet had too much experience of her mother's moods not to lead Mrs Gibson away almost by main force, she protesting all the while.

Once in her own room, Lady Harriet said, 'Now, Clare, I'll tell you all about it; and I think you'll have to believe it, for it was Mr Preston himself who told me. He made both papa and me promise not to tell; but papa did – and that's what mamma has for a foundation.'

'But Cynthia is engaged to another man – she really is. And another – a very good match indeed – has just been offering to her in London. Mr Preston is always at the root of mischief.'

'Nay! I do think in this case it must be that pretty Miss Cynthia of yours who has drawn on one man to be engaged to her – not to say two – and another to make her an offer. I can't endure Mr Preston; but I think it's rather hard to accuse him of having called up the rivals, who are, I suppose, the occasion of his being jilted.'

'I don't know. Cynthia has a way of attracting men. I will speak to her; I will get to the bottom of the whole affair. Pray tell Lady Cumnor that it has so fluttered me the way she spoke, about my dress and all. And it only cost five guineas after all, reduced from eight!'

'Well, never mind now. But, do you know, mamma is so much pleased to have you here!'

And so Lady Cumnor really was, in spite of the continual lectures which she gave 'Clare', and which poor Mrs Gibson turned under as helplessly as the typical worm. Still it was something to have a countess to scold her; and that pleasure would endure, when the worry was past. When she looked back upon her visit, as she drove home in the solitary grandeur of the Towers carriage, there had been but one great enduring rub – Lady Cumnor's crossness – and she chose to consider Cynthia as the cause of that. Mrs Gibson sate down despondingly in her own little easy-chair, and in reply to Cynthia's quick pleasant greeting of –

'Well, mamma, how are you?' she replied dolefully –

'It has not been such a happy visit that I should wish to prolong it.'

'What has been the matter?' asked Cynthia.

'You! Cynthia – you! I little thought, when you were born, how I should have to bear to hear you spoken about. It is not pleasant for me to hear first of my daughter's misdoings from Lady Cumnor, and then to be lectured about her, and her flirting, and her jilting, as if I had anything to do with it.'

Cynthia was brought to bay.

'Would you mind telling me what they said? Here's Molly' (as the girl entered the room). 'Molly, mamma has come back from the Towers, and my lord and lady have been doing me the honour to talk over my crimes and misdemeanours, and I am asking mamma what they have said.'

'They say you've gone and engaged yourself to Mr Preston, and now refuse to marry him; and they call that jilting.'

'Do you wish me to marry him, mamma?' asked Cynthia, her face in a flame, her eyes cast down.

'No,' said Mrs Gibson. 'Of course I don't; you've gone and entangled yourself with Roger Hamley, a very worthy young man; but nobody knows where he is, and if he's dead or alive; and he has not a penny, if he is alive. You've entangled yourself with him, and you've done something of the sort with Mr Preston, and got yourself into such an imbroglio' (Mrs Gibson could not have said 'mess' for the world, although the word was present to her mind), 'that when a really eligible person comes forward you have to refuse him. You'll end an old maid, Cynthia, and it will break my heart.'

'I daresay I shall,' said Cynthia quietly. 'I sometimes think I'm the kind of person of which old maids are made!' She spoke seriously, and a little sadly.

'I don't want to know your secrets, as long as they are secrets; but when I am constantly blamed for your misconduct, I think it's very hard.' Mrs Gibson began to cry. Just then her husband came in.

'You here, my dear! Welcome back,' said he, coming up to her and kissing her cheek. 'Why, what's the matter? Tears?'

'Yes!' said she, raising herself up, and clutching after sympathy of any kind, at any price. 'I'm come home again, and I'm telling Cynthia how Lady Cumnor has been so cross to me, and all through her. Did you know she had gone and engaged herself to Mr Preston, and then broken it off! Everybody is talking about it, and they know it up at the Towers.'

For one moment his eyes met Molly's, and he comprehended it all.

'Cynthia,' said he, very seriously.

'Yes!' she answered softly.

'Is this true? I had heard something of it before – not much;

but there is scandal enough about to make it desirable that you should have some protector – some friend who knows the whole truth.'

At last she said, 'Molly knows it all.'

'Yes! I know that Molly knows it all, and that she has had to bear slander and ill words for your sake, Cynthia. But she refused to tell me more.'

'She told you that much, did she?' said Cynthia, aggrieved.

'She didn't name your name,' said Mr Gibson. 'At the time, I believe, she thought she had concealed it – but there was no mistaking who it was.'

'Why did she speak about it at all?' said Cynthia.

'It was necessary for her to justify herself to me – I heard my daughter's reputation attacked for the private meetings she had given to Mr Preston – I came to her for an explanation. There's no need to be ungenerous, Cynthia, because you've been a flirt and a jilt.'

Cynthia looked at him.

'You say that of me, Mr Gibson? Not knowing what the circumstances are, you say that?'

He had spoken too strongly; he knew it. But he could not bring himself to own it just at that moment. The thought of his sweet innocent Molly prevented any retraction at the time.

'Yes!' he said, 'I do say it. I do say that Molly has had a great deal to bear, in consequence of this clandestine engagement of yours, Cynthia – there may be extenuating circumstances, I acknowledge – but you will need to remember them all to excuse your conduct to Roger Hamley, when he comes home. I asked you to tell me the full truth, in order that, until he comes, and has a legal right to protect you, I may do so. Here are you engaged to two men at once, to all appearances!' No answer. 'To be sure, the gossips of the town haven't yet picked out the fact of Roger Hamley's being your accepted lover; but scandal has been resting on Molly, and ought to have rested on you, Cynthia – for a concealed engagement to Mr Preston – necessitating meetings in all sorts of places unknown to your friends.'

'Papa,' said Molly, 'if you knew all, you wouldn't speak so to Cynthia. I wish she would tell you all that she has told me.'

'I am ready to hear whatever she has to say,' said he. But Cynthia said –

'No! you have prejudged me. I refuse to give you my confidence or accept your help. People are very cruel to me' – her voice trembled for a moment – 'I did not think you would have been. But I can bear it.'

And then, in spite of Molly, who would have detained her by force, she tore herself away, and hastily left the room.

'Oh, papa!' said Molly, crying, and clinging to him, 'do let me tell you all!' And then she suddenly recollected the awkwardness of telling some of the details of the story before Mrs Gibson, and stopped short.

'I think, Mr Gibson, you have been very, very unkind to my poor fatherless child,' said Mrs Gibson. 'I only wish her poor father had been alive, and all this would never have happened.'

'Very probably. Still I cannot see of what either she or you have to complain. As much as we could, I and mine have sheltered her; I have loved her; I do love her, almost as if she were my own child – as well as Molly, I do not pretend to do.'

'That's it, Mr Gibson! you do not treat her like your own child.' But in the midst of this wrangle Molly stole out, and went in search of Cynthia. But Cynthia was locked into her room, and refused to open the door.

'Open to me, please,' pleaded Molly. 'I have something to say to you – I want to see you – do open!'

'No!' said Cynthia. 'I don't want to hear what you have got to say. I don't want to see you. Go away. I cannot bear the feeling of your being there – waiting. Go downstairs – out of the house. It is the most you can do for me now.'

## CHAPTER 46

# 'Troubles Never Come Alone'

Molly crept away, as she was bidden. It was long past lunch-time, when once again she stole up to her room. The door opposite was open wide – Cynthia had quitted the chamber. Molly arranged her dress and went down into the drawing-room. Cynthia and her mother sate there in the stern repose of an armed neutrality. Cynthia was netting away, as if nothing unusual had occurred. Not so Mrs Gibson; her face bore evident marks of tears, and she looked up and greeted Molly's entrance with a faint smiling notice. Molly took up a book to have the semblance of some employment.

At length Cynthia spoke, but she had to begin again before her words came clear.

'I wish you both to know, that henceforward all is at an end between me and Roger Hamley.'

Molly's book went down upon her knees.

'Cynthia – think of him! It will break his heart!'

'No!' said Cynthia, 'it will not. But, even if it did, I cannot help it.'

'All this talk will soon pass away!' said Molly; 'and, when he knows the truth from your own self' –

'From my own self he shall never hear it. I do not love him well enough to go through the shame of having to excuse myself. Confession may be an ease of mind if one makes it to some people – to some person – and it may not be a mortification to sue for forgiveness. I cannot tell. All I know is – and I know it clearly, and will act upon it inflexibly – that –' And here she stopped short.

'I think you might finish your sentence,' said her mother.

'I cannot bear to exculpate myself to Roger Hamley. And the truth is, I do not love him. I like him, I respect him; but I will not marry him. I have written to tell him so. And I have written to old Mr Hamley. It is such a relief to feel free again. It wearied me so to think of straining up to his goodness.'

When Mr Gibson came home, she asked to speak with him, alone, in his consulting-room; and there laid bare the exculpation of herself which she had given to Molly many weeks before. When she had ended, she said –

'And now, Mr Gibson – I still treat you like a friend – help me to find some home far away, where all the evil talking and gossip mamma tells me of cannot find me and follow me. It may be wrong to care for people's good opinion – but it is me, and I cannot alter myself. You, Molly – all the people in the town – I haven't the patience to live through the nine days' wonder. I want to go away and be a governess. I have broken it all off with Roger. I wrote this morning. If he ever receives that letter, I hope to be far away by that time; in Russia, may be.'

'Nonsense. An engagement like yours cannot be broken off, except by mutual consent. You've only given others a great deal of pain without freeing yourself. Nor will you wish it in a month's time. When you come to think calmly, you'll be glad to think of the stay and support of such a husband as Roger. You have been in fault, and have acted foolishly at first – perhaps wrongly after- wards; but you don't want your husband to think you faultless?'

'Yes, I do,' said Cynthia. 'At any rate, my lover must think me so. And it is just because I do not love him even as so light a thing as I could love, that I feel that I couldn't bear to have to tell him I'm sorry, and stand before him, like a chidden child, to be admonished and forgiven.'

'But here you are, just in such a position before me!'

'Yes! but I love you better than Roger. And I would have told you, if I hadn't expected and hoped to leave you all before long. I should see if the recollection of it all came up before your mind; I should see it in your eyes, I should know it by instinct. I have a fine instinct for reading the thoughts of others, when they refer to me. I almost hate the idea of Roger judging me by his own standard, which wasn't made for me, and graciously forgiving me at last.'

'Then I do believe it's right for you to break it off,' said Mr Gibson. 'That poor, poor lad! But it'll be best for him too. And he'll get over it. Still, take till tomorrow before you act upon your decision. What faults you have fallen into have been mere girlish faults at first – leading you into much deceit, I grant.'

'Don't give yourself the trouble to define the shades of blackness,' said Cynthia bitterly. 'I'm not so obtuse but what I know them all, better than anyone can tell me. Oh, sir! I think, if I had been differently brought up, I shouldn't have had the sore angry heart I have now. No, don't! I should always have wanted admiration and worship, and men's good opinion. Those unkind gossips! To visit Molly with their hard words! Oh, dear! I think life is very dreary.'

She put her head down on her hands; tired out, mentally as well as bodily. So Mr Gibson thought. He left the room, and called Molly. 'Go to Cynthia!' he whispered, and Molly went. She took Cynthia into her arms with gentle power.

'Oh, my darling!' she murmured. 'I do so love you, dear, dear Cynthia!' and she stroked her hair, and kissed her eyelids; Cynthia suddenly started up, stung with a new idea, and looking Molly straight in the face, said –

'Molly, Roger will marry you! You two good' –

But Molly pushed her away, with a sudden violence of repulsion. 'Don't!' she said. She was crimson with shame and indignation. 'Your husband this morning! Mine tonight! What do you take him for?'

'A man!' smiled Cynthia. 'And therefore, if you won't let me call him changeable, I'll coin a word and call him consolable!' At this moment, Maria entered. She had a scared look.

'Isn't master here?' asked she.

'No!' said Cynthia. 'I heard him go out five minutes ago.'

'Oh, dear!' said Maria. 'And there's a man come on horseback from Hamley Hall, and he says as Mr Osborne is dead, and that master must go off to the Squire straight away.'

'Osborne Hamley dead!' said Cynthia, in awed surprise. Molly was out at the front door, round into the stable-yard, where the groom sate motionless on his dark horse, flecked with foam. Molly laid her hand on the hot damp skin of the horse's shoulder; the man started.

'Is the doctor coming, Miss?'

'He is dead, is he not?' asked Molly in a low voice.

'There is no doubt according to what they said. But there may be a chance. Is the doctor coming, Miss?'

'He is gone out. I will go myself. Oh! the poor old Squire!' She went into the kitchen – went over the house with swift rapidity, to gain news of her father's whereabouts. The servants knew no more than she did. Upstairs sped Molly to the drawing-room, where Mrs Gibson stood at the door.

'What is it, Molly? Why, how white you look, child!'

'Osborne Hamley is dead!'

'Dead! Osborne! Poor fellow! I knew it would be so, though – I was sure of it. But Mr Gibson can do nothing, if he's dead!'

'He will not be long,' thought Molly, 'or he would have left word where he was going. But oh! the poor father all alone!' And then she acted. 'Go to James, tell him to put the side-saddle on Nora Creina!'

So, down Molly came, equipped in her jacket and skirt; quick determination in her eyes.

'Why, what in the world' – said Mrs Gibson – 'Molly, what are you thinking about?'

'I must go. I cannot bear to think of him alone. When papa comes back, he is sure to go to Hamley, and if I am not wanted, I can come back with him.'

They rode quick, and when they came in sight of the square stillness of the house, shining in the moonlight, Molly caught at her breath. One yellow light burnt steadily.

'It's the old nursery. They carried him there. The Squire broke down at the stair-foot, and they took him to the readiest place.'

Molly dropped down from her seat, before the man could dismount to help her. She gathered up her skirts and ran along the once familiar turns, and swiftly up the stairs, and through the doors, till she came to the last; then she stopped and listened. It was a deathly silence. She opened the door – the Squire was sitting alone at the side of the bed, holding the dead man's hand, and looking straight before him at vacancy. He did not stir at Molly's entrance. Molly came up to him with the softest steps, the most hushed breath that ever she could. After a moment's pause, standing by the old man's side, she slipped down to the floor, and sat at his feet. There they sate, silent and still, he in his chair, she on the floor; the dead man, beneath the sheet. Time had never seemed so without measure, silence had never seemed so noiseless as it did to Molly, sitting there.

Her father stood by them both, before either of them was aware. 'Go downstairs, Molly,' said he gravely; but he stroked her head tenderly as she rose. Now she trembled with fear, as she went along the moonlit passages. It seemed to her as if she should meet Osborne, and hear it all explained: how he came to die – what he now felt and thought and wished her to do.

## CHAPTER 47

# Squire Hamley's Sorrow

It seemed very long before Mr Gibson came down.

'He's gone to bed,' said he at length. 'Robinson and I have got him there. But, just as I was leaving him, he called me back and asked me to let you stop. I'm sure I don't know – but one doesn't like to refuse at such a time.'

'I wish to stay,' said Molly. 'Papa – what did Osborne die of?' She asked the question in a low, awe-stricken voice.

'Something wrong about the heart. When I saw him on Thursday week, he seemed better. But one never can calculate in these complaints.'

'You saw him on Thursday week? Why, you never mentioned it!' said Molly.

'No. I don't talk of my patients at home. Besides, I didn't want him to consider me as his doctor, but as a friend. Any alarm about his own health would only have hastened the catastrophe.'

'Papa, I ought to tell you something. I know a great secret of Osborne's, which I promised solemnly not to tell; but the last time I saw him, I think he must have been afraid of something like this. Osborne was married.'

'Married! Nonsense! What makes you think so?'

'He told me. And six months ago, last November, when you went up to Lady Cumnor, he gave me his wife's address, but still under promise of secrecy.'

'Where is this wife of his?'

'Near Winchester. He said she was a Frenchwoman and a Roman Catholic; and a servant.'

'Phew!'

'And,' continued Molly, 'he spoke of a child.'

Mr Gibson sate down, put his hands in his pockets, and began to think.

'Well!' said he at last, jumping up, 'nothing can be done tonight. Poor little pale face!' – taking it between both his hands and kissing it; 'poor, sweet, little pale face!' Then he rang the bell, and told Robinson to send some maidservant to take Miss Gibson to her room. 'He won't be up early,' said he, in parting. 'I'll be here again before ten.'

Late as it was before he left, he kept his word.

'Now, Molly,' he said, 'you and I must tell him the truth between us. It may comfort him, but I've very little hope.'

'Robinson says he has gone into the room and locked the door on the inside.'

'Never mind. I shall send up Robinson to say I am here, and wish to speak to him.'

Mr Gibson was growing impatient before they heard the Squire's footstep on the stairs; he was evidently coming slowly and unwillingly. He came in almost like one blind, groping along, and taking hold of chair or table for support or guidance, till he reached Mr Gibson. He did not speak when he held the doctor by the hand; he only hung down his head, and kept on a feeble shaking of welcome.

'I'm brought very low, sir. I suppose it's God's doing; but it comes hard upon me. He was my firstborn child.'

'Here's Molly,' said Mr Gibson, choking a little himself, and pushing her forwards.

'I beg your pardon; I did not see you at first.' He sate heavily down, and then seemed almost to forget they were there.

'Where's Roger?' said Mr Gibson. 'Is he not likely to be soon at the Cape? You will be glad to have Roger at home as soon as may be, I think, sir. Some months must elapse first; but I'm sure he will return as speedily as possible.'

The Squire said in a very low voice. 'Roger isn't Osborne!' And Mr Gibson spoke more quietly than Molly had ever heard him do before.

'No! we know that. I wish that anything that Roger could do, or that I could do, or that anyone could do, would comfort you; but it is past human comfort.'

'I do try to say, God's will be done, sir,' said the Squire, looking up for the first time; 'but it's harder to be resigned than happy people think. He was my first child, sir; my eldest son. And of late years we weren't – we weren't quite as good friends as could be wished; and I'm not sure – not sure that he knew how I loved him.' And now he cried aloud, with an exceeding bitter cry.

'Better so!' whispered Mr Gibson to Molly. 'Tell him all you know, exactly as it happened.'

Molly began. The Squire did not attempt to listen, at first, at any rate.

'One day when I was here, at the time of Mrs Hamley's last illness, I was in the library, and Osborne came in. He said that I was not to mind him; so I went on reading. Presently, Roger came along. He did not see me, and said to Osborne, "Here's a letter from your wife!"'

Now the Squire was all attention; 'His wife! Osborne married!' Molly went on –

'They made me promise never to mention it to anyone, or to allude to it to either of them again. I never named it to papa till last night.'

Still the Squire hung on her lips.

'Some months ago Osborne called. He was not well. He spoke to me of his wife for the first and only time since the affair in the library. He said his wife was a good woman, and that he loved her dearly; but she was a French Roman Catholic, and she had been a servant once. I have her address at home. He wrote it down and gave it me.'

'Well! well!' moaned the Squire. 'He and I to live together with such a secret in one of us! It's no wonder to me now – nothing can be a wonder again, for one never can tell what's in a man's heart. Married so long! Oh, Osborne, Osborne, you should have told me! And Roger too! He could know it all, and keep it from me!'

'Osborne evidently had bound him down to secrecy, just as he bound me,' said Molly; 'Roger could not help himself.'

'Osborne was such a fellow for persuading people, and winning them over,' said the Squire dreamily. 'Oh, my lad, my lad – thou might have trusted thy old dad!'

'Well, but, Squire,' said Mr Gibson, 'to return to his wife'–

'And the child,' whispered Molly to her father.

'What?' said the Squire. 'Is there a child? Husband and father, and I never knew! God bless Osborne's child! I say, God bless it!' He stood up reverently, and the other two instinctively rose. He closed his hands, as if in momentary prayer. Then, exhausted, he sate down again, and put out his hand to Molly.

'You're a good girl. Thank you. – Tell me what I ought to do, and I'll do it.' This to Mr Gibson.

'I think there must be some written confirmation, which perhaps ought to be found before we act. Most probably this is to be discovered among Osborne's papers. Will you look over them? Molly shall return with me, and find the address that Osborne gave her, while you are busy'–

'She'll come back again?' said the Squire eagerly. 'You – she – won't leave me to myself?'

'No! She shall come back this evening. I'll manage to send her somehow. But she has no clothes but the habit she came in, and I want my horse that she rode away upon.'

'Take the carriage,' said the Squire. 'I'll give orders. You'll come back again, too?'

'No, I'm afraid not. I'll come tomorrow, early. Molly shall return this evening, whenever it suits you to send for her.'

'This afternoon; the carriage shall be at your house at three. I dare not look at Osborne's papers without one of you with me; and yet I shall never rest till I know more.'

As they rode away, Mr Gibson said –

'Some one must write to Mrs Osborne Hamley. She must be told that the father of her child is dead. Shall you do it, or I?'

'Oh, you, please, Papa!'

'But she may have heard of you as a friend of her dead husband's.'

'If I ought I will do it.'

Mrs Gibson gave Molly a warm welcome. For one thing, Cynthia was in disgrace; for another, Molly came from the centre of news; for a third, Mrs Gibson was really fond of the girl, in her way.

'To think of it all being so sudden at last! Not but what I always expected it! And so provoking! Just when Cynthia had given up Roger! What does the Squire say to it all?'

'He is beaten down with grief,' replied Molly.

'Indeed! I should not have fancied he had liked the engagement so much.'

'What engagement?'

'Why, Roger to Cynthia, to be sure. I asked you how the Squire took her letter, announcing the breaking of it off?'

'Oh – he hasn't opened his letters today. I saw Cynthia's among them.'

'I hate to look at such things in a mercenary spirit, but it is provoking to see Cynthia throw over two such good matches. First Mr Henderson and now Roger Hamley. When does the Squire expect Roger? Does he think he will come back sooner for poor dear Osborne's death?'

'I don't know. He hardly seems to think of anything but Osborne. But perhaps the news of Osborne's being married, and of the child, may rouse him up.'

Mrs Gibson exclaimed, 'What *do* you mean, child? Osborne married! Who says so?'

'Oh, dear! I suppose I ought not to have named it. I'm very stupid today. Yes! Osborne has been married a long time; but the Squire did not know of it till this morning. I think it has done him good. But I don't know.'

'Who is the lady? Who is the lady? Do tell me all you know about it, there's a dear.'

'She is French, and a Roman Catholic,' said Molly.

'French! They are such beguiling women; and he was so much abroad! You said there was a child – is it a boy or a girl?'

'I did not ask.'

Just then, Cynthia came wandering into the room with a careless, hopeless look in her face.

'Molly, darling! Is that you? The house isn't the same when you are away!'

'And she brings us such news too!' said Mrs Gibson. 'I'm really almost glad you wrote to the Squire yesterday; for, if you had waited till today he might have thought you had some interested reason for giving up your engagement. Osborne Hamley was married all this time unknown to everybody, and has got a child too.'

'Osborne married!' exclaimed Cynthia. 'Poor Osborne!'

'It was a great piece of deceit, and I can't easily forgive him for it. Only think! If he had paid either of you any particular attention, and you had fallen in love with him! Why, he might have broken your heart, or Molly's either. I can't forgive him, even though he is dead, poor fellow!'

'Well, as we neither of us did fall in love with him, I only feel sorry that he had all the trouble and worry of concealment.' Cynthia spoke with a pretty keen recollection of how much trouble and worry her concealment had cost her.

## CHAPTER 48

# Unlooked-for Arrivals

Molly went into the drawing-room. The Squire was standing in the middle of the floor, awaiting her – in fact, longing to go out and meet her, but restrained by a feeling of solemn etiquette in that house of mourning. He held a paper in his hands, which were trembling with excitement and emotion.

'It's all true,' he began; 'she's his wife, and he's her husband – was her husband! Poor lad! poor lad! it's cost him a deal. Pray God, it wasn't my fault. Read this, my dear. It's a certificate. It's all regular – Osborne Hamley to Marie-Aimée Scherer – parish-church and all, and witnessed. Oh, dear!' He sate down in the nearest chair and groaned.

'There are some letters,' said she; 'may I read them?' At another time she would not have asked; but she was driven to it now by the speechless grief of the old man.

'Ay,' said he. 'Maybe you can. I can only pick out a word here and there. I put 'em there for you to look at; and tell me what is in 'em.'

Molly managed to translate into good enough colloquial English some innocent sentences of love, and submission to Osborne's will – as if his judgment was infallible – and of faith in his purposes; little sentences in 'little language' that went home to the Squire's heart.

In examining the papers, she came upon one in particular. 'Have you seen this, sir? This certificate of baptism of Roger Stephen Osborne Hamley, born June 21, 183–, child of Osborne Hamley and Marie-Aimée his wife' –

'Give it me,' said the Squire, his voice breaking now. '"Roger", that's me, "Stephen", that's my poor old father. And Osborne – Osborne Hamley! One Osborne Hamley lies dead on his bed – and t'other – t'other I've never seen, and never heard on till today. He must be called Osborne, Molly. There is a Roger – there's two for that matter; but one is a good-for-nothing old man; and there's never an Osborne any more; we'll have him here, and get a nurse for him; and make his mother comfortable for life in her own country. I'll keep this, Molly. You're a good lass for finding it. Osborne Hamley! And if God will give me grace, he shall never hear a cross word from me – never! He shan't be afeard of me. Oh, *my* Osborne, *my* Osborne.'

From the general tone of the letters, Molly doubted if the mother would consent, so easily as the Squire seemed to expect, to be parted from her child. Still, it was not for Molly to talk of this doubt of hers.

There were not many people who had any claim to be invited to the funeral, and of these Mr Gibson and the Squire's hereditary man of business had taken charge. But when Mr Gibson came, early on the following morning, Molly referred the question to him, which had suggested itself to her mind, though apparently not to the Squire's, what intimation of her loss should be sent to the widow.

'She must be told,' said Mr Gibson, musing.

'Yes, she must,' replied his daughter. 'But how?'

'A day or two of waiting will do no harm,' said he. 'Suppose you write, and say he's very ill. I daresay they've indulged themselves in daily postage, and then you can follow it up next day with the full truth.'

The writing this letter was difficult work for Molly, and she tore up three copies before she could manage it to her satisfaction. The next day was easier; the fact of Osborne's death was told briefly and tenderly. But, when this second letter was sent off, Molly's heart began to bleed for the poor creature, bereft of her husband, in a foreign land, and he dead and buried without her ever having had the chance of printing his dear features on her memory by one last long lingering look. With her thoughts full of the unknown

Aimée, Molly talked much about her that day to the Squire. He would listen for ever to any conjecture, however wild, about the grandchild, but perpetually winced away from all discourse about 'the Frenchwoman', as he called her. He would treat her with respect as his son's widow. He would make her an allowance to the extent of his duty: but he hoped and trusted he might never be called upon to see her.

And all this time a little young grey-eyed woman was making her way towards the dead son, whom as yet she believed to be her living husband. She knew she was acting in defiance of his expressed wish; but he had never dismayed her with any expression of his own fears about his health; and she, bright with life, had never contemplated death coming to fetch away one so beloved. He was ill – very ill, the letter from the strange girl said that; but Aimée had nursed her parents, and knew what illness was. And was she not his wife, whose place was by his pillow? So, Aimée made her preparations, swallowing down the tears that would overflow her eyes, and drop into the little trunk she was packing so neatly. And by her side, on the ground, sate the child, now nearly two years old; and for him Aimée had always a smile and a cheerful word. So Aimée caught the evening coach to London and there the Birmingham coach. When the coach set her down at Feversham she asked for a man to carry her trunk, and show her the way to Hamley Hall.

'Hamley Hall!' said the innkeeper. 'Eh! there's a deal o' trouble there just now.'

'I know, I know,' said she, hastening off after the wheelbarrow in which her trunk was going, and breathlessly struggling to keep up with it, her heavy child asleep in her arms. To her, a foreigner, the drawn blinds of the house, when she came in sight of it, had no significance.

'Back-door or front, missus?' asked the boots from the inn.

'The most nearest,' said she. And the front-door was 'the most nearest'. Molly was sitting with the Squire in the darkened drawing-room, reading out her translations of Aimée's letters to her husband. The Squire was never weary of hearing them; the very sound of Molly's voice soothed and comforted him. Suddenly there came a ring at the front-door bell, pulled by an ignorant, vigorous hand. Molly stopped reading; she and the Squire looked at each other in surprised dismay. They heard Robinson hurrying to answer the unwonted summons. They listened; but they heard no more.

The old servant opened the door, and right into the midst of them came the little figure in grey, looking ready to fall with the weight of her child.

'You are Molly,' said she, not seeing the Squire at once. 'The lady who wrote the letter; he spoke of you sometimes. You will let me go to him.'

Molly did not answer, except that at such moments the eyes speak solemnly and comprehensively. Aimée read their meaning. All she said was – 'He is not – oh, my husband – my husband!' Her arms relaxed, her figure swayed, the child screamed and held out his arms for help. That help was given him by his grandfather, just before Aimée fell senseless on the floor.

'*Maman, maman*!' cried the little fellow, now fighting to get back to her, where she lay; he fought so lustily that the Squire had to put him down, and he crawled to the poor inanimate body, behind which sat Molly, holding the head; whilst Robinson rushed away for water, wine, and more womankind.

'Poor thing, poor thing!' said the Squire, bending over her. 'She is but young, Molly, and she must ha' loved him dearly.'

'To be sure!' said Molly quickly. She was untying the bonnet, and taking off the worn, but neatly-mended gloves; there was the soft luxuriant black hair, shading the pale, innocent face, – the little, notable-looking brown hands, with the wedding-ring for sole ornament. The child nestled up against her with his plaintive cry: '*Maman, maman*!' At the growing acuteness of his imploring, her hand moved, her lips quivered, consciousness came partially back. She did not open her eyes; but great, heavy tears stole out from beneath her eyelashes. Molly held her head against her own breast; and they tried to give her wine, which she shrank from; water, which she did not reject, that was all. At last she tried to speak. 'Take me away,' she said, 'into the dark! Leave me alone!'

So Molly and the women lifted her up and carried her away, and laid her on the bed, in the best bed-chamber in the house, and darkened the already-shaded light. She offered neither assistance nor resistance to all that they were doing. But, just before Molly was leaving the room, she felt rather than heard that Aimée spoke to her.

'Food – bread-and-milk for baby!'

In the hurry, the child had been left with Robinson and the Squire. When Molly came down, she found the Squire feeding the child, with more of peace upon his face than there had been for all these days.

'She is lying very still, but she will neither speak nor eat. I don't even think she is crying,' said Molly.

'We must let her rest,' said the Squire. 'And I do believe this little chap is going to sleep in my arms. God bless him!'

But Molly stole out, and sent off a lad to Hollingford with a note to her father. Her heart had warmed towards the poor stranger, and she went up from time to time to look at the girl, scarce older than herself. By-and-by, the Squire said in a whisper –

'She's not like a Frenchwoman, is she, Molly?'

'I don't know. I don't know what Frenchwomen are like.'

'And she looks like a gentlewoman, I think. I hope she's got friends who'll take care of her, – she can't be above twenty. I thought she must be older than my poor lad!'

'She's a gentle, pretty creature,' said Molly. 'But – but I sometimes think it has killed her; she lies like one dead.'

'Nay, nay!' said the Squire. 'It's not so easy to break one's heart. Sometimes I've wished it were. But one has to go on living – "all the appointed days", as is said in the Bible. But we'll do our best for her.'

The February evening drew on; the child lay asleep in the Squire's arms, till his grandfather grew tired and laid him down on the sofa. Presently – but it seemed a long, long time first – Molly heard the quick, prompt sounds which told of her father's arrival. In he came – to the room as yet only lighted by the fitful blaze of the fire.

CHAPTER 49

# Molly Gibson's Worth
# Is Discovered

Mr Gibson came in rubbing his hands after his frosty ride. He greeted the Squire, who, signing to his friend to follow him, went softly to the sofa and showed him the sleeping child.

'Well! this is a fine young gentleman,' said Mr Gibson, returning to the fire. 'And you've got the mother here, I understand. Mrs Osborne Hamley, as we must call her, poor thing! It's a sad coming home to her; for I hear she knew nothing of his death.'

'Yes! She's felt it a terrible shock. I should like you to see her, Gibson, if she'll let you. We must do our duty by her, for my poor lad's sake. I wish he could have seen his boy lying there; I do. I daresay it preyed on him to have to keep it all to himself. He might ha' known me, though. He might ha' known my bark was waur than my bite. It's all over now, though; and God forgive me if I was too sharp! I'm punished now.'

Molly grew impatient on the mother's behalf.

'Papa, I feel as if she was very ill; perhaps worse than we think. Will you go and see her at once?'

Mr Gibson followed her upstairs, and the Squire came too. They went into the room where she had been taken. She lay quite still, in the same position as at first. Her eyes were open and tearless, fixed on the wall. Mr Gibson spoke to her, but she did not answer.

'Bring me some wine at once, and order some beef-tea,' he said to Molly.

But when he tried to put the wine into her mouth, as she lay there on her side, she made no effort to receive it, and it ran out upon the pillow. Mr Gibson left the room abruptly. The Squire stood by in dumb dismay, touched in spite of himself by the death-in-life of one so young, and who must have been so much beloved.

Mr Gibson came back two steps at a time; he was carrying the half-awakened child in his arms. He did not scruple to rouse him into yet further wakefulness – did not grieve to hear him begin to wail and cry. His eyes were on the figure upon the bed, which at that sound quivered all through; and, when her child was laid at her back, and began to scramble yet closer, Aimée turned round, and took him in her arms, and lulled him and soothed him with the soft wont of mother's love. Before she lost this faint conscious-ness, which was instinct rather than thought, Mr Gibson spoke to her in French. It was the language sure to be most intelligible to her dulled brain.

Mr Gibson extorted from her short answers at first, then longer ones, and from time to time he plied her with little drops of wine, until some further nourishment should be at hand.

Mr Gibson gave some instructions to one of the maid-servants as to the watch she was to keep, and insisted on Molly's going to bed. When she pleaded the apparent necessity of staying up, he said –

'Now, Molly, you will have enough to do to occupy all your strength for days to come; and go to bed you must now. I only wish I saw my way as clearly through other things as I do to your nearest duty. I wish I'd never let Roger go wandering off; he'll wish it too, poor fellow! Did I tell you, Cynthia is going off in hot haste to her uncle Kirkpatrick's. I suspect a visit to him will stand in lieu of going out to Russia as a governess.'

'I am sure she was quite serious in wishing for that.'

'Yes, yes! at the time. I've no doubt she thought she was sincere in intending to go. But the great thing was to get out of the un-pleasantness of the present time and place; and uncle Kirkpatrick's will do this as effectually, and more pleasantly, than a situation at Nishni-Novgorod in an ice-palace.'

He had given Molly's thoughts a turn, which was what he wanted to do. Molly could not help remembering Mr Henderson, and his offer, and all the consequent hints; and wondering and wishing – what did she wish? Before she had quite ascertained this point, she was asleep.

After this, long days passed over in a monotonous round of care; for no one seemed to think of Molly's leaving the Hall during the woeful illness that befell Mrs Osborne Hamley. It was not that her father allowed her to take much active part in the nursing; the Squire gave him *carte-blanche*, and he engaged two efficient hospital-nurses to watch over the unconscious Aimée; but Molly was needed to receive the finer directions as to her treatment and diet. It was not that she was wanted for the care of the little boy; the Squire was too jealous of the child's exclusive love for that, and one of the housemaids was employed in the actual physical charge of him; but he needed some one to listen to his incontinence of language, both when his passionate regret for his dead son came uppermost, and also when he had discovered some extraordinary charm in that son's child; and, again, when he was oppressed with the uncertainty of Aimée's long-continued illness.

Perhaps Mr Gibson did not spare her enough; one day, after Mrs Osborne Hamley had 'taken the turn', as the nurses called it, when she was lying weak as a new-born baby, but with her faculties all restored, and her fever gone – when spring buds were blooming out, and spring birds sang merrily – Molly answered to her father's sudden questioning, that she felt unaccountably weary; that her head ached heavily, and that she was aware of a sluggishness of thought which it required a painful effort to overcome.

'Don't go on,' said Mr Gibson, with a quick pang of anxiety. 'Lie down here – with your back to the light.' And off he went, in search of the Squire. He had a good long walk, before he came upon Mr Hamley in a field of spring wheat, where the women were weeding, his little grandson holding to his finger in the intervals of short walks of inquiry into the dirtiest places, which was all his sturdy little limbs could manage.

'Well, Gibson, and how goes the patient? Better? I wish we

could get her out-of-doors! It would make her strong as soon as anything.'

'It's not about her. May I order the carriage for my Molly?' Mr Gibson's voice sounded as if he was choking a little.

'To be sure,' said the Squire. 'What's the matter, man? Speak!'

'Nothing's the matter,' said Mr Gibson hastily. 'Only I want her at home under my own eye'; and he turned away to go to the house. But the Squire kept at Mr Gibson's side. He wanted to speak, but his heart was so full he did not know what to say.

'I say, Gibson,' he got out, 'your Molly is liker a child of mine than a stranger; and I reckon we've all on us been coming too hard upon her. You don't think there's much amiss, do you?'

'How can I tell?' said Mr Gibson, almost savagely. But any hastiness of temper was instinctively understood by the Squire; and he was not offended. He felt as if he should not know what to do without Molly. He stood by, while Mr Gibson helped the tearful Molly into the carriage. Then the Squire mounted on the step and kissed her hand; but when he tried to thank her and bless her, he broke down; and, as soon as he was once more safely on the ground, Mr Gibson cried out to the coachman to drive on. And so Molly left Hamley Hall.

And when they came home, Mr Gibson did not leave her, till he had seen her laid on a sofa in a darkened room. Then he came away, leading his wife, who turned round at the door to kiss her hand to Molly, and make a little face of unwillingness to be dragged away.

'Now, Hyacinth,' said he, 'she will need much care. She has been overworked, and I've been a fool. We must keep her from all worry and care – but I won't answer for it that she'll not have an illness, for all that!'

The illness which he apprehended came upon Molly; not violently or acutely, so that there was any immediate danger to be dreaded; but making a long pull upon her strength, which seemed to lessen day by day, until at last her father feared that she might become a permanent invalid. There was nothing very decided or alarming to tell Cynthia, and Mrs Gibson kept the dark side from her in her letters. As Mrs Gibson said to herself, it would be a pity to disturb Cynthia's pleasure by telling her much about Molly. But it so happened that Lady Harriet – who came, whenever she could, to sit awhile with Molly – wrote a letter to Cynthia. All the first part of the letter was taken up with commissions; but then she went on to say –

'I saw Molly this morning. Twice I have been forbidden admittance, as she was too ill to see anyone out of her own family. I wish we could begin to perceive a change for the better; but she looks more fading every time, and I fear Mr Gibson considers it a very anxious case.'

The day but one after this letter was despatched, Cynthia walked into the drawing-room at home, with as much apparent composure as if she had left it not an hour before. Mrs Gibson started up.

'Cynthia! Dear child, why have you come back?'

'Because I never knew – you never told me – how ill Molly was.'

'Nonsense! Molly's illness is only a nervous fever; but you must remember nerves are mere fancy, and she's getting better. Such a pity for you to have left your uncle's. Who told you about Molly?'

'Lady Harriet.'

'But you might have known she always exaggerates things. Not but what I have been almost worn out with nursing. Perhaps, after all, it is a very good thing you have come, my dear. Although I can't think how you could come off in this sudden kind of way; I am sure it must have annoyed your uncle and aunt. I daresay they'll never ask you again.'

'On the contrary, I am to go back there as soon as ever I can be easy to leave Molly.'

'"Easy to leave Molly." Now that really is nonsense, and rather uncomplimentary to me, I must say: nursing her as I have been, daily, and almost nightly; for I have been wakened, times out of number, by Mr Gibson getting up, and going to see if she had had her medicine properly.'

'I'm afraid she has been very ill?' asked Cynthia.

'Yes, she has, in one way; but not in another. It was what I call more a tedious, than an interesting illness.'

'I wish I had known!' sighed Cynthia. 'Do you think I might go and see her now?'

'I'll go and prepare her. Ah; here's Mr Gibson!' Cynthia thought that he looked much older.

'You here!' said he, coming forward to shake hands.

'I never knew Molly had been so ill, or I would have come directly.' Her eyes were full of tears. Mr Gibson was touched: he shook her hand again, and murmured, 'You're a good girl, Cynthia.'

'She's heard one of dear Lady Harriet's exaggerated accounts,' said Mrs Gibson, 'and come straight off. I tell her it's very foolish, for Molly is a great deal better now.'

'Very foolish,' said Mr Gibson, echoing his wife's words, but smiling at Cynthia. 'But sometimes one likes foolish people for their folly, better than wise people for their wisdom. And now I'll run up and see my little girl, and tell her the good news. You'd better follow me in a couple of minutes.'

Molly's delight at seeing her showed itself, first in a few happy tears, and then in soft caresses and inarticulate sounds of love. Once or twice she began, 'It is such a pleasure,' and there she stopped short. But the eloquence of these five words sank deep into Cynthia's heart. She had returned just at the right time. Cynthia's tact made her talkative or silent, gay or grave, as the varying humour of Molly required. She listened, too, with the semblance, if not the reality, of unwearied interest, to Molly's continual recurrence to all the time of distress and sorrow at Hamley Hall. Cynthia instinctively knew that the repetition of all these painful recollections would ease the oppressed memory, which refused to dwell on anything but what had occurred at a time of feverish disturbance of health. So she never interrupted Molly, as Mrs Gibson had so frequently done, with, 'You told me all that before, my dear. Let us talk of something else.'

So Molly's health and spirits improved rapidly after Cynthia's return; she was able to take drives, and enjoy the fine weather; it was only her as yet tender spirits that required a little management. All the Hollingford people forgot that they had ever thought of her except as the darling of the town; and each in his or her way showed kind interest in her father's child. Miss Browning and Miss Phoebe considered it quite a privilege that they were allowed to see her a fortnight before anyone else; Mrs Goodenough stirred dainty messes in a silver saucepan for Molly's benefit; the Towers sent books, and forced fruit, and new caricatures, and strange and delicate poultry; humble patients of 'the doctor' left the earliest cauliflowers they could grow in their cottage gardens, with 'their duty for Miss'. The last of all, though strongest in regard, most piteously eager in interest, came Squire Hamley himself. When she was at the worst, he rode over every day to hear the smallest detail, facing even Mrs Gibson (his abomination), if her husband was not at home, to ask and hear, till the tears were unconsciously stealing down his cheeks. Every resource of his heart, or his house, or his lands, was searched and tried, if it could bring a moment's pleasure to her; and, whatever it might be that came from him, at her very worst time, it brought out a dim smile upon her face.

## CHAPTER 50

# An Absent Lover Returns

And now it was late June; and to Molly's and her father's extreme urgency in pushing, and Mr and Mrs Kirkpatrick's affectionate persistency in pulling, Cynthia had gone back to finish her interrupted visit in London, but not before the bruit of her previous sudden return to nurse Molly had told strongly in her favour in the fluctuating opinion of the little town. Her affair with Mr Preston was thrust into the shade; while everyone was speaking of her warm heart.

One morning, Mrs Gibson brought Molly a great basket of flowers, that had been sent from the Hall. Molly had just come down, and was now well enough to arrange the flowers for the drawing-room, and, as she did so with these blossoms, she made some comments on each.

'Ah! these white pinks! They were Mrs Hamley's favourite flower; and so like her! This little bit of sweet briar, it quite scents the room. Oh, mamma, look at this rose! I forget its name, but it is very rare, and grows up in the sheltered corner of the wall, near the mulberry-tree. Roger bought the tree for his mother with his own money when he was quite a boy; he showed it me, and made me notice it.'

'I daresay it was Roger who got it now. You heard papa say he had seen him yesterday.'

'No! Roger! Roger come home!' said Molly, turning first red, then very white.

'Yes. Oh, I remember you had gone to bed before papa came in. Yes, Roger turned up at the Hall the day before yesterday.'

Roger, two months before, had received the intelligence of

311

Osborne's death, as well as Cynthia's hasty letter of relinquish-
ment. He did not consider that he was doing wrong in returning
to England immediately, and reporting himself to the gentlemen
who had sent him out, with a full explanation of the circumstances
relating to Osborne's private marriage and sudden death. He offered, and they accepted his offer, to go out again for any time that
they might think equivalent to the five months he was yet engaged
to them for. They were most of them gentlemen of property, and
saw the full importance of proving the marriage of an eldest son,
and installing his child as the natural heir to a long-descended
estate. This much information Mr Gibson gave to Molly in a very
few minutes when he returned. She sat up on her sofa, looking
very pretty with the flush on her cheeks, and the brightness in
her eyes.

'Well!' said she, when her father stopped speaking.

'Well! what?' asked he playfully.

'Oh! How is he looking?'

'He looks broader, stronger – more muscular.'

'Oh! is he changed?' asked Molly.

'No, not changed; and yet not the same. He's as brown as a berry
for one thing; and a beard as fine and sweeping as my bay-mare's
tail.'

'A beard! but go on, papa! Does he talk as he used to do? I
should know his voice amongst ten thousand.'

'I didn't catch any Hottentot twang, if that's what you mean.'

Mrs Gibson had come into the room and Molly fidgeted.

'Tell me, how are they all getting on together?'

'Roger is evidently putting everything to rights in his firm,
quiet way.'

'"Things to rights." Why, what's wrong?' asked Mrs Gibson
quickly. 'The Squire and the French daughter-in-law don't get on
well together, I suppose? I am always so glad Cynthia acted with
the promptitude she did; it would have been very awkward for her
to have been mixed up with all these complications. Poor Roger!
to find himself supplanted by a child when he comes home!'

'You were not in the room, my dear, when I was telling Molly of the reasons for Roger's return; it was to put his brother's child at once into his rightful and legal place. So now, when he finds the work partly done to his hands, he is happy and gratified in proportion.'

'Then he is not much affected by Cynthia's breaking off her engagement? I never did give him credit for very deep feelings.'

'On the contrary, he feels it very acutely. He and I had a long talk about it, yesterday.'

Both Molly and Mrs Gibson would have liked to have heard something more about this conversation; but Mr Gibson did not choose to go on with the subject. The only point which he disclosed was, that Roger had insisted on his right to have a personal interview with Cynthia; and, on hearing that she was in London at present, had deferred any further explanation or expostulation by letter, preferring to await her return.

Molly went on with her questions on other subjects. 'And Mrs Osborne Hamley? How is she?'

'Wonderfully brightened-up by Roger's presence. They are evidently good friends; and she loses her strange startled look when she speaks to him. I suspect she has been quite aware of the Squire's wish that she should return to France, and she hasn't had anyone to consult as to her duty until Roger came, upon whom she has evidently firm reliance.'

'I should think he would come and call upon us soon,' said Mrs Gibson to Molly.

'Do you think he will, papa?' said Molly, more doubtfully.

'I can't tell, my dear. Until he's quite convinced of Cynthia's intentions, it can't be very pleasant for him to come on mere visits of ceremony to the house in which he has known her; but he's one who will always do what he thinks right, whether pleasant or not.'

Mrs Gibson could hardly wait till her husband had finished his sentence, before she testified against a part of it.

'Convinced of Cynthia's intentions! I should think she had made them pretty clear! What more does the man want?'

'He's not as yet convinced that the letter wasn't written in a fit of temporary feeling. He needs the full conviction that she alone can give him.'

'Poor Cynthia! My poor child!' said Mrs Gibson, plaintively. 'What she has exposed herself to by letting herself be over-persuaded by that man!'

Mr Gibson's eyes flashed fire. But he kept his lips tight closed. Molly, too, had been damped by an expression or two in her father's speech. 'Mere visits of ceremony!' Was it so, indeed? Whatever it was, the call was paid before many days were over. That he felt all the awkwardness of his position towards Mrs Gibson – that he was in reality suffering pain all the time – was but too evident to Molly; but, of course, Mrs Gibson saw nothing of this.

Molly was sitting in her pretty white invalid's dress, half-reading, half-dreaming; for the June air was so clear and ambient, the garden so full of bloom, the trees so full of leaf, that reading by the open window was only a pretence at such a time. It was after lunch when Maria ushered in Mr Roger Hamley. Molly started up; and then stood shyly and quietly in her place, while a bronzed, bearded, grave man came into the room, in whom she at first had to seek for the merry boyish face she knew by heart only two years ago. But his voice was the same; that was the first point of the old friend Molly caught, when he addressed her in a tone far softer than he used in speaking conventional politenesses to her stepmother.

'I was so sorry to hear how ill you had been! You are looking but delicate!' letting his eyes rest upon her face with affectionate examination. Molly felt herself colour all over. To do something to put an end to it, she looked up, and showed him her beautiful soft grey eyes, which he never remembered to have noticed before. She smiled at him, as she blushed still deeper, and said –

'Oh! I am quite strong now to what I was. It would be a shame to be ill when everything is in its full summer beauty.'

'I have heard how deeply we – I am indebted to you – my father can hardly praise you'–

'Please don't!' said Molly, the tears coming into her eyes in spite of herself. He seemed to understand her at once; he went on as if speaking to Mrs Gibson: 'Indeed, my little sister-in-law is never weary of talking about '*Monsieur le Docteur*', as she calls your husband!'

'I have not had the pleasure of making Mrs Osborne Hamley's acquaintance yet,' said Mrs Gibson, 'and I must beg you to apologise to her for my remissness. But Molly has been such a care and anxiety to me – for, you know, I look upon her quite as my own child – that I really have not gone anywhere; excepting to the Towers, perhaps I should say, which is just like another home to me. And then I understood that Mrs Osborne Hamley was thinking of returning to France before long? Still it was very remiss.'

The little trap thus set for news of what might be going on in the Hamley family was quite successful.

'I am sure Mrs Osborne Hamley will be very glad to see any friends of the family, as soon as she is a little stronger. I hope she will not go back to France at all. I trust we shall induce her to remain with my father. But at present nothing is arranged.' Then he got up and took leave. When he was at the door, he looked back, having, as he thought, a word more to say; but he quite forgot what it was, for he surprised Molly's intent gaze, and sudden confusion at discovery, and went away as soon as he could.

'Poor Osborne was right!' said he. 'She has grown into delicate fragrant beauty, just as he said she would; or is it the character which has formed her face? Now, the next time I enter these doors, it will be to learn my fate!'

Cynthia returned to Hollingford and, in answer to her mother's anxious inquiries on the subject, would only say that Mr Henderson had not offered again. Why should he? She had refused him once, and he did not know the reason of her refusal.

Underneath there were other feelings; but Mrs Gibson was not one to probe beneath the surface.

## CHAPTER 51

# 'Off with the Old Love,
# and on with the New'

The next morning Cynthia had already received a letter from Mr Henderson before she came down to breakfast – a declaration of love, a proposal of marriage; together with an intimation that he was going to follow her down to Hollingford, and would arrive at the same time that she had done herself on the previous day. Cynthia said nothing about this to any one. She came late into the breakfast-room. Molly was not as yet strong enough to get up so early. Mr Gibson went about his daily business, and Cynthia and her mother were left alone.

'Mamma, I expect Mr Henderson will come and call this morning.'

'Oh, my precious child! – But how do you know? My darling Cynthia, am I to congratulate you?'

'No! I have had a letter this morning from him, and he's coming down by the "Umpire" today.'

'But he has offered?'

Cynthia looked up, like one startled from a dream.

'Offered! yes, I suppose he has.'

'And you accept him? Say "yes", and make me happy!'

'I shan't say "yes" to make anyone happy except myself, and the Russian scheme has great charms for me.' She said this, to plague her mother, it must be confessed; for her mind was pretty well made up. But it did not affect Mrs Gibson, who affixed even less truth to it than there really was.

'You always look nice, dear; but don't you think you had better put on that pretty lilac silk?'

'I shall not vary a thread or a shred from what I have got on now.'

'You dear, wilful creature! you know you always look lovely in whatever you put on.' So, kissing her daughter, Mrs Gibson left the room, intent on the lunch which should impress Mr Henderson at once with an idea of family refinement.

Roger had heard from Mr Gibson that Cynthia had come home and, resolving, as ever not to interfere with the morning hours that were tabooed to him of old, he rode slowly; compelling himself to quietness and patience.

'Mrs Gibson at home? Miss Kirkpatrick?' he asked of the servant, Maria, who opened the door.

'I think so – I'm not sure! Will you walk up into the drawing-room, sir? Miss Gibson is there, I know.'

So he went upstairs, all his nerves on the strain for the coming interview with Cynthia. It was either a relief or a disappointment, he was not sure which, to find only Molly in the room: – Molly, half-lying on the couch in the bow-window which commanded the garden; draped in soft white drapery, very white herself.

'I'm afraid you are not so well,' he said to Molly, who sat up to receive him, and who began to tremble with emotion.

'I'm a little tired, that's all,' said she; and then she was quite silent. He took a chair and placed it near her, opposite to the window. He felt he ought to talk, but he could not think of anything to say. The merry murmur of distant happy voices in the garden came nearer and nearer; Molly looked more and more uneasy and flushed. He could see over her into the garden. A sudden deep colour overspread him. Cynthia and Mr Henderson had come in sight; he, eagerly talking to her as he bent forward to look into her face; she, her looks half averted in pretty shyness, was evidently coquetting about some flowers, which she either would not give, or would not take. Just then, Maria was seen approaching; apparently she had feminine tact enough to induce Cynthia to leave her present admirer, and to go a few steps to meet her and receive the whispered message that Mr Roger Hamley was there, and wished to speak to her. She turned to say something to Mr Henderson before coming towards the house. Now Roger spoke to Molly hurriedly.

'Molly, tell me! Is it too late for me to speak to Cynthia? I came on purpose. Who is that man?'

'Mr Henderson. He only came today – but now he is her accepted lover. Oh, Roger, forgive me the pain!'

'Tell her I have been, and am gone. Send out word to her. Don't let her be interrupted.'

And Roger ran downstairs at full speed, and Molly heard the passionate clang of the outer door. He had hardly left the house, before Cynthia entered the room, pale and resolute.

'Where is he?' she said.

'Gone!' said Molly, very faint.

'Gone. Oh, what a relief! It seems to be my fate never to be off with the old lover before I am on with the new, and yet I did write as decidedly as I could.'

Mr Henderson was handsome, without being conceited; gentlemanly, without being foolishly fine. He talked easily, and never said a silly thing. He was good-tempered and kind; but he wanted something in Molly's eyes – at any rate, in this first interview, and in her heart of hearts she thought him rather commonplace. But of course she said nothing of this to Cynthia, who was evidently as happy as she could be. Mrs Gibson, too, was in the seventh heaven of ecstasy. Mr Gibson was not with them for long; but, while he was there, he was evidently studying the unconscious Mr Henderson with his dark penetrating eyes.

The next time Mr Gibson found Molly alone, he began –

'Well! and how do you like the new relation that is to be?'

'It's difficult to say. I think he's very nice in all his bits, but – rather dull on the whole.'

'I think him perfection,' said Mr Gibson, to Molly's surprise; but in an instant she saw that he had been speaking ironically. 'I don't wonder she preferred him to Roger Hamley. Such scents! such gloves! And then his hair and cravat!'

'Now, papa. He's a great deal more than that.'

'So was Roger. However, I must confess I shall be only too glad to have her married. She's a girl who'll always have some love-affair on hand, and will always be apt to slip through a man's fingers if he doesn't look sharp.'

Whatever else Mr Henderson might be, he was an impatient lover; he wanted to marry Cynthia directly – next week – the week after; at any rate before the long vacation, so they could go abroad at once. Mr Gibson, generous as usual, called Cynthia aside a morning or two after her engagement, and put a hundred-pound note into her hands.

'There, that's to pay your expenses to Russia and back. I hope you'll find your pupils obedient.'

To his surprise, Cynthia threw her arms round his neck and kissed him.

'You are the kindest person I know,' said she; 'and I don't know how to thank you in words.'

'If you tumble my shirt-collars again in that way, I'll charge you for the washing. Just now, too, when I'm trying so hard to be trim and elegant, like your Mr Henderson.'

'But you do like him, don't you?' said Cynthia pleadingly. 'He does so like you.'

'Of course. We're all angels just now, and you're an archangel. I hope he'll wear as well as Roger.'

Cynthia looked grave. 'That was a very silly affair,' she said. 'We were two as unsuitable people' –

'It has ended, and that's enough.'

Mr and Mrs Kirkpatrick sent all manner of congratulations in a letter praising Mr Henderson, admiring Cynthia, and insisting into the bargain that the marriage should take place from their house in Hyde Park Street, and that Mr and Mrs Gibson and Molly should all come up and pay them a visit. There was a little postscript at the end. 'Surely you do not mean the famous travel-ler, Hamley, about whose discoveries all our scientific men are so much excited. You speak of him as a young Hamley, who went to Africa. Answer this question, pray, for Helen is most anxious to know.' In her exultation at the general success of everything, and desire for sympathy, Mrs Gibson read parts of this letter to Molly; the postscript among the rest. It made a deeper impression on Molly than even the proposed kindness of the visit to London.

## CHAPTER 52

# Bridal Visits and Adieux

The whole town of Hollingford came to congratulate and inquire into particulars. Even Lady Cumnor was moved into action. She who had only once been to see 'Clare' in her own house – she came to congratulate after her fashion. It was but eleven o'clock, and Mrs Gibson would have been indignant at any commoner who had ventured to call at such an untimely hour; but in the case of the Peerage the rules of domestic morality were relaxed.

The family 'stood at arms', as it were, till Lady Cumnor appeared in the drawing-room; and then she had to be settled in the best chair before anything like conversation began. She was the first to speak; and Lady Harriet, who had begun a few words to Molly, dropped into silence.

'I have been taking Mary – Lady Cuxhaven – to the railway station on this new line between Birmingham and London, and I thought I would come on here, and offer you my congratulations. Clare, which is the young lady?' – putting on her glasses, and looking at Cynthia and Molly, who were dressed pretty much alike. 'I did not think it would be amiss to give you a little advice, my dear,' said she, when Cynthia had been properly pointed out to her as bride-elect. 'I have heard a good deal about you; and I am only too glad, for your mother's sake – your mother is a very worthy woman – I am truly rejoiced, I say, to hear that you are going to make so creditable a marriage. I hope it will efface your former errors of conduct – which we will hope were but trivial in reality – and that you will live to be a comfort to your mother. But you must conduct yourself with discretion in whatever state of life it pleases God to place you, whether married or single. You must reverence your husband, and conform to his opinion in all things. Look up to him as your head, and do nothing without consulting him.' – It was as well that Lord Cumnor was not amongst the audience; or he might have compared precept with practice – 'Keep strict accounts; and remember your station in life. I understand that Mr –', looking about for some help as to the name she had forgotten, 'Henderson – Henderson – is in the law. Although there is a general prejudice against attorneys, I have known two or three who are very respectable men; and I am sure Mr Henderson is one, or your good mother and our old friend Gibson would not have sanctioned the engagement.'

'He's a barrister,' put in Cynthia. 'Barrister-at-law.'

'Ah, yes. Attorney-at-law. Barrister-at-law. I understand without your speaking so loud, my dear. What was I going to say before you interrupted me? When you have been a little in society, you will find that it is reckoned bad manners to interrupt. I had a great deal more to say to you, and you have put it all out of my head. There was something else your father wanted me to ask – what was it, Harriet?'

'I suppose you mean about Mr Hamley?'

'Oh, yes! we are intending to have the house full of Lord Hollingford's friends next month, and Lord Cumnor is particularly anxious to secure Mr Hamley.'

'The Squire?' asked Mrs Gibson, in some surprise.

'The famous traveller – the scientific Mr Hamley, I mean. I imagine he is son to the Squire. Lord Hollingford knows him well; but, when we asked him before, he declined coming, and assigned no reason.'

Had Roger indeed been asked to the Towers and declined? Mrs Gibson could not understand it. Lady Cumnor went on –

'Now, this time we are particularly anxious to secure him, and my son, Lord Hollingford, will not return to England until the very week before the Duke of Atherstone is coming to us. I believe Mr Gibson is very intimate with Mr Hamley; do you think he could induce him to favour us with his company?'

And this from the proud Lady Cumnor; and the object of it

Roger Hamley! Mrs Gibson could only murmur out that she was sure Mr Gibson would do all that her ladyship wished.

'Thank you. You know me well enough to be aware that I am not the person, nor is the Towers the house, to go about soliciting guests. But in this instance I bend my head.'

'Besides, mamma,' said Lady Harriet, 'papa was saying that the Hamleys have been on their land since before the Conquest; while we only came into the county a century ago; and there is a tale that the first Cumnor began his fortune through selling tobacco in King James's reign.'

If Lady Cumnor did not exactly shift her trumpet and take snuff there on the spot, she behaved in an equivalent manner. She began a low-toned, but nevertheless authoritative, conversation with Clare about the details of the wedding, which lasted until she thought it fit to go; when she abruptly plucked Lady Harriet up, and carried her off.

Nevertheless, she prepared a handsome present for the bride: a Bible and a Prayer-book bound in velvet with silver-clasps; and also a collection of household account books.

'If you are driving into Hollingford, Harriet, perhaps you will take these books to Miss Kirkpatrick,' said Lady Cumnor, after she had sealed her note with all the straightness and correctness befitting a countess of her immaculate character. 'I understand they are all going up to London tomorrow for this wedding, in spite of what I said to Clare of the duty of being married in one's own parish-church. I advised her to repeat to Mr Gibson my reasons for thinking that they would be ill-advised to have the marriage in town; but I am afraid she has been overruled. That was her one great fault when she lived with us; she was always so yielding, and never knew how to say "No".'

'Mamma!' said Lady Harriet, with a little sly coaxing in her tone, 'do you think you would have been so fond of her, if she had said "No", when you wished her to say "Yes"?'

'To be sure I should, my dear. I like everybody to have an opinion of their own; only, when my opinions are based on thought and experience, which few people have had equal opportunities of acquiring, I think it is but proper deference in others to allow themselves to be convinced. I am not a despot, I hope?' she asked, with some anxiety.

'If you are, dear mamma,' said Lady Harriet, kissing the stern uplifted face very fondly, 'I like a despotism better than a republic; and I must be very despotic over my ponies, for it's already getting very late for my drive round by Ash-holt.'

But when she arrived at the Gibsons', she was detained so long there by the state of the family, that she had to give up her going to Ash-holt. Molly was sitting in the drawing-room, pale and trembling. She was the only person there when Lady Harriet entered; the room was all in disorder, strewed with presents and paper, and boxes.

'You look like Marius sitting amidst the ruins of Carthage, my dear! What's the matter? Why have you got on that woe-begone face? This marriage isn't broken off, is it? Though nothing would surprise me where the beautiful Cynthia is concerned.'

'Oh, no! that's all right. But I've caught a fresh cold, and papa says he thinks I had better not go to the wedding.'

'Poor little one! And it's the first visit to London too!'

'Yes. But what I most care for is the not being with Cynthia to the last; and then, papa – papa has so looked forward to this holiday, – and seeing – and – and going – oh! I can't tell you where; but he has quite a list of people and sights to be seen – and now he says he should not be comfortable to leave me.' Just then Mrs Gibson came in.

'My dear Lady Harriet – how kind of you! Ah, yes, I see this poor unfortunate child has been telling you of her ill-luck. It is a great mortification to a girl of her age to lose her first visit to London.'

'Now, Clare! you and I can manage it all, I think, if you will but help me in a plan I've got in my head. Mr Gibson shall stay in London; and Molly shall be well cared for, and have some change of air and scene too. I can carry her off to the Towers, and watch her myself; and send daily bulletins up to London, so that Mr Gibson may feel quite at ease. What do you say, Clare?'

'Oh, I could not go,' said Molly; 'I should only be a trouble to everybody.'

'Nobody asked you for your opinion, little one. If we wise elders decide that you are to go, you must submit in silence.'

Meanwhile Mrs Gibson was rapidly balancing advantages and disadvantages. Amongst the latter, jealousy came in predominant. The 'ayes' had it.

'What a charming plan!'

So Molly was driven off in state the next day. All morning, Cynthia had been with her in her room, attending to Molly's clothes, and rejoicing over the pretty smartnesses, which, having been prepared for her as bridesmaid, were now to serve as adornments for her visit to the Towers. Only when the carriage was announced, and Molly was preparing to go downstairs, Cynthia said –

'I'm not going to thank you, Molly, or to tell you how I love you.'

'Don't,' said Molly, 'I can't bear it.'

'Only you know you are to be my first visitor; and, if you wear brown ribbons to a green gown, I'll turn you out of the house!'

So they parted. Mr Gibson was there in the hall, to hand Molly in. He had ridden hard; and was now giving her two or three last injunctions as to her health.

'Think of us on Thursday,' said he. 'I declare I don't know which of her lovers she mayn't summon at the very last moment to act the part of bridegroom. I'm determined to be surprised at nothing, and will give her away with a good grace to whoever comes.'

When Molly arrived at the Towers, she was convoyed into Lady Cumnor's presence by Lady Harriet. Lady Cumnor was positively gracious.

'You are Lady Harriet's visitor, my dear,' said she, 'and I hope she will take good care of you. If not, come and complain of her to me.' It was as near an approach to a joke as Lady Cumnor ever perpetrated, and from it Lady Harriet knew that her mother was pleased by Molly's manners and appearance.

'Now, here you are in your own kingdom; and into this room

I shan't venture to come without express permission. Here's the last new *Quarterly*, and the last new novel, and the last new essay. Now, my dear, you needn't come down again today, unless you like it. Parkes shall bring you everything and anything you want. You must get strong as fast as you can, for all sorts of great and famous people are coming tomorrow and the next day, and I think you'll like to see them.'

When Molly went down to lunch, she found Sir Charles Morton, the son of Lady Cumnor's only sister: a plain, sandy-haired man of thirty-five or so; immensely rich, very sensible, awkward, and reserved. He had had a chronic attachment, of many years' standing, to his cousin, Lady Harriet, who did not care for him in the least. Lady Harriet was, however, on friendly terms with him and told him what to do, and she had given him his cue about Molly.

'Now, Charles, the girl wants to be interested and amused without having to take any trouble for herself; she's too delicate to be very active either in mind or body. Just look after her when the house gets full, and place her where she can hear and see everything and everybody, without any fuss and responsibility.'

So Sir Charles did not say much to her; but what he did say was thoroughly friendly and sympathetic; and Molly began, as he and Lady Harriet intended that she should, to have a kind of pleasant reliance upon him. Then, in the evening, while the rest of the family were at dinner – after Molly's tea and hour of quiet repose, Parkes came and dressed her, and did her hair in some new and pretty way, so that, when Molly looked at herself in the cheval-glass, she scarcely knew the elegant reflection to be that of herself. She was fetched down by Lady Harriet into the formidable drawing-room which had haunted her dreams ever since her childhood. At the further end sat Lady Cumnor at her tapestry-work; the light of fire and candle seemed all concentrated on that one bright part where presently Lady Harriet made tea, and Lord Cumnor went to sleep, and Sir Charles read passages aloud from the *Edinburgh Review* to the three ladies at their work.

When Molly went to bed, she was constrained to admit that

staying at the Towers as a visitor was rather pleasant than other-wise. For the first time for many weeks, Molly began to feel the delightful spring of returning health.

## CHAPTER 53

# Reviving Hopes and
# Brightening Prospects

'If you can without fatigue, dear, do come down to dinner today; you'll then see the people one by one as they appear, instead of having to encounter a crowd of strangers. Hollingford will be here too.'

So Molly made her appearance at dinner that day; and got to know, by sight at least, some of the most distinguished of the visitors at the Towers. The next day was Thursday, Cynthia's wedding-day; bright and fine in the country, whatever it might be in London. And Molly came downstairs to the late breakfast. She looked so much better that Sir Charles noticed it to Lady Harriet; and several of the visitors spoke of her this morning as a very pretty, lady-like, and graceful girl. On Friday, as Lady Harriet had told her, some visitors from the more immediate neighbourhood were expected to stay over the Sunday; but she had not mentioned their names, and, when Molly went down into the drawing-room before dinner, she was almost startled by perceiving Roger Hamley in the centre of a group of gentlemen. He made a hitch in his conversation, lost the precise meaning of a question addressed to him, answered it rather hastily, and made his way to where Molly was sitting. He had heard that she was staying at the Towers; but he was almost as much surprised by her looks, as she was by his unexpected appearance, for he had only seen her once or twice since his return from Africa, and then in the guise of an invalid. Now, in her pretty evening-dress, with her hair beautifully dressed, Roger hardly recognised her. He began to feel that admiring deference which most young men experience, when conversing with a very pretty girl: a sort of desire to obtain her good opinion, in a manner very different to his old familiar friendliness. He was annoyed when Sir Charles came up to take her in to dinner and found himself watching them from time to time. In the evening he sought her out, but found her preoccupied with one of the young men staying in the house, who had had the advantage of two days of mutual interest, and jokes and anxieties, of the family circle. Molly could not help wishing to break off all this trivial talk and to make room for Roger: but, though both wanted to speak to the other more than to anyone else in the room, Lord Hollingford carried off Roger to the clatter of middle-aged men. Mr Ernest Watson, the young man referred to above, kept his place by Molly, as the prettiest girl in the room, and almost dazed her by his never-ceasing flow of clever small-talk. The ever-watchful Lady Harriet sent Sir Charles to the rescue; and, after a few words with Lady Harriet, Roger saw Molly quietly leave the room, and a sentence or two which he heard Lady Harriet address to her cousin made him know that it was for the night. Those sentences might bear another interpretation than the obvious one.

'Really, Charles, considering that she is in your charge, I think you might have saved her from the chatter of Mr Watson; I can only stand it when I am in the strongest health.'

Why was Molly in Sir Charles's charge? why? Then Roger remembered many little things that might serve to confirm the fancy he had got into his head; and he went to bed puzzled and annoyed. It seemed to him such an incongruous, hastily-got-up sort of engagement, if engagement it really was. On Saturday they were more fortunate: they had a long *tête-à-tête* in the most public place in the house – on a sofa in the hall where Molly was resting at Lady Harriet's command, before going upstairs after a walk. Roger was passing through, and saw her, and came to her. Standing before her, and making pretence of playing with the gold fish in a great marble basin close at hand –

'I was very unlucky,' said he. 'I wanted to get near you last night, but you were so busy talking to Mr Watson, until Sir Charles Morton came and carried you off – with such an air of authority! Have you known him long?'

'No! not long. I never saw him before I came here – on Tuesday. But Lady Harriet told him to see that I did not get tired – you know I have not been strong. He is a cousin of Lady Harriet's, and does all she tells him to do.'

Molly stood up.

'I must go upstairs,' she said; 'I only sate down here for a minute or two, because Lady Harriet bade me.'

'Stop a little longer,' said he. 'This is really the pleasantest place; this basin of water-lilies gives one the idea of coolness; besides – it seems so long since I saw you, and I've a message from my father to give you. He is very angry with you.'

'Angry with me!' said Molly in surprise.

'Yes! He heard that you had come here for change of air; and he was offended that you hadn't come to us – to the Hall, instead. He said that you should have remembered old friends!'

Molly did not at first notice the smile on his face.

'Oh! I am so sorry,' said she. 'But will you please tell him how it all happened? Lady Harriet called the very day when it was settled that I was not to go to'– Cynthia's wedding, she was going to add, but she suddenly stopped short, and changed the expression – 'go to London, and she planned it all in a minute, and convinced mamma and papa, and had her own way. There was really no resisting her.'

'I think you will have to tell all this to my father yourself, if you mean to make your peace. Why can you not come on to the Hall when you leave the Towers?'

'I should like it very much, some time. But I must go home first. They will want me more than ever now'–

Again she felt herself touching on a sore subject, and stopped short. Roger became annoyed at her so constantly conjecturing what he must be feeling on the subject of Cynthia's marriage. He determined to take the metaphorical bull by the horns. Until that was done, his footing with Molly would always be insecure.

'Ah, yes!' said he. 'Of course you must be of double importance, now Miss Kirkpatrick has left you. I saw her marriage in *The Times* yesterday.'

His tone of voice was changed in speaking of her; but her name had been named between them, and that was the great thing to accomplish.

'Still,' he continued, 'I think I must urge my father's claim for a short visit, because I can really see the apparent improvement in your health since I came – only yesterday. Besides, Molly,' it was the old familiar Roger of former days who spoke now, 'I think you could help us at home. Aimée is shy and awkward with my father, and he has never taken quite kindly to her – yet I know they would like and value each other, if some one could but bring them together – and it would be such a comfort to me, if this could take place before I have to leave.'

'To leave – are you going away again?'

'Yes. Have you not heard? I didn't complete my engagement. I'm going again in September for six months. And it is not likely I shall ever make the Hall my home again; and that is partly the reason why I want my father to adopt the notion of Aimée's living with him. Ah, here are all the people coming back from their walk. However, I shall see you again; perhaps this afternoon we may get a little quiet time, for I've a great deal to consult you about.'

They separated then, and Molly went upstairs very happy; very full and warm at her heart. There was no opportunity for renewed confidences that afternoon, but on the Sunday evening, as they all were sitting and loitering on the lawn before dinner, Roger went on with what he had to say about the position of his sister-in-law in his father's house; the mutual bond between the mother and grandfather being the child, who was also, through jealousy, the bone of contention and the severance.

The next day Molly went home; she was astonished at herself for being so sorry to leave the Towers. She had gained health; she had had pleasure; the faint fragrance of a new and unacknowledged hope had stolen into her life.

CHAPTER 54

# Molly Gibson at Hamley Hall

How charming the place looked in its early autumnal glow! And there was Roger at the hall-door, watching for her coming. He retreated, apparently to summon his sister-in-law, who came now timidly forwards in her deep widow's-mourning, holding her boy as if to protect her shyness; but he struggled down, and ran towards the carriage, eager to greet his friend the coachman, and to obtain a promised ride. Roger did not say much; he wanted to make Aimée feel her place as daughter of the house; but she was too timid to speak. She took Molly by the hand and led her into the drawing-room; where, as if by a sudden impulse of gratitude for all the tender nursing she had received during her illness, she put her arms round Molly and kissed her long and well. And after that they came to be friends.

It was nearly lunch-time, and the Squire always made his appearance at that meal, more for the pleasure of seeing his grandson eat his dinner than for any hunger of his own. Aimée seemed to forget her English in her nervousness, and to watch, with the jealous eyes of a dissatisfied mother, all the proceedings of the Squire towards her little boy. They were not of the wisest kind, it must be owned; the child sipped the strong ale with relish, and clamoured for everything which he saw the others enjoying. Aimée could hardly attend to Molly for her anxiety as to what her boy was doing and eating; yet she said nothing. After the boy's first wants were gratified, the Squire addressed himself to Molly.

'Well! I thought you were going to cut us, Miss Molly, when I heard you was gone to the Towers. Couldn't find any other place to stay at, while father and mother were away, but an earl's, eh?'

332

'They asked me, and I went,' said Molly; 'now you've asked me, and I've come here.'

'I think you might ha' known you'd be always welcome here, without waiting for asking. Why, Molly! I look upon you as a kind of daughter more than Madam there!' dropping his voice a little. 'Nay, you needn't look at me so pitifully; she doesn't follow English readily.'

'I think she does!' said Molly, in a low voice – not looking up, for fear of catching another glimpse at Aimée's sudden forlornness of expression and deepened colour. She felt grateful when she heard Roger speaking to Aimée the moment afterwards in the tender terms of brotherly friendliness.

'He's a sturdy chap, isn't he?' said the Squire, stroking the little Roger's curly head. 'And he can puff four puffs at grand-papa's pipe without being sick, can't he?'

'I san't puff any more puffs,' said the boy resolutely. 'Mamma says "No", I san't.'

'That's just like her!' said the Squire. 'As if it could do the child any harm!'

Molly made a point of turning the conversation from all personal subjects after this, and kept the Squire talking about the progress of his drainage. He offered to take her to see it; and she acceded. But, in the evening, when Aimée had gone to put her boy to bed, and the Squire was asleep in his easy-chair, she was virtually *tête-à-tête* with Roger. And so it went on during all the time of her visit.

Molly had grown very fond of Aimée; when the latter was at her ease, she had very charming and attaching ways. One day Aimée suggested a nutting expedition – another day they gave little Roger the unheard-of pleasure of tea out-of-doors; and it was Roger who arranged these simple pleasures – such as he knew Molly would enjoy.

On Molly's last morning at the Hall, Aimée came down, grave and anxious: her boy had not had a good night, he had fallen into a feverish sleep now. Immediately, the table was in a ferment. Molly quickly proposed that the carriage should come round immediately and bring back her father at once. Her proposal was agreed to, and she went upstairs to put on her things. She came down into the drawing-room, expecting to find Aimée and the Squire there; but word had been brought that the child had wakened in a panic, and both had rushed up to their darling. But Roger was in the drawing-room awaiting Molly, with a large bunch of the choicest flowers.

'Look, Molly!' said he. 'I gathered these for you before breakfast.'

'Thank you! You are very kind.'

'Then do something for me,' said he. 'I have no right to ask, Molly. Will you give me back one of those flowers, as a pledge of what you have said?'

'Take whichever you like,' said she, eagerly.

'No; you must choose, and you must give it me.'

Just then the Squire came in. Molly exclaimed –

'Oh, please, Mr Hamley, do you know which is Roger's favourite flower?'

'A rose, I daresay. The carriage is at the door, my dear' –

'Here, Roger – here is a rose!'

And the Squire took her to the carriage, talking of the little boy; Roger following, and hardly heeding what he was doing. He kept asking himself: 'Too late – or not? Can she ever forget that my first foolish love was given to one so different?'

## CHAPTER 55

# Roger Hamley's Confession

Roger felt more and more certain that she, and she alone, could make him happy. To love her, that was already done. And yet, was not this affair too much a mocking mimicry of the last – again just on the point of leaving England – if he followed her now – in the very drawing-room where he had once offered to Cynthia? And then, by a strong resolve, he determined on his course and he kissed the rose that was her pledge of friendship. Until his return he would not even attempt to win more of her love than he already had. But, once safe home again, no weak fancies as to what might or might not be her answer should prevent his running all chances, to gain the woman who was to him the one who excelled all. Till then he would be patient.

Molly sent her father to the Hall; and then sate down to the old life in the home drawing-room, where she missed Cynthia's bright presence at every turn. Mrs Gibson was in rather a querulous mood.

'Considering all the trouble I had with her trousseau, I think she might have written to me. Just a letter. My poor heart is yearning after my lost child! Really, life is somewhat hard to bear at times.'

Then there was silence – for a while.

'I wonder how the poor little boy is!' said Molly.

'Poor little child! When one thinks how little his prolonged existence is to be desired, one feels his death would be a boon.'

'Mamma! what do you mean?' asked Molly, much shocked.

'I should have thought the Squire desired a better-born heir than the offspring of a servant. And I should have thought it mortifying to Roger to find a little interloping child, half-French, half-English, stepping into his shoes!'

'You don't know how fond they are of him – the Squire loves the little boy as much as his own child; and Roger – oh! what a shame to think that Roger –' And she suddenly stopped short, as if she were choked.

'I don't wonder at your indignation, my dear!' said Mrs Gibson. 'It is just what I should have felt at your age. But one learns the baseness of human nature with advancing years. I was wrong, though, to undeceive you so early – but, depend upon it, the thought has crossed Roger Hamley's mind! My dear, let us talk on some more interesting subject. I asked Cynthia to buy me a silk gown in Paris, and I said I would send her word what colour I fixed upon – I think dark blue is the most becoming to my complexion; what do you say?'

Molly agreed, sooner than take the trouble of thinking about the thing at all; she was far too full of her silent review of all the traits in Roger's character that gave the lie to her stepmother's supposition.

They heard Mr Gibson's step downstairs. But it was some time before he made his entrance.

'How is little Roger?' said Molly eagerly.

'Beginning with scarlet fever, I'm afraid. It's well you left when you did, Molly. You've never had it. If there's one illness I dread, it is this.'

'Will he have it badly?' asked Molly.

'I can't tell. I shall do my best for the wee laddie.'

Whenever Mr Gibson's feelings were touched, he was apt to recur to the language of his youth. For some days there was imminent danger to the little boy; for some weeks there was a more chronic form of illness to contend with; but, when the immediate danger was over and the warm daily interest was past, Molly began to realise that, from the strict quarantine her father evidently thought it necessary to establish between the two houses, she was not likely to see Roger again before his departure for Africa.

One evening after dinner, her father said –

'As the country-people say, I've done a stroke of work today. Roger Hamley and I have laid our heads together, and we've made a plan by which Mrs Osborne and her boy will leave the Hall.'

'What did I say the other day, Molly?' said Mrs Gibson, interrupting, and giving Molly a look of extreme intelligence.

'And go into lodgings at Jennings' farm; not four hundred yards from the Park-field gate,' continued Mr Gibson. 'The Squire and his daughter-in-law have got to be much better friends over the little fellow's sick-bed; and I think he sees now how impossible it would be for the mother to leave her child, and go and be happy in France. But that one night, when I was very uncertain whether I could bring him through, they took to crying together, and condoling with each other; and it was just like tearing down a curtain that had been between them; they have been rather friends than otherwise ever since. Still, Roger and I both agree that his mother knows much better how to manage the boy than his grandfather does. And it makes her impatient, and annoyed, and unhappy, when she sees the Squire giving the child nuts and ale, and all sorts of silly indulgences. Yet she's a coward, and doesn't speak out her mind. Now, by being in lodgings, and having her own servants not ten minutes' walk from the Hall, so that she and the little chap may easily go backwards and forwards as often as they like, and yet she can keep the control over the child's discipline and diet. In short, I think I've done a good day's work,' he continued, stretching himself a little; and then, with a shake, making ready to go out again, to see a patient who had sent for him.

'A good day's work!' he repeated to himself as he ran downstairs. 'I don't know when I have been so happy!' For he had not told Molly all that had passed between him and Roger. Roger had begun a fresh subject of conversation, just as Mr Gibson was hastening away from the Hall.

'You know that I set off next Tuesday, Mr Gibson, don't you?' said Roger.

'Of course. I hope you'll be as successful in all your scientific objects as you were the last time, and have no sorrows awaiting you when you come back.'

'Thank you. Yes. I hope so. You don't think there's any danger of infection now, do you?'

'No! If the disease were to spread through the household, I think we should have had some signs of it before now.'

Roger was silent for a minute or two. 'Should you be afraid,' he said at length, 'of seeing me at your house?'

'Thank you; but I think I would rather decline the pleasure of your society there at present. Besides, I shall be over here again before you go. I'm always on my guard against symptoms of dropsy. I have known it supervene.'

'Then I shall not see Molly again!' said Roger, in a tone and with a look of great disappointment.

Mr Gibson turned his keen, observant eyes upon the young man. Then the doctor and the father compressed his lips and gave vent to a long intelligent whistle. 'Whew!' said he.

Roger's bronzed cheeks took a deeper shade.

'You will take a message to her from me, won't you? A message of farewell!' he pleaded.

'Not I. I'll tell my womenkind I forbade you to come near the house, and that you're sorry to go away without bidding good-bye. That's all I shall say.'

'But you do not disapprove? – I see you guess why. Oh! Mr Gibson, just speak to me one word of what must be in your heart, though you are pretending not to understand why I would give worlds to see Molly again before I go!'

'My dear boy!' said Mr Gibson, more affected than he liked to show, and laying his hand on Roger's shoulder. 'Mind, Molly is not Cynthia. If she were to care for you, she is not one who could transfer her love to the next comer.'

'You mean, not as readily as I have done,' replied Roger. 'I only wish you could know what a different feeling this is from my boyish love for Cynthia.'

'I wasn't thinking of you when I spoke; but, however, as I might have remembered afterwards that you were not a model of constancy, let us hear what you have to say for yourself.'

'Not much. I did love Cynthia. Her manners and her beauty

bewitched me; but her letters, – short, hurried letters – sometimes showing that she really hadn't taken the trouble to read mine through – I cannot tell you the pain they gave me! Twelve months' solitude, in frequent danger of one's life – face to face with death – sometimes ages a man like many years' experience. Still, I longed for the time when I should see her sweet face again, and hear her speak. Then the letter at the Cape! – and still I hoped. But you know how I found her – engaged to Mr Henderson. I saw her walking with him in your garden. I can see the pitying look in Molly's eyes as she watched me. And I could beat myself for being such a blind fool as to – What must she think of me! how she must despise me, choosing the false Duessa!'

'Come, come! Cynthia isn't so bad as that. She's a very fascinating, faulty creature.'

'I know! I know! If I called her the false Duessa, it was because I wanted to express my sense of the difference between her and Molly as strongly as I could. You must allow for a lover's exaggeration. Do you think that Molly, after seeing and knowing that I had loved a person so inferior to herself, could ever be brought to listen to me?'

'I can't tell. And, even if I could, I wouldn't. Only, if it's any comfort to you, I may say what my experience has taught me. Women are queer, unreasoning creatures, and are just as likely as not to love a man who has been throwing away his affection.'

'Thank you, sir!' said Roger. 'I see you mean to give me encouragement. And I had resolved never to give Molly a hint of what I felt till I returned – and then to try and win her by every means in my power.'

'Now, Roger, I've listened to you long enough. If you've nothing better to do with your time than to talk about my daughter, I have. When you come back, it will be time enough to inquire how far your father would approve of such an engagement.'

'He himself urged it upon me the other day – but then I was in despair – I thought it was too late.'

'And what means you are likely to have of maintaining a wife. I'm not mercenary – Molly has some money independently of me

– that she by the way knows nothing of – not much; – and I can allow her something. But all these things must be left till your return.'

'Then you sanction my attachment?'

'I don't know what you mean by sanctioning it. I can't help it. I suppose losing one's daughter is a necessary evil. Still, it is but fair to you to say, I'd rather give my child – my only child, remember! – to you, than to any man in the world!'

'Thank you!' said Roger, shaking hands with Mr Gibson, almost against the will of the latter. 'And I may see her, just once, before I go?'

'Decidedly not. There I come in as doctor as well as father. No!'

'But you will take a message, at any rate?'

'To my wife and to her conjointly. I will not in the slightest way be a go-between.'

'Very well,' said Roger. 'Tell them both, as strongly as you can, how I regret your prohibition. I see I must submit. But, if I don't come back, I'll haunt you for having been so cruel.'

'Come, I like that! Give me a wise man of science in love! No one beats him in folly. Good-bye.'

Mr Gibson gave Roger's message to his wife and to Molly, that evening at dinner. It was but what the latter had expected, after all her father had said of the very great danger of infection; but, now that her expectation came in the shape of a final decision, it took away her appetite. She submitted in silence; but her observant father noticed that, after this speech of his, she only played with the food on her plate, and concealed a good deal of it under her knife and fork.

'Lover *versus* father!' thought he, half sadly. 'Lover wins.' And he, too, became indifferent to all that remained of his dinner. Mrs Gibson pattered on; and nobody listened.

The day of Roger's departure came. Molly tried hard to forget it in working away at a cushion she was preparing as a present to Cynthia. It was a rainy day, too; and Mrs Gibson, who had planned to pay some calls, had to stay indoors. This made her restless and fidgety. She kept going backwards and forwards to different windows in the drawing-room, to look at the weather, as if she imagined that, while it rained at one window, it might be fine weather at another.

'Molly – come here! who is that man wrapped up in a cloak – there – near the Park-wall, under the beech-tree – he has been there this half-hour and more, never stirring, and looking at this house all the time! I think it's very suspicious.'

Molly looked, and in an instant recognised Roger.

'Why, mamma, it's Roger Hamley! Look now – he's kissing his hand; he's wishing us good-bye in the only way he can!' And she responded to his sign; but she was not sure if he perceived her modest, quiet movement, for Mrs Gibson became immediately so demonstrative that Molly fancied that her eager foolish panto-mimic motions must absorb all his attention.

'I call this so attentive of him,' said Mrs Gibson, in the midst of a volley of kisses of her hand. 'Really, it is quite romantic. It reminds me of former days – but he will be too late! I must send him away; it is half-past twelve!' And she took out her watch and held it up, tapping it with her fore-finger, and occupying the very centre of the window. Molly could only peep here and there, dodging now up, now down, now on this side, now on that, of the perpetually moving arms. She fancied she saw something of a corresponding movement on Roger's part. At length, he went away slowly, slowly, and often looking back, in spite of the tapped watch. Mrs Gibson at last retreated, and Molly quietly moved into her place, to see his figure once more, before the turn of the road hid him from her view. He, too, knew where the last glimpse of Mr Gibson's house was to be obtained, and once more he turned, and his white hand-kerchief floated in the air. Molly waved hers high up, with eager longing that it should be seen. And then, he was gone! and Molly returned to her worsted-work, happy, glowing, sad, content, and thinking to herself, how sweet is friendship!

When she came to a sense of the present, Mrs Gibson was saying –

'Upon my word, though Roger Hamley has never been a great

favourite of mine, this little attention of his has reminded me very forcibly of a very charming young man – Lieutenant Harper – you must have heard me speak of him, Molly?'

'I think I have!' said Molly absently.

'Well, you remember how devoted he was to me, when I was at Mrs Duncombe's, and I only seventeen. And, when the recruiting party was ordered to another town, poor Mr Harper came and stood opposite the school-room window for nearly an hour, and I know it was his doing that the band played "The girl I left behind me", when they marched out the next day. Poor Mr Harper! It was before I knew dear Mr Kirkpatrick! Dear me! How often my poor heart has had to bleed, in this life of mine! not but what dear papa is a very worthy man, and makes me very happy. He would spoil me, indeed, if I would let him. Still, he is not as rich as Mr Henderson.'

Having married Cynthia, as her mother put it – taking credit to herself as if she had had the principal part in the achievement – she now became a little envious of her daughter's good fortune in being the wife of a young, handsome, rich, and moderately fashionable man, who lived in London. She naïvely expressed her feelings on this subject to her husband, one day when she was really not feeling quite well.

'It is such a pity!' said she, 'that I was born when I was. I should so have liked to belong to this generation.'

'That's sometimes my own feeling,' said he. 'So many new views seem to be opened in science, that I should like, if it were possible, to live till their reality was ascertained, and one saw what they led to. But I don't suppose that's your reason, my dear, for wishing to be twenty or thirty years younger.'

'No, indeed! To tell the truth, I was thinking of Cynthia. Without vanity, I believe I was as pretty as she is – when I was a girl, I mean; I had not her dark eyelashes, but then my nose was straighter. And now – look at the difference! I have to live in a little country-town with three servants, and no carriage; and she, with her inferior good looks, will live in Sussex Place, and keep a man and a brougham, and I don't know what. But the fact is, in this generation there are so many more rich young men than there were when I was a girl.'

'Oh, oh! so that's your reason, is it, my dear? If you had been young now, you might have married somebody as well off as Walter?'

'Yes!' said she. 'Of course I should have liked him to be you. I don't believe Walter will ever be so clever as you are. Yet he can take Cynthia to Paris, and abroad, and everywhere. I only hope all this indulgence won't develop the faults in Cynthia's character. It's a week since we heard from her, and I did write so particularly to ask her for the autumn fashions, before I bought my new bonnet. But riches are a great snare.'

'Here's medicine for you, mamma,' said Molly, entering with a letter held up in her hand. 'A letter from Cynthia.'

'Oh, you dear little messenger of good news! The letter is dated from Calais. They're coming home! She's bought me a shawl and a bonnet! The dear creature! Always thinking of others before herself. They've a fortnight left of their holiday! Their house is not quite ready; they're coming here. Oh, now, Mr Gibson, we must have the new dinner-service at Watts's I've set my heart on so long! "Home" Cynthia calls this house. I'm sure it has been a home to her, poor darling! I doubt if there is another man in the world who would have treated his step-daughter like dear papa! And, Molly, you must have a new gown.'

'Come, come! Remember, I belong to the last generation,' said Mr Gibson.

'And Cynthia won't mind what I wear,' said Molly, bright with pleasure at the thought of seeing her again.

'No! but Walter will. I must have a new gown, too.'

But Molly stood out against the new gown for herself, and urged that, if Cynthia and Walter were to come to visit them often, they had better see them as they really were, in dress, habits, and appointments. When Mr Gibson had left the room, Mrs Gibson softly reproached Molly for her obstinacy.

'You might have allowed me to beg for a new gown for you, Molly, when you knew how much I admired that figured silk at

Brown's the other day. And now, of course, I can't be so selfish as to get it for myself, and you to have nothing. You should learn to understand the wishes of other people. Still, on the whole, you are a dear, sweet girl, and I only wish – well, dear papa does not like it to be talked about. And now cover me up close, and let me go to sleep, and dream about my dear Cynthia and my new shawl!'

# Concluding Remarks
## (By The Editor of the *Cornhill Magazine*)

Here the story is broken off, and it can never be finished. What promised to be the crowning work of a life is a memorial of death. A few days longer, and it would have been a triumphal column, crowned with a capital of festal leaves and flowers; now it is another sort of column – one of those sad white pillars which stand broken in the churchyard.

But if the work is not quite complete, little remains to be added to it, and that little has been distinctly reflected into our minds. We know that Roger Hamley will marry Molly, and that is what we are most concerned about. Indeed, there was little else to tell. Had the writer lived, she would have sent her hero back to Africa forthwith; and those scientific parts of Africa are a long way from Hamley; and there is not much to choose between a long distance and a long time. How many hours are there in twenty-four when you are all alone in a desert place, a thousand miles from the happiness which might be yours to take – if you were there to take it? How many, when from the sources of the Topinambo your heart flies back ten times a day, like a carrier-pigeon, to the one only source of future good for you, and ten times a day returns with its message undelivered? Many more than are counted on the calendar. So Roger found. The days were weeks that separated him from the time when Molly gave him a certain little flower, and months from the time which divorced him from Cynthia, whom he had begun to doubt before he knew for certain that she was never much worth hoping for. And if such were his days, what was the slow procession of actual weeks and months in those remote and solitary places? They were like years of a stay-at-home life, with liberty and leisure to see that nobody was courting Molly meanwhile. The effect of this was, that long before the term of his engagement was ended all that Cynthia had been to him was departed from Roger's mind, and all that Molly was and might be to him filled it full.

He returned; but when he saw Molly again he remembered that to her the time of his absence might not have seemed so long, and was oppressed with the old dread that she would think him fickle. Therefore this young gentleman, so self-reliant and so lucid in scientific matters, found it difficult after all to tell Molly how much he hoped she loved him; and might have blundered if he had not thought of beginning by showing her the flower that was plucked from the nosegay. How charmingly that scene would have been drawn, had Mrs Gaskell lived to depict it, we can only imagine: that it would have been charming – especially in what Molly did, and looked, and said – we know.

Roger and Molly are married; and if one of them is happier than the other, it is Molly. Her husband has no need to draw upon the little fortune which is to go to poor Osborne's boy, for he becomes professor at some great scientific institution, and wins his way in the world handsomely. The Squire is almost as happy in this marriage as his son. If anyone suffers for it, it is Mr Gibson. But he takes a partner, so as to get a chance of running up to London to stay with Molly for a few days now and then, and 'to get a little rest from Mrs Gibson.' Of what was to happen to Cynthia after her marriage the author was not heard to say much; and, indeed, it does not seem that anything needs to be added. One little anecdote, however, was told of her by Mrs Gaskell, which is very characteristic. One day, when Cynthia and her husband were on a visit to Hollingford, Mr Henderson learnt for the first time, through an innocent casual remark of Mr Gibson's, that the famous traveller, Roger Hamley, was known to the family. Cynthia had never happened to mention it. How well that little incident, too, would have been described!

But it is useless to speculate upon what would have been done by the delicate strong hand which can create no more Molly

Gibsons – no more Roger Hamleys. We have repeated, in this brief note, all that is known of her designs for the story, which would have been completed in another chapter. There is not so much to regret, then, so far as this novel is concerned; indeed, the regrets of those who knew her are less for the loss of the novelist than of the woman – one of the kindest and wisest of her time. But yet, for her own sake as a novelist alone, her untimely death is a matter for deep regret. It is clear in this novel of *Wives and Daughters*, in the exquisite little story that preceded it, *Cousin Phillis*, and in *Sylvia's Lovers*, that Mrs Gaskell had within these five years started upon a new career with all the freshness of youth, and with a mind which seemed to have put off its clay and to have been born again. But that 'put off its clay' must be taken in a very narrow sense. All minds are tinctured more or less with the 'muddy vesture' in which they are contained; but few minds ever showed less of base earth than Mrs Gaskell's. It was so at all times; but lately even the original slight tincture seemed to disappear. While you read any one of the last three books we have named, you feel yourself caught out of an abominable wicked world, crawling with selfishness and reeking with base passions, into one where there is much weakness, many mistakes, sufferings long and bitter, but where it is possible for people to live calm and wholesome lives; and, what is more, you feel that this is, at least, as real a world as the other. The kindly spirit which thinks no ill looks out of her pages irradiate; and while we read them, we breathe the purer intelligence that prefers to deal with emotions and passions which have a living root in minds within the pale of salvation, and not with those that rot without it. This spirit is more especially declared in *Cousin Phillis* and *Wives and Daughters* – their author's latest works; they seem to show that for her the end of life was not descent amongst the clods of the valley, but ascent into the purer air of the heaven-aspiring hills.

We are saying nothing now of the merely intellectual qualities displayed in these later works. Twenty years to come, that may be thought the more important question of the two; in the presence of her grave we cannot think so; but it is true, all the same, that as mere works of art and observation, these later novels of Mrs Gaskell's are among the finest of our time. There is a scene in *Cousin Phillis* – where Holman, making hay with his men, ends the day with a psalm – which is not excelled as a picture in all modern fiction; and the same may be said of that chapter of this last story in which Roger smokes a pipe with the Squire after the quarrel with Osborne. There is little in either of these scenes, or in a score of others which succeed each other like gems in a cabinet, which the ordinary novel-maker could 'seize'. There is no 'material' for him in half-a-dozen farming men singing hymns in a field, or a discontented old gentleman smoking tobacco with his son. Still less could he avail himself of the miseries of a little girl sent to be happy in a fine house full of fine people; but it is just in such things as these that true genius appears brightest and most unapproachable. It is the same with the personages in Mrs Gaskell's works. Cynthia is one of the most difficult characters which have ever been attempted in our time. Perfect art always obscures the difficulties it overcomes; and it is not till we try to follow the processes by which such a character as the Tito of *Romola* is created, for instance, that we begin to understand what a marvellous piece of work it is. To be sure, Cynthia was not so difficult, nor is it nearly so great a creation as that splendid achievement of art and thought – of the rarest art, of the profoundest thought. But she also belongs to the kind of characters which are conceived only in minds large, clear, harmonious and just, and which can be portrayed fully and without flaw only by hands obedient to the finest motions of the mind. Viewed in this light, Cynthia is a more important piece of work even than Molly, delicately as she is drawn, and true and harmonious as that picture is also. And what we have said of Cynthia may be said with equal truth of Osborne Hamley. The true delineation of a character like that is as fine a test of art as the painting of a foot or a hand, which also seems so easy, and in which perfection is most rare. In this case the work is perfect. Mrs Gaskell has drawn a dozen characters more striking than Osborne since she wrote *Mary Barton*, but not one which shows more exquisite finish.

Another thing we may be permitted to notice, because it has a great and general significance. It may be true that this is not exactly the place for criticism, but since we are writing of Osborne Hamley, we cannot resist pointing out a peculiar instance of the subtler conceptions which underlie all really considerable works. Here are Osborne and Roger, two men who, in every particular that can be seized for description, are totally different creatures. Body and mind, they are quite unlike. They have different tastes; they take different ways: they are men of two sorts which, in the society sense, never 'know' each other; and yet, never did brotherly blood run more manifest than in the veins of those two. To make that manifest without allowing the effort to peep out for a single moment, would be a triumph of art; but it is a 'touch beyond the reach of art' to make their likeness in unlikeness so natural a thing that we no more wonder about it than we wonder at seeing the fruit and the bloom on the same bramble: we have always seen them there together in blackberry season, and do not wonder about it nor think about it at all. Inferior writers, even some writers who are highly accounted, would have revelled in the 'contrast', persuaded that they were doing a fine anatomical dramatic thing by bringing it out at every opportunity. To the author of *Wives and Daughters* this sort of anatomy was mere dislocation. She began by having the people of her story born in the usual way, and not built up like the Frankenstein monster; and thus when Squire Hamley took a wife, it was then provided that his two boys should be as naturally one and diverse as the fruit and the bloom on the bramble. 'It goes without speaking.' These differences are precisely what might have been expected from the union of Squire Hamley with the town-bred, refined, delicate-minded woman whom he married; and the affection of the young men, their kindness (to use the word in its old and new meanings at once) is nothing but a reproduction of those impalpable threads of love which bound the equally diverse father and mother in bonds faster than the ties of blood.

But we will not permit ourselves to write any more in this vein. It is unnecessary to demonstrate to those who know what is and

# About this Compact Edition

*Wives and Daughters* first appeared in the *Cornhill Magazine* as a monthly serial from August 1864 to January 1866. It was not quite complete, since Elizabeth Gaskell had died on 12 November 1865, but her friend Frederick Greenwood, editor of the magazine, summarised her intentions in some concluding remarks. These are printed at the end of this present edition, which omits or prunes some of the groupings of minor characters and background descriptions which do not relate to the main action. There are some reductions, too, in overlong dialogue acceptable in a serial which had to reach so many words to fill the monthly quota of pages. Throughout only Mrs Gaskell's words are used, and these display her fine humour, often compared with Jane Austen's, an exquisite sense of period and place, narrative expectation, and a sympathetic presentation of character.